This book is for the Bumblebee Queens, who wake early in the Spring, hungry and alone, prepared to work for all of us.

"Laughter is the sun that drives winter from the human face."
-Victor Hugo

BOOK TWO IN THE
LAUGHTER OF THE SUN SERIES

THE
SORROW
OF
BEES

ANDIE HOLMAN

Book Cover by Richard Ljoenes
Edited by Kenneth Zink
Formatted by Lorna Reid

Edition One 2025.

Also by the author:
The Mermaid's Wrath—Book One in The Laughter of the Sun series

ONE

MORI

I was restless, with no purpose. After Terrun's dark magic left me hovering in the Sliver, one foot in both worlds, neither dead nor alive, Jelly had coaxed me back with the promise we'd do beautiful things for the world. So far, our grand plans hadn't materialized. We hadn't even discussed them.

"Mori, where's your head?" Mew's brow wrinkled as he helped me up from the mat where he'd sent me sprawling. I'd completely missed blocking his kick, leaving my ears ringing. We were training in his dojo in the village.

"Just preoccupied."

"Trouble at home?"

I snorted. This wasn't my home. Not really. "Mako and Jelly have been fighting all week." I rubbed my temple, throbbing from Mew's hit. His face was curious, a touch troubled, and he grazed his fingers across my brow, lifting away the sting. I blinked at him. "Thanks, Mew."

His eyes narrowed. "Do you want to talk about it?"

I shrugged my shoulders. "Not much to say. They're in a snit over something and don't want to share. They're hissing like two wet cats in a pillowcase, but never with claws, which must be a fated mates thing. I'd have drawn blood by now. Shouldn't it be easier? Anyway, neither of them will explain why they're so pissy. I'm iced out."

He nodded sagely. "They are new to the bond, but that's not fun to live with." He patted my shoulder. "You're too distracted to train today. Go lose yourself in your books."

I puffed out my cheeks in resignation. "I think I will." I tipped my head. "You're a good friend, Mew. You listen to me. I appreciate it." What I didn't voice was that I was lonely, and Mew was the one constant companion I could rely on, even if he beat the snot out of me.

Fate stole my friend from me; at least, that's how I saw it. Despite her voluminous powers, Jelly lost her sharp edge. She was like an octopus, ever changing to fit her environment, adapting her persona to suit the situation. She always looked at Mako before answering a question, like she needed permission for her feelings. Old Jelly, my childhood friend, was unapologetically opinionated, and I didn't care for this newer version.

I closed the leather cover of my latest encyclopedia on the Fae, treating it with the care it deserved. Gazing out the window of the library in the small village, people were closing shop, meaning it was time for me to leave my small cocoon and face the calamity at the Fields' house, namely Mako and Jelly.

I glanced over at the notes I'd made on the Fae. They weren't all bad; just pathologically self-serving. We didn't have any books on them back at the reef, and I bathed in the vast knowledge I had at my fingertips. Given the village was a sanctuary for magic, no one twitched as I translated the old books from my cozy corner on the third floor, away from the bustle and hushed voices.

I gathered my two tomes and left them at the main desk. Jared, the librarian, looked up, saw it was me, and blushed. "Had enough for today?" He pushed up his blue-rimmed round glasses, smiling shyly as I slid the thick books toward him.

"My head's about to explode. Their language is so tricky.

Too many consonants and not enough vowels. But I'm getting the rhythm of it." I tossed my curls over my shoulder, leaning in to smile at him beguilingly, my arm on the desk, reaching over to twiddle a pen near his fingers.

His dark brown hair fell forward as he logged the books under my name, his lips moving as he wrote in a red-covered journal, which subtly flashed as he closed it. If I had to guess, I'd say he was a Mage. I dropped my voice. "Hey Jared, can I ask you something, and promise to keep it to yourself?" I leaned in, coaxing him to come closer. "Do you know if there are side effects of forced fusion rituals?"

His eyes sprang wide, and he looked around, fearful of eavesdroppers. "That's dark magic, Mori. You shouldn't mess around with that."

"It's already happened. To a friend of mine."

Jared narrowed his eyes at me. "I'm supposed to report it."

I waved him off casually. "Oh, it was in England. But what do you know? My friend is struggling to manage the magic."

"I'm not surprised. You shouldn't force magic on people. How many strands? One? Two?

My lips turned down. "Seven."

"Seven! Shit, Mori! I'm surprised she's still alive! There's always a cost to using the dark arts. Maybe her difficulties are because of that." He shook his head, muttering, "Seven."

He raised his chin and swallowed, making the apple at his throat bob. "Since we're opening up to each other, can I ask you a question? It's somewhat personal. I've researched it, but the Mers are notoriously secretive, and the information we have here is vague." He gave me a half-smile. "With you being estranged from the surface and all."

I tapped the tip of the pen, letting it knock against his hand, making contact without touching him. He tried to hide his gasp. I purred in an innocent voice. "Of course. Anything." I fluttered my eyelashes. Poor man. He couldn't hide his nerves as his throat worked overtime.

He steeled himself. "I know the Mers recharge themselves through intimacy. Do you take the magic from the person? Deplete them?"

"Steal it?" I traced my other hand against my chest in faux horror, drawing his eyes to my deep vee neckline, a hint of lace peeking through. "No. It's an internal process. I mean, someone could bolster the replenishment by *giving* their magic, but it doesn't hurt them. We're not vampires." His relief was palpable, tension breaking from his shoulders.

I leaned in further, as if sharing a secret, my fingers grazing his. He couldn't meet my eyes, so enamored with my decolletage. "It's always appreciated if someone donates their magic to a mermaid, like adding spice to a meal, but it's unnecessary for the boost. It's still nourishing." I winked at him. "We can do it for ourselves, but it's more fun with a friend."

The apple bobbed up and down, making me unable to hide my smile. He was vibrating with magic, and a tendril of it curled toward me before he drew it back, an invisible whisper on my skin. He wasn't really my type, but starved for affection, I flirted with him. He said, "I understand. Good to know. Thank you." He finally tore his stare from my breasts, blinking from behind his glasses. "See you tomorrow?" His voice held longing, as if my regular visits were the highlight of his day.

"Can't wait." I retrieved my helmet and leather jacket from the staff room, a perk I'd secured immediately, casually pouting that I had nowhere to put them. Jared offered his locker with a stammer, saying he rarely used it. Feeling his eyes on me, I tossed back my long hair, and swiveled my hips while pulling on the jacket. Completely unnecessary, but fun, especially when I caught the small groan escaping his throat.

Mako taught me to ride a motorcycle after I'd moaned about

being trapped on the gorgeous estate his family owned. I'd learned quickly, desperate to have my freedom from watching him and Jelly navigate their sudden fated status. Thankfully, I'd mastered it before the friction between them started a week ago.

I kicked the engine to life, slapped down my visor, and twisted my wrist, leaving the village behind. My shoulders relaxed as the trees raced by, the road curving and carving along the coast. I pulled into a rest stop overlooking the ocean, the bike idling between my thighs as I set down a foot, waiting for a sense of homesickness as I stared at the blue horizon. It didn't come. My life was here on the surface now. With a check over my shoulder, I sped back on the road toward the compound.

Magic snapped over my body as I pulled into the driveway, reminiscent of swimming into the bubble around the reef, although this was for protection from attack, not microplastics. I shuddered involuntarily, remembering when the Eators invaded this place, aiming to take Jelly's pearl. We'd seen neither hide nor hair of the vile creatures, and for that I was glad. Still, they were out there, undoubtedly waiting.

I glimpsed Roan roaming the house in nothing but shorts. I stared at his imposing body, completely covered in magical ink. He was airing his thick hair, the warrior style braid unbound. He kept the sides shaved tight, displaying more tattoos on his skull. The bike idled as I watched, the engine hot. We'd been attempting to outdo each other's seductions, almost torturing each other with innuendos.

To be honest, I loved the tension, the thrill of the chase, hovering on the edge of submission, but we were both too stubborn to give in, for whoever succumbed first would be the loser; though losing would be sweeter than pie. Of that, I had little doubt. But I avoided going too far, of leading him too deeply into temptation, as feelings were dangerous, and I wasn't looking for attachments. Flirting was safer.

Leaving the bike in the garage, I headed down the side path toward my small house on the property when I heard shouting floating toward me on the salted breeze. Jelly and Mako were fighting again, this time outside. They'd see me if I continued on, and it would be awkward. I'd asked Jelly what was wrong several times, but she brushed me off, telling me it was teething pains. She'd demoted me as her confidant, which stung more than I wanted to admit. In the small places of my heart, I felt abandoned by her. I didn't need the reminder.

I turned, heading straight for the pool, needing a soak after sitting for so long. Not to mention my low back was screaming from the heavy deadlifts Mew insisted I needed for efficient fighting.

I left the helmet and my clothes on the lounger, jumping in the pool in my underwear. Everyone was used to my near nudity by now, swimming in a thong and a bra, and if it bothered anyone, they hadn't complained, so I didn't care. I swam to the deep end of the pool in one breath, kicking my legs like a frog, purring in my throat as I reached my goal.

Admittedly, I'd grown lazy, relying on the tumultuous thundering of the pool jet to get my magical recharge. If I used sex, it would be much stronger, but that meant actually interacting with someone. My mind wandered to Jared. He was cute in that geeky, brainiac way. Shy, but that didn't matter. I could sense the power strumming in his mind, making him attractive.

After his earlier question, I could easily convince him to slip away, undetected in a dusty corner of the old building for a quick recharge, but keeping him on my hook was better, made him more helpful. He gave me access to rare books normally encased behind glass. Plus, he let me sneak my cinnamon-dusted cappuccinos into the library. I shook my head. This was much cleaner.

I leaned heavily on my elbows, letting the water pulse against my lower body, causing my breath to catch as I got into position.

I scrunched my eyes closed as the water deliciously assaulted me, my teeth clenched so I wouldn't moan out loud as the crescendo built at a furious pace. My muscled tightened, so close...

A deep voice mocked me, jarring me from my bliss. "Playing in the pool again, lass?" I flung myself backward.

"Roan." Frustration gripped my teeth as my orgasm slipped away in the cool water. I clenched my jaw around his name.

I watched with narrowed eyes as he strolled toward me, taking his time to toss his towel on the lounger, knowing he had a rapt audience. He looked over with a grin, his green eyes twinkling. "Did I interrupt something?"

I gave him my best scowl. "You know you did." The throb of my power dot, my nickname for the exquisite female organ at the apex of my thighs, slowly died down, but the roar in my blood did not, especially as the enormous man gracefully split the surface and swam to my side. "What do you want, Roan?"

He chuckled, water running down his thick muscles as he leaned on an elbow on the pool edge, right next to where I gripped with my fingers. The droplets shimmered against his dark tattoos. "Ye know what I want, Mori." I loved the way my name rolled from his tongue, like he savored it inside his mouth. He burned me with his stare. I scoffed, dismissing him as I flicked my wet curls off my shoulder. He watched my every move with hunger.

I felt my magical boosting slide away, leaving me more tired and sore. My question came out harsher than I wanted, especially since I needed his help. "Are you going back to England soon?" I spun my legs through the cool water, still annoyed at being disturbed.

"Are ye looking to be rid of me, lass?" His deep voice carried mirth, grinning at my surly expression.

I dropped my irritation. "I'm bored, Roan." I waved my hand at the pool and the gorgeous house. "This is great, but I want more."

He roughed a meaty hand across his tight beard, evaluating my words. "Ye want more? Not one for a life of comfort, eh? Ye need action." With his beard wet, I could see a tattoo on his throat. It was tempting to tip his head back to look closer. He waited for me to answer, and I tore my mind away from touching him.

I said, "It's not so much action. I want to heal the rift between the land and the sea. We've shown we can work together; at least in our group. I want to take it wider, meet more Surfecti, and show them the Mers are ready to negotiate a truce. With you and Richard as Wizardy co-chairs, and Anna the most powerful witch in Europe, surely you can make introductions."

"What about Jelly?"

"What about her? She's busy with Mako. She probably wouldn't notice if I left."

His eyes flashed sympathetically. "Ah. Fated mates. Give them some time, lass. They're new to the bond."

I ignored his words. "Jelly's happy here. She's got her work with Simmi, her new instant family, and I'm…I'm…" I threw my hand in the air, feeling like a spoiled princess who couldn't appreciate her good fortune.

"Stagnant." He dropped his hand to swirl the water on the surface. "Aye, lass, I could introduce ye. Do the Mers support ye? I won't show ye around unless I know for certain they're game."

"I'll confirm with my father and the shaman. They were restructuring the government the last time we spoke. If he says yes, you'll take me? We'll go?" I couldn't help the hope in my voice.

"Aye, lass. We'll go." I stopped myself from flinging my arms around him. I bit my lip in excitement, and his eyes dropped to my mouth as he spoke. "I'll take ye to meet everyone important." I spread my palms on the cool cement, ready to push myself out, when he stopped me with a heavy hand on my shoulder. "Does Jelly know yer plans?"

"No. We barely speak alone anymore. I told you. She's busy with Mako."

"Ah," he said, leaving it at that.

I hauled myself out, secretly smiling as Roan inhaled a sharp breath at my wet thong. I grabbed my gear from the lounger, swaying my hips as water streamed down my body. Roan called out my name, making me pause and turn at the edge of the clover lawn. He'd swum to the shallow end of the pool and stood up, his hands on his hips. "Lass, I could help ye recharge yer magic. A pool jet can't kiss ye."

The afternoon sun threw warm light on his body, glistening wet, his eyes glinting with emerald fire. Tempting. So tempting. I perused his body with my gaze. "It also doesn't talk back. I'm good, Roan, but thanks for the offer."

"Yer loss, lass."

I grinned with a flirty smile that didn't reach my heart. He was probably right.

I ate dinner alone in my small house, comfortable, elegant, with all the modern amenities a woman could want. I contemplated finishing what I'd started in the pool, but didn't have the energy. I snuggled in early with a historical novel and a cup of chamomile tea. My eyes grew heavy, and I sprawled across the massive bed like a starfish, using all the pillows as props for my tired body, and dreamed.

Roan was there, as if my subconscious needed to follow through on the teasing. And Gods, he could kiss. A little on the rough side, just like I liked it, his fingers gripping my curls as he devoured me. I thought I'd catch fire as my knees weakened along with my will, letting him take control. My arms wound round his neck, pulling him closer. Closer. More. Gods, yes, more. His calloused fingers fell from my hair to my body and I panted in his mouth as his eyes flashed a brilliant green, a male groan in his throat as his hand slid down and found…

Sadly, the dream ended. The sounds of my own moans roused me, tangled in the sheets, my throat dry, the echo of my wantonness ringing in my ears. I was feverish and soaked in sweat. Cursing, I drank the water on my bedside table, fluffed the pillows, and moved to the other side of the bed that wasn't damp.

I tossed for ages, unable to escape the vividness of the dream; his beard rasping my skin, his fingers wrapped in my hair, the scent of him flooding me like fresh pine. Jelly and I called him my surly bear, and in my dream, I'd pictured him leaning his back on a tree, naked, beckoning me with the crook of his finger, and I'd gone to him with a willing desperation, so different from reality.

TWO

JELLY

It wasn't the smell of singed hair that roused me, nor the frantic noise Mako made as he slapped orange flames from his thighs. My lover's shout snapped me from the dream. "Jelly! The bed is on fire!" Through half-lidded eyes, I threw a pitcher of water on him, belatedly realizing I'd made things worse. Now we lay in sodden, scorched sheets, the bitterness of burning still in the air.

I scanned his skin, seeing it bald and red, but not blistered. "Oh, Mako, I'm so sorry." I looked down at myself, noting I was intact. The flames hadn't reached for me. I bit my lip, embarrassed. "That's the second time this week." He looked at my chagrin and softened, pulling me over the wet mess to the other side of the bed, tucking me against his chest. I frowned at my dream, the cause of the fire. "I was in a strange place, surrounded by peculiar fruit. People shouted, but their mouths weren't moving. I saw flashing red eyes, so an Eator, but he looked different, more human. I must have reacted to my panic in my sleep."

The light was strange, wavering across the walls in a loop. I glanced with confusion at the levitating lamp, the cord straining from the socket like an over-filled balloon. I searched inside, found the purple thread of magic and pulled, intending to set it gently back down, but the lamp crashed to the bedside table, tottered, and fell to the floor, smashing the light bulb with a pop, plunging us into darkness. Mako held me tighter, reaching over to flick on the lamp on his side of the bed, light catching on his chest.

I traced my fingertips along the intricate scales of his wave tattoo. It wasn't a tattoo; not exactly. Mother Kokuro marked Mako, claiming him as her own, and in doing so, she enhanced his Fae, the half he'd inherited from his father. When Mako pulled on his Fae magic, he grew in size and power, and his fighting skills morphed into something delightfully feral. His other half was Mers, from Sophia, a legend on the reef. She hadn't returned after a procreation mission, disregarding Mers law, choosing to stay on the surface with Sebastian.

Unlike Mako, I had been fully Mers when Kokuro claimed me during the forced fusion ritual, extending her powers to me, and I'd almost died from the pain of her marking. She'd given me an exquisite symbol on my back, a yin yang with mermaid fins flicking outside the circle, a sun at the top and a new moon in the bottom. My turquoise eyes also ringed in black. My magic morphed with Kokuro's claiming, letting me shoot turquoise fire. That's when it worked. Right now, it was frenetic.

Mako smoothed my sweaty blue hair from my forehead before kissing it. "Does Leoht have any insight?"

I called to the teardrop black pearl at my throat, the one handed down through my family. The Fae King sent her to Mother Kokuro for safekeeping after discovering his son was abusing her. The Mother then sent Leoht to the Mers, after Leoht complained of being cooped up. We bonded during the ritual and communicated telepathically or in pulses when she wasn't in the mood to talk. *Leoht, any ideas?*

She answered with two pulses. No.

I groaned and rolled away from Mako. "She doesn't know." I glanced back at my fated mate, my lover, my staunchest ally, and recently, the source of all my frustration. He poked his finger through the hole in the sheet, his lips turned down. "Which means I'll be facing a monster amongst rotten fruit at some point. Terrific." He said nothing; didn't even look up. "Mako, I'm going to burn the house down. Seven new strains and I can't control any of it." I swept my hands down my body. "This hot mess is only getting hotter." He still didn't speak. My eyebrows hitched up with impatience. "I set you on fire."

I stared at the broken lamp on the floor. Resignation filled my voice as I looped over the argument we'd been having earlier. "I want to train with the Surfecti. Something's wrong." Mako frowned as the volume of my voice crept higher. "Mako, I'm serious! I need to talk to them about the dream I had last week. We know where Leif is! Don't you want to get him back?"

He scowled at me. "Of course I do!"

"I've done as you asked and kept it a secret, but clearly, this is beyond me. I need to talk about it." His countenance deepened, his face showing some internal struggle he wasn't willing to share. I swung my legs off the soggy mattress and stomped to the bathroom.

When I came out, Mako was stripping the bed. He rolled the ruined sheets into a ball and tossed them in the corner. He kissed me and magic tickled the nerves of my spine, momentarily stalling my anger. He ran his hand through my hair, keeping his voice neutral. "We have training. Mew will be here soon."

I pulled back and stared into his cobalt-blue eyes, blinking at me innocently as if I hadn't just demanded to learn my new magic. My anger spiked. "Have you at least told Sebastian and Sophia about my dream yet?" Seven days ago, Mother Kokuro, a giant magical oyster, had pulled me to her while I slept, telling me where Mako's missing brother was. Leif was stuck in a Fae place called the Hellhole. She said I must not attempt a rescue until I found my yellow, but hadn't explained what that meant.

His heavy breath puffed at his hair. "No. I haven't told my parents. I don't want to get their hopes up." He looked at my expression and rushed to finish before I started yelling. "I'm not saying you can't find your yellow, but we're talking about the Hellhole, Jelly! A dimension where only Leoht can safely go because she's fully Fae. And even she doesn't want to!"

My fists cracked against my hips as I stepped out of his grasp. "Damn it, Mako, it's bigger than just Leif. Both Samara and Mother Kokuro told me I was missing something and needed to find it. Samara is an ancient Fae-Mers Seer, and she said we were part of a prophecy and that I needed my yellow. You don't ignore Seers. You follow their directives." He remained aloof, causing my anger to surge.

I poked a finger at his chest. "Tell your parents. They deserve to know we have a lead on your brother." I jabbed him harder. "And get your damned Hai Matau already. Kokuro warned you. She told you to wear it." A car door slammed in the distance and I steamed with frustration. "Mew's here, and he's early."

I yanked on my sweatpants, threw my hair into a bun, and ran out the door without Mako. I'd moved into his house at the far end of the property, living together since our fated mates revelation, but I desperately missed rooming with Mori, my best friend from the reef. She was in another house, much smaller, further up the path. I knocked on the door to collect her, but silence greeted me. Either she was ignoring me or she was already in the main building. I knocked again, a flash of guilt racing through me. I'd neglected her since becoming fated to Mako. I hadn't even asked her how she was taking the news.

With no reply, I ran to the modern home, all glass and concrete, skittering through the door on the lower level to the home gym. It was more than a space filled with standard weights. The ceilings were high, bearing anchors for long ropes, along with balance beams perched thirty feet in the air. Nets lay flat against the wall like spider webs, waiting to be pulled up and secured in case we slipped while training on the beams. The walls were padded, and wooden targets nested in the blue foam. I stared at the spot where I'd flung Mako across the room the first time I'd met him, the indent of his skull still evident.

We'd left Bermuda once Simmi recovered, returning to the Fields' compound, and I'd helped promote Simmi's laundry strips. As much as I adored Mako's sister, and enthusiastically approved of her invention to replace plastic jugs, this wasn't what I wanted to do with my life. I had the niggling sensation destiny expected far more, and it had everything to do with my new magic, as well as my best friend.

Mori had shown little interest in soap and spent most of her time in the village. She'd cajoled Roan to join us here, saying he needed some beach time, but she had an ulterior motive. She wanted firsthand details of the Surfecti, the magical races on the land. She took copious notes as he explained the nuances, her eyes flashing with excitement. He loved her enthusiasm, and she wallowed in his attention, her flirtation one step below scandalous. She was a skilled seductress, and Roan was barely keeping his head above water, although he often gave as good as he got.

I scanned the room and grinned as Mori pinned Roan to the target board with throwing stars while blindfolded. I didn't see a drop of blood on the man. Mori cackled as she tugged the silk from her eyes, stepping close to his body to haul her stars from the target. His arms were out wide, the stars embedded mere fractions from his skin. "Got you again, Roan. The blindfold wasn't a hindrance." He growled at her good-naturedly, his green eyes flashing as she gloated.

"Aye, lass. Yer quick and bloody accurate." Roan inspected his elbow, his multiple dark tattoos catching the early light. "Not a single graze." He looked up and saw me. "Mornin' Jelly. Ye look frazzled. What's got ye het up?"

About to reply, my legs swept out from under me. I crashed to the mat with a grunt, and maroon magic flared and crackled inside me, causing my chin to explode in white fur. Mori howled with laughter and I scowled as I tugged the magic back into line. Mew straddled me, reaching down to yank out a rogue whisker.

Roan sucked his teeth. "Ah. The magic's still wild, I see."

Snarling, I hooked one leg behind Mew and rolled us. Despite his outweighing me, the maneuver was successful, and I held him down for exactly two seconds before he tossed me away and jumped up. I rolled with fury. "Why would you say that? I'm clearly killing it, Roan!" I spun to face Mew, staring up at his gentle face, knowing underneath that small smile was a beast. "And you! I wasn't ready!"

He chuckled. "We're never ready, Jelly. That's why we train." His head turned as Mako entered, wearing his dark thoughts like a crown. Mew frowned at the smooth skin on Mako's legs, obvious compared to his hairy shins. "Did she set you on fire again, or have you started shaving your thighs for some reason?"

Roan scowled and crossed his beefy arms. "Jelly, lass, ye can't go on like this. That's Gray's magic that's out of control. What about the others? Any success with them?"

I lifted a hand in the air, Mew grasping it and hauling me to my feet. I turned to Roan. "No. It's not only Gray's flames. This morning, I levitated a lamp, Richard's magic, which smashed on the ground when I tried to pull the magical thread, and then, well, you just saw Simon's wolf bursting out of my face like a pricker bush." I brushed back my loose hair with impatient fingers, tapping my foot. "I want Surfecti training, straight from the source, but someone is stalling." I tossed my chin in Mako's direction.

Mako toed the thick mat at his feet, looking down, hands

on his hips. Mori slid up beside me, swiping back her curls to touch her temple, letting her communicate in my head telepathically. *He looks angry. Like he has all week.*

I set his legs on fire in reaction to a premonition. Eator. We've been fighting about my magic. I want to go to England to get a handle on it, and he's dragging his feet.

Mori gaped at me. *Why? Doesn't he want you to understand it?*

It doesn't seem to matter what I want. I'm losing patience with him.

Roan cleared his throat, obviously eavesdropping. His ability to listen to people's thoughts was a hefty part of his magic. He came closer, his voice a soft growl in my ear. "Be gentle with him, lass. Yer both new to the mate bond. It takes time to learn to negotiate."

I shoved him out of my space. "Stop listening in, Roan. It's rude. Also, when are you going to teach us to speak without needing to touch our temples? You said you would. Anyone who knows us can see we're having a private conversation, emphasis on private, not that you care."

Mori chimed in. "Yeah, you did. What's the holdup?" She stood toe to toe with him, glaring mischievously at his green eyes while cocking out a hip. Roan stiffened, affected by her close proximity. He took a step back. Mori stepped in. Roan's eyes narrowed at her challenge. The rough spark between them broke when Mew tackled me from behind, flinging me to the floor to grapple, and Mori burst out laughing from the shriek I let out.

"Mew!" I slipped away from him like a wet fish. "I was having a conversation!" He positioned himself in a cross-legged posture. I adjusted my wayward bun, fuming. "You can't just barrel into me without preparation!"

He smiled at my outrage. "Use your magic on me, Jelly. I want to see it. Throw it all at me, everything you've got." I whipped out a hand and blasted his reposed lotus, using my Mers scream. He shielded, letting my turquoise magic flow around him like a gentle caress rather than the hurricane I intended. He arched up an eyebrow. "Oh, come on, Jelly, that was your Mers. Too easy. Let's see this cockamamie magic, the stuff you clearly can't control."

Goddess, damn it. He knew that comment would tick me off.

I flung out my other hand. Double-barreled blue energy shot at the smug expression on his face. He blinked and looked at me with disappointment as it slid over him, which only fueled my fury. I pulled on Gray's magic, orange flames leaping from my hands and stretching toward his head. At least he didn't have any hair to burn. But before it could reach him, it ricocheted and lit my sweatpants on fire. I squealed.

Mew lifted a fist and snuffed the flames, shaking his head. "Try harder, Jelly."

I called the red line inside me, blasting at Mew with pulses so strong they made my arms tremble. That was Branko's gargoyle magic, and considering I wasn't a Shifter, I didn't know what it would do. I was hoping for wings one day.

Mew swatted the pulses away, staring at his nails. "Whenever you're ready."

I roared in frustration and drew on every piece of magic inside me, Mers, Fae, and Surfecti. I was sick of my inability to direct my power, exasperated with my ineptitude. My feet unintentionally left the mat with purple magic, but I didn't falter. Hovering a few inches in the air, I assembled the different threads, weaving a bolt from eight strands of magic, aiming at Mew's condescending smirk with my palms. My muscles strained from the effort as I put all my rage into the bolt. This would shut him up.

But before I could send it, I lost hold of the maroon thread, and a heavy white tail ripped out of my charred pants. Turquoise fire shot to the ceiling, narrowly missing a beam, and the purple thread evaporated, dropping me. I collapsed on the floor, deflated, letting it all drain away. The green thread from Roan's magic allowed me a wisp of Mew's thoughts.

She's worse than I thought.

My unbidden tail lashed against the mat in frustration until I found the maroon line and squelched it. I dropped my face in my hands, trying to tame the chaos inside me. Mew's voice was soft. "Our training isn't working, Jelly. I thought I could get it out of you in a cohesive manner, but you're completely out of control. Your anger is getting in the way."

I slammed my palm down, the violence of it stinging. "My anger? My anger is all I have, Mew! It calls my magic!"

"Not so, Jelly. You are far more than anger."

His gentleness stoked the fire inside me. "Am I? I'm a mermaid with a furious scream, capable of exploding the world, and yet, now that I'm mixed with all this extra magic, I can't make it work anymore! And Mako won't let me get help, and I'm setting the sheets on fire, and smashing up the room, and he's...he's..."

I bit back the words, literally snagging my lip in my teeth. I wanted to say he was a chicken-shit spineless jellyfish who had no faith in his mate and her abilities, faltering as they may be. Mew's eyebrows raised. I wondered if he'd caught my unspoken thoughts.

Mako's voice was icy as he stalked toward us. "He's what, Jelly? Go on. Tell us your true feelings."

I slapped both hands on the mat, needing to hit something. "Damn it, Mako! This is how we're doing it? With an audience? Fine! I've had seven foreign strains of magic thrust into me, and I can't command a single piece of it. You brush me off, thinking that with enough time, I'll master it. I can't, okay? I can't fucking control it! I need help!" I buried my face in my hands.

Mori came to my side, crouching down to lay her hand on my shoulder, speaking on my behalf. "Gods, Mako. She was just managing the influx of power from the pearl when you all did the forced fusion ritual. You never taught her how to wield the magic, and it comes out at inopportune moments, leaving her with a sense of failure." I swallowed thickly while Mori kept speaking. "Mother Kokuro claimed her, although not a drop of Fae blood runs naturally in her veins. How must that be for her? You were there, Roan. You saw how shocked she was when she first turned to Fae form."

Roan agreed solemnly, stepping closer. "Aye. I saw. Drop yer hands, lass. Look at my face." I complied unenthusiastically. "I saw how ye struggled to command the magic, but ye did. Remember that, lass. Ye made it work."

I threw a hand in the air, exasperated. "Only because it was do or die! Terror took the wheel that day, Roan. I want to use this magic proficiently when I call it, when I command it. Right now, it's carnage!"

Mori glanced between me and Mako. She narrowed her eyes as he postured defiantly, certain of his justified stance. She spoke aloud, wanting witnesses to his answer. "Is he holding you back?"

I stared at the ceiling, neither confirming nor denying.

Mori glared at Mako. "If she says she needs help, then she needs it." I glanced at her gratefully, letting her fight my corner, peeking at Mako, who was turning a furious shade of red.

Mori jerked up her chin and seethed at Mako, vitriol rolling off her. "You're her mate. You're supposed to support her, but you're ignoring her requests. She needs you! Gods, Mako! Do better!"

Mako's restraint snapped. "Supposedly, what she needs is yellow, whatever the fuck that means, because we can't go to the Hellhole without it!" He sucked in a breath as everyone stared at him. I groaned at his slip of the tongue. I'd wanted to tell Mori about my dream privately.

Mori's jaw dropped open as she sprang to her feet. "What yellow? What Hellhole?" She spun to me. "Jelly? What happened? What's he talking about?"

Mako dropped his forehead into his hand, shaking his head. I cleared my throat and flung an accusatory finger at my mate. "What happens now is directly your fault, Mako. You let it slip, not me." I cringed, instinctively drawing up my shoulders, knowing things were about to get messy. "Mother Kokuro came to me in a dream. She knows where Leif is."

Roan, Mori, and Mew roared collectively. "What?"

Roan recovered first. "Leif's alive?"

I swallowed. "He's trapped in a Fae dimension, the Hellhole, and we're meant to get him, but I'm missing yellow, and I can't go until I have it, but we can't figure out what it is."

Mori's face was a crumple of hurt. "Why didn't you tell me? When did this happen?" She sank to her knees in front of me. "I would have helped you." She glanced over at Mako with venom in her eyes. "He told you to keep it a secret, didn't he?"

Mako snarled, his lips pulling back. "Kokuro said she won't survive without her yellow, and I'm not letting her die for my brother! But we have to go. We have to get him. I've been trying to figure it out. Gods almighty, this isn't straightforward, Mori!" His body tensed with anger. "And while I appreciate Jelly is your best friend, she's my mate. My. Mate. I know what's best for her."

My jaw dropped open, too stunned to counter his statement.

Mori rose and faced him, her voice scathing. "Oh, I'm fully aware she's your mate, Mako. Believe me, I've keenly noticed her absence. But as for you knowing what's best, you and I clearly have different opinions about that." Her fists curled at her sides as she stepped into his space. Guilt swallowed me. I'd shunned my friend and her brilliant mind because my mate had asked me to. When had she and I last been alone together? I couldn't remember. They circled each other with hostility in their eyes.

I needed to stop them. "No fighting! Look, I need help. It's clear to everyone that I can't handle this Surfecti power. And maybe I won't find my yellow until I do." I clamped my palms over my eyes. "I need to find whatever is missing. It's not just Leif. I need it for me! Mako, why can't you understand?"

As it was all in the open, he unleashed. "I'm worried about you! It's called love!" Mako's face reddened as his eyes sparked with blue magic. He was losing his grip on his emotions. I could sense his desperation, and a good mate would try to calm him. I wasn't that person.

I rolled my eyes. "Oh! Love is it? Not that I have much experience, but controlling someone isn't loving!" I was angry, embarrassed, hurt, and frustrated; a whole slew of emotions I couldn't carry with grace. Typically, this was when I would lose it and blow something up.

Thankfully, Leoht was keeping her cool. She rattled the pearl at my throat. *Calm down. This helps no one.*

My lip curled up. *Help me or butt out.*

Don't let them fight, Jelly. You need everyone on the same side.

I looked up just as Mori pushed Mako back, a sneer on her face. I'd missed whatever they'd slung at each other. Roan got between them before blows could fly, and held a palm on each of their chests, separating them. He said, "All right, enough now."

Mew watched silently, pensive. I stewed, still sitting on the mat opposite him. I pointed a finger at him and said, "You started this, Mew. You made me lose my temper. I'm finishing it. I'm going for a swim. Mori? Join me?" Mako turned toward the door as well. I stopped him. "No, Mako. Just Mori. I need some time with her alone." Pain flashed through his dark eyes at the rejection. He spun around, giving me his back.

Mew interjected with a creased brow. "Jelly, we're not done here."

My laugh was sharp, with no humor. "Yes we are, Mew. I can't control a lick of my magic, and I'd rather not rub my face in my failure. I'm done."

Mori wove her arm through mine, and we marched for the door. I had my ass in the breeze from the accidental tail shredding my pants, but held my whisker-free chin high. When we got outside, I exhaled. I looked over my shoulder as Roan shook his head and pinched the bridge of his nose. Mew's eyebrows drew down on his wide face, rubbing over his bald head.

My heart stuttered as Mako watched us go, his face mournful like he'd lost his best friend. I swung my chin forward and walked.

THREE

MAKO

As the love of my heart stormed away, I slammed my fist into the punching bag, hard enough for it to reverberate up my tendons. Running my fingers through my hair in frustration, I tugged and muttered under my breath.

Roan's voice boomed across the gym. "Aye, well fook if that's not a mess. Why ye didn't tell us about Leif? And what is this yellow? We're yer family, Mako. Ye shouldn't keep secrets from family."

I spun on him, ready to defend my choices, but my anger dropped when I faced him and Mew, both standing with their arms crossed, eyes narrowed. Roan looked more imposing, with his full body tattoos and cut muscles, but I knew better. Mew typified a jolly giant with his kind eyes, bald head, and extra padding, appearing to be an older, paunchy male, but he was insanely powerful, both in strength and magic.

I scowled at them. "I had my reasons for keeping it a secret."

Roan snorted, running a hand over his thick braid. "Oh, aye, and that's going well. Jelly is ready to flay ye."

Mew tilted his head, the light flashing off his bald head. "Why are you avoiding England?"

I fisted my hand, irritation hot in my skin. "She's been

practicing grasping the different strains of magic, but they're elusive, reluctant to bend to her. If we go to England, it's an admission of weakness and I was trying to spare her. She hates feeling weak." I swept my hand toward my bald thighs. "But she's a mess. She burned the bed again."

Roan chuckled, his lips twisted into a grin. "Any reason she went for yer jewels?"

I leveled a glare at him and rolled my shoulders back, but my bravado quickly faded. I exhaled loudly, ready to lay it all out. Frankly, it was a relief to talk about it. I shook my head, my eyes cast down in defeat. "We've argued about it constantly. She's wanted to tell you since she had the dream. I asked her to wait. She's ready to go tearing into the unknown without being fully equipped. I'm trying to protect her."

"From what?" Mew looked genuinely puzzled.

I stared at him as if he were dense. My tone was incredulous. "From herself!" Roan snorted and widened his stance. I threw a hand in the air. "Seriously, you guys? The Fae dimension? To a place called the Hellhole? She's in a sprint toward danger, and I can't let her. I won't let her. End of discussion." I crossed my arms defiantly, the three of us mirroring each other.

Mew rubbed his bald head, absorbing my words. He slowly dropped his hand, continuing to scrutinize me as if judging my sincerity. When I didn't falter, his eyes widened and his mouth frozen open in shock. He blinked twice. He said, "You're protecting her from danger? No…wait. You *are* serious."

I barked my reply. "I am."

Mew stared, baffled, and burst into great guffaws, honking like an asthmatic donkey as he brayed in my direction. He tried to speak, holding up a finger. He glanced at my darkening scowl, which caused him to double over, slapping his thighs as tears leaked from his eyes. He waved his hand, grasping for breath, but ended up sinking to his knees to pound on the mat.

I snapped at him. "Fuck off, Mew. It's not that funny."

At that, he collapsed and rolled onto his back, grabbing his belly as his entire body shook. Damn if it wasn't contagious. Roan snickered, trying to stay neutral, until he threw his head back and roared at my expense. This set Mew off further. Mew struggled to inhale and wiggled on the floor, squealing like a baby pig. My lips twitched, my stubbornness sliding apart.

Mew could barely speak, choking on his words. "You…you…you!"

Roan's hands were on his hips, his torso bent forward as he gasped for air through his laughs.

I half-grinned through a surly chuckle. "You both suck."

Roan finished Mew's thought, his tattooed fingers rubbing his chin as a smile split his face. "Yer bent because yer girl wants to chase danger? Christ, man, have ye met her? She's a fuokin' typhoon! And ye think ye can stop her?" He buckled with laughter again, causing Mew to squirm, the donkey honks taking over the squeals.

The smile that had formed on my lips dropped away. "She's not just my girl. She's my mate! It's different!"

Mew rolled over and panted, humming in his throat as he struggled to contain himself. He lay on his stomach, his ruddy face turned toward me and resting on his forearms, random chuckles still slipping from his lips. He wore a ridiculous grin as he wiped his eyes with his fingertips. "Oh, Mako, Mako, Mako. It's hard to be on this side of the fence, isn't it?"

He stood with a grace that didn't suit his massive size. He clapped a hand on my shoulder, his brown eyes twinkling. "Now you know what you put your parents through. All your secret missions, risking your life without a thought for anyone else… I can't wait to tell your father about this."

I shook my head. "Don't, Mew. Not yet. I haven't told them about Jelly's dream."

Roan sighed, clearing the mirth from his throat. "Yeah, so she said. Why not?"

Rubbing my temples, I exhaled. "What if she can't do it? Get this yellow? We don't even know what it means. What if she's lost in the Hellhole? And let's say she finds this yellow thing, goes to the Hellhole, and we can't find Leif? What then? It would crush my parents. I don't think Mom would survive."

Roan slapped me on the back of the head, hard enough to make me step forward. I turned to him with bared teeth, my Fae magic close to the surface. He rolled his eyes contemptuously. "Yer a dumb fook sometimes. Yer mother is the leader of your family. She's yer glue. The woman's got a steel spine and grit for days. And your Da? Have ye ever seen him falter? He's bloody Fae, ye daft muppet."

I opened my mouth to counter, but Roan kept talking. "He gets frustrated with ye now and again, but he's always had yer back, Mako. He's supported ye even when it scared the hair off his chest. Cutting up nets, alone in the dead of night, in shark infested water. Ye fookin' twit. Now ye understand what it's like having someone ye love go tearing off into the wilds."

I grimaced as guilt slashed at my heart. Since Leif's disappearance, I caused my parents to worry, but I'd never considered how terrifying my activities were for them. Mew drew me away from Roan by the shoulders, looking me square in the eye. He smiled broadly, deep lines crinkling his cheeks. "Do you remember when I showed you…me?"

Mew had bailed me out of jail, arrested for attempting to sabotage a whaling vessel, sparing my parents the heartbreak. As we sat on the steps outside the police station, I resisted his vehement plea to give up my illegal pursuits, despite them landing me in a cell. He'd told me to keep defending the ocean, but to restrain myself from actions that could end with imprisonment. He could only do so much without involving them.

I'd told him to mind his own business. When he said that I was his business and making his job impossible, I'd rolled my eyes and said something snarky. My attitude changed in a heartbeat when he showed me his higher form, available only to me. I remember I'd stuttered and scooted away. He wasn't from this realm. He never explained exactly what he was, but it didn't matter. He'd made his point. He was my guardian, and I was making him work overtime with my hazardous activities.

Mew sighed and squeezed my shoulders. "You and Jelly are so alike. It's no wonder you're fated for each other." He lifted his eyes to the sky and frowned, as if cursing his life's assignment. He dropped his face back to mine. "She's powerful, Mako, and she won't allow you to treat her like glass. Don't forget who you fell in love with. You call her the savage queen for a reason."

All the tension in my soul dropped at his words. He was right. I loved that about her, and I was trying to squash it. He dropped his hands and smiled at me kindly.

Roan chuckled. "Aye, we want to wrap the ones we love in cotton wool, and tuck 'em in cozy so the world never touches them. But ye can't. Not with Jelly. She is wild. It's her nature, and ye can't pin her down like a butterfly. She won't stand for it."

Mew frowned as I absentmindedly roughed my fingers over my throat, thinking about the part of Jelly's dream that I hadn't shared with them. Mother Kokuro told her I needed my necklace. Jelly had pestered me about it until I lashed out at her, shutting her down. Mew said, "You still aren't wearing your Hai Matau, your pendant. You need to put it on and reclaim its gifts."

I scowled as I dropped my hand, fisting it on my hip. "Your psychic abilities are freaky, Mew."

A wide grin split his round face. "Not psychic. Observant."

Roan stepped closer. "What's this? Tell me the story." He sank to the floor, stretching out meaty thighs, inked all the way to his toes. Internally, I groaned. I wouldn't escape this. I sat across from him, cross-legged, and Mew dropped beside me.

My voice was soft. "I'm sure I've told you." Roan shrugged, reaching for his feet to stretch his hamstrings. I picked at a thread on my shorts, not meeting their eyes. "A friend of Dad's gifted me a Hai Matau at birth. An orca tail in jade. It's special. Leif loved it and always wanted it. I haven't worn it since the day he disappeared. We hovered over a deep hole, far back in the cave Dad expressly said not to enter, daring each other to go down. I offered a trade, egging him on, saying I'd give him the necklace if he brought up a handful of sand. He went in and never came back. I couldn't wear the Hai Matau after that. It only reminded me of him, and my part in his disappearance." Unbidden, tears gathered in my chest.

I cleared my throat as Roan and Mew remained silent. "I should be grateful that he's alive, and I am. Trust me, it does a lot to ease my guilt. But he's stuck in a Fae dimension, lost in the Hellhole, and Jelly's been told she won't survive a rescue attempt without her yellow, and that neither of us are welcome since we aren't pure Fae. We'll need Leoht to take her true form and guide us. Leoht is not happy about it. Jelly told me she's terrified." I scrubbed my hands over my face. "I want to support Jelly. I do. But…" I shook my head. "Losing Leif sent me on a destructive path. If I lost Jelly…" I swallowed down a lump of emotion.

Mew spoke softly. "So it's *your* fear that's holding her back. You want to shield her from danger because you're frightened of how you'll respond if it goes wrong."

I yanked on the loose thread in my shorts, causing the fabric to bunch up. I smoothed out the wrinkle. "If Jelly died, I'd burn the world to the ground. She's not afraid of anything, champing at the bit to find her missing piece, desperate to understand her magic; magic we thrust into her, and I'm holding her back. She's ready to dive into the darkest dimension of the Fae world to find Leif." The skin around my eyes crinkled in a twist of disbelief and worry. "She's never even met him."

Mew smiled. "No, but he's important to you. And she saves and protects the innocent. Mako, that's who she is." He tipped his head as he watched his words settle in. "May I correct you on an earlier assumption?" I shrugged and waved him on. "When arguing with Jelly, you said, 'I'm worried about you. It's called love.' Now, that's confusing your fear with love. Can you see why she's upset? Especially given her background with the Trident muzzling her?"

I blinked, then dropped my face into my hands, moaning as I slid them through my hair to grab at the roots. I looked at Mew with haunted eyes. "We're fated mates. I thought that was enough. How does anyone survive relationships?"

Roan made a noise, somewhere between a grunt and a laugh. Mew grinned. "Trial and error. But mostly, communication. Lots of communication. Own your fear. Explain your projections. Reassure her. Sometimes manning up means eating crow." He chuckled to himself, winking at me. "Actually, it means eating a lot of crows." He looked at the large tattooed man beside him. "And you said you'd teach them hands-free telepathy. They will need it."

I spun to him, hope making my voice squeak. "Wait, what do you know?"

Mew shrugged. "Jelly needs her yellow."

I edged closer to him. "Do you know what it is? Where to find it?" Mew pressed his lips together tightly. I said, "Oh, come on, Mew, can you give me a hint at least? You have power. You have connections. Please."

Mew squinted his eyes at me in a rare show of impatience. "You know that's against the rules, Mako. I need to remain impartial or face painful consequences." He leaned in, looking around before he spoke, as if the padded walls had ears, his lips grazing the shell of my ear. "Get your necklace." He sat back and stared at me, his eyes intense. Then he squeezed them shut as if in pain. He blinked back tears and pressed the heels of his hands to his temples.

I sat forward, alarmed. "Mew? Are you okay?"

"It's fine." He ground out the words between clenched teeth. His body sagged after the shortest migraine I'd ever seen. He rubbed the back of his skull, his face twitching.

Roan looked back and forth between us. "What do ye mean, connections? What's yer magic, Mew?"

Mew smiled, his headache forgotten, eyes exploding with delighted mischief. "Ah, well, Roan, pass a challenge. Pin me down for five seconds to find out."

I cocked my head. "You've said that to Jelly. Why could you tell me?"

Mew shrugged his shoulders jovially. "Because you're my responsibility."

Roan rolled his neck. "Five seconds? We're roughly the same size, same weight. All right. Let's go." Mew grinned and clapped his hands together, vanishing. Roan snarled at the emptiness left behind. "Nah. That's playin' dirty. Show yerself." A second later, he was flat on his stomach with an arm twisted behind him, his back arching painfully. He slammed his free hand on the mat. "I can't fight a ghost."

Mew's voice echoed throughout the gym, filling every crevice with the sound. "I'm no ghost, Roan. Five seconds. Again." Roan leaped to his feet, his hands outstretched for Mew, thinking he was merely invisible. A tap on his shoulder sent him spinning around, grasping at empty air before his knees buckled and he fell hard on the mats.

He froze, his eyes wide, his voice stiff. "Is that a blade at me throat?"

Mew's voice chuckled. "Not exactly. Feels like it though, doesn't it?" I could see, and Mew held the edge of a feather to Roan's skin.

Roan swallowed thickly and said, "I yield. I'd rather check on the lasses than have my ass handed to me. Mako, let's go to the beach and find yer girl. Mew, ye come too, ya bald bastard." Mew's deep laughter filled the air. Mew shimmied into view and held a hand out to Roan, helping him to his feet. Roan dusted himself off and sucked his teeth. "Five seconds for yer secrets, eh?"

Mew grinned. "That's right. Five seconds and I'll tell you. Even better, I'll show you. But there are rules. Five seconds."

I turned off the lights as we left, turning toward the steep stairs that led to the beach. Mew stopped me. "It's time. Go get it."

I swallowed my hesitation. "Okay. It's up in my old room."

I ran for the sliding glass doors and slipped through, hoping to skirt past my mother, but she had a sixth sense about things. "Mako? What are you doing, honey? I thought you were training." I rounded the corner, finding her in the living room, a laptop balanced on a cushion on her legs.

"Hey, Mom. We are. Were. We're going down to the beach." I kissed her cheek, wanting to avoid Jelly's dream, her strange magic, Leif, the Hellhole…anything. She hummed in her throat and looked at me with curiosity. I laughed awkwardly, my fingers twitchy, nerves alight.

She said, "Ask Mew if he'll stay for lunch. Fish tacos. His favorite." Suspicion crept up my spine. Her insight was uncanny, like she'd developed psychic abilities and not told me.

I tried to sound natural. "Perfect, I'll tell him. See you later." I bolted up the stairs, glancing over my shoulder to see her watching my departure with wistful eyes. She shook her head and returned to her work. I paused outside my childhood door.

I hadn't been here in years. I'd moved to the small house on the far edge of the property when I turned sixteen, my parents happy to give me more space as I'd been a terror after Leif disappeared. Mom had turned my room into an art studio.

I stepped through the various easels she had set up, admiring her work. Her oils were rich and thick, mostly stills of plump fruits, whereas her watercolors were loose like smoke, dawn rising on the ocean in pale blue and orange. I paused at a charcoal sketch of me and Jelly in an embrace. It was beautiful, capturing my mate in a moment of joy, something I hadn't seen often enough.

Love shone through her eyes as she smiled at me, my hand gently cupping her face. Her head tilted as though she were leaning into my touch, her lips soft, her face hopeful. Had I put that look on her face? How long had it been since I'd last seen it? Mom had given most of her attention to Jelly's expression. For me, there were quick lines shaping my face and the drape of my hair, my lips curled up. But she'd done my eyes, and they glowed with fascination. I lifted my fingers and traced over Jelly's profile in the air, careful not to smudge the drawing.

A pang struck me, and I regretted my previous words to Jelly. I thought I was being protective, an act of love. I rubbed the back of my neck ruefully. I'd completely misunderstood how she would receive my concern. Truthfully, though, we barely knew each other. All we'd shared since the moment we met was chaos. We now lived in the still between storms, and neither of us could navigate the calm.

I moved to the closet and stopped to breathe. Old guilt and shame rose in my chest, but I pushed past them, refusing to let the ghosts haunt me. I rustled around, sliding little-used winter coats along the rail, moving snow boots and ski boots into the room so I'd have space to lift the loose floorboard. I jiggled it, hearing it groan after so many years of slumber. I dug against the wall but couldn't find a purchase, my fingers much larger than when I hid it.

I cursed and spun to the room, searching for a tool. There. One of Mom's palette knives. Careful not to nick the smooth edge, I wiggled it against the wall and popped up the board.

My breath stalled as I stared at the box.

I steeled myself and picked up the small black square, noticing the hum of energy that met my skin. Was it pleased? Angry? I slipped it into my pocket and tapped down on the board before returning the closet to itself. I stopped in front of our portrait once more, desperate to see that expression on Jelly more often. She looked so happy. I rushed downstairs and flew out the door without a word to my mother. I wouldn't be able to lie if she asked me why I'd been in my room.

Mew and Roan were sitting on the wall by the pool, admiring the new sculpture Dad had found after Jelly blew up the concrete mermaid. It was a fanciful piece; three young nymphs gathered around a fat koi spouting water out of pursed lips. Roan looked up as I approached. "Ye set, mate?" I nodded and turned for the stairs. We descended together, both men quiet behind me despite their enormous size. When my feet hit the sand, I scanned for her, hearing her laugh from the water.

FOUR

MORI

The wheels in my mind churned as Jelly explained her dream from Mother Kokuro. I couldn't fathom what yellow meant. Was it a strain of magic? Something a Surfecti needed to give her? Or was it an aspect of herself? Yellow, yellow, yellow. I tapped my fingers on my lips, turning over possibilities.

Jelly finished speaking, combing her hand through her hair in frustration. I said, "Well, she told you to ask your witch. There's your answer. You need Anna to find this missing yellow, and she could have helped you seven days ago, but no, you've been keeping it a secret, setting the sheets on fire, and I don't mean that in a good way. Plus a tail and whiskers? Levitation? Jelly, you've got to train with the Surfecti. There's no alternative. You're going to hurt someone."

I huffed at her and wrapped an arm around my middle, chewing on my thumbnail, her week-long rejection of my talents still stinging. I couldn't keep the bitterness out of my tone. "I can't believe you kept this from me, Jelly. I mean it. I'm really hurt. I'm the brains in this operation, remember?"

Jelly groaned and stared at the sky, unable to meet my eyes. "Mako asked me not to tell anyone. Not even you. That was a mistake. I'm sorry, Mori." She dropped her face and gently reached for my thumb, pulling it from my agitated teeth. We were deep enough for her to float with her tail, but shallow enough for me to stand. My head poked out of the gentle waves.

I dunked my head to cool the angry tears in my eyes, wiping the salt from my face when I came up. "Well, I'm at a loss for words. You don't need Mako's permission. It's your life, Jelly. Your magic." I tipped my head at her. "Your responsibility."

Jelly flicked her tail in the water, looking down. "I wanted to respect his request. Leif is his brother."

"Sure, but you're the one missing something. Maybe that's why your magic is so unhinged."

Jelly's eyes scrunched up as she laughed. "Unhinged is the perfect word."

Now I understood the source of her snappiness, I said, "Contact Anna and get this sorted. Clear?"

"Crystal." She suddenly frowned and put her hand on my shoulder, lifting her fingers of her other hand to her temple. Someone from home was calling her. As she was touching me, I could listen in.

The Shaman's voice sprang into my head. *Jelly, are you there? Is Mori with you?*

Jelly smiled. *Hi Synchi. Yes, she's here. What's up?*

My Dad's familiar voice piped in, curling around me like a hug. *Mori? Hello, my little fish. I'm here with the Shaman.*

Toto! I grinned like a lunatic, picturing my enormous father with long red hair and matching beard.

Jelly smiled at my joy. *Hi Tro!*

Getting a conference call from them was odd. My eyebrows drew down. *Toto, why are you both calling?*

The Shaman replied. *Mori, I wanted to ensure you are being judicious with your transformation potion. Don't use it recreationally. If you need more, I can send it via Hannah, but it won't be easy.*

Jelly frowned. *Why not? She can come with the next round of mermaids.*

My dad answered to quickly. *We're just taking precautions. Nothing to worry about.*

I shook my head at Jelly. They were being too vague. Concern filled my voice. *Tell us what's going on. You're hiding something.*

The Shaman sighed, probably pulling on the braid on her chin. *Simply put, there's been an uprising. Since you two went to the surface and stayed, mermaids are demanding their rights. They want to surface for fun, with no expectation of getting pregnant, and the old mermen don't like that. We're attempting to restructure the Trident, but it's proving more difficult than we'd hoped. They're keeping everyone in the bubble. We're in lockdown.*

I gasped with shock, turning wild eyes to Jelly. *They've stopped the Procreation Missions?*

Jelly snarled in my head, wearing her fury on her face. *And are still controlling the mermaids, just different, making them prisoners instead of slaves.*

My dad's voice was calm. *Don't come home. Not right now. I'm sure it will blow over. Lady Amphi is working on swaying the Trident members to loosen their stranglehold, but they're facing the possibility of losing power, so obviously, they're fighting back.*

I picked at my nails, nervous for my father but not voicing it. Jelly chewed on her lip. The Shaman cleared her throat before speaking. *What is happening up there? Anything exciting? Jelly, how is your new magic?*

The smooth skin of Jelly's forehead creased as the corners of her mouth turned down. She was trying to figure out how to fudge. I rolled my eyes, catching Jelly's stare and holding it as I babbled before she could stop me. *Mother Kokuro told her she needs to find a missing yellow to rescue Leif, Mako's brother, from the Hellhole. She had the dream a week ago, and she kept it from me.*

Jelly's eyes flew wide as I confessed her secret. Then they scrunched up as she prepared herself. As expected, the Shaman's reply was sharp with anger. *What??? Jelly. Explain. All of it.*

Jelly mouthed 'thanks a lot' before telling my father and the Shaman her dream, and her lack of control over her magic, but she'd left out one critical part.

Like a child, I blurted. *And Mako isn't supporting her. He's holding her back.* Jelly pinched my arm in retaliation, falling into our childhood behaviors.

Both of them sighed. My father spoke gently. *It's difficult being fated. A mate is the person who will force your growth the most. So be patient, Mori. You've known Jelly far longer than Mako. He'll get there. Give him a chance.*

Damn it. Roan and Mew had said the same thing.

The Shaman's voice was stern. *Jelly, Mori, are you taking the contraceptive potions Anna gave you?* We both said yes, although I shouldn't bother. A pool jet couldn't get me pregnant. The Shaman chortled. *Tro, take that scowl off your face. They're grown mermaids and need to recharge. I'm simply ensuring they're being safe. Jelly, go to Anna. You're an idiot to ignore Mother Kokuro's advice. Keep me posted on your magic and this missing yellow. And Mori, no transforming unless you need to.*

I rushed in. *But you're okay, Shaman? Toto? Has anyone threatened you?*

There was a smile in his voice as my father replied. *We're fine. I promise. I love you.*

I love you too.

Jelly said goodbye and dropped her fingers, spinning to me in anger. "I wasn't ready to tell them!"

I crossed my arms. "Bad habit you've picked up. Secrecy."

Jelly flicked her tail, rubbing the sand on my legs. "So, the Trident. Do you think we should worry?"

I shrugged. "Toto says they have it handled. But no more missions. How crazy is that?"

Jelly frowned. "Yeah. It's weird. Not much we can do from here."

We fell silent for a while. I prodded the skin around my nails again, nervous to broach the topic foremost in my mind. I dropped my hand, squaring my shoulders. "So, um, can I talk to you about something?"

"Of course. What's wrong?"

"It's Roan."

"Oooh! What? Have you finally shagged him? Is he pierced? Down there? I mean, I wouldn't put it past him, with the tattoos and pierced nipples. He's probably got a pain kink." When I didn't reply, her eyes narrowed as she growled. "What? Did he hurt you? I'll rip out his throat if he did."

I choked on a breath. "What? No! I don't know if he's pierced. One more image to torture myself with. I haven't even kissed him. It's not that."

Jelly tilted her head. "What aren't you telling me? Mori, you can always come to me, especially when it concerns Roan."

I dug my toes into the sand, pouting. "You're always busy with Mako."

She groaned and threw her hands in the air. "I already apologized! We're trying to learn how to communicate, and I'm used to you, I guess, someone who knows me as well as their own face. I'm struggling with the whole fated mate thing, having to think of him all the time."

I scrunched up my brow. "Watching you and Mako doesn't give me the greatest of confidence in fate. No offense."

Jelly snorted. "None taken. We've fought nonstop since my dream." She frowned with hurt in her eyes. "I thought that being mated meant it would be sunshine and unicorns. It's not."

"Hmm," I said noncommittally. She'd just confirmed my stance on relationships. They were trouble.

She said, "So, Roan. What's going on?"

My dreams for Europe, for the unification of magic, hovered on the tip of my tongue. I just needed to word it properly so she wouldn't freak out. I opened my mouth, inhaling to explain, but she stopped me with a hand on my shoulder, her eyes lifting over my head. Her lips pressed together in a tight frown, but her eyes softened. "Mori, Mako is swimming toward us. Can we have a moment alone?"

Seriously? Now? We'd barely had half an hour together. "All you've had are moments alone. But sure, I get it. You need to kiss and make up." I tucked away the rejection and leveled my gaze at her. "Stick up for yourself. You need control over your magic. You need your yellow, and you aren't finding it here."

Mako's head popped up. I squeezed Jelly's shoulder, glaring at him. Idiot. He needed to trust her, not smother her. I sighed, relegated to a secondary position in the dynamics, and dipped underwater, pushing away from them. I looked back, seeing their tails close together, one cobalt, one turquoise. Bitterness flared in my throat as I surfaced for breath.

I swam for the beach, my legs kicking in the waves. I missed my tail. I scowled, wishing someone had blasted me with Fae magic, allowing me to transform whenever I wanted. But no, no such luck. I was stuck with my legs. And now I couldn't go home if I wanted to. I strolled through the surf toward Roan, who stood transfixed, watching me.

He'd pulled off his shirt, his inked body soaking in the morning sun. My eyes flicked over his ridged abs, the low sling of his shorts, and damn if he didn't subtly flex his pecs, making those barbell piercings catch the light. He stepped forward and handed me a towel, his eyes greedy as they ate up my pale skin, hovering too long on my soaked top. I took his stare leisurely, enjoying the hunger on his face. I swept the rough cloth down my limbs with slow attention, hearing Roan's breath shorten as my ass lifted higher. I loved having this imposing man in my thrall.

I should stop pouring it on so thick. Mew confirmed my thoughts with a chuckle. My eyes flitted over to his grinning face. Mew. He was other. That much was clear from our training. He was an enigma, shrouded in mystery, and one I intended to uncover, but I'd never be able to pin him to the mat. I'd have to find another way to get him to spill his secrets.

His smile widened as his gaze flitted between me and Roan, knowing exactly what I was doing and how I affected Roan. My seduction skills were, after all, exemplary. My lips twitched. I had Roan paralyzed, his nostrils flaring as he absorbed my every movement. I squeezed the water from my long red curls and twisted the towel around my waist. I'd worn the white bikini to torture Roan, and it was working. He couldn't tear his eyes from me.

I snapped my fingers in his face to break the spell. "Did Mako tell you everything about Jelly's dream?"

Roan wiggled his head, my words pulling him from his trance. He sighed roughly and ran his fingers over his beard. "Aye. He did. We need to go to the Coven. We need Anna."

"That's what I said."

Roan grunted with annoyance. "He should have told us. We could have helped sooner."

"Also what I said." I smiled at him. "Seems we agree."

"Aye, on some things." His eyes flashed hot as I readjusted my top. Then they fell to my legs, encased in the towel. "Does it bother ye, lass? Being stuck in this form? I imagine it's like a part of ye is missing without yer tail."

His astute observation shocked me. I stepped closer to him, my fingers lightly touching his thick forearm. "Something fierce.

I'm jealous that Jelly and Mako can change back and forth. I'd love to do that." Gratitude rustled through me along with an ache in my heart. "Thank you for noticing."

His chin tucked down and he leaned close, so close, too close. "Ye know I watch ye, lass. I can read ye." The growl of his voice shot to my center, exploding like fireworks, and the scratch of his beard on my cheek made my breath hitch. It was too much like my dream. I pulled away my hand and leaned back, unnerved by his words. My heart thumped in a frenzy.

I blurted the first thing I could think of. "Your beard is ticklish. You should shave it off."

He grinned, green eyes twinkling. "Give me a reason to, lass."

I stepped further away, flustered, putting distance between us. I turned my back to him and shaded my eyes with my hand, watching Jelly and Mako in the water. She'd crossed her arms, then uncrossed them as she flung a hand in the air. He floated like a statue, taking it. She was angry and yelling. Fated mates. It didn't look fun.

FIVE

MAKO

I kept a small distance between us to respect Jelly's space. She was justifiably upset. I said, "Jelly, I'm sorry. I wasn't listening to what you need. I get you want to understand your magic. I want that too. I thought I could keep you from danger, but Roan and Mew made me see I was wrong. I've acted like you're mine to defend, to control. I'm an idiot."

She didn't speak. If she had her legs, her foot would tap a rapid staccato. I sighed. Crow time. "I've behaved like the Trident, blocking you from your autonomy."

"And my friends."

I dropped my eyes in shame. "And your friends." I froze, suddenly worried. "Are you and Mori okay? I haven't…I haven't ruined anything, have I?"

Jelly frowned, her eyes glancing at the beach. "No. The trouble between me and Mori is my fault. I kept the dream from her, and that was my decision, but she's hurt. She and I are a team, Mako. She's all I had before you, and I alienated her. You're my mate, but she's my soul sister. Besides, as Anna would say, she's bloody brilliant, and we're both idiots for keeping her in the dark. If anyone can figure out my missing yellow, it's her."

She bit her bottom lip, making my heart flip over, her habit of teething her mouth still heating my blood. She said softly, "Share me, okay? I need Mori."

I stroked her cheek with my fingers. "I'm sorry, Jelly. I didn't think it through. I did what I thought was right."

She closed the gap between us, her tail fin curling around mine. "I'm sorry too. I'm frustrated with myself, and that turns to rage. I'm sorry about the fire this morning. I'm sorry about yelling at you and airing our troubles in public. You're acting from love."

Forgiven, I wrapped my arms around her waist, our tails wafting in the waves to keep our heads above water. "It wasn't love. It was fear, my terror, that something would happen to you. My fear is why I've been reluctant to talk about magic or yellow or Leif or anything. I just want to breathe before we rush into danger."

She pulled my face to hers, her turquoise eyes wide as they gazed into mine. Our lips were fractions away, and we shared a breath. "Tro was the same, when I was leaving for my surface mission, when I met you. He was also terrified." She scanned my eyes for understanding. "I'll tell you what I told him. I need your faith, Mako, not your fear."

I'd met Tro, Mori's father, who raised Jelly as his own after her parents died. She'd lived with the Shaman, but Tro was a major influence in her life, training her to be a warrior from childhood. He'd given me the man-to-man talk right after Jelly and I became mates, telling me that loving her would challenge my every limit and that my life no longer belonged to just me, but also a ferocious mermaid, who raged through the world with wild passion. He'd grinned and said that fate was fickle, and I'd met my match, literally.

I swept her hair into my fist and pressed my lips to hers in a fevered kiss, pouring my dedication and belief into her. Our kisses were always magical, but this one was a promise. I rested my forehead on hers, tightening my fingers in her blue tresses, overcome with my responsibility to her. "You have my faith. You're my savage queen. I will always be at your side. But I can't lose you, Jelly." I tugged hard enough to make her gasp.

Her breath was throaty. "You won't, Mako. Trust me to do this."

She kissed me, drowning me in her magic. I groaned, about to suggest we settle on the bottom and play further, but a sharp whistle from the beach turned our heads. Mew waved at us to return. Jelly frowned and said, "What does he want?" She kissed me again, quickly, and held my face. "I love you, Mako."

"And I love you." I cleared my throat and released her hair. "So, Jelly, I did something. Something you've ever so sweetly nagged me about. I got my necklace from the closet." Jelly's eyes blinked wide, our amorous kissing forgotten. She'd relentlessly badgered me to collect it, and I'd stubbornly refused, too nervous in case it rejected me. I'd thought it was better to let sleeping dogs lay still in case they showed teeth.

Jelly grabbed my hand, tearing toward the beach at incredible speed, her forceful tail pumping. I laughed as we zoomed for the shore. She let go, closing her eyes and concentrating. Her tail split in two, forming the long legs I adored, and I watched with pride as she no longer winced. Once, it had been tortuous for her.

She scowled at me with impatience. "Come on, Mako. Hurry."

I transformed and followed her as she strode purposefully through the surf, taking the towel that Mori offered before slipping on her sundress, shouting to Mew and Roan that they could turn around. She passed me the towel, and I wrapped it around my waist, shaking the water from my hair. Four sets of eyes stared at me expectantly. I swallowed my nerves, my voice wavering. "I'm not getting out of this, am I?"

Mew laughed. "No, Mako. You're not."

Mori said, "Wait. What have I missed? What is he doing?"

Jelly answered in a controlled tone, her body betraying her inner turmoil, with her arms tightly crossed, toes tapping the sand. "He's putting on his Hai Matau."

Mori gasped, her eyes wide. "His necklace?"

Jelly tried to mask her fear but failed. "Yes. His necklace."

I pulled on my shorts and dropped the towel, my heart thumping. I slipped my hand in my pocket, reaching for the innocent box, and Jelly moved to my side, holding her breath. I swallowed my trepidation and opened it, the small hinges creaking from age. My heart flew out of my chest as the green whale's tail shimmered in the sunlight. I stroked a fingertip over it, blinking back tears. Its magic strummed against my touch.

The leather cord glistened, perfectly preserved as if years hadn't passed. Jelly's fingers wrapped around the box, taking it from me as I lifted my Hai Matau. I swallowed a few times. Everyone was silent, waiting. Leif's face flashed in my mind, so similar to mine, with his dark hair and blue eyes. Hearing his laugh in my mind, I slipped the leather over my head with trembling fingers, and when the jade pendant touched my skin, right over the whirlpool Mother Kokuro had marked on my chest, I dropped to the sand like a stone.

SIX

LEIF

The guards were on our trail. We twisted down the dark, steamy passage, the walls of the maze stretching high over my pointed ears. I sniffed the air, sulfuric and heavy, with a trace of dark magic. "Xeno! Trix! Hurry!" My voice was a hiss through my teeth. We needed to reach the water, but the twin girls were exhausted, emaciated, their feet dragging against the slick stones as they stumbled and knocked together. We wouldn't make it at this pace.

Heavy footsteps pounded behind us, at least three sets of feet echoing against the walls. I yanked Trix onto my back, wrapping her thin arm around my neck. "Hold tight." I peered in the pitch black, sweeping Xeno into my arms. Trix hung like a cape, dragging my spine in the wrong direction. I hunched over, and with a small cry, her legs hooked around my waist, her nails digging into my skin. Xeno was barely conscious. Her lips gaped open, the whites of her eyes alarming.

I sprinted, digging my claws into the stone as adrenaline pumped through my muscles. We were an ungainly creature, our balance awkward, and I careened around the corner, leaping into the black void. We landed heavily on the ledge, and I pressed us against the wall. Trix buried her face in my neck as the guards dashed past us, luckily not looking down. I walked into the strange water, both icy and hot simultaneously. "Trix, Hold your breath. Do not let go or you'll die. Xeno is out. I'm going to cover her mouth and nose. Here we go."

I dove, commanding my transformation from Fae into Mers, cursing silently that I'd lose the pants I was wearing. Usually, I'd stash them in a hole in the wall, but we didn't have time for me to undress. We descended deeper into the water, freezing my skin yet making me sweat as it pricked into my nerves. I held Xeno like a doll in one arm, my hand over her face, pinching her nostrils. Trix's grip loosened, her thighs floating away from me, and I grabbed her wrists, locking her to my neck. I swam harder, forcing my tail to move faster through the dark tunnel. Soon, we surfaced in a cave lit with tiny green worms.

Trix groaned in my ear, and I swung around so she could grab the slick wall. "Climb up, Trix. I need to hand you Xeno. Don't quit now." Her breathing labored as she dragged herself over the edge, reaching down. I held Xeno high, my tail thrashing the water, needing to get out of the strange magic.

"I have her." Trix gasped for breath as she hoisted her sister, and with a final push and pull, Xeno was safe. I hauled myself out, swapping my tail for legs, rocking from the quick change. My muscles spasmed from the energy in the water. I dropped to my knees, peering over Xeno and checking her pulse. It was slow, but it was there. I sat back on my heels and swiped a hand over my face.

Trix looked puzzled. "How do you stand it? It's poisoned."

"The water? I'm half Mers. I guess it overpowers whatever is in there, although let me assure you, it's not pleasant." I pulled on a pair of threadbare pants, hoping they'd last a little longer. Clothing was scarce down here.

Trix rubbed a hand down her arm, shivering. "How did I?"

"I was touching you. You wouldn't be able to swim through it without me. Come. I have food and blankets. We need to wake Xeno so she can eat. You're both skin and bones." I gathered the limp girl in my arms and twisted along a tunnel to another cave, looking up into the dark nothingness above me.

I collected the lava rocks together and whispered an incantation, encouraging their glow. Placing Xeno close to the warm stones, I covered her with all the blankets I had, save the one I draped over Trix after handing her a sack with three holes for the head and arms. "Wring out your clothes, Trix." Trix nestled beside her sister, close to the heat.

Now that we were safe, I studied them. I hadn't looked closely during their rescue. They were identical twins except for a marking on Trix's leg. Blond hair reached their hips, and both had enormous brown eyes, the color of rich soil. Their skin was a deep golden yellow. Today was the first time I'd been able to slip past the guards as they changed shifts, the new replacements running late. Luckily, the ones leaving didn't wait, grumbling with hunger. After a quick debate, they decided leaving the girls unsupervised for a few minutes wouldn't matter.

I handed Trix a strip of dried meat. "It's salamander. Not very tasty, I'm afraid. But it's fatty and will help you rebuild your strength. You'll need it."

She recoiled at my offering. "I can't eat that."

I blinked at her in surprise. "It's all I have, Trix. You need to eat."

With trembling fingers, she took the meat, closed her eyes and hushed a prayer in a foreign language. She wiped back a rogue tear that rolled down her cheek and took a bite. She mumbled through a mouthful of tough meat. "What do I need strength for?"

I ran a hand through my long dark hair, loosening through the matted knots to let it dry. "Our escape. Someday, somehow, we're getting out of here. But you'll need to build muscle. We almost didn't make it." She sighed and kept chewing.

I stared up at the inky circle above us, knowing that in the other world, my family still missed me. At least, I hoped they did. In my mind, Simmi cried, begging me not to go down in the well. I wished I had listened. I gnawed on the jerky, lost in my thoughts.

Trix swallowed, her face pained as she did. "When did you get here?"

I rubbed my palm on my knee. "I'm not sure how long I've been stuck. Years, I would guess, but then Fae time works differently. It might be a momentary blip on the surface. Maybe it's been decades. There's no sun here to judge. It's just constant dark horror."

When I first fell through, I didn't move, huddled on the floor in Fae form. I'd stayed Fae since I landed. I'd seen my family calling for me, echoing their screams with my own. Mom came every high tide, her face contorting with agony as she swam to the bottom. She had transformation potions to give her a tail, the one she'd lost when she left the Mers, but it came at a cost. It hurt her.

She'd curl into a ball and sob my name, begging me to come back to her. I wailed for her to hear me, but she never did. She'd swim up as the tides changed, her tail pumping weakly, her skin torn from the tumultuous water pushing her against the rough edges of the walls. Twelve hours later, she'd return, and I would sit beneath her and die a thousand times.

Trix took another nibble and spoke through the mouthful. "Is anyone looking for you?"

I frowned at my memories. Dad came as Fae when the water was low, and I was certain he could break down the barrier between us. His electric blue magic chipped rocks from the walls, gathering at his feet in a pile as he blasted and blasted the circle beneath him repeatedly. He'd roar in frustration, destroying and rebuilding the rocks daily. One day, he stopped coming.

I answered quietly. "Not for a while."

Mako had tried the longest. He was so brave. He came day and night, high tide and low. He'd scream my name until his voice broke. I wept, watching him fall apart. He cried to me, saying he was sorry, and to please come home. He was right there, his cobalt blue tail so close I thought I could touch it. So close, but impossible to reach. To my horror, he'd taken off his Hai Matau. I yelled into the void to stop being stupid, to put it back on.

Trix cocked her head as she stared at me. Her large brown eyes went vacant. She refocused. "Your brother still suffers from terrible guilt. He believes he's responsible."

My jaw dropped open. "Are you a Seer?"

She shrugged a bony shoulder. "Something like that. Tell me about him. Tell me about the whales. He's surrounded by the energy of orcas."

"Mako has a Hai Matau, a talisman, shaped in an orca tail. The bonds in orca families are unbreakable. Orcas are gregarious, playful, but they're also deadly killers. Mako is like that. He's easy-going, but if you cross him? Threaten someone he loves? He turns vicious."

"Hmm." She mused over my words. "You love him deeply."

I smiled, the first genuine one in a while. "When Mako was born, I was ecstatic. I had a best friend in life, the greatest gift ever. The moment the talisman touched his skin, the orca magic snapped over me. When Simmi, our sister, was born a year later, the magic claimed her as well." My cheeks heated with shame. "But the love got twisted."

Oh, how I'd wanted that necklace. I'd burned with envy when Mako got it. The jade carving was so delicate, so fine. A master or mistress of the trade had created it. I wanted the power of the orcas. I was the oldest, the first son. I should hold us together. But I didn't have a talisman. I never received a sacred gift. So when he offered it in a dare, I lunged for it.

"Oh! You…" Her eyes squeezed shut, as she grasped at her head, sending her wet blond hair over her shoulder with the sudden violence of the motion.

"What Trix? What's wrong?"

Her voice sounded broken; broken for me. "You believe you caused your fall." She blinked her eyes. I dropped my face, unable to meet her open stare. When I first fell into the Hellhole, an old Fae lived in the cave beside mine, and tired of listening to my wailing, he explained by throwing his voice through the wall that Fae magic responded to emotion. He said I must have done something awful to deserve my fate.

I mumbled to Trix. "I did."

"Tell me."

I looked at the strange girl with her enormous, wise eyes, and told her the story with a heavy heart. When I'd reached the bottom of the well, I was full of scorn and avarice, mocking my brother for his innocence. He never should have made that dare. I'd sneered, lusting for the power I'd have with his necklace, power that would make me feel important. I deserved that. As soon as my fingers touched the sand, my vision had blurred, my heart ripped with panic, and I fell into the Hellhole with a scream.

She'd stopped eating to listen, her face contorted in dismay at my confession. Then she blinked, shaking her head, looking like she wanted to correct me, but she didn't speak. I waved at her meat. "Finish that, Trix."

Mako's necklace was the secret to them finding me. I was certain of it, but he'd taken it off the day I disappeared. He'd hovered over me, heartbreakingly explaining that he didn't deserve its gifts. I'd raged, screaming until I was hoarse that he needed to wear it, and torn up my fists from punching the sharp walls. Eventually, he stopped coming. I waited on my side of the well, watching obsessively, praying they'd return and free me. But hope had shrunk to a grain of rice that sat heavy in my heart, swamped by grief.

Xeno coughed and rolled dangerously close to the lava rocks. Trix caught her in time and pulled her back, helping her sit up. Xeno's eyes were bleary, her speech slurred. "What happened?"

Trix smoothed back her sister's hair. "Leif saved us. We were almost dead." She glanced up at me. "How did you do that?"

"I've been here a long time. I've avoided detection because I can swim in the waters, and you can't reach this cave by foot, plus it's where I last saw my family, so I stay. There's a whole network of tunnels, with the lava rock mine at the center. As for why? You were about to die. When the guards left you unattended, I saw a chance, and I took it. You've been bound and bled for ages."

What I didn't voice aloud was that this was my penance, putting my life at risk to save others. Some of the Fae I rescued called me a hero, but I shut that down. I was unworthy of the praise.

"Vingor will look for us," Xeno said weakly.

I nodded. "He will. But I haven't seen his guards touch the water. Can you eat?" Trix whispered furtively in her ear. Xeno glanced sadly at her sister and took the jerky. She blessed it before nibbling on the end.

Her body sagged over. "I'm too weak to sit up." I rushed to help her, not wanting Trix to spend her energy. Xeno groaned as I propped her against the wall. She said, "You've put yourself in danger for us."

I snorted softly, tucking the blanket around her. "This entire place is danger. That's nothing new." I looked at the thin girl, wondering what magic was in her blood. Blood that Vingor wanted. I shuddered. I'd seen what he did, capturing Fae and stealing their power. He collected their blood methodically, labeling each bottle carefully. The large cave behind the bleeding room carried shelving that spanned the entire wall, with hundreds, maybe thousands, of small bottles. I'd only glimpsed him a few times, an unnerving experience.

Vingor had the kind of handsomeness reserved for movie stars, but those playing the villain, dark and broody, with chiseled features accentuated by a scar that traced across his cheek, three white stripes, as though he'd been clawed. Rather than detracting from his good looks, the scar added to them, making him appear all the more wicked. It was clear he was the boss of this place, but for what, I didn't know.

Trix's voice faltered. "We can't escape. He said he'd never let us go." Tears wobbled in her eyes. She held up her wrist, a small black x on the inside. Xeno weakly showed hers. I lifted my arm, showing them mine. It had appeared with a flaming singe when I fell through the well.

I glanced behind her. In caves beyond this one, connected by long tunnels, other rescued Fae bundled together to survive. With the addition of the twins, we numbered over twenty. None of us could leave, branded with the small mark. I taught the others to catch salamanders, bringing them bait on a regular rotation. I was the only one who could swim the water unassisted, so I took it upon myself to be their protector, and when the bleeding room was empty, which wasn't often, I snuck in to pilfer whatever I could, gathering sacks, blankets, containers, and rope. I kept us as comfortable as I could.

Trix spoke with a soft, sad tremble. "We're just a burden on you now."

I watched her face sag in despair, mirroring mine. "Did you come through a hole like me?"

Xeno swallowed her mouthful and answered. "No. Someone stole us. We're… Rare. Powerful." She glanced at her sister. "Trix and I are…" Her words cut off as Trix violently shook her head.

My brows bunched together. "You can trust me. I won't hurt you."

Xeno coughed through a laugh. "Oh, we're not scared of you. You're a hero. They call you the Ghostfish."

I snorted. "Ghostfish?"

Xeno grinned. "Vingor's guards call you that. You have quite the reputation of slipping in undetected and freeing people. They worry you'll come on their watch."

I ran a hand through my damp hair. "You've been under extra guard. Vingor thinks you're important."

Trix nudged her toe against a warm rock. "We are. We're Amphibi." Her eyes welled up.

Xeno sighed, the sound strumming with sorrow. I gave them some space and left to check my traps, pleased to see two salamanders lured by the slimy orange eels. I learned you could stun the eels by squeezing their heads. I'd eaten them initially, but they made me heave for days.

I brought my fresh bounty close to the lava rocks, slicing and skinning the prize. Both girls turned their heads in dismay, refusing to watch. The wheels turned in my head slowly. Amphibi. Amphibians. Salamanders. They were eating their kin. Oh Gods.

I swallowed thickly. I had nothing else to give them. "I'm sorry. About the salamanders. I've searched for alternatives, but they are the only things we can eat." I made quick work of the meat, hating I had no other option for them. I cleared my throat. "Amphibi magic is incredibly rare. No wonder he wanted you. What does he get from it?"

With a glance at her sister, Trix answered. "Our blood is toxic. One drop could kill ten grown men. He told us we were special, and he could create an army from us." My face must have paled, because she rushed to soothe me. "We've learned to contain our poison. In our brethren, our skin is lethal, but we've adapted. If I said *Phyllobates terribilis* to you, would you know what that is?"

I shook my head. I hadn't seen a book in years.

She sighed. "We're endangered. We come from the line of the golden frog, but more important is our contribution to—"

Xeno cut her off. "No. No more, Trix. If we survive this, we'll tell him." She changed the subject. "You carry the mark as well. Have you tried to escape?"

I finished my salamander, rubbing my greasy fingers on my pants, trying not to snag them with my claws. "As soon as I get close to the entrance, I'm thrown back. I've tried all of them."

Trix wiped her face. "The mark must be some sort of binding spell. If you have one too, there's no hope. We'll just hide until we're caught or we starve." Her thin shoulders rolled forward in defeat.

I shook my head. "I don't believe that. There has to be a way out."

The Hellhole was a labor camp; a place where Fae went to die. I'd seen them mining the strange rocks. They chipped hunks of it from the higher walls to avoid being burned, but the skin on their hands blackened and peeled. When someone collapsed from the backbreaking work, guards unceremoniously rolled them into the glowing pit, their bodies becoming ash instantaneously. I collected the rocks without injury from a pile of discards, scampering to deliver them among my people.

Ordinary Fae, with lesser magic, usually ended up in the Hellhole for political reasons, having stupidly dared to criticize the ruling family. Loyalists reported them and they wound up here. Without the x on their wrists, they could leave, and I'd helped many find their freedom, leading them through the maze of tunnels to various entrances. The Fae I'd rescued from the bleeding room were different. They had deep magical powers, bore marks, and couldn't escape. If I saw the x, I brought them here, the only place I could guarantee their safety.

Trix gestured toward the lava rocks. "Do you know what those are?"

I shrugged. "They're cold until you whisper over them and heat them. Are they some kind of fuel?"

Trix nodded solemnly. She tipped her head to the side, studying me. "Not everyone can activate them. You have the power. It's very curious, Leif. You can swim in the waters and light the rocks. And the eels? You touch them with your bare hands?"

"They give a shock if you don't catch them just right."

She frowned. "They're elecatraba eels. They're toxic. Usually, just brushing against them would kill you. I wonder what the connection is. For some reason, there are parts of you I can't read. Your energy is clouded, murky."

She suddenly shrieked with fright, making me spin. Flower, a wizened and mischievous Fae, stepped out of the cave wall. I introduced her and chastened her for scaring the girls. "Flower, some people think it's rude to eavesdrop. Or glamor themselves to camouflage with the walls."

She cackled and shrugged up a shoulder, causing her beige sack to lift, displaying knobbly knees. She pointed at me, speaking to Trix. "He bears an uncanny resemblance to someone I used to know, but I can't be certain, so I shall not assume. Leif, I came to ask for more eels. Please bring them when you can." She hummed to herself as she tottered off down the tunnel, leaving us alone.

Xeno pressed her hand to her mouth. "May I have some water?" She waved at the wall, holding my water-catching contraption. I'd rummaged through the storage area behind the bleeding room, finding large glass containers I'd jimmy rigged with rope. A fresh stream came through a crack at various times, brackish but drinkable. I handed her a chipped cup of the turbid liquid. Trix waved for it when Xeno was done.

Trix took a sip, looking up at the ceiling. She screeched in alarm, tossing the cup in the air, kicking the lava rocks, and backpedaled to the wall next to Xeno with wide eyes. I shouted, gripping up my knife. "What?" I following her frozen gaze. My breath escaped me and I rubbed my eyes while shaking my head. Impossible. Impossible!

It was Mako. He was much older, his chin wider, with long hair but the same cobalt blue eyes. Ink covered most of his chest and arms. He was shouting, gesticulating wildly, but there was no sound. Falling forward from his neck was the Hai Matau.

I laughed like a fool, tears streaming from my eyes. My brother had finally found me.

SEVEN

MAKO

"LEIF!" I roared out his name, pummeling on the separation between us. It was like thick glass, the surface sparking as I hit it. "LEIF!" He was laughing and crying as he watched me struggle. I scanned all around him, memorizing the details. He was in a cave. A pile of glowing rocks sat in the center of the dark floor. A few of them lay to the side, kicked by the girl. The two thin and young Fae stared at me with slack jaws against the wall. One of them stood and pulled at his hand. Her mouth moved. He pointed at me, grinning.

"Leif! Talk to me!" I pounded on the glass. The girl looked at him with raised eyebrows and shook her head, staring right at me. Leif's face puzzled. Then he said something to her, his gestures excited. She went back to her identical sister and sat with her arms wrapped around her knees, both of them still staring at me with shocked expressions.

Leif's eyes shone at me with relief. He lifted his finger to his lips, telling me to calm down. I stopped slamming my fists, my breath ragged. He pulled on an ear and shook his head. He couldn't hear me. He put his hands on his cocked hips, tilted his head, and pointed to his mouth. I carefully read his lips as he spoke. *Miss me?*

Did I miss him? Unbelievable. I wished we knew sign language. That would be handy right now. I snorted and replied, intoning the word slowly to make sure he grasped it. *Yes, you dumb fucker.*

His eyes flew wide. We'd been children the last time we'd seen each other, and our parents did not tolerate foul language. I laughed at his shock, grateful tears sliding from my eyes. I found Leif. I swiped a hand across my nose. He tipped back his head and smiled at me, the dull light of the cave highlighting his pointed canines. Amazing. He was living in his Fae form.

He seemed in good shape, with wiry muscles and not a drop of fat on his body. I frowned. He wouldn't do that for aesthetics; he was probably starving. His hair was a tangled mass, fashioned in small braids, or matted locks, to keep it away from his face. He wore thin and tattered trousers, one knee split, the hems ragged, and they hung loose on his hips, held up with a piece of frayed rope.

Leif dropped his eyes, scanning the ground wildly. He grimaced and picked up his knife, wiping the guts of something on the thigh of his pants. He carved into the stone beneath him. HELLHOLE, waving his hand behind him to show he was in a different dimension. I nodded madly. He dropped the knife and cocked his head. He pushed his hair over his pointed ears, tugging on one. I nodded enthusiastically to show I understood.

His eyes glassed up. He formed a word with a contorted expression. *Mom?*

I smiled. *Good. Dad too. And Simmi.* It wasn't the time to explain we'd just freed her from the clutches of an evil Fae prince named Terrun, assisted by a team of Surfecti, a group of Bermudian Fae-Mers, and two powerful mermaids, one of whom I was married to, or mated to. I splayed out my hands on the glass. *I miss you.* My throat closed over as I fought down my tears. I wanted to bawl like a baby from the guilt and relief, but it would probably annoy him.

He saw the torture on my face and put his hand on his heart. *Me too.* He waved his hand in the air. *Hellhole. Fae.* He confirmed again, in case I had missed it, pulling his sharp ear.

I pointed to the girls over his shoulder, jerking my chin in question. *Who are they?*

He followed my gesture with his eyes and shrugged before swinging back to face me, carefully enunciating a question. *Can you find me?*

I ran a hand through my hair. How could I explain Jelly and her missing yellow in a few words?

Shit. Something was happening. I was being drawn away. I pressed my palms to the glass in a panic. I screamed, "Stay alive! We're coming!" His eyes flew wide and anguish colored his face. He stretched up his hand as if trying to grab me.

The world went dark.

The first sense to return was taste. Blood. I smelled salted caramel and heard the roll of the ocean waves. When I blinked my eyes open, Jelly hovered above me. "Mako!" Tears filled her eyes as she gasped my name through her torn and dripping lip. "Oh, thank the Goddess. I didn't know if it would work."

She'd given me a blood kiss, pulling me back through her magic and the mate bond, retrieving me. I winced as I felt my split lip. She must have bitten me. She scooted back as I sat up, my head spinning. I grasped at the Hai Matau, gripping it between tight knuckles.

"I saw Leif," I said, my voice disbelieving.

Jelly rocked back on her heels. "You saw him? Was it a vision?"

"No. I was there. We saw each other. But something divided us. I couldn't break it."

Jelly stroked back my hair. "Close your eyes and tell us everything before you forget."

Everyone gathered close on the sand as I told them what happened. When I finished, I blinked at Mew, who had paled to a disturbing shade of ash. Shock marred his face, and his voice was tremulous as he grappled to speak. "Mako. Are you certain twin girls were with him? Describe them. Every detail."

"Long blond hair, stick straight, but it was wet, so I can't be sure. Brown eyes, at least the one who got close. Really thin, like skeletons. Narrow chins, very delicate features. Maybe less than five feet tall? They were tiny. If I had to guess, I'd say they were young, but I can't be sure."

Mew held his breath as his eyes darted to and fro. I'd never seen him this upset. His brown eyes scanned mine. "Birthmarks?"

I closed my eyes again, searching for anything I'd missed in my story. There. On one of the girl's thighs. The one who stood up. "There's something like an arrow on one of them? On her right thigh. Wait. She had a black x on her wrist." My eyes flew open. "So did the other. So did Leif."

Mew slumped back, all the blood draining from his face. He looked close to fainting. "The girls are in the Hellhole." He held his cheeks in his trembling hands, shaking his head slowly from side to side. "This can't be happening."

Jelly licked at her bloodied lip. "Who are they?"

Mew paused and dropped his hands. "I can't say."

Roan growled at his statement. "Mako just traveled to the fookin' Hellhole and ye can't say? Ye can't say a fookin' thing? What use are ye?"

I rolled my neck, stiff from the vision. "Whoever they are, Leif has them. For now, they look safe. Well, as safe as they can be."

Jelly, ever insistent, repeated her question. "Who are they?"

Mew sighed, glancing at Jelly, then Roan. "There are things

I can't divulge. There are repercussions if I do. So please, do not ask again." He gave me a worried look. "You're sure they're safe?"

I shrugged. "Mew, they are alive. Skinny and scared, but Leif has them. That's all I can tell you." I caught Roan's eye. "We were mouthing to each other, trying to read lips. I need to talk to him to understand what we're up against."

I turned my gaze on Jelly. "And you, savage queen, are going to get your wish. We're going to England after we talk to my parents. We're finding your yellow and we're going to Leif. I'm so sorry I didn't listen to you. You were right. We should have acted immediately."

I reached out and waved my hand to Roan, sensing I needed his strength to stand upright. He gripped it and hauled me up. I swayed on my feet, Jelly rushing to steady me against her. I kissed her head and said, "Let Roan take me. I don't want to knock you down if I fall. I'm kind of dizzy." She frowned and reluctantly handed me off to the burly man. He wrapped his arm around my shoulders and helped me stagger across the soft sand.

Jelly was right behind me, Mori at her side. They spoke to each other in hushed tones. Roan pricked up when his name floated past us. I chuckled in my throat. "You've ruined telepathy for them. They can't talk in private with you around." He grunted and half dragged me up the steep stairs. "Roan, you're going to teach us that soon, right?"

"Aye, we'll start straight away." He dropped his voice. "I have to admit, I've enjoyed eavesdropping on the wee fishies behind us. I'll also have to teach ye to block, or ye'll get overwhelmed by the incessant chatter people have in their heads." He paused when I slowed down, grasping the railing for breath. The world was spinning. "What's wrong with ye?"

"I don't know. Maybe traveling to a Fae dimension drained me."

"Hmm. Or yer overwhelmed by yer necklace. Could be the unleashing of the magic. Come on. Steady on, now." I steeled my jaw and forced my legs to work, my knees buckling a few times from the effort. We reached the top to find my parents with Simmi. She rushed to my side.

"Mako? What's wrong!" She drew back with a gasp before stepping closer, trailing her fingers over my Hai Matau. "We sensed it."

My eyebrows drew together in puzzlement. "Sensed what?"

She rolled her eyes. "The orca magic, dummy. It's like a homing device. I was playing my flute with the birds and a flare went off in my chest. All of us ran to the cliff. We saw you on the beach, and you were thrashing around and then Jelly straddled you and kissed you. We figured since you had her and everyone else, you'd be okay. So what's going on? Why did you put it back on? It's been years since you've worn it."

I lifted my eyes to my parents. Dad had his arm around Mom's shoulder, squeezing her to his side. He kept his face smooth, but she looked ragey. I said, "We need to talk. And we need to sit down for it. At least, I do."

Dad eyed my necklace silently, kissed Mom's head, and took her hand, leading her into the spacious living room, thick with lush green plants and large black and white photographs of ocean scenes. Once settled, I took a deep breath, letting the exhale escape in a slow blow. Jelly entwined her fingers with mine for moral support. Mom raised her eyebrow at me. Her voice was tight. "Out with it. You're wearing your Hai Matau. Something made you put it on. You were rumbling around upstairs, but I didn't realize it was for your necklace."

I held her gaze, getting straight to the point. "I saw Leif."

"How?" My father sprang to his feet, his face so close it made my eyes cross. His voice was icy with fury. "Mako Fields, if you went back in that cave, so help me Gods…"

"Dad, I didn't go in there! I swear. At least, not physically. But maybe? Sit down and let me explain."

When he reclaimed his seat, Jelly cleared her throat beside me, nerves warping her tone. "Um, I think I should go first. I had a dream. Mother Kokuro told me where to find Leif."

"What?" Mom's voice pitched high, hope shining in her eyes. "Last night?"

Jelly swallowed, her jaw clenching. "No. A week ago." Her knuckles whitened as she gripped my hand harder. She rushed an apology. "I'm sorry. I should have told you sooner, straight away." She glanced at me quickly, ready to take the fall if I needed an out.

My mother's face hardened as she stared at my lover in disbelief, her lips pulled down in an angry scowl. "A week?"

I sat straighter. "No, don't blame Jelly. It was me. I asked her to keep it a secret."

"Son, why?" Dad's face was heartbroken, and it speared me to the bone. "We could have been looking for him." Mom covered her mouth with her hand, struggling to keep from either yelling or crying. I couldn't tell what side she was leaning toward.

I sighed. "It's complicated. I wanted to protect Jelly. She's missing something and we don't know what it means."

Mom swung her intelligent eyes to Jelly. "Where is he?"

Jelly's face paled. "The Hellhole."

"WHAT?" Dad looked apoplectic, the veins in his forehead bulging. I expected smoke to come out of his nostrils. "Tell us everything, Jelly."

Jelly dutifully recounted her dream. Dad stroked a hand over his chin, the movement rough as he stared at me with grave disappointment. I squirmed as if I were six years old with frosting in my hair after pilfering a cake on the counter, but the discomfort was short-lived as my sister threw herself at our parents and hugged them, breaking the thick air.

There were tears in her eyes. "This is the only lead we've

had since he left. This is good news." Simmi crossed her arms and scowled at me. "But Mako, you're a moron for keeping this from us. And for what? To protect Jelly?" She giggled. "She's more likely to protect you!"

Jelly murmured under her breath, her voice dripping. "See? You shouldn't doubt me. Your sister has faith."

Mom smiled. A small one, but a smile nonetheless. She leaned forward in her seat, gesturing at me. "Your turn. Tell us about Leif."

I gave them every detail from my brief glimpse at the Hellhole. When I mentioned the twins, especially the one with the birthmark, Dad's face whipped to Mew, sharing a silent moment of horror. Mori noticed. "Why do these girls upset everyone? What aren't you telling us?"

Mew shook his head. "I can't, Mori. I just can't."

Dad glanced at Mew before staring at his hands; hands that flexed nervously. "But I can. A little. These girls…they can't be in the Hellhole. Their blood, their magic. It's special." Mew cleared his throat abruptly. Dad's shoulders sagged. "And apparently, that's all I can say. Look, there is an ancient pact to protect their kind and keep them secret, but if they're with Leif, we must assume he will keep them safe. He's stayed alive so far."

We fell into silence, lost in our thoughts, and I broke first, turning to the tattooed man who watched my father with a frown. "Roan, is there a way to access Leif with blood magic? We need more information."

He stroked his chin thoughtfully. "Aye, possibly. But we'll need Anna to do it." He tossed his head at Jelly. "And ye need Anna to find yer yellow."

Simmi's voice tightened with barely restrained excitement. "Will Simon be there?"

Roan grinned at her. "It'd be best. Can't have Jelly growing whiskers like a fookin' Santa. She'll need Simon to teach her how to tame it."

He lightly scuffed on his beard with his fingertips and looked at my parents. "Ye ready to go back to England?" When they emphatically said yes, he pulled out his phone, hit a number on speed dial, and walked toward the kitchen. "Richard, it's Roan. We're coming to ye. That's right, the lot of us. Mako put on his necklace. Aye, ye heard right." His voice faded into a background rumble as my parents glowered at me, upset on so many levels.

Jelly excused herself, heading to the kitchen after Roan, leaving me to my fate. When I turned from my parents' silent accusatory eyes, I caught the anger on Mori's face just before she straightened it. I hung my head, running my fingers through my hair. I'd pissed everyone off by keeping quiet, thinking I was acting in Jelly's best interest.

Not one to hold her tongue, Mori slipped over to perch on the arm of the sofa. Her voice was firm yet hushed. "Mako, I respect Jelly is your mate and you want to protect her, but this is clearly bigger than you. You're going to be rattled by seeing your brother, meaning that you may not be capable of keeping a cool head. I can. I've been with Jelly for twenty-seven years, weathering all of her storms, and I will stand by you as well. Let me help, okay?" Her hand landed on my shoulder heavily and she squeezed.

I twisted to look at her, seeing the determination in her golden hazel eyes. I swallowed, embarrassed that I'd shunned her, given she was exceptionally bright, not to mention my mate's sister at heart. "Thank you, Mori. And you're right. I am rattled. If I'd put on the necklace sooner…"

My breath caught in my throat as I realized the gravity of my mistake. Tears pooled in my eyes, and I hid my face in my hands. Her hand soothed down my back and left, replaced by powerful arms that lifted me to my feet and curled around me.

I choked, my voice cracking. "I'm so sorry, Dad. I didn't know. I didn't know the necklace was the key. It's my fault he's been stuck all these years."

He held me close, his hand cradling my head, just as he'd done when I was small. "It's okay, Mako. Shh. It's okay. It's my fault more than yours. I should have protected him better. It's my fault you hid the necklace. I knew wearing it upset you, so I didn't push you to put it back on." Another pair of arms snaked around me from behind, followed by a third. Mom and Simmi squeezed while Dad swallowed thickly, holding us together as a family. His voice was determined. "We'll get him back. Hellhole or not, we're bringing Leif home."

Jelly returned to the room. "What's going on? Ah hell." She clamped herself to our group hug. "Now you're all gonna make me cry." She squeezed us tight. I opened my eyes to smile at her, catching Mori standing awkwardly to the side.

My voice was rough. "Mori, come here. You're family and belong in this hug." She hesitated before bounding to us, flinging herself around Mom and Simmi. We crushed each other, soaking in hope. I gasped for a breath. "I'm sorry, everyone. I'm sorry I didn't say something sooner."

Mew came close and weaved a hand through the multiple bodies to lay it on my shoulder, gently squeezing. "Mako, before you lose yourself in a flushable swirl of guilt and self-loathing, you didn't have visions as a child, did you?" I grunted no, the best I could do given the octopus of arms banding my ribcage. He smiled. "No, you didn't. What does that mean to you?"

My eyebrows drew down as I frowned. The bodies around me eased slightly, allowing me to turn my head and speak. "Don't make me guess. Just tell me, Mew."

He grinned, his brown eyes and bald head catching the light overhead. "It's Jelly. As your mate, she's connected to Leif through the Hai Matau. Her pearl prompted the vision."

I blinked as his words sunk in. "Jelly did this?"

She squirmed closer to nuzzle my cheek. "Technically, I'm guessing Leoht did."

Roan walked back in the room, done with his call, and chuckled. "I see ye kissed and made up. Anna will be here as soon as we're ready. I've called Simon, Gray, and Branko, asking them to return and help Jelly with her magic. Anna's collecting them now. Got room for one more?"

I heard Mori's soft gasp and looked over my shoulder, seeing her pressed from behind by Roan, his massive body swamping her as he reached around with burly, tattooed arms. He leaned in further to ruffle my hair, squishing her against my mother. I waited for her snark, telling him to back off and give her some space, but she grinned, the freckles on her nose scrunching up.

I winked at her. She winked back.

EIGHT

MEW

Everyone scattered to get packed, leaving me alone in the living room on the pale wooden bench, carved with a pattern of waves. Searing pain lurched through my head and I gasped, buckling over. A piercing voice snapped my name. *Bartholomew!* It was multi-tonal, hitting every note on the scale, the sharps highlighted to fully capture my attention. It clanged through my brain until I adjusted my hearing to whittle out the highest and deepest notes.

Ma'am?

What are you doing? You must not interfere!

Sweat pooled on my lip as her stabbing voice caused tension to grip my muscles tight. No small feat, as I was a giant. I fought for breath. *Boss, I'm not interfering. I'm encouraging creative thinking.*

You're dropping hints. Changing fate. What's going on with your charge? I saw him writhing on the beach like a fish.

I grunted through tight teeth. *Can you tone it down, please?* The invisible grasp on my body released. I sighed and sat up. *Thank you.* I rubbed my hand on my bald head. I had to choose my words carefully or she would instantly rip me from this world, and I needed to protect Mako and the others. *Mako put on the Hai Matau, which activated the orca magic, and he slipped into a vision of sorts and hovered above the Hellhole. He saw Leif inside…*

My voice dropped off, reluctant to admit who else was in that gods awful place.

And?

I winced in advance, steadying myself. *And the Rana twins are with him.*

Her voice shrilled like an ice pick in my skull. *The twins are in the Hellhole? No, no, no. This is catastrophic!*

Good. We agreed. *I know it is. Boss, I swear I'm not directly telling them what to do, but can you give me a little leeway? We have to get the girls back. Gaia must be losing her mind. Literally.*

Fine. You may drop vague hints, but any outright suggestions will result in your punishment. I already had to ping you once. Do you understand?

Yes, ma'am.

Very well. Keep me posted.

Her retreat was a balm to my nervous system. I didn't tell her I was with Sebastian, but I didn't need to. The boss knew everything. The appearance of the Rana twins indicated the prophecy had begun. But with them in the Hellhole… It was disastrous, our worst nightmare.

What a mess. I snapped my fingers and disappeared, needing a suitcase of my own. I was going with them to England.

NINE

JELLY

Mako was already inside, throwing clothes into a duffel bag. His movements were urgent, and he spared me a quick glance before shoving shoes on top, soles up. "Get packed, Jelly. We need to go." I leaned on one leg, pushing out my hip and crossing my arms. He spoke again when I didn't move. "Jelly. Did you hear me?"

"Oh, I heard you just fine. I heard bossiness." I tapped a foot on the hardwood floor. "Mako, is this what you're like when you're stressed? You're short-tempered, and I get it, but I'm not a punching bag. Understand?"

He didn't look up as he replied. "In the past, when I had a singular mission, I steamrolled everyone." He grimaced as he stuffed socks inside my tall boots. "My parents would ask what I was doing and where I was going, and I'd blow them off and storm from the house. It must have driven them nuts. So, yes. This is me stressed. This is me on a mission. Jelly, quit looking at me like that and keep packing." He hadn't looked up to see my face, but knew me well enough to know it was surly.

I tossed my sneakers into the suitcase. "I'm upset that it took seeing Leif to drive a call to action. In the future, when I say something's important, I want you to act on it."

He dragged his hand through his hair, finally pausing to look at me. "Jelly, I'm a wreck, a fucking blistering mess. I took off my necklace fifteen years ago. That's why he's there, why he's stuck, and I hate myself right now." There was agony in his eyes. "Jelly, *please*. Please, can we talk about this later? We need to go."

Dear Goddess, he was just like me. As we hurried up the path, the wheels on my suitcase struggled through the stones, causing me to stop and jiggle it. Mako vibrated in frustration. His voice was terse. "Here, switch with me." He passed me the compact duffel and grunted as he lifted my suitcase. "What did you put in here? Rocks?"

I raised my eyebrow at him. "You packed it." He sped past the house where Mori stayed. I waved him on. "I'm going to check on Mori. She overthinks packing. Go. We're right behind you." He snatched the duffel from me and careened up the path, his muscles straining. I entered without knocking. As I suspected, Mori's bed was a mountain of clothes, and she stood frozen, staring at it. I laughed. "Okay, speed packing. We leave in five minutes. Get your toiletries."

She called to me from the bathroom. "I need those wool shirts, the merino ones. Those will be good in England."

I frowned as she returned with her arms full. "It's summer. You don't need wool."

She smirked. "You clearly weren't paying attention. It's always raining and cold. I'm not getting caught out again with linen pants as my only option. Merino is hydrophilic, so it keeps you from getting clammy if you get wet, and English rain busts from the sky with no warning. Plus, wool keeps you from stinking." She looked at me with great seriousness. "Stinking is not sexy."

I quickly folded the shirts. "Look at you, spouting facts about natural fibers. But who are you being sexy for? Roan? No, you would've acted on that already. Branko? Or do you plan to wrangle Simon and Gray and see what secrets they keep? Or will you roll them into a heap of male bodies, and jump in the middle like a dog in a leaf pile?"

Mori paused. "Maybe?" She fanned at her face and plucked her shirt. "Thinking about them all makes me hot. Physically burning. I'm roasting."

I rolled trousers up tightly. "What's happening with Roan? You mentioned him earlier, but we didn't get to finish the conversation." Mori picked at a thread on the blanket. I leaned forward, scrutinizing her expression. She tried to keep her face blank but failed spectacularly as she groaned and fell backward on the bed among her clothes, flinging an arm over her face. I looked at her curiously. "What's going on with you two?"

She rolled to her side and propped her head on her hand. Her voice was vulnerable. "I'm terrified of making a mistake."

I lay down to face her. This was important. Mako could wait. "Mistake? I don't follow."

She rolled her eyes impatiently. "I've been watching you and Mako bicker at each other like old hens. Peck, peck, peck. Nag, nag, nag. You toss out a hand, he crosses his arms, you sigh like you're dying. He scowls and growls and you yell back." She grinned. "I'm really proud of you for yelling back, by the way. I'd have to smack you if you just took his shit without fighting. But my gods, it's exhausting watching you two."

I nudged her ribs with my knuckle, making her wriggle away. "And yet…Roan is on your mind."

She rolled onto her back, studying the ceiling. "And yet, Roan." She faced me again, dropping her voice. "He wants more. He keeps saying I came back from death for him. I didn't." I raised an eyebrow. Her brow wrinkled. "I didn't! I came back because he promised to teach me hands-free telepathy. And I came back for you."

I stroked her cheek. "Don't forget your powerful influence on the world of magic. That's what Samara said."

"Yes. But remember? She said another would join us. But she didn't say who. She wanted it to be a surprise for me. She's a Seer, Jelly. She deliberately chose to keep me in the dark, making me second guess myself. She said he would make himself known. But Roan was already with us. The other Surfecti, too. So, what if I haven't met him yet? What if I miss the one I'm supposed to be with? I assume this other person is for me, but maybe not." She sighed so deeply her hair blew back. "Ugh. None of it matters anyway. I don't want to be tied down by one person."

I grimaced. I had no good words of advice for her. I was barely hanging on to my own relationship, and fate had flung us together. Mori squinted at me, her face softening. "Do you regret it?"

"Regret what?"

"Having your mate chosen for you?"

I stared at the cobalt blue band on the index finger of my left hand, my mate mark. "Sometimes. Mother Kokuro said we embraced the ultimate sacrifice with love in our hearts, so she bound us when we'd made the choice, albeit without knowing we were, and she cemented it. Mostly, it's amazing."

I flopped onto my back. "Although, right now, he's making me crazy, but I can't walk away. That's the part that frustrates me, trying to find this middle ground. We both have such forceful personalities, and when we butt heads, we get nowhere. It's a stalemate for who will break first."

Mori said, "If he'd trusted you from the start, we'd already be in England sorting out your magic. Instead, we're a week behind, and magic can go weird in an instant. Especially yours. But what do I do about Roan?"

I chewed on my lip, changing the subject. "What do you

think my missing yellow is?" Mori's face flashed with annoyance, but it was so brief I waved it off.

She braced her head on her elbow. "I've been mulling it over. I have some ideas, but I don't want to share them until we see Anna. I don't want to send us off in the wrong direction."

"Look at you keeping secrets."

Mori rolled her hazel eyes. "Hardly! I'm being judicious. Well, none of our conversation makes Roan any more clear for me. Maybe I should let fate take over and stop fussing over who I should get frisky with."

I poked her ribs playfully. "As much as I like to talk about your sex life, we really need to get going."

She said under her breath, "What sex life?"

We shoved her clothes in her suitcase with no rhyme or reason until it overflowed. She had to sit on the suitcase so I could close it, stuffing in rogue fabrics with quick fingers while tugging the zip, encouraging the teeth to hold. We lurched up the path, carrying the bulging suitcase between us. The rest of our group assembled in the living room, and Mew came through the front door just as Anna flashed in, her long dark hair in her trademark low bun. She looked at Mori's bursting luggage with a touch of trepidation. "Goodness, Mori. How long do you plan to stay?"

A strange flush of guilt crossed her face. Mori said, "Is it a problem? Teleporting this much stuff?"

Anna smiled. "No. It's fine. Well, hello everyone. Here we are again. Oh, we haven't met, I'm Anna."

I watched with keen interest as Mew shook her hand. When she'd first met me, she'd tested my magic, causing a ricochet spark to scald my palm. Mew would likely fly across the room, given the magic he possessed.

But there was nothing. Not even a wince. I sucked my teeth in disappointment. Not that I wanted Mew hurt, I just wanted to see Anna zap someone besides me. So far, she never had.

We hauled our bags to the center of our circle. Sebastian locked the doors and cast a protection spell on the house. Anna called for us to join hands, and I sought Mako. His palm was sweaty. He really was nervous. I squeezed his hand tightly as Anna spoke the teleport incantation, and my stomach dropped out as a white light flashed and we disappeared.

We landed in the foyer of the New Forest Coven Headquarters, where Anna was the Lead Witch. I wobbled on my feet, Mako holding me up, and blinked a few times to clear my vision. I beamed with pride. Usually, with teleporting, I ended up on my hands and knees, trying not to vomit. The vast entrance was the same, antique brass lights and candles illuminating the space. I shivered from the drop in temperature. "Leave your bags," Anna said. "Come, everyone's in the library."

It seemed like years since I was last in the beautiful room, with its high ceilings and forest green walls with dark mahogany wainscoting. Curlicue holdbacks tamed the heavy cream drapes, letting the gloomy weather show through the ancient casement windows. I gazed over the grounds and my heart fluttered at the oak sentinels along the property, their massive trunks sturdy, leaves gently trembling in the faint rain. Logs puttered and sparked in the stone fireplace, and I grinned at the familiar faces that turned at our arrival.

"Jelly!" Gray was the first to reach me, and when he held open his arms, I raised an eyebrow at him cautiously. He laughed and stared closely. "Look. No gold flecks, no seduction magic. Just brown. Just me." Then he engulfed me. "Gods, it's good to see you. I've missed you." He reached for Mori next. "All of you." Mako waited for his turn, stepping slightly away so Gray would go to him.

Gray and Mako hugged tightly, childhood friends reunited, both of them wiping their eyes when they broke apart. They spoke too softly for me to eavesdrop, but from the way Mako gesticulated and pointed to his necklace, he was talking about Leif. Gray grabbed him at the back of the neck and pressed his forehead to his before breaking away, clearing his throat. Mako squeezed his shoulder, turning away.

Gray shouted across the room. "Roan! No one drinks whiskey like you do! Finally, a partner in crime." They thumped each other on the back.

Simmi chatted with Anna, darting glances around the room, observing the group dynamics, her eyes often falling on Simon. After her rescue, she'd been weak, a shell of her normal self, and she hadn't met the others beyond cursory greetings. Simon and Branko left Bermuda well before we did, as we waited for Simmi to fully recuperate. Anna leaned close to Simmi, and her eyes flew wide at whatever she'd shared.

As Richard kissed my cheeks, I saw Branko and Mori in an extra long hug. He must not have shifted recently. When in his gargoyle form, his skin turned ice cold, and took a while to thaw. She was blushing at something he said. Then she tipped back her head and laughed. His steel-gray eyes twinkled as he watched her with delight.

I noticed Roan staring at them with a scowl as Mori stroked up and down Branko's bare arm, chatting excitedly. I hip checked him as I strolled by to say hello to Simon, the wolf shifter, known professionally as The Drifter. I pinched Roan's side to get his attention. "Your jealousy is showing. Tuck it in." Roan grunted and turned away as I hugged Simon, friendly as ever.

"Hey, Jelly! How are you?" Simon's pale hair was longer than before, hanging free, and he'd kept his trademark goatee.

I tugged on his darker blond whiskers. "Well, not so good. I grow one of these when I try to use your magic!"

His light-blue eyes widened with horror. He pulled on his chin. "We need to change that, like, pronto. No offense, but I'm not sure you can carry off facial hair." His smile grew wider, and

I glanced over my shoulder to find Branko right behind me. I turned to greet him.

"Hi Branko," I said. He opened his arms. I stepped in. I'd never hugged Branko before. It was like squeezing a cool wall of concrete.

His voice rumbled in my ear like rocks in a tumbler. "Ah, this is nice. Anna transported me this time, so I didn't need to shift into cold stone to fly. It's good to give everyone hugs."

I pulled back and teased him. "Didn't pick you for the hugging type."

He smiled softly, almost sadly. "I rarely have the chance, working with gargoyles. We're all stony." He chuckled, the sound a deep rasp. "Nor do I have many people I wish to embrace."

Richard called to us all, asking us to please sit. An unfamiliar witch brought in a massive tray bearing three steaming teapots, multiple china cups and saucers, milk, sugar, spoons, and a tower of ginger cookies. She maneuvered her burden through the room with ease, though it dwarfed her, and weighed quite a bit from the strain of her biceps. Anna introduced her as Veda.

She set the tray down and faced me, cocking her head to the side. Through squinted eyes, she stared from my head to my toes. She whispered to Anna, who nodded, her lips in a tight line. Veda scanned over Mori, frowned, and left without a word. Odd.

Anna poured the tea while Gray dressed it to our preferences, me taking it with two sugars and a spot of milk. Richard passed the plate of cookies delicately through the air with his levitation magic, careful not to tumble them. With everyone served, Anna sat primly on her chair, took a sip of her tea and sighed. Her sharp eyes settled on me. "Here we are again, gathered because Jelly is out of control. And I say this with great affection. Are we surprised?" Her lips twitched, and I laughed, so different from the first time we met.

I waved my hand with a flourish. "What can I say? I'm consistent." I set my china cup on its matching saucer of scattered pale violets. "But all joking aside, I'm a mess. A bona fide mess. The magical strains are in complete disarray and don't respond to a single command." I sighed and took a sip of my tea. "Even worse, they come out inappropriately. I set the bed on fire this morning and smashed a lamp, both things happening while I was asleep." Everyone looked at me with great concern.

Mori giggled. "That's not all. While training, she sprouted a beard and then a tail. A thick white one, Simon, like yours, but tipped in turquoise. Bust right through her pants after she torched them with Gray's magic. She thumped it on the floor with exaggerated irritation." She waved her hand back and forth with brisk movements. "Slap, slap, slap, slap."

I scowled at her. There was no need to humiliate me. Simon's eyes grew wide. He gasped in genuine horror. "Oh, shit!"

Richard's brows drew down as he struggled to keep a straight face. Branko's jaw ticked. Simmi's hand covered her mouth while Gray snuffled and coughed, clearing his throat. Roan rocked back on his heels and crossed his arms, watching everyone's reactions with twinkling eyes. Anna looked positively delighted as she set down her tea.

Finally, someone sniggered. That's all it took. The entire room collapsed into boisterous guffaws and feminine shrieks. Mew began honking, which set off a fresh cascade. I crossed my arms with a huff, trying to look unimpressed, but eventually broke down and laughed until my stomach ached.

TEN

MAKO

My heart lurched as the Surfecti in the room listened closely to Jelly's dream. They took her seriously, asking pertinent questions, and clarifying her answers. At one point, Gray looked at me with condescendingly arched eyebrows, suggesting he thought I was a fool.

Anna recapped succinctly. "Mother Kokuro found Leif in the Hellhole. Neither Jelly nor Mako will be welcome there. The pearl, Leoht, will need to take Fae form to escort them, and Jelly needs her yellow first, or she will die." She swept a rogue strand of hair behind her ear, her voice flat. "And somehow, I'm to help you find this missing piece of yourself."

Jelly bit her lip nervously. "Yup. That's it."

Anna looked at her husband. She and Richard held gazes for a while, having a conversation in their heads before she turned to me. "Mako, you're next. Tell us about Leif."

I explained what I'd seen. To my surprise, no one responded to the arrow tattoo on the thin girl's leg. No one except Mew and my dad, who both shifted in their seats uncomfortably. Mori, Gods bless her, noticed, and said something, sharing my suspicion the girls were important.

Her eyes narrowed as she called out to the room. "What is

so special about these girls?" When met with blank faces, she pointed between Mew and my father. She tilted her chin. "Sebastian, you can say more than Mew. Go on."

Dad glanced at Mew cautiously, his voice anxious. "I am limited in what I can say, so read between the lines. It might seem off point, but all of it is important. Mew, stop me if I go too far. The Fae live in different dimensions, with time working strangely to ours on the surface. The Earth, Gaia, has her own timeline, her own age, different from the Earth plane and the Fae. She is four and a half *billion* years old." He waited to let that sink in before continuing.

"What is less understood is the Earth's spirit. She is a living entity, a sentient being like you or me. She has emotions, and she expresses these regularly. She causes natural disasters when upset. As you would expect, volcanoes and fires show her anger, floods depict grief, and hurricanes and typhoons are her frustration. Earthquakes, too, when she wants to give us a good shake. Sometimes we need her to clear the air with her storms, to encourage fresh growth, but lately, she's more violent."

Dad frowned ruefully. "All of this happens simultaneously. Imagine having such cataclysmic feelings in such an enormous field, impacting so many beings."

Richard frowned. "I'm certain I'd be quite mad, literally climbing the walls with insanity." We all murmured in agreement.

Dad's voice dropped deep, making us all lean in. "She has ways of speaking to us, if we're clever enough to pay attention. At the moment, we're approaching the solar maximum period for Solar Cycle Twenty-five. Can anyone explain what that is?"

Simon piped in. "I can. They're the Northern Lights. But I'm not really clear on the science behind them if it's important."

Richard said, "Energized particles from the sun hit the Earth's atmosphere and funnel toward the poles through the planet's magnetic field, causing The Northern Lights. This current cycle, number twenty-five, is perhaps the most powerful in five hundred years. People in Florida and India are seeing the lights. That's unheard of. Is it a message?"

Dad inched forward in his seat. "What do they make us do?"

The rest of us looked at him blankly, but Mori's reply was instant. "Look up."

Dad sat back and ran his hands over his cheeks. He echoed Mori. "We look up." Dad paused, collecting his thoughts. He met Mori's eyes, sensing she was the enigmatologist in the room, the one to figure out puzzles. "Pay attention." Mori watched every muscle on my father for silent tells. He spoke quickly, as if needing to get the words out with speed. "The Earth has guardians for her soul, beings who protect her from losing control and causing harm."

Mori said immediately, "The twin girls."

Dad did not nod or respond, but his eyes bored into Mori's as he fisted his hands. "And these guardians are critical to her mental health. If she's troubled, she lets us know."

Mori spoke quickly, thinking out loud. "The intense northern lights are a distress call because the twins are in the Hellhole? She's trying to get our attention?" Dad exhaled and sat back, his slack face an affirmation.

I leaned forward. "What will happen if the earth goes insane?"

Branko shook his head sadly. "What normally happens when a woman loses her mind?"

Roan answered gruffly. "She either explodes, destroying everything in her path, or she shuts down and freezes ye out."

I swallowed thickly, so grateful my mate preferred fire over ice. I said, "Prince Terrun couldn't kill the humans and take over the Earth because we stopped him. So maybe taking the twins makes her, Gaia, kill the humans. Same result, different approach."

Richard's voice was grave. "The most recent hurricanes to hit the East Coast of America were devastating, reaching places they shouldn't have. She may be responding to their kidnapping."

I turned to Anna. "So, we have to get them back to save Gaia's mind? How is this connected to Jelly? Kokuro said to ask you specifically for Jelly's missing yellow. Maybe she needs another strain of Surfecti magic? Maybe from a witch?"

Branko was thoughtful as he rubbed his ear, his face drawn down in a frown. "I have a colleague with yellow."

Gray nodded. "I remember several from university. But who? We can't have random mages and gargoyles blasting her with magic just to see if it works."

Mori groaned, shaking her head. "No, you're going down the wrong path. Kokuro explicitly said 'Ask your witch.' I don't think it's male energy, at least, not like the fusion ritual. Gaia is female. We'll find the yellow through Anna or a witch."

A voice spun our heads. "You have a problem with yellow?" It was Veda, the one who had brought us the tea. She wore a bright green sari that wrapped around her body, baring a warm brown sliver of midriff, and a black bindi adorned her forehead. She stood at the door with a fresh batch of cookies. Veda tipped her head. "If it's yellow, there is likely a block in her Manipura."

"Mani-what?" Jelly asked.

Veda flipped her shiny dark braid over her shoulder, walking toward us. She set the cookies on the table. "Manipura. It's the name for the navel chakra." She leaned closer and pointed at Jelly's belly. "Also called the solar plexus chakra." She stood straight and stared at our group expectantly.

Mori's eyes widened. "Is Manipura's color yellow?" When Veda broke into a wide smile, Mori clapped her hands together. "Is this the yellow she needs?"

Veda glanced at Anna questioningly. Anna nodded for her to continue. Veda studied Jelly, then frowned. "Manipura controls intellect, ego, aggression and will. When in balance, you are confident. When not, it manifests in low self-esteem and control issues, most commonly anger. It is the seat of your personal power. If there's an issue, start there."

Jelly threw up her hands. "My power is all over the place! That is the problem!"

The witch raised an eyebrow at Jelly's flare of anger. "Indeed. There is another possibility. Gold is associated with the ninth chakra, a gold ball above the body, which contains the blueprint of the soul, all the skills and abilities you have acquired in all lifetimes and incarnations. Yours looks…" She squinted above Jelly's head. "Confused. Gold or yellow. It is unclear which is truly in distress, but there is definitely a hole in your belly."

She turned to Anna with a nod of her chin. "With the swirls of color inside her, it is difficult to diagnose, but I cannot see yellow at all. Perhaps it hides. I cannot be sure. She must learn to differentiate the magics."

I stared at the miraculous stranger, the first to have an inkling of a solution. "How long will that take?" My voice bordered on frantic.

Veda shrugged. "The sooner you start, the better." She swept from the room, the smell of chamomile and cardamom fading behind her.

Anna said, "Veda is an exceptional healer. She works primarily with the body's energies and can read colors. But you're too jumbled for her to see clearly. Jelly, which magic seems the most out of control?"

Jelly exhaled and slumped her shoulders, struggling to pick just one. I took her hand and said, "Well, the most dangerous of them is Gray's fire." I resisted the urge to display my singed thighs. "It bursts out when she's under duress, like this morning, coming out of a dream."

"I've had nightmares. Premonitions." Jelly shuddered and made a sour face. "This morning I saw fruit and an Eator."

Anna's face pinched. "Do you know where you were?"

Jelly slowly shook her head. "Nowhere I recognized."

Richard tipped his chin, curiosity in his eyes. "What fruits?"

Jelly threw her hands up in exasperation, separating hers from mine, slowly sliding them down her blue hair. "None I've seen before. They were a dark purple, shaped like boy balls." Her lips twitched as I chuckled beside her. "Small at the top and filling out to a bulb. Full of tiny, tiny seeds, sort of pinkish inside."

Roan said, "Sounds like figs. Were ye fighting?"

She patted her hips over the soft leather holster that carried her knives, one a stiletto, the other a knuck. "No. I just saw him and ran."

He pressed further. "No magic? No colors ye could see?"

She shook her head no. "It was incredibly noisy, with tons of humans, weird fruit, and a face with red eyes. That's it. I get the sense I wasn't alone, but no other faces were clear."

Gray pushed off from his lean against the fireplace, pulling his hands from his pockets. "We'd better get started. Let's adjourn to the training level. I like this room. I'd hate to see it torched to the ground." As Jelly and Mori followed the others from the room, Gray stopped me. "How bad is she? Mako, be honest with me."

I searched the concern in his eyes. "She burned the hair off my legs this morning. Second time this week she's set the bed on fire. It always happens from her dreams." I pinched the bridge of my nose, swaying between loyalty to my mate and truth to my friend. Truth won.

I dropped my hand, worried. "She's a mess, Gray. She's completely out of control. When she tries to wield the magic, it comes out jumbled and mixed. Then she gets angry. This morning, after soaking me with water to put out the fire, she levitated the lamp, lost control, and it smashed to the floor. Then the whiskers and the tail. She can pull a single thread, but as soon as she loses focus, or tries to use another, it blows up in her face. Then she gets angry and lashes out, usually at me."

Gray's mouth turned down. "You're an idiot for not speaking up sooner."

"I'm trying not to pressure her for this yellow, but Gray...I'm losing it, man. We need to know what it means. Where to find it. I need her to do this. Seeing Leif... I have to get him back. Like yesterday. I feel...I don't even know how to express how I feel. Relief? Shame? Horror? All of it together. We have to free him."

He tipped his head at me, seeing right through me. "So, this frustration is about your needs?"

Damn all these enlightened people. I ran a hand through my hair. "What if she fails? Can I still love her?" My voice tightened. "It's affecting everything. I thought she could figure it out for herself, but she can't, and I'm angry that she can't. I'm an asshole for saying that, but it's true. I mean, I love her, of course I do, but Gods damn it, I'm having a hard time with all the fighting."

I dropped my chin down, shaking my head. "We've been at each other's throats. And I swing side to side. One minute I want to protect her from the Hellhole, and the next, I'm angry she's not getting there fast enough."

Gray clamped his hand on my shoulder. "How does she feel?"

I exhaled a loud sigh. "Frustrated. Mostly with herself, but then she gets mad when I make a suggestion. I can't win."

Gray chuckled. "Welcome to relationships."

I shook my head. "Does it get better?"

He shrugged his shoulders. "Wouldn't know. I tend to avoid them."

ELEVEN

MORI

Everyone gathered in the basement, standing far away from Gray and Jelly as they faced each other on the mats. I shifted my weight from foot to foot, doing a form of pacing while standing. Yellow. Yellow. Manipura. Solar plexus. Solar. Solar. Sun. Sun flares. Personal power. Yellow. Girl guardians. Solar. Shit. I couldn't find a clear path. My chin jerked up as Anna snapped her fingers and a safety dome fell over their Jelly and Gray to contain errant flames. We could still hear them speak.

"Just draw on the orange," Gray said. "Focus solely on that one."

Jelly closed her eyes tight and breathed, searching inside for Gray's magic. "I have it."

He spoke calmly. "Throw flame at me. It won't hurt me." She struck out her hand, blasting flames at the tall man, causing his brown eyes to squint with delight. He caught the fire easily in his palm, absorbing it. "That was great, Jelly! Do it again!" She repeated the task flawlessly.

Anna scowled at my side. "There's nothing wrong with her magic."

I snorted before I replied. "She's in a magical bubble with a friend, playing with flames that won't hurt him. If you put in another man, I'll bet the magic will get confused. Go on, test my theory."

Branko's cool skin brushed my arm as he passed, making me involuntarily shiver, but not from the cold. His voice was so deep it resonated in my core. "I will go in. Out of all of us, fire will hurt me the least."

Gray stopped Jelly when Branko approached. Anna's dome shimmered as he stepped through, returning as he spun to face Jelly. His baritone voice vibrated the air. "Now, do mine." Jelly concentrated, searching within for his strand, and she sent a pulse of magic to Branko, the color bright red like fresh blood. He grinned. "Very good. Now do Gray's and then mine, alternating."

Jelly took a deep breath and lifted her hands. For a beautiful moment, she held both the flame and a ball of red energy in her palms, looking as cool as a sea cucumber, and ready to play. She winked at the men and fired. And that's where the beauty ended.

As soon as she mixed the magic, the others exploded from her body. Her feet lurched up on a purple cushion of light, the orange fire wild while the red magic scattered toward the men, simultaneously making horns sprout from her head. She had the wherewithal to throw her palms up, blasting the shield with a kaleidoscope of color, warping the bubble above her as it strained to withstand the madness.

"Drop it!" Branko's voice was sharp from behind the shelter of stone wings, covering both him and Gray. They were right to be worried; Jelly was a force of untamed power. Jelly's face strained, her eyes vacant, and she jerked on all the magic, falling to the floor in a crumple. When she lifted her head, pointed ears showed above her blue tangles, and she bared sharp teeth in frustration before tugging hers back inside herself, making her Fae features disappear, but she pulled on her round ear to be sure.

I muttered under my breath. "What a mess." I tapped Anna's shoulder. "See what I mean? She needs to practice one at a time. Trust me. Doing it like this will make her more frustrated, and she'll lose what small hold she has."

Anna called to the men. "Gray, step out." He strode to my side, his face pale as he faced his mother.

His voice shook with quiet alarm. "Mum, we don't have defensive magic against someone with eight strains. We can't do this."

Her voice was steel. "We can and we will." She clipped at a trot to Jelly and Branko, jostling the bun at her nape. I followed, with Mako right behind me. Anna lowered the shield. "Jelly, stand up. Get up, now!" I helped her to her feet, twisting my arm around her waist when she faltered. Anna was brisk. "One at a time, then. Can you do that?"

Jelly croaked, embarrassed by her failure. "Yes."

Anna turned. "Mako? You're first."

Branko frowned. "But she's intimately familiar with Mako's magic."

Anna tucked a loose strand behind her ear and turned away. "Precisely." I lingered, reluctant to leave, wanting to help Jelly somehow. A large, cool hand guided me forward, heavy yet gentle, barely pressing into my lower back. I stepped forward obediently as Mako passed me toward Jelly, his face troubled.

Branko leaned close to my ear, the coolness of his breath refreshing on my skin. "She feels chaotic. Why would this be?"

I stepped away from the others, motioning with my head he should follow. I stared at his shimmering steel eyes, so sharp they could cut. I resisted the urge to smooth the frown from his face. With no eyebrows, only the furrow of his brow showed his concern. That and the downturn of his thick lips. Lips that looked incredibly kissable. Lips I wanted to touch. I tucked my twitchy fingers into the deep pockets of my trousers. My voice was hushed. "I think it's embarrassment. Jelly's never been a good beginner. She likes to be an expert from the start."

The lines in his forehead grew deeper. "But that is ridiculous. How can she expect to wield seven strange strains without instruction?" He straightened, taking his coolness with him, leaving me burning hotter with the desire to touch him. I knew what he looked like in the nude, phenomenally male. I'd seen him fully shifted as well, with massive clawed wings, horns on his head and jutted fangs. He didn't frighten me. He intrigued me. He gazed over my head toward Jelly and Mako, and I reluctantly tore my eyes from Branko to give them my full attention.

With the shield resurrected, they faced each other. He said something to make her smile, and her shoulders relaxed. She lifted her hand and coaxed forward the cobalt-blue strand, Mako's magic. It came easily and spilled across the shield like water, flowing in a flirtatious manner as it snaked up Mako's arm. He answered her call, his power joining hers, teasing and playing, pulling her hair and making her laugh.

Branko smiled at them fondly. "Mates. She trusts him. She has no fear with his magic."

My eyes widened. "That's it!" I rushed to Anna. "Put someone else in there with them. Mako makes all the difference." I scanned the Surfecti. "Sebastian. Let him go in."

Anna gasped and clamped her hand on my shoulder. "Yes, of course! Sebastian? If you will?"

He walked to the shield and waited for them to notice, pulsing his magic once to get their attention. Sebastian stepped in. He spoke in a soothing tone, almost hypnotic. "Jelly, keep hold of Mako's magic. Son, drop yours. Jelly, pull on my magical thread within yourself. I'm here if you need help. Electric blue, and remember, it's zippy, not like Mako's. See if you can control them both."

She inhaled and held the breath, coaxing out the zinging

spark of Sebastian's Fae magic. It danced on her palm like glitter. She sent it out, and it whizzed and flashed amid the flowing cobalt. Her arms trembled from the effort of holding them both, but she was doing it. Sebastian smiled. "Excellent, Jelly. Can you take more?"

"Not yet. Let me get used to these first." Her jaw ticked as she focused.

Mako asked quietly, not wanting to break her concentration. "Can you add yours?"

She nodded, sweat beading her face. Turquoise fire wrapped around the cobalt first, chasing it like a puppy. Sparks broke away and danced with the flashes. Her face exploded with joy as she maneuvered all three together. Sebastian laughed. "Perfect! Jelly, draw in Mako's thread, keeping mine active. Easy now." That's when she lost control.

We yelped and jumped back as the shield burst open and blue Fae magic scattered across the ceiling. Branko yanked me behind him, winding his arm backward, pressing me against him protectively. His body was an icy wall of stone, right on the edge of transforming, and every cell in my body sparked. I peeked around his side, and seeing no danger, stepped out next to him, peering up. "Thank you, Branko. Quick reflexes."

He rolled his shoulders, shaking off his magic. "I didn't want you hurt." His face was pensive, his lips parted on a breath. Steel eyes watched me guardedly as he uncharacteristically skated a cold finger down my spine, just barely touching. I arched with surprise at the iciness and had to bite my lip to keep from audibly groaning. A roar tumbled in my belly, heat bursting out of my body, accompanied by an odd gurgling noise. I caught Roan's glare as he watched us and excused myself with a choke of air, crossing to Jelly.

She bent over, panting, her hands on her knees. Sweat rolled off of her nose. She shook her head in dismay. "I lost it when I dropped Mako's magic." She turned to Sebastian, failure in her eyes. "Why can't I do it alone?"

I stepped closer, grateful for the distraction from Branko. "Listen, I have a theory. When you're ready, try again with someone besides Sebastian, but keep Mako in the bubble with you. Draw his magic first, then call out another." I turned to the assembled Surfecti. "Who wants to go next?"

Roan stepped forward. "I'll go." He smiled at Jelly mischievously. "I'll twirl with the tornado." As he passed me, he touched my temple, causing sparks to flash before my eyes. He winked at me before swaggering toward Jelly, making her lips twitch in amusement. He tapped her and Mako, both of them gasping like I had. "That's opened yer minds. Yer going for green, lass. Green, cobalt, and turquoise, nothing more." I went back to the others, but kept some distance from Branko to avoid embarrassing myself in case he touched me again.

Mako stood by her side, the two of them facing Roan, who rolled his neck and shook out his hands. He nodded once, and Anna resealed the bubble. Jelly quickly pulled up the cobalt and turquoise, comfortable with those. Roan spread his feet, bracing. "Now, Jelly, when ye pull my green thread, I also want ye to use it. Get it up in yer hand and I'll coach ye."

She focused, and quickly, a ball of emerald green magic sat tightly in her upturned palm. Roan spoke in a deep growl. "Good, lass. Relax. Let it play." The green light began thrumming, vibrating and shuddering in her hand as her face visibly softened.

I squawked as Roan's voice filled my head. *Ye lasses want me to teach ye telepathy? Let's go.* He grinned in my direction. *Lesson One: keep yerself straight when someone talks in yer head. Mori, that means take the shock off yer face.* I blinked and composed myself, twisting my fingers together tightly. Roan chuckled at me, the sound of it shooting straight to my center. *Good lass. Now, Jelly, say something back.*

Jelly's voice sounded strained. *This is more difficult than I expected.*

I gawked as Mako spoke next, finding it easier than Jelly. *Keep your focus. You're doing great. Mori? Say something to make Jelly laugh. Try to break her concentration.*

I didn't want to shake her personally, as she was already on edge from the magic. I chose a different target. I spoke in a sultry tone, soaked with every drop of my seduction magic. *Roan, take off your shirt, nice and slow. Peel it off. I need to see your tattoos. I need it real bad, surly bear, real, real bad.*

Jelly jolted and laughed, her eyes flicking to mine as I stood casually, one hip cocked, my head tilted on Roan as if judging a pony in a show.

When Roan answered, his voice was rough and teasing. *Ye want to play? Aye, lass, I'll strip for ye. But it won't be slow. I don't want Jelly too distracted.* He ripped off his shirt, yanking it over his head, turning to me with a smoldering stare. I hummed at the sight of his thick torso, soaked in dark ink save the red roses that covered his scar. He lifted his arms wide, the smile on his face devastating me. He wore his jeans low, and my eyes dove to the muscles on his hips, pointing south.

Voices sounded around me, one of them Branko, commenting on Roan's behavior with surprise, but they were distant, as if under water. I kept my focus, not wanting to drop the thread connecting our minds. *Really Roan? You're that easy? Tsk. I'd hoped you'd make me sweat for that skin. How about you, Mako? Want to show me your abs?*

He answered with a grin. *I only get naked for my mate, you dirty mermaid.*

I rolled my eyes and huffed into our minds. *That's not fair to the rest of us, Mako. Come on, let's see it.*

Roan's voice was teasingly deep. *Ye plan to strip the room naked, lass?*

I grinned at the fire in Roan's eyes, licking my lips. *I wouldn't say no. It could be fun.*

Mako ran a hand through his hair, laughing, watching Jelly's brow as it creased and flexed with effort. He seemed impervious to my seduction. Must be a mate thing. His voice edged with laughter in my head. *You'll leave me and my mate out of your fantasies.*

Roan chuckled. *Yer not my type, Mako.*

I bit my lower lip as he stared, loving this ability to flirt with a straight face. I twirled a red curl in my fingers. *So what is your type, Roan? Do you like them subservient, or prefer feisty girls? Fiery girls?*

The look on Roan's face destroyed me, so full of want and promise. It was as if his rich voice was right in my ear, breathing heat into my body. *Oh, fookin' aye, lass. The hotter the better. I like playing with fire.* Blood flushed to my cheeks. Damn it. He was out-seducing me.

The green wobbled in Jelly's hand as she giggled at our banter. Roan coaxed her to push harder. *Say something, Jelly. Use the magic and speak to us.*

Her jaw clenched tight as she concentrated. *It's… so… hard!*

Without missing a beat, Roan replied in a deep growl. *Aye, that's what she said.*

I squealed loudly in my head, my hands flying up to slap against my mouth, which hadn't made a sound. Jelly doubled over laughing, dropping the magic. She lifted her shirt to wipe the sweat from her face, beaming up at Roan. "That was amazing!"

Roan chuckled and picked up his shirt, and I groaned in my head without thinking. *I'm the one on fire after that.* Roan slowly turned to face me, his hand clenching the fabric. He took a small step to the side, holding my eyes, and I willed myself not to peer down at his jeans, but I couldn't stop myself. My breath caught. I didn't think to filter my thoughts. *Sweet goddess, he's fucking glorious.*

Roan chuckled. His emerald green eyes flashed at me wickedly. *I'd make ye sweat, lass, till it runs off yer body like rain. That I can promise.*

I coughed and choked, glancing at Mako and Jelly, but they were murmuring to each other, completely unaware of Roan's words. He'd said that only to me. Simon sniffed the air, looked at me curiously, followed my gaze, still hooked on Roan, and grinned.

Branko reached for me with concern when I flapped at my face. His hand slid through my hair, throwing ice on my neck, which did nothing to cool me off. If anything, it had the opposite effect. His deep voice sent more of a shiver down my spine than his chilly hand. "You're burning up, Mori. Are you unwell?"

I looked down, certain my shirt was on fire, positive Gray had accidentally set me aflame. I managed to gasp, "I'm fine," and spun on my heel to fetch water for Jelly. Yes. For Jelly. I tore up the stairs, bursting into the kitchen, and opened the faucet, dropping my mouth to drink from the stream directly. Goddess, I was parched. I wiped my chin with the heel of my hand, slapping my wet hand on my neck, my head falling forward as I struggled for breath. Roan won that round for certain. I'd have to do better.

A voice rang out from the pantry, startling me. "My, my, you are thirsty." Veda stepped out, holding two cans of coconut milk. "And I mean that as slang, not specific, although we have glasses on the top shelf." A wide smile stretched her face as she witnessed my confusion and distress. I was still blushing from Roan's parting words and Branko's touch.

Her deep brown eyes lost focus, and the bindi on her forehead flared, morphing from simply a black dot to one surrounded with white squiggles like the sun. I held my breath as it spun and her voice changed, deep and rattly, but she wasn't talking to me. "Yes, I can see it. She has an imbalance in Svadhishthana." She frowned. "Anahata and Muldhara as well."

She blinked, and the bindi stopped turning, lying still as if merely decoration. She pointed at the space below my navel. "You are dehydrated. Thirsty. You draw too much prana from your kidneys." She stepped closer, staring at my stomach. "Not enough pleasure. There is interest. So much interest, but no satisfactory release." She looked up. "Svadhishthana churns like a volcano. It is unstable."

I squirmed under her astute evaluation. "Prana? As in life force?" She nodded. "What do you mean by thirsty? And how can you read me but not Jelly?"

She laughed, the sound like crystals rubbing shoulders. "Too many magics muddle her. Your colors are pure." She pointed slightly lower than my bellybutton. "Svadhishthana. Sacral Chakra. Orange. The seat of sexuality. Yours looks terribly overstimulated, yet disgruntled. Not happy." I snorted. That was putting it mildly. She pointed to my heart. "Anahata is too pale. It should be bright green. Yours is dull." She pointed to my crotch. "And Muldhara is also weak. Do you struggle with this physical form?"

"You mean legs?" I shrugged. "It's not my normal state, so maybe?"

"Hmm. You need red."

"Red?" My thoughts went directly to Branko and his bright crimson magic.

She waved a finger up and down my body. "Your heart is wounded. Have you recently lost someone close? Not death; I don't see that. Something else, but it's similar."

I swallowed as she summarized my feelings. "My best friend found her soulmate."

She nodded with understanding, but it wasn't a nod, it was more of a shake. Maybe it was cultural, but it was confusing. "You feel left behind."

I played at nonchalance. "Kind of. Sometimes." She arched a sculpted eyebrow. I admitted with a sigh. "Fine, yes, I do."

"Ah. And you distract yourself with sexual temptation, almost too much, but you don't follow through. That's why Svadhishthana churns like lava." She patted my cheek softly. "Get hydrated, thirsty girl." She turned from me abruptly and walked back to the pantry. I reached for a glass from the cupboard and gulped three before refilling it and returning to the basement.

Jelly thanked me as I passed her the glass. She drank it in one go. "That's better."

My cheeks heated as I caught Roan staring at me. "That telepathy was cool."

She laughed at my expression, tracking my eyes. "I've never seen a man outfox a mermaid before. Mind you, he is a Mage, but his seduction skills are strong. You had to leave the room from something he said."

I clenched my fists to stop from fanning my face. She drew back and crossed her arms, looking at me from under deep brows. "What have you done with Mori? Where's my friend who bounces from bed to bed? Roan's right there like low fruit. You wouldn't even have to try."

I stuck my thumbnail in my mouth, biting down, making it bend under my teeth. Jelly pulled it away before I could rip it off. I shook my head without giving her an explanation. I didn't want to distract her from her magic.

Her eyebrows bunched in. "Fine. Don't answer me." She sighed, changing the subject. "I don't see how we'll do the telepathy on our own, though. I have the green thread, but what if you want to call me?"

Roan's voice sounded behind me. "Lesson Two, lass.

Patience. We'll get to that." My lady parts turned molten as his beard tickled my ear from behind. I wanted to lean into him and feel the roughness of his chin on my throat. "Ye all right, lass? Ye look rattled. Was it our wee chat?"

I gasped and stepped away from his body heat. "I'm fine. Totally fine." He chuckled and let me be. I grabbed Jelly's elbow and steered her away from the group. "Veda just gave me a reading. Apparently, I'm imbalanced and thirsty." I put my fingers to my temple to speak with her privately and dropped them in frustration, not wanting Roan to listen in. I hissed right in her ear. "Sexually frustrated."

"Oh," she said, her eyes twinkling. "So do something about it." She tipped her chin at Branko, Roan, Gray, and Simon, who stood in a circle talking. I followed her stare over my shoulder. Both Branko and Roan looked over, desire open on their faces. Jelly smirked. "Two candidates right there, ready to play. Don't sweat it, Mori, just pick one." She purred in her throat and grinned excitedly. "I've always lived vicariously through your sexual adventures, Mori. Don't let me down now."

What she didn't understand, and what I couldn't possibly explain, was that I liked them, both of them, probably more than I should, and if I gave in, it could only end in disaster. I wouldn't be the wedge in their friendship. Someone would get hurt, and the chance of it being me was too high.

TWELVE

JELLY

By the end of our first training session, the only magic I could fully control was Mako's. With him in the shield, I'd held Sebastian's magic successfully for a brief time, Roan's somewhat adequately, and Gray's with only minimal scorching. But I couldn't hold the threads from Branko, Simon, or Richard, even with Mako at my side.

After I toppled over like a stone statue, Branko stepped out of the bubble. He muttered he couldn't help me. When I rapidly shifted in and out of a turquoise wolf, crying with pain at each change, Simon had also bowed out. Richard tried the longest, so patiently, as we floated together to the ceiling, pushing straight through Anna's bubble from the force of our combined purple magic. I'd fallen, but he caught me, holding me suspended in the air. He settled me down gently and I burst into tears of frustration. I was drained.

Sophia came to me first and hugged me. "It might take a little time."

I wiped my nose on my arm. "Time we don't have."

She squeezed harder. "Jelly, we've danced to this tune before. Don't do this." She pulled back, holding me by the shoulders. "I was aggressive about Simmi's rescue, forcing you to act before you were ready. I won't do it again with Leif. He's stayed alive so far, and no one is strapping him down and bleeding him. He's Fae. He's smart." She pulled me close again. "What we need is for you to be whole. We will not risk losing you in the Hellhole, Jelly."

Mori snaked into the hug, reaching her arms around me to hold Sophia, squishing me between them. "You did really well, Jelly. You pulled each thread by itself, and while you didn't necessarily wield them, you could pick them out one by one. That's significant progress compared to the shitshow you've been until now."

Mako walked over and stole me from their arms. Mori grumbled as he tugged me away, but he insisted. "You need to recharge. I'm taking you upstairs."

I shook my head. "We can go a few more rounds."

He was adamant. "Jelly, let's go. Upstairs, now." I balked at his tone, wanting to fight back, but I was too tired. Walking up all the stairs leveled me, and I dragged my feet step by step. I was more drained than I realized. Mako said, "See? I can tell when you're depleted. You could barely stand up."

I sighed. "You're right. I'm exhausted." He pushed open the door to our room, and I greedily eyed the king-sized four-poster bed. In the small sitting area, a crystal vase of yellow roses perfumed the air. I padded to the table and stroked a petal between my finger and thumb. I spun to Mako, who was tossing the decorative cushions into a pile on the floor.

He flopped on the bed, patting the space next to him. I crawled over his body with a groan and collapsed face down against the fluffy pillow. He turned on his side, facing me, looking serious. He stroked a finger down my cheek. His voice was quiet, almost hesitant. "Jelly, do I make you happy?"

My answer was pat, far too quick. "Of course you do! What a silly question."

Sorrow touched his brief smile. "And of course you'd say that. It's a serious question. Are you happy?"

I pouted, too tired for a deep conversation, but the concern in his eyes made me pause before dismissing him. I looked across the bed to avoid his face. "Mako, you're my mate."

"Still not an answer." He slid his fingertips to my chin, gripping lightly as he forced me to meet his eyes. "Are you?"

I frowned. No one had ever asked me that before. "I'm happy when we have sex." I crooned the words, unease in my belly. His question unsettled me.

His cobalt eyes flashed. "Mmm. That's passion. Tell me about joy."

"Joy?"

"Joy. Unbridled joy, a pleasure from being alive. Are you content with your life?" When I didn't respond, he continued. "Aristotle believed there were two types of happiness. Hedonia happiness, derived from pleasure, and eudomonia, which comes from seeking virtue and meaning; having a purpose."

I shrugged. "I have the hedonistic down, and then the other one? Um." Biting my lip, I hesitated, unsure I knew what true happiness was. I shook my head free of his fingers and turned on my side to face him, stroking his dark hair from where it had spilled onto his cheek. "I have purpose. It's great when I fulfill it, like teaching young turtles to avoid plastic bags, and I was happy when we defeated Terrun."

"That sounds like career satisfaction, not joy. Do you ever wake up delighted?"

My eyebrows drew down as I puzzled his words. "Briefly, I guess. At the start of our relationship, I couldn't believe my good fortune."

He coughed a sharp laugh. "At the start? We've barely been mates for a second!"

I sighed and met his stare. "Look, you asked me a heavy question, and I'm tired. You don't get to approve or disapprove of my answer. Let me figure this out. If you want more than my temper, don't rile it."

"Fair enough. Keep going."

I rolled onto my back, my forearm over my head. "The ocean is my purpose for living. At least, it was, until we became mated. Now, I always have to think about you. How will this affect Mako? Will this upset Mako? What will Mako think?" There was a snip in my tone, but he wanted honesty; here it was. "I worry about how you perceive my actions." I turned my head sideways to look at him. "I feel judged."

"What about Mori? Does she make you feel like that?"

I flicked my wrist. "Mori's different. She's family. We stick by each other by default." I shouldn't be so flippant or assuming, not after she'd told me I'd hurt her, but I didn't want to derail what was clearly an important discussion for Mako. I shifted again to face him. "Mako, you're my mate. Yet it's like you don't trust me, not fully. I thought being fated meant never questioning each other, but it's like you magnify my every small fault by looking too closely."

His lips turned down as he searched my eyes. "I don't mean to do that. If I call attention to your mistakes, it's only to strengthen you so you don't repeat them." He reached out to stroke my face. "But I want you to be happy. I want to give that to you."

I flopped away on my back, this time covering my eyes with my arm. "I've been blaming you for my discontent. Before that, it was the Trident, or my parents' deaths. But I think happiness must be an inside deal, and I'm the only one who can find it. You, personally, can't give it to me. I have to do it myself. I guess

I've never given it much thought, always so busy with the sea life or fighting against the Trident's tyranny. Then came Terrun. Happiness was never high on my list of priorities."

I rolled over to face him. "But now Leif is depending on us. If anything, I feel anxious, not joyful. Time breathes down my neck like a monster, making me worry I won't succeed." I saw a flicker in his eyes. I'd hit on a shared concern. My throat bunched into knots as the truth settled in my bones. "What if I don't? What will that mean? To us?" Tears sparked my eyes. I covered them with my hand. My voice dropped, broken, as sorrow raced through me. "Fuck… I don't think I've ever been happy. I don't think I even know what it is."

He moved closer, gently uncovering my face, hovering near, his breath warm. "Tell me what you need."

I swallowed thickly, my voice cracking. "That's the problem, Mako. I'm not sure what I need."

He looked at my lip, currently trapped in my teeth, as I bit back tears of bewilderment. This conversation had thrown me. He leaned closer and sucked my lip between his, sliding his tongue against mine. I groaned in my throat as his magic teased at my edges, coaxing me away from dark thoughts.

He was good at that.

Our lovemaking was quick, perfunctory, a means to an end to recharge our magic, with precious few moments of teasing or tenderness. Mako passed out almost instantly, gently snoring, his lips and body slack. Unbidden, my brain started chewing on our problems like tough meat, over and over, grinding at me. I couldn't wield my magic. I couldn't force it to behave. Leif was in danger, and I was the key to his freedom. Plus, Mako was upset with me, although he didn't outright admit it, but my ineptitude had frustrated him tonight, even though I'd tried as hard as I could.

I worried and fussed in my mind, wondering why I was so

unanchored. Since trying to tame the magic, I'd only become more untethered from myself. I knew one thing for certain.

I sure as shit wasn't happy.

I slipped from the bed, and Mako snuffled and rolled over. I splashed water on my face, pushing my arms through the robe I found hanging on the back of the bathroom door. It was dark outside, but I wouldn't sleep, not like this, not with my brain in overdrive. I closed the door softly behind me, leaving Mako sleeping like the dead.

THIRTEEN

MEW

I'd holed up in my room after watching Jelly repeatedly fail to manipulate the magic. I'd vanished, knowing no one would miss me, too distracted by Jelly. I sat in the wing-back, a pale golden color that mocked me with its hue. At this rate, Jelly wouldn't find her yellow in time.

I called out in my head. *Boss? Do you have a minute?*

Instantly, her multi-phonic voice filled my brain. *I'm getting reports that Gaia is upset.*

I tried to keep the defeat from my voice but failed. *Yes, a slew of vicious hurricanes with tornados just ripped through the Atlantic. We have mudslides, flooding. Random forest fires are breaking out. Gaia is angry.*

What about the mermaid? Is she any closer to retrieving the twins?

My voice dropped deeper in resignation. *Jelly is picking her way through the magic, but she needs her mate at her side to do it.*

Is that a problem?

I rubbed my bald head in thought. *It means she's reliant on Mako.* I grit my teeth, preparing for the pain as I spoke the next words. *It's happening too slowly. I need to give them more hints. A* searing pick of heat flared through my temple as she reprimanded me.

It released as fast as it had come as she spoke. *Fine. You may use an intermediary. Or you may speak in riddles, but nothing too overt. No outright assistance or you risk upsetting the balance. If it placates you, Bartholomew, know that I wish you could explain, but even we have rules.*

Yes, ma'am. Thank you, ma'am.

My stomach growled. Infernal beast. Sometimes I hated being in this form, needing to care for it with food, water, and soap. I hoisted out of the chair and shimmered, dropping my muscles and bones for bright light, reappearing in the kitchen, startling the staff. Damn. I thought it would be empty at four in the morning.

The woman who'd brought us tea stifled a squeal as she watched me take shape, flinging her hands from inside the deep bowl, a cloud of flour rising in the air. She dropped to her knees on the floor with her head bowed, her bindi pressing to the stone beneath her, chanting ancient words of praise and reverence. I rushed to her side and tapped her back. "You have to get up. They'll ask questions if they see this. Please, get up! Veda, was it?"

She sat back on her heels, staring at me in awe. I coaxed her up, holding out a hand to help her. Her fingers shook as she hesitated, nervous to touch me, and then she grasped and I lifted her. "You…you…" She stared at me, spluttering. "Your aura is gold and white light!" Her eyes were like a rabbit's, wide and darting all around me.

"Shh. No one knows. Well, Mako has seen me, but he doesn't know specifically what I am."

"Is Mako your charge? The mermaid's mate?" She smoothed down her sari, streaking the fabric with flour, her fingers still trembling.

"Yes."

"How can I help you, Faithful One?" She seemed close to falling to her knees again.

I grinned. "You can start by calling me Mew, and hiding that you're familiar with my kind." I tipped my head, eyeing her with curiosity. "How is that?"

She laughed, a pretty sound, and the bindi on her forehead grew white spikes and began spinning. "I see your colors, Faithful, ahem, Mew, and yours are not from this plane. A thick blessing of gold permeates your energy, and the white light is blinding."

"Have you seen my kind before?"

"Only once when I was a girl. That's when I received the gift." She tapped her finger on her bindi, still wide-eyed. "Given to me by one of you."

I smiled at the fawning woman. "You are more than a healer. You have the Sight, but Anna said nothing. Why not?"

She cocked up an eyebrow, her voice dry. "Because when you tell people you hear voices, they tend to lock you up. I keep it to myself."

She was perfect. I couldn't have asked for a better wing woman. "Veda, I need your help."

She clapped her hands together, a white puff of flour surrounding them. "Of course, Faithf-uh, Mew…anything."

"You saw Jelly's chaos, yes?"

Her brow furrowed down. "The poor girl is in scattered pieces. She's frenetic with colors that don't belong to her, not organically. What happened to her?"

"They did a Coactus Fusionem on her to defeat the Fae Prince, Terrun."

Veda clutched at her chest. "Forced fusion?" She paled, her brown skin turning ashen. "How many?"

I grimaced. "Too many. One Fae, one Fae-Mers, two Shifters, and three Mages. It was necessary at the time."

"That's awful! No wonder she's muddled. With so many

threads thrust with such violence… I can't pick that apart." She shook her head, frowning, eyes brimming with tears. "Poor thing. I'm sorry, Great One. I don't think I can help."

"You said that her Manipura is the issue."

"I said it was likely. If she's searching for yellow, that would be the center to watch. That one or the ninth above her head. But with such a propulsion of new magic…" Her bindi spun at an easy pace before going faster, taking her attention to another place. She spoke to someone else, her guides, I imagined.

She hissed under her breath. "Yes, I'm aware of who he is! No, I don't–" She sucked in and gestured with her head, almost making circles as she nodded and shook it at the same time. She clutched her dusty hands in her sari, worrying and fidgeting as she listened. "Yes, yes, I understand." She glanced at me, her face paling more. "I see. Yes, I do. I will tell him."

Her voice was tight with alarm. "I am told she lost a piece of her soul with the forced fusion. The power of it went for her weakest link. My guides say she's always been volatile, and that anger depleted her solar plexus. Receiving the bolt of magic from seven men knocked it from her. This is no simple matter. No simple matter at all. She must find it. She has no balance, no stability."

The bindi spun like a top, and she clutched the counter to stay steady. Her eyes went to a faraway place. "Oh! OH!" She blinked and refocused, gaping at me with enormous eyes. "Mother Kokuro claimed her and made her a Fae? A mermaid turned into a Fae! No wonder I couldn't read her." Her eyes went unfixed, and she swayed as she received more messages. "The pearl she wears is a being? They bonded? What madness is this?"

I scrubbed my face with my hands. "Yes, the pearl is a Fae creature, changed to a pearl for her protection. She bonded with Jelly during the ritual, I believe, simultaneously with Kokuro's marking. From what you say, if a piece of her dislodged, she needs a Soul Seeker, a rare breed, and I know of only one."

Our eyes collided and together we hushed a name, cautious of speaking it out loud. "Sundidarta."

Sundidarta was beyond secretive. She only appeared when offered a great sacrifice, and she was fickle, often dismissing the gift out of spite. Veda's face fell. "I have nothing of value to give her. But you…you could offer a feather?"

I stared at her in appalled disbelief, my jaw loosening as my eyes widened. "A feather. You want *me* to give *her* a feather?"

Veda shrugged and spread open her hands, almost in apology. "It is a worthy offering to gain an audience."

I pinched the bridge of my nose, worried about the consequences of her suggestion, but it was a solid idea. "A feather. She would accept that."

A piercing pain rang through my brain, setting my teeth on edge. *Bartholomew! You will do no such thing!*

I winced as a drop of blood fell from my nose. *Boss, she needs her soul in one piece. She can't get the twins without it.* The pain eased, and I gasped for breath.

The voice swirled, puncturing my ears as she scowled. *Well…not a gold one.*

Understood. Not a gold one. I'll give her a bit of fluff, nothing more.

She snorted contemptuously at my suggestion. *Fluff will not do. Give her a young one; one without so much wisdom.*

Yes, ma'am.

Veda's eyes were enormous. "Were you just speaking with…with…her?" I nodded, grabbing a tissue to push at my nostrils. I threw the bloody mess in the trash and turned to face Veda again. She'd plunged her hands back in the bowl, kneading and fisting with a frenzy. She frowned at my nose. "She is not happy with you. She hurt you."

"She is not pleased, but she agrees a feather will suffice." I watched Veda attack the dough, slapping it around with great vigor. "How much can you say? What will your guides allow?"

She dropped her eyes. Her bindi spun lazily as she shaped the dough into a large ball, draping a clean cloth over the bowl for its first rise. She rinsed her hands and dried them before speaking. Her jaw was tight. "I cannot tell her she is missing a piece of her soul. But I can dance around it and hope she is clever enough to understand."

"We're in a similar boat then."

She nodded. "That we are." Our heads swung together as the door pushed open.

Jelly looked up and squeaked, flinging her hand to her chest. "Goddess! You scared me! I thought everyone was in bed." Her turquoise eyes caught the light, and Veda peered a little closer, studying her. Jelly tilted her head. "Are you looking at my energy? Mori said you read hers. And you gave Mori advice, something about staying hydrated. Can you help me? With my yellow?"

Veda's head bobbled as she chose her words. "I must not say too much." She squinted at Jelly again and huffed out a breath. "Please forgive the insult, but can you call on your friend? The one with the problem?" She waved at her nether region. I covered my mouth and swallowed my laugh as Veda suggested Mori's rampant frustrated desire.

Jelly scratched her head. "Who? Mori?"

Veda nodded. "Mori. The one with red hair."

Jelly shrugged. "Sure, but why?"

Veda grinned. "She is very smart. She will hear what I am saying without me saying it, and I need her to hear what I have to say."

Jelly rubbed her face with her hands. "Okay, well, that's not confusing at all." She pressed her fingers to her temples. I scuffed at the floor, eavesdropping. Neither woman was aware I could listen to their thoughts, and in a minute, I'd wish I hadn't.

Mori? Are you up? Mori? Mori! Wake up! Wakeupwakeupwakeup! MORI!

Mori's voice was bleary. *What?? Jelly? Jelly! Damn it! I was in the middle of a spectacular sex dream!*

Jelly's mouth flew wide with a silent gasp. Downright rascality lit her face as she scanned back and forth with her eyes, biting her lip to hold back giggles. *Who with? Branko or Roan?*

Ugh. Both! I can't believe you woke me up! I'll never get it back now, and I was right in a good part. Such a good part. They were just about to… Gods damn it.

Jelly grinned. *I'm sorry, Mori. Sincerely, I am. But I need you in the kitchen. It's important.*

Mori blew out an aggravated breath. *The second I'm getting some action, you wake me up.* With that, the connection ended.

Jelly dropped her fingers. "She's on her way. But she's mad. Be ready."

I slowly exhaled the breath I'd held, trying not to laugh.

Minutes later, a red-headed hurricane punched through the door, swinging it on its hinges, hitting the back wall with a bang. "What is so damned critical you dragged me from bed?" She saw me and Veda and stalled. "Oh, hi guys. What's up?"

Jelly pointed at Veda. "Veda said she could help me, but she wanted you here because apparently, I'm not smart enough to understand the code she's about to speak in."

Mori gathered her dressing gown closer. "Code?"

We all jumped when the door swung wide again. Roan strode in wearing only his boxers, his hair disheveled, unbound from its typical thick braid. It swept off to one side, and he ran his fingers through it in frustration. His eyes fell on Jelly first. "Ye have a bad habit of waking me from sleep. What's all the shouting about?"

Jelly blinked. "We weren't shouting."

Roan snorted. "Oh, so the bloody yelling that just rattled me skull wasn't ye two?"

Mori paled. "You heard us?"

His green eyes bored into Mori as his voice dropped. "Ye were dreaming of me, lass, a lush, steamy one from the sounds of it, but just to be clear, I don't share."

She slapped his arm with a crack, instantly turning red. "I told you to stop doing that! Stop listening in!"

He pretended to rub away a bruise from where she'd smacked him, a half-grin on his face. "Until I teach ye to block me, yer talking in my head. Now what's going on?"

Veda inhaled, ready to speak, when the door pushed open again, softly this time, and Mako entered, rubbing his eye with the heel of his hand. He was still half asleep. "Why are you all yelling?"

Mori covered her face, her red curls falling forward as she groaned.

Mako grinned. "I was waiting for details about the dream." He shrugged at Roan, mischief dancing in his eyes. "I was curious about the good part. I'd hoped you would describe it. I'm sure Roan wants to know." Jelly swatted him first, with Mori bunched up behind her. Mori fumed, staring at the floor, probably loathing her fair skin, currently a flaming beetroot red. I cleared my throat, not admitting that I'd listened too.

Roan chuckled at Mori's mortification. "I kept us connected through the green thread, and we'll stay hooked in until I teach ye all the workings of the magic. Lesson Three: Assume everyone's listening."

Mori rolled her eyes. "You could have told us that." She shook out her shoulders and lifted her chin proudly, only to blush further when she eyed Roan's state of undress. "For Goddess's sake! You couldn't find pants?"

"Ah, lass, I didn't think it was necessary since ye had me divested of clothes in yer dream." He waggled his eyebrows at her. Mori's jaw dropped, steam bursting from her ears as she grappled for a comeback.

I rescued her, drawing everyone's attention. "Before Mori combusts, let's get to the reason we called her downstairs. Veda, if you would?"

Veda had watched the drama with delight, her head bobbing and weaving as each person delivered a quip. She beamed at us and clapped her hands together. "The dynamics between you are breathtaking! Such spark!" Her smile dropped as the weight of her task engulfed her. "The Faa, ahem, Mew has asked me to speak with you regarding Jelly's energy. As I told her, I cannot burst forth with the answer, but must step on light toes in hopes you will put the pieces together. Are you ready? I can only say this once." She steeled her eyes on Mori, who perked up under the attention.

"A rainbow consists of multiple hues. Green, purple, orange, two reds, and three blues. The color that's missing has gone into space, held by a creature who wants a large taste." She stopped speaking, looking at Mori with a hopeful expression.

Mori's face turned grumpy and sour. "That's it? That's what you're giving me? Okay, fine. Obviously, you're talking about Jelly's missing yellow." Veda's head bobbled between a nod and a shake.

Jelly held up a hand. "Veda, can you give us a thumbs up or a thumbs down when we're getting close? I'm afraid I can't read your gestures."

Veda glanced at me apprehensively. She'd probably already stepped too far. I nodded to her and said, "Warm."

Both Mori and Jelly gave me blank looks. Mako explained. "Warm means you're on the right path. Keep going, Mori."

Mori stared at me while speaking, looking for tells. "The

rainbow is the ritual." Mori closed her eyes, her lips reciting Veda's words. Her eyelids snapped open. "The ritual broke something in Jelly, sent it away from her."

My voice gathered momentum. "Warmer." I rolled a hand at her, praying she could figure this out before the Boss chastised me for interfering.

Mori's voice rose to a shout. "Someone has her yellow piece and wants to eat it?"

"Hot! Red hot! Arrrhhh!" My knees gave way as a slashing dagger of pain seared through my head. I clutched it as I crashed to the floor, blood streaming from my nose onto my lips.

Jelly leaped for me. "Mew, what the hell?" She skidded across the floor, still dusting with flour, and snapped her teeth against her cheek. Her eyes ransacked my face as she grabbed my head, preparing to give me a healing blood kiss.

"Jelly, no!" Mako sprinted to draw her away from me. "No, you can't."

She wrestled him. "He's in pain! I can help!"

"It's not like that for him!" Mako's voice was wild, fearful for his mate, as he should be. The door slammed open and the rest of the house's occupants poured through, staring at me bleeding on the floor. Sebastian instantly sussed what was wrong and shooed Jelly and Mako away from me.

His voice was low in my ear. "How can I help?"

I sounded like a croaking frog. "Water. On my head."

Sweet relief arrived swiftly as Sebastian poured a bowl on my skull. Mako pulled up the pink liquid with his magic, funneling it down the drain. Slowly, the pain faded, leaving a halo in my vision. Each person's energy flickered around them. This must be what Veda saw.

I stared at Jelly. She was a tangle of spaghetti-like threads, squirming together in no discernible pattern. But cobalt and turquoise flowed in one line, tightly intertwined. My heart dropped. So bound to Mako, she couldn't differentiate her own magic, but she'd have to undertake the soul retrieval without him. I hauled myself onto a stool, staring at the alarmed faces surrounding me.

"Mew! What was that?" Jelly hissed from a distance.

"That was me saying too much."

Mori was indignant on my behalf. "All you said was warm and hot! You said nothing!" She turned to everyone. "The ritual knocked something out of Jelly's center, her yellow. Someone has it and wants to eat it."

Anna stifled a yawn. "Good Lord, that's atrocious. Veda, kindly make us tea? We're all up. We might as well work. I doubt we'll sleep again."

Veda scampered to the kettle and filled it, worry on her face as she glanced at me. I gave her a small nod to show I was fine. She did her nod and shake of her head combination, clearing her throat delicately. "Would anyone prefer coffee?" Several hands went up, and Simon trundled over to her side, smiling.

Mori piped in. "Extra cinnamon on mine, please."

Simon stilled Veda with a hand on her shoulder. "I'm happy to make the coffees, Veda, if you wouldn't mind putting together some toast or something?" He scanned the room. "Is anyone else hungry or just me?"

I let my head fall back so the blood would drain down my throat. I giggled. I'd originally come into the kitchen for food. I lifted a weak hand. "Me. I am. I'm famished."

FOURTEEN

JELLY

I paced back and forth before the fire, which Gray had stoked, chewing on my lip as I thought. A piece of my soul was missing, and I hadn't noticed, probably because I'd been flush with so much new power. Veda and Simon arrived with breakfast, the sun still sleeping, unlike us. I nibbled an edge of buttered sourdough toast. Veda perched like a green parrot in a chair, sipping her herbal tea as she watched me with bright eyes.

Mori sat on the sofa next to Mako and Sophia, and set her cappuccino on the table, turning to Anna. She bunched her red curls into a rough knot. "Who do you know who eats colors?"

Anna set down her mug with care, her lips pursed. She crossed her legs, a ridiculously fluffy slipper dangling from her toes. She tapped her fingers on her mouth, thinking. "This will not be straightforward. It's not about the color. It sounds like Jelly needs a Soul Seeker…" She let her thoughts drift off.

Mori sat forward. "Soul Seeker?" Her brow crunched down. "From what I remember, I think there's only one left. It's almost impossible to see her." Her face rumpled further. "She needs a gift to even get her attention, and even then, you're not guaranteed she'll help you, but I don't see another option, do you?"

Anna frowned. "We need something formidable to draw her out." She shook her head. "But my first thought isn't feasible. I can only think of Jelly sacrificing her pearl."

I spun on her with bared teeth. "What? NO!" Everyone jolted at my shout, too strong for the situation. "I'm sorry. I didn't mean to blast you. But, no, absolutely not. Leoht is not an option. We have to find something else." My heart stuttered as I made a suggestion. "Can I give up some of my magic? Would that be enough?"

Veda shook her head emphatically. No weave or bobble in the motion. "No. You must not. You can't lose any more of yourself. The piece that's missing is already sizeable. You would not survive giving more away."

Mew cleared his throat from where he stood in the background. He stepped forward. "Leave the gift to me. I have something she wants. I can't tell you what it is, but it will secure an appointment."

Roan ran his hands down his thighs, now clad in gray sweatpants and a faded black t-shirt emblazoned with a rock band's logo. "Gods. Sundidarta. She's a terror."

Mew winced, as if anticipating an attack. "You need to talk to the twins first." He hissed in a breath, clutching at his head, the words coming forward through clenched teeth. Blood coagulated in his nostrils, about to flow.

I paused in my pacing, wondering if I needed to throw more water on Mew. He staunched the flow, tipping back his head, waving me away as I approached with a vase of flowers, ready to chuck the blossoms to the floor. Anna and I shared a look, coming to the same conclusion.

Anna tipped down her chin. "Blood ritual. We'll do it in your room." She stood and crossed to Mako. "I will send you physically into the vision, as you have the strongest connection to Leif, with Jelly and Roan observing. I won't have the strength for all of you to go in, and you won't have much time."

I bunched my blue hair into a messy bun, slipping over an elastic band to secure it. "Why not?"

Sebastian answered me. "Because it's the Hellhole. Fae time. It's too easy to get lost in there." Disappointment was on his face as he addressed Mako. "Son, I would go—" He didn't finish the sentence, swinging his eyes to Mori as she cut him off.

Mori cocked her head. "But you can't. Why not? It's something to do with Terrun calling you Sebastio, isn't it? I've wanted to ask you since I fell in the Sliver, but it seemed rude, so I've been waiting for the right time. Who are you to Terrun? Vingor? You know a lot, but can't say much."

"Gods, Mori, back off." I glared at her, wondering why she was pushing so hard, but she had that look on her face, and she would not drop it.

She stepped closer. "What is your connection to all this? You're Fae, we know that much. You must have inside information. You're under a silencing spell, aren't you? Can you break it? Can you tell us something? One word to give us a hint? You could help us figure this out. Will you try?"

Sebastian opened his mouth to speak when his lips slammed together in a fierce line, his eyes bulging. Sophia jumped up and moved to him. He leaned against the bookcase, huffing, his muscles straining as he fought for control of his voice. She slid her arm around her husband. Her eyes were wide with worry. She said, "Mori, stop."

Sebastian shook his head, determined, and began trembling. His face turned bright red, and the veins on his forehead stood out. He panted as though about to free dive to the bottom of the ocean. Finally, he spat out one word, the garbled cry barely discernable. "Brother!" With a wail of anguish, thin ropes of dark smoke circled his neck, choking him. He collapsed on the floor, taking Sophia down with him.

Mew was there in an instant, as if he'd flashed across the room. He lifted Sebastian and ran for the stairs, cradling Sebastian in his arms like a child. He shouted over his shoulder. "Sophia. Your room. Now!"

Tears rolled down Sophia's face as she fumbled to stand with Simmi's help. Her voice shattered like glass. "Brothers? They're brothers? But Terrun almost killed Simmi!" Simmi was pale as a ghost and pulled her mother to stumble after Mew.

I spun Mako around as he stepped to go with them, horror all over my face. He closed his eyes, and when they reopened, he looked crushed, sick. "I always knew Dad was powerful. But Gods, never this. I have to help Mew." He turned and ran, following his family, the blood ritual forgotten.

Shock made my heart race, and I stood paralyzed, the repercussions of Sebastian's admission freezing me to the spot. I couldn't move. The pearl vibrated so hard it lifted the chain, drawing me from my stupor. I stepped away from everyone. *Leoht? Did you know?*

She replied in a tremulous voice. *He saved me. He's the one who appealed to his father. I owe my life to Sebastio.*

Anger consumed me as I spat at her in reply. *His father? You mean the Fae King? You didn't think it was important to tell me he was brothers with the Fae that tried to kill us?*

Her answer was quiet. *What would it have changed?*

I was a chess piece in an unfathomable game. Leoht could have told me a hundred times who Sebastian was. That my mate, my damned mate, was Fae royalty. I didn't know what it meant, but it meant something. I'd been bumbling along, trying to keep us all alive, operating in outrageous ignorance all this time. Fury gathered in my throat as I unraveled.

Magic poured out of me, spitting and hot. Flames dripped

onto the carpet, then levitated in the air, threatening to catch the drapes. Gray sprang to my side, dousing the fire, and yelled for help. Whiskers and horns slashed out of my body before sucking back in, leaving me nauseous. More fire sparked in different colors as my magic mixed up, trying to escape the boundaries of my skin.

Mori jumped to my side, coming too close, drawing back with a hiss. "Jelly! Jelly, stop!"

I stared at her, unseeing, my rage and sense of betrayal taking over all sense.

Roan knocked the wind from my lungs as he lunged for me, whipping me over his shoulder and bursting out the side door. Mori came after us, yelling for me to calm down. I couldn't. I was vibrating, coming undone at the edges as a tail ripped my pants, fangs tearing my mouth.

Roan grunted in pain as more fire escaped me. "Sorry about this, lass." He slung me from his back, holding me by a wrist and an ankle, and spun once for momentum before flinging me away from the house. I surged through the open sky, my sight growing dim as the magic inside me congregated into a furor. When I hit the ground, I exploded, a wail bursting out of my throat. Mori screamed my name.

Spasming magic gripped my body. I thought I would burn alive. Then everything went cold, ice cold, and the world around me turned black. I had no senses. I must be dead. Overarching grief snuffed out my anger, drilling a hole where my heart lived.

"Stop being so dramatic." The voice hit notes of deep bass along with light bells.

I tested my throat in the void. "Leoht? I can't see a thing."

"Ah. Just a moment." She flicked on a floodlight in the darkness. I blinked at her, my eyes taking a moment to adjust. She was just as I remembered, at least six feet tall, thickly built, with dark skin the color of vantablack, gleaming in this strange light she'd produced. She tipped her head, her long fangs playing with her bottom lip.

Her eyes were electric purple with a shocking pink pupil, ringed in turquoise by my magic. White, silky hair swung around her hips as she strode toward me. She sank down, sitting cross-legged near where I sprawled. She wore what looked like a second-skin swimsuit, wrapping her torso in supple, black leather. She tilted her head the other way as she studied me, her long pointed ears tipped in silver, poking through her hair.

"You're a mess, Jelly."

The anger resurfaced. "Explain yourself, Leoht. All this time, you said nothing. Why?"

She ignored my question. "Mother is worried about you." She blinked her strange eyes and leaned closer. "Hmm."

"Hmm, what?" I dragged myself up to sitting.

"I can see what Veda was saying about your energy. You're a mangle of magic with a great hole in your center. That must be your missing piece. The one we need to find."

"Leoht, answer my question. Why didn't you tell me about Sebastian?"

She had the courtesy wear embarrassment on her face, but only for a moment. She squared her shoulders. "You would have mistrusted him. I kept quiet out of respect. I suspected at some point he would challenge his brother's curse, and now we are here." Her words resonated. She was right; I would have judged Sebastian.

I looked around in the void. "Where are we? What happened to me?"

"Somewhere safe. Your body is fine. The stone man protects it. He immediately came to your aid." She sighed, and I swear she swooned a little, her pink pupils growing larger.

"Branko?"

"Mmm. Soon they will rush to wake you, so listen carefully.

Vingor is the eldest, Terrun is the baby. Sebastio is the middle child, the most honorable and decent of Fae to exist. The other two, well, you met Terrun. He is greedy and serves only himself."

She shuddered and rubbed her hands on her sinewy arms. "Vingor is hungry for the crown, and has been since a child. He wants to return to the old ways when the Fae ruled over all. He started bleeding powerful Fae, siphoning magic to increase his own as well as create demons. Terrun stumbled upon his experiments. During this time, I was Terrun's lover." She frowned, reminiscing. "He used to be good."

Her shoulders drooped further at the memory, and her voice grew softer, making me lean in closer. "One night, he bit me. Not uncommon during relations, but…he drank. That was new. He drank my blood, and I realized he was stealing my power. My blood enhances energy, either good or bad."

She wiped under her eyes. "There was a seed of darkness in him. A hunger for control. Terrun…he went mad after that night and started stealing the light of souls. I gave him the power to change others, to nurture their darkness. Not on purpose, of course. Even so, it's my fault."

"He created the Eators from your blood?"

She nodded. "He became obsessed. He started with weaker Fae and drained them dry, like a vampire. He became so hungry. When I threatened to go to the King, Terrun knocked me unconscious and took me to the Hellhole." A shimmering bright silver tear slipped down her black cheek. She looked so fragile.

"Did Vingor bleed you?"

The quicksilver of her tears ran true. She choked back a sob. "Terrun watched. He didn't want to kill me, thinking it was more useful to keep me alive, so he handed me to his older brother."

My heart stalled, thinking of Leoht in such a terrible place, betrayed by her lover. My voice cracked. "How long were you there?"

Leoht wiped her eyes, silver drops on the back of her hand. She didn't answer the question, clearing her throat to continue. "By this point, Sebastio discovered the terror in the castle was Terrun. He caught him biting into a gentle yet powerful fairy, a young man who worked in the kitchen, and stopped him, encasing Terrun in chains and dragging him before the king."

"Sebastian's father." I confirmed, still not fully believing.

"Yes. Their mother, the queen, was worried about me. I was one of her close guards, her friend. Terrun had told her I'd taken leave, but she knew I wouldn't go without saying a word. She demanded an audience with me. Under duress, Terrun confessed where I was. The King summoned Vingor to bring me."

She rose and began pacing the edge of our spotlight. "It was explosive. Queen Raya shrieked when she saw me…I was so thin. So weak. She demanded retribution, despite the instigators being her sons. Vingor cited an ancient text protecting royalty from prosecution; something about power siphoning, claiming I was a tool to be used. Raya, full of rage, hissed in the King's ear to save me. He transformed me into a pearl on the spot and gave me to her as decoration. She later whisked me to Mother, hiding me."

"I thought the King hid you."

She shook her head. "The Queen was loyal to me, but the King changed me in front of his sons. It didn't take Terrun too long to figure out his mother sent me to the ocean, but he didn't know where, and Mother Kokuro keeps to herself. Sebastio was so disgusted at the lack of justice, he said he was leaving the kingdom."

"And Terrun put a curse on him. Forbidding him to speak of it."

Leoht frowned. "Yes. The King didn't argue. Sebastio was abandoning them, and therefore, he should be silenced. But

Jelly, I don't think Leif is in the Hellhole by accident. What if it's a trap? For me. A single drop of my blood is overwhelmingly powerful. My magic can manipulate and amplify any hint of darkness in a soul. It's almost impossible to resist. Terrun knows your bloodline carries the pearl. He knows you're mated to Mako. What if Leif is bait?"

"That doesn't make sense. Leif has been missing for fifteen years. How could they possibly know? But you've been a pearl for ages, so I'll take it into consideration, but I think you're being paranoid."

She crouched down, level with my eyes. "Terrun said he wanted to exterminate humanity to save the Earth from their destruction, but Vingor has other plans. He wants to enslave them. Jelly, Terrun failed in the ocean attacks. He failed when we rescued Simmi. Knowing about Sebastio's family, and that you're mated to Mako, if they've figured out Leif is there, it's obvious you'll try to save him and the twins, and I have to guide you through the Hellhole to free them. It's the perfect opportunity to grab me."

I shook my head. "But if they're aware of Sebastian's children, that means Mako and I…Was our meeting a set up by Terrun?" Horror coiled in my gut. "Is our fate bond a fake?"

Leoht startled. "What? No! Mother Kokuro oversaw that. Do not doubt her. Do not doubt Mako. You are forever connected to Sebastio, to his family." She stood and paced on light feet, turning in circles. "They must not capture me." She stalled, panic on her face.

"Leoht…" My voice carried an edge of desperation, frightened she was trying to back out.

She cut me off with a wave of her hand. "I said I would take you. I stand by my word." Leoht's purple eyes squinted as she leaned closer. "But be aware. Terrun and Vingor are ancient, and terribly, terribly smart. You must be careful." She crossed her arms. "They're working on your body. You will wake soon."

"Leoht, I'm sorry for what happened to you. Truly, I don't know what else to say. I don't mean to belittle your concerns about a possible trap. I'm taking you seriously. And I am so sorry we have to go back there. Do you see we don't have a choice? But I swear we won't go until you're ready." I reached for her hand and squeezed. Her skin was on the cool side, but not icy like Branko's.

She nodded crisply, standing and backing away. "Think about what I said. Time's up." The light faded, and she slipped into the darkness. I traced her with my eyes, catching the light of her purple iris as she vanished.

I inhaled in a rush, bitterly cold air in my throat, my bones frozen stiff. When I tried to move, Branko spoke from somewhere around my feet. "She's waking up." Warmth flooded me, burning away a painful chill.

Mori breathed in my face. "Jelly? Can you open your eyes?"

I blinked. Was it raining? My face and neck were wet. Was I bleeding? I wiped at my face with a trembling hand. Water, not blood, and clear sky above, the first light of day creeping through the trees. Branko rumbled. "I froze you, Jelly. You are currently in a thaw." My neck creaked as I turned it, seeing Gray cocooning me in gentle flames.

Everyone but the Fields family surrounded me. Roan rubbed his beard, then his face, and finally his head. He dropped into a crouch near my face, resting his forearms on his knees. He looked distraught. "I'm sorry I chucked ye, love. I didn't want ye to blow up the house." His voice cracked. "Branko jumped ye and smothered the flames."

"Flames?" I squeaked the word.

Mori nodded, her face close to mine. "You burst into turquoise fire. It was like your magic wanted to burn the others out of you." She swallowed with tears in her eyes. She glanced over her shoulder at Branko, hidden from my view behind the others. "Branko shifted and covered you with his wings." She blinked at him with gratitude and awe, a healthy dose of fiery desire in her eyes. She turned back to me. "He saved your life."

Feeling less of an icicle, I groaned and sat up. I patted myself down and lifted a tremulous hand to my face. It was smooth and normal. I leaned over my knees, my long blue hair following me. I hadn't scorched it. "Branko? Where are you?"

The enormous man kneeled beside me, everyone moving away. I wanted to hug him, but couldn't touch him. His skin would be dry ice, having just shifted. His wings, horns, and claws were nowhere in sight. His skin was pale gray, his eyes a deep steel. He looked at me somberly. I swallowed as he stared at me, waiting for me to find my words. "Did I hurt you?"

He grinned softly. "You did not. It takes hours for fire to distort stone. You burned bright, but not hot. I am fine."

My eyes closed with relief. "Thank you, Branko. I owe you one."

He leaned a little closer, chilling me with his skin. His steely eyes widened with curiosity. "Where did you go? You were baying in pain, and then you stopped. Did you simply pass out, or did you travel?"

I looked around, noticing everyone had sat or kneeled on the cold ground, the dew dampening their clothes. All of them were silent, waiting for my answer. "Leoht took me somewhere. We spoke."

I called to Leoht. *May I tell them?*

One pulse in reply.

I nodded to no one in particular. "She's given me permission to share her story." I stared at them all with wide eyes. "We should go back in the house. It will take me a while, and it's cold. Mori is shivering."

Roan moved to Mori. "Take my heat, lass." He wrapped his body around hers. She melted into him, sighing. Branko stood, disappointment on his face, and stormed toward the house. I watched him go, tasting his bitterness on my tongue. Simon and Gray hauled me up, settling me between them. They sauntered toward the house as my cold muscles jerked and stuttered, remembering how to move. Urgency nipped at me, but I could only do so much. Once inside, they put me near the fire, and Anna pressed a healing tea, sweet with honey, into my hands.

The Fields family and Mew were still absent. I opened my mouth to ask for them when Mori and Roan walked in; her laughing at something he'd said. Branko's lips drew down. My heart went to him. Such a kind soul, trapped in a skin that repelled close touch. Mori scanned the room, noticed who was missing, and said, "I'll go check on them. Don't start without me." She thundered away, her footsteps sounding on the marble in the foyer and fading once she hit the carpeted stairs.

Both Roan and Branko watched her go.

FIFTEEN

MAKO

Mew put Mom and Simmi in a trance-state to work on Dad. They sat on a shared loveseat, their eyes closed. He left me be, seeing as how I'd already seen his true form. Dad lay on the bed, stiff and pale, his jaw wide open as if screaming.

Mew pulled sticky dark strings like spiderwebs from Dad's throat. They stank like gasoline in the sun, and Mew was very careful to set them inside a lapis lazuli crystal bowl he'd retrieved from somewhere. Once full, he stirred the contents with a golden feather he'd plucked from one of his wings. The strands hissed and squirmed like worms before shrinking and puffing away on acrid smoke. He set the feather on the lip of the bowl and kept pulling.

Mori knocked softly, calling my name, and Mew glanced at the door in alarm. "Don't let her in here." Beads of sweat rolled down his shiny head. I opened the door just a crack and slid out, careful to keep Mori from peeking inside. She tried, but I blocked her with my body, forcing her to step back.

Mori tugged my sleeve, trying to drag me away. I wavered, wanting to stay with Dad, but then she spoke. "Jelly set herself on fire after losing control of her magic. Like, big time. Branko smothered the flames by icing her. Gray thawed her out. She says

Leoht took her somewhere. She's awake now. She needs you." Magical words, those three. I raced down the stairs to my mate, who sat on the bench before the fire, hugging a mug to her chest.

She peeked up from under her lashes. Her gaze was bleary. I cupped her cheek in my hand, startling from the low temperature. "What happened? Are you okay? You're freezing!" I pressed my warm hands to her chilled face and kissed her, rushing her full of my magic. She jolted, sloshing hot tea on her fingers. I took her mug as she wiped her hands on my pants. I turned to the room. "Dad's okay. Mew is working on him. He's ah, he's um…"

"No need to explain, Mako," Richard said. "We don't need the details."

I turned back to Jelly. "Mori said you lit up, then you went with Leoht. What happened?"

"Sit down, Mako. You'll want to sit down." With my hand in hers, she recounted Leoht's story, her eyes never leaving mine, until she sagged back at the end. Everyone in the room was silent, staring at me. So much fell into place. I came back to the present when Jelly gently shook me. "Mako? Roan asked you a question." I stared at them all in a daze, my mind reeling.

Roan repeated himself. "I asked if ye were alright. Judging yer face, I'd say no."

I slowly shook my head, clearing my thick throat before attempting to speak. "No." My head spun. I came from royal Fae blood. I stood and paced, pulling at my hair and staring at the oaks outside. What did this mean? I stalled mid-step, my fingers gripped and tugging, incoherent mutters stealing my breath as I struggled to digest Leoht's story. Gray redirected me to the bench, making sit before I dropped. Despair hit me next, thinking of Leif as bait. Doom sat heavily on my shoulders. The entire mission was a setup.

Jelly squeezed my hand, wrapping her other arm around me

and holding tight. A voice floated through my mind. It sounded like an orchestra tuning, finding the same note through multiple instruments. *Breathe, Mako. All is not lost. I am Leoht. Look around you. Power surrounds you. And Mori, you've made me laugh so hard through the years. You've been a wonderful friend. Roan, I am pleased to speak with you. Thank you for connecting their minds.*

Mori squealed and covered her mouth, her eyes flying wide. Roan stroked over his chin, nodding. Leoht wasted no time. *Listen carefully, all of you. You must do the blood ritual right now. Terrun will sense that his curse is being lifted from Sebastio. If he's working with Vingor, they will double their efforts to find the twins. That must not happen.*

I swayed where I sat, snatching my hand from Jelly's, clutching the bench beneath me. My jaw was so tight I might chip my other teeth. I leaped to my feet, shocking everyone around me with the abruptness. Roan was already up, pacing, looking at me with wild eyes. I spun to Anna. "We need to do the ritual." When she stared at me without moving, all politeness escaping me as I bellowed. "Now!"

She jerked. "Good heavens, Mako! What's gotten into you?"

"Leoht just spoke to us. Mew is lifting a silencing curse from Dad, which will trigger an alarm for his brothers." I choked on the word. "We have to warn Leif."

I hauled Jelly to her feet and ran for the stairs. As Anna and Mori raced for the room containing the magical relics and items they needed, Jelly and I burst into ours. She hastily pulled up the covers, pushed the pillows against the wooden headboard, and sat, having done this before.

Roan climbed on the bed to face her. I paced, willing Anna to hurry. The others filtered in, taking up spots by the window. Gray stopped me from tearing out my hair. He spoke measuredly. "Mako, take a breath. Be calm."

I exhaled a forceful breath, trying to rid myself of anxiety. "Just…what if it doesn't work? What if I don't reach him in time? What if they've already caught him?"

Gray held me by the shoulders, stalling my attempt to resume pacing. My friend's deep brown eyes bored into me. "It will work. Trust, Mako. It will all be okay. It has to be." He turned me to face Jelly and Roan, both of them sitting with eyes closed, breathing deeply as they prepared. "Go sit with them. Collect yourself. You need clarity for the ritual. Go."

My thoughts went to Dad. "Gray, knock on Mom's door and tell Mew what we're doing. I don't think it affects anything, and it doesn't matter because we're doing it, anyway. He won't open the door, so just knock and then speak."

Gray nodded. "On it." With a squeeze to my shoulders, he pushed me toward the bed and left. I perched next to Jelly, willing my breathing to steady.

A small voice sounded from the floor. "Oh, thank Bastet. I made it in time. I ran as fast as I could. Move over, Mako. I need to jump up. You're in the way." I grinned, shifting to peer at Icy, who had helped us before when rescuing Simmi. She was a Seer. The chubby white cat lashed her tail.

Jelly whooped beside me, startling Roan, his green eyes flying open as he scowled. Jelly scrambled over me to peer over the side of the bed. "Icy! You're back!"

"I am, and now you're in my way." Icy wiggled her haunches and leaped up, digging in her claws for the final ascent. She reached the top and sat back, twisting to smooth out her fur with a pink tongue before marching across the pale quilt to stand before me.

I scratched her under her chin, right where she liked it. "Hi, Icy." She purred, making chirping noises amidst the rumbling.

"What's she doing here?" Roan looked at her suspiciously.

Her ears flattened at his tone. I withdrew my hand,

knowing how quick she was to bite. She said, "Tell the big man I am here to escort you. You'll need extra assistance to travel to the Faelands." She narrowed her pale blue eyes at me. "Especially to the Hellhole. I will keep the portal open for your safe return."

Moments later, Anna and Mori came through, their hands full of various items. Anna visibly sagged with relief when she saw the cat. "Oh, Icy, thank goodness. I was fussing about how to do this. It's going to take a lot of magic." Icy nodded to her silently.

Anna turned back to us. "You all need to undress. Down to your shorts. Clothing mutes your energy. Leoht grants entrance to the Hellhole as she's been there before, which means Jelly needs to be there. Roan will allow you to communicate. Mako, your job is to focus on your brother's energy through the orca to ensure you land near him. Any questions?"

I slid my pants down my legs, tossing them in a heap on the floor. Mew arrived and leaned heavily in the doorway, mopping his brow with a cloth. I nodded to him. "Warn Leif. Get a message from the girls. Anything else?" Mew shook his head and left.

Mori set two black candles on our left and two on our right. Under Anna's instruction, she placed a wide silvery black bowl, almost a platter, between us. With steady fingers, she handed each of us a different black crystal and stepped back.

Anna explained. "These are the strongest stones I have for protection."

Jelly cleared her throat with trepidation. "Everything is black. Isn't that bad?"

Anna tsked. "Superstition. Black is protective during shadow work. The bowl is hematite, powerfully grounding. It is high in iron, amplifying your blood, and it will guide you back home. Hold the crystal in your dominant hand. I need to cut both palms."

Anna murmured a spell. The power in my stone was potent,

making the base of my spine tingle as the magic of it snapped into place. Anna approached us with her jewel-encrusted knife, chanting under her breath. The air in the room grew thicker. Anna muttered, half in a trance. "Hold the stone with your index finger and thumb, stretching your palm out as much as you can. Coat the stone in your blood and place it in the bowl. Make sure they touch." She looked at Icy. "If you will take the position you need, please?"

Icy said, "Try not to get blood on me. I don't like the taste." I relayed her words to Roan, who stared at her intently as she curled herself around the hematite bowl. Anna exhaled and sliced my palms first. A rush of nerves washed through me as I rolled the stone between my bloody hands, placing it gently in the bowl. Roan was next, his face stoic, and he set his shiny shungite beside my tourmaline. Jelly chomped the inside of her cheek as Anna dragged the knife across her flesh. She wrapped her stone in her hands, whispering her own prayer to her sea goddess before setting it in the bowl.

Anna's voice dropped an octave as she chanted, holding her hands over the bowl. Icy began purring as loudly as she could, the vibration of it a physical caress. After a long exhale, Anna said, "Mako, think of your love for Leif. Hold hands and be safe."

Roan spoke in our minds. *If I sense danger, Mako, I'm bringing ye out. Understand? Ye'll be able to hear us. So will Leif. We'll be brief.*

I heard Jelly in my head. *I love you.*

I looked at my fierce mate and nodded once. *I love you, too.* I held out my hands, blood pooling in the centers. I pictured Leif's face in my mind, in the cave with the glowing red rocks. I saw him in Fae form in tattered clothes, holding that knife. I pulled on the familial bond of my Hai Matau, praying for it to find my brother.

As skin touched skin, I transported through a black tunnel

filled with screaming sounds and hot air; terrifying. My eyes streamed and burned, smelling rancid oil, tasting something akin to leather. I choked, trying not to breathe, wondering if my lungs would burst. I landed, hard, and rolled across a stone floor, splashing into a pool of liquid acid. Strong, wiry arms yanked me out, and I coughed, gasping for breath, my face close to slimy orange eels that lay flayed on the rock.

"MAKO?" Leif screeched my name as I retched. I looked down, noting all I wore were wet boxers. "Mako, what the fuck are you doing here? I'm trying to leave, not have you come in!" He rushed to rub me down with a blanket, muting the sting on my skin. "You're in Fae form!" He tugged at the sharp tip of my ear. "How are you Fae? What the hell, Mako? You stupid idiot! What is wrong with you?"

"Nice to see you too," I said wryly, grinning at the wild Fae hovering over me. With a cry, he wrapped me in his arms and squeezed so tightly my spine popped. He was so lean. Too lean. I wheezed through his hug. "We're doing a blood ritual. I had to talk to you. As for how I'm Fae, that's a long story. What about you? How are you Fae?"

He pulled me to my feet, staring at me. "It happened as soon as I fell in here. You're all grown up. How long have I been gone?" His previous affection dropped away as he looked me over.

My voice was hoarse, stripped by the water. "Fifteen years."

His eyes filled with tears of disbelief. "Fifteen years?" His agonized voice bounced off the slick walls, echoing over his next words. "Fifteen years to put on the necklace?" He bared his sharp teeth. I recoiled with horror, thinking he might go for my throat. I stepped back.

Roan's voice shattered the tension, sounding all around us. "Lads, no time to fight. Leif, take Mako to the twin girls."

Leif's jaw dropped open as he scattered his eyes around the ceiling. "ROAN? Is that you?"

"Aye. Now go."

Leif snarled and grabbed my arm, digging in with his claws, dragging me deeper into the cave, keeping me upright as I tripped on the uneven floor and stumbled into a larger space. Two identical small faces blinked at me. One of them waved. She lifted and crossed to me on thin, stick-like legs, an arrow on one thigh. She laid her tiny hand on my chest, under the Hai Matau, pressing against the whirlpool Mother Kokuro had marked me with. A zing of power seized my heart.

She looked up with tears in her brown eyes. "Hello, brother." Leif stared at her, stunned.

The other girl approached shyly. At her sister's encouragement, she also slid her hand to my chest, exhaling as she connected with the mark. Leif made a quick introduction. The girl with the arrow was Trix. The other was Xeno.

I turned to Leif, who watched us with a slack jaw as the girls seemed to know me through my tattoo. "Leif, my mate needs to find a piece of her soul. Then we can come. We're working on–"

"Your mate?" His eyes blinked incredulously. He ran a clawed hand through his matted hair. "You're mated?" Another pang of guilt shot through me. I'd been living on the surface, finding love, and he'd been here, surrounded by acidic water and darkness.

Jelly's voice rang through the cave. "I'm Jelly. I'm his fated mate. As soon as I'm whole, we're coming for you. All of you." Both Trix and Xeno grasped each other around shuddering, bony shoulders.

Roan's voice sounded around us. "Trix, Xeno, can ye hear me?" Both girls nodded, not at all startled by a disembodied voice. "Do ye have something to tell us?"

Xeno scanned the dark ceiling, calling out in a shaky voice. "Find liquid gold."

Jelly's voice strummed with shock. "Is that my yellow?"

Xeno shook her head, frustrated. She dropped her gaze from the ceiling to meet mine. Her glower bored into my skull. "Two pet names. You plus her."

I leaned closer, swamping over the girl in height. "What do you mean, pet names?"

Trix drew her back by the arm. "She cannot say more." She hissed at her sister. "You must not say more." Xeno glared at her, stomping her small foot on the floor, sending a reverberation through the cave.

Roan's voice echoed around us. "Mako, Icy's purr is fading. Give him the warning!"

I steadied myself, hating to deliver this news when I was about to leave. "Dad is…Gods, Leif…Dad's a Fae Prince. He's brothers with Vingor and Terrun."

Leif gaped at me. "Dad… Why hasn't he tried to get me? He should be able to go anywhere!" Tears of fury and betrayal edged his eyes.

I grabbed him by the shoulders. "It's not that easy. You don't know Terrun's story yet. He kidnapped Simmi, bled her, used her to turn humans into things called Eators. We assume Vingor is doing something similar. That's why he has them." I nodded to the twins.

The blood drained from Leif's face. Xeno and Trix both burst into tears.

Leif drew back his lips in a snarl. I shook him. "They'll be looking harder for you now, so extra caution. Don't do anything risky."

His voice was savage as he hissed at me. "Risky? You have no idea what it's like down here. I've lost fifteen years, Mako. Fifteen! Tell our royal father to get me the hell out of here. Now!"

I nodded, swallowing down tears. "I will. We will."

"Mako!" Roan's voice was urgent, laced with a touch of panic.

I grabbed the back of Leif's neck, my fingers digging in as I slammed our foreheads together. My voice broke. "I am so, so sorry. I love you. Stay alive." He inhaled to reply, but the stinking and burning dark tunnel yanked me away before he could sound out the words.

SIXTEEN

MORI

Roan was sweating buckets, rivulets racing down his nose and catching in his beard as his body shook. His eyes squeezed with pain as his jaw worked back and forth, his teeth grinding. Jelly looked no better, her chin tucked into her chest as she took short, quick breaths. Leoht vibrated at her throat, not lifting on the chain, but definitely involved. Mako's eyes darted back and forth behind his closed lids, his body tight, his knuckles white as they gripped Roan and Jelly. I listened with alarm as the cat's purr stuttered, breaking off as she hauled in more breath to continue.

Roan roared, the sound weakening my knees, and I yelped as Mako's eyes flew wide and he lurched to the side of the bed. I was ready. I held the bucket under his face, turning my head to the side as his stomach released in a stream. I clenched my teeth and breathed through my mouth. He spat and sat up, clutching his head, smearing blood on his temples. Jelly snapped her teeth on her lip and kissed him. Ew.

Roan buckled over, knocking the bowl with his knee as he splayed out his hands to catch himself. Bloodied crystals rolled over, landing on Icy. She didn't have the energy to hiss a complaint or open her eyes. She lay panting through an open mouth.

She gave a weak meow, a questioning one from the tone, and Jelly spoke through a ragged breath. "All here."

Richard handed them mugs of Anna's healing tea, and they each sucked it down greedily. Anna sank into a chair, panting. Jelly's head hit the wood behind her, and the pearl finally lay still. She lifted a hand to it, exhaling a long breath. Roan shifted his vast body and sprawled on his back across the foot of the bed, gasping. Mako's eyes went wide, and he motioned to me. Up came the tea. I gagged as he spat. Simon handed him a wet cloth, which he took with a muttered thanks, wiping his mouth. Simon grinned at my expression and grabbed the bucket from my hands, disappearing into the bathroom.

I had a thousand questions banging on my tongue, but I waited for them to speak first. Jelly cleared her throat, the black ring around her eyes more pronounced. "He's there with the girls. Mako found them." She smoothed her hand down Mako's leg. "Can you talk?"

Richard handed him more tea, which he sipped slowly this time. Roan groaned when Icy struggled to him and lay on his chest. His big hand came down gently, resting on her belly as she flopped over. He spoke in a soft growl. "Don't bite me, ye wee terror." She choked out a purr, I assumed a laugh, and fell asleep.

Mako cleared his throat, testing his voice. It was rough and raspy. "Gods. That was awful. The stench of the tunnel." He grimaced and wiped his face again. "I can't get the taste out of my mouth." He leaned back on the pillows, collecting his thoughts. "Everyone is fine. As well as they can be. I..." Tears formed in his eyes, one spilling silently down his cheek. He shook his head. Jelly held his hand, taking over.

Her voice wobbled. "We saw the girls, and they recognized Mako, calling him brother when they held their hands to his chest, over the mark. One twin, Xeno, told me to find liquid gold. When I asked if it was my yellow, she stared at Mako as if trying to eat him and said, 'two pet names, you and him,' and then the other twin, Trix, made her stop."

Footsteps at the door turned my head. It was Mew, looking bedraggled. I hadn't noticed him leave once the ritual started. I stepped out of the way as he approached Mako on the bed. He set a hand on Mako's shoulder. "Your father is sleeping. He will be out for a while." His eyes gathered the bloody crystals, dried a deep rust, the bowl, and healing cuts on their hands. His voice dropped to a faint rustle. "I felt you and Leif." His lips turned down. "Also Terrun and Vingor. They are furious." Jelly and Mako both stiffened.

Mew's turned and his eyes settled on me, almost pleading, begging for me to understand. "Sawel. North of the river, beyond the lit eye, to a split bridge where truce-breakers die." His teeth gritted as he spoke, his words turning tight, the muscles of his shoulder bunching up. Only Anna and I noticed he was speaking. "To avoid her pale hand…" He fell to his knees, swooning as he gripped his head as if trying to keep it attached. Blood dripped onto his lip. "Protection…high in the…brand."

I dropped to my knees beside him, patting him in a panic. "Simon! Get water!"

Simon rushed in with the bucket he'd rinsed and dumped it on Mew's head. He gasped and collapsed on the floor, barely breathing. Simon raced for more water. I pressed my ear against his moving lips. I barely caught the words as they came out with a sigh. "She must not fail."

"Mew?" I shook him. "Mew?"

Simon barked from above me. "Cover his nose and mouth." I protected his airway as more water soaked into the carpet. He turned for the bathroom again. I flinched as Mako suddenly appeared beside me.

Mako said, "Simon, stop. He's breathing. He'll come back

around." His eyes turned to me. "What did he say to you? I couldn't hear him."

Anna looked shaken. "He must have only spoken to me and Mori. The word 'sawel' means soul in the ancient language. He was telling us where to find the Seeker." She quickly recounted his riddle to everyone else.

Richard's eyebrows clung to each other. "What did he whisper at the end? I saw his lips moving."

I grabbed a tissue and held it to Mew's bloody nose, staunching the flow. "He said she must not fail."

Jelly put her fear to the side. She swung her legs off the bed and poked Roan, who was snoring lightly along with the cat, although I could swear Icy had one eye cracked open. "Roan. Get up. We have work to do. Don't step on Mew."

He roughed a hand over his face. "What's this now? What happened?"

Jelly pointed to the floor. "Mew passed out on the floor. He gave Mori a riddle about my soul piece. Get up. We need to figure it out."

Richard said, "I have an idea for part of it. Come. Let's go back downstairs where we can all sit." He and the others departed, leaving me, Roan, Mako, and Jelly, the four of us, staring at the unconscious man on the floor. Branko was the last to leave, staring at me with his steel eyes as if he wanted to say something but chose not to.

Jelly sniffed under her arm with a sour face. "I need a quick shower. I stink of fear." Mako said he would join her. She stepped over Mew and pulled Mako's hand, the two of them stumbling for the bathroom with hushed voices. The water turned on.

Roan stared at me from the bed, his head twisting at an awkward angle. He caught me in his emerald eyes, hypnotizing me, and a memory of something struggled to work its way forward in my mind. I broke the stare and leaned to the right, grabbing a cushion from the chair to place under Mew's head, but when I turned back, he was gone. Only the outline of his body in the sodden carpet remained.

I dropped the embroidered pillow. "Where did he go? He was right here!" I sucked back a sob and slapped my hands to my cheeks, shaking my head. "No, no, NO! What is happening? I can't…" I was clearly losing my mind. Roan shifted the sleeping cat and rolled from the bed, kneeling before me.

I rocked back and forth. It was all too much. Forced fusions, blood rituals, fighting mates, missing souls, hellish dimensions, the twin girls, secret royalty…it was all too much for my brain to grasp, and my grip on reality slid away. I wanted to scream and scream and scream. Roan's warm hands wove under my wrists and grasped the back of my skull as I shook. I clutched at his shoulders for balance. He dropped his forehead to mine. His voice was raspy. "Lass. Breathe. Ye can't fall to pieces now."

His fingers were firm, giving me an anchoring point as he pulled back to look at my face. My eyes stared wide, seeing nothing. He stroked his thumbs along my jaw, leaning in close. "Mori, yer shaking. That's not like ye, lass. Ye been thinking too hard, burning through magic. When did ye last recharge?" I dipped my chin down. "Answer me." When I still didn't speak, incapable of finding my tongue from the way his touch burned me, his grasp tightened. "I interrupted ye at the pool. I should have let ye finish. Aye, fook."

I jerked my eyes to meet his, wanting to snap at him to leave me be, but not finding the words. I was too close to a full burnout to answer. He scanned my face with worried green eyes. "Yer running on fumes, lass. Let me help ye." I opened my mouth to speak, but nothing came out. There was churning in my body below my navel, twisting and turning as if its own beast. He leaned closer, his lips mere centimeters from mine. "Lass, ye fookin' dream of me. Say yes to me."

Whatever was happening in my belly burst open, pushing me over the edge with a yearning I couldn't resist. I curled my fingers in his beard, yanking his mouth to mine. I opened my lips, diving into his invitation, a deep moan escaping me as my tongue found his. His fingers bruised my neck as he kissed me, one hand sliding wide on my back, pushing my chest firmly against his.

Just as greedily, I grabbed his skull, my fingers squirming into his thick braid and pulling, needing him closer. His deep voice crooned in my head. *That's right. It's all for ye to take.* His kiss rushed with power, causing my body to throb.

I cried out in the kiss, lost in the sensation of his magic. My body took control, overpowering the thoughts that kissing Roan would lead to complications. The fire in my lower belly consumed me, and I pressed more of myself against him when he spread his knees wide and sat back, yanking me onto his lap. I squeezed my thighs around him, locking my ankles. Legs. Wide legs. Legs clamping his body, clad only in black briefs. My stomach gushed magma.

With one arm around my hips, he moved me over him, over and over, never breaking the kiss. He was everywhere as the fire inside devoured me. I wailed in my head. *Yes! More! More, Roan!* His arm tightened as he rocked me harder, his other tangled in my hair, his beard roughing my face, my lips bruised, my breath gone. Painful pressure raged in my body, like fire fighting against the confines of glass, roaring within a closed container. Gods, I was desperate for him, but I wavered, fearful of claiming his magic, frightened by the intensity of my longing.

His magic pounded against me, seeking entrance. I was so close, yet still holding back, a thin thread of mental awareness screaming for me to resist. This would cause feelings. Too many feelings. My skin roasted, too hot, and my belly pitched and whined in a fervor. I couldn't hold back. I had to let go. He snarled in my head. *Take it, lass!*

I exploded into pieces of stars, flung from this time, gone from this place, hovering in the dark sky before falling, plummeting to earth, crashing like waves on the sand as his magic consumed me in a rush of power. I shook and shook and shook, my body releasing, then recharging in a roar of flame that burned me from the inside. My brain was white noise, my ears dull ringing. I hauled air into my lungs, aware that I'd stopped breathing.

I slowly settled back into my body, drawing the sensation of flames around me like a blanket. A thick hand was stroking my spine. My fingers ached from gripping someone's shoulders. My face was wet from tears, my breath ragged to my ears. A deep voice rolled through my head, the sound comforting. *Ah, lass, ye needed that, didn't ye? Shh. It's okay now.*

I blinked my lids open, staring directly into endless pools of emerald. His eyes were soft and twinkling. "Roan? Why am I in your lap? What…" My voice trailed off, feeling his body beneath me, so hard, so thick. He cupped my face in his huge hand, wiping tears from my cheeks. The other continued to stroke my spine in long sweeps.

"The magic took ye, lass. Yer body pushed your brain to the side." It rushed back to me, what I'd just done. I'd begged him. Oh, gods. This was awful. I steeled myself, waiting for a snarky remark, a smug comment that he'd won this battle of wills. It didn't come. He was tender with me, so different from what I expected. I unlocked my ankles and shifted, sliding my body back slightly, slipping toward his knees. The hand on my back froze like he couldn't bear to release me. He said with a rumble, "Thank you for letting me see ye." He looked almost shy.

My heart pounded. What did this mean between us? Would he expect more? Would he expect me to return the favor? Now?

Later? I'd completely lost control of my body. Would this happen again? Could I stop it?

He smiled. "Ach, yer overthinking it, aren't ye? Yer pulse is a gallop. Don't worry, lass. Ye'll get no chains from me." A twisted image of him strapping me down filled my head, bringing another rush to my belly. He chuckled, as if reading my mind. "Now, lass, I need ye off my lap. I can't sit in a polite company like this." My eyes flew wide as I gaped at him. I scrambled out of his embrace, stumbling to my feet. He grinned as he looked up at me, adjusting his boxers.

"I…I…" I had no words.

He rose and pulled me close, his hand sliding behind my head again, the other wrapping possessively around my hips. "Ye'll be wanting to shower, lass. Yer soaked, and the sweet scent of ye is thick in the air." His words stunned me, as did his hardness against my stomach. My belly lurched again, almost dragging me away with its insatiable need. He dropped his mouth to mine, kissing me slowly, his tongue teasingly gentle as he stroked, stoking my fire hotter, urging me to go for another round, and then another. The water turned off in the bathroom.

"That'd be yer cue, lass. Go wash up." He turned me in his hands and moved me forward with his wide palm at the small of my back. I lost all sense of direction, lurching out of the room in a haze. With a rumble in his throat, he left me at my door, sauntering down the hallway with his clothes in his swinging hand, whistling a cheerful tune. I stared after him. His voice laughed through my mind. *Stop looking at me ass. Go bathe.*

I blinked, incredulous at his gall. I wasn't looking at his…yes. Yes, I was. My shower was quick, cold, and I moved methodically, stunned. I toweled off, noting I was calmer, certainly energized, but baffled by my loss of control. That had never happened before. I was always in control. I braced my palms on the bathroom counter, inhaling and exhaling slowly.

My mind was sharp and electric, the synapses zinging with power.

I dressed in shorts and a tank top, scowling at the stacks of merino wool in my dresser, my hair pulled up to expose my neck. I tugged at my scant clothes and the overwhelming heat in my body. I fanned myself as I walked down the stairs. When I entered the library, Veda's eyes flew wide with delight. She clapped her hands together with glee. "Oh yes, that's much better!"

My cheeks flushed red, and I rushed for a worn velvet wingback as Branko looked at me quizzically. He delicately sniffed at the air as I walked past him and rumbled deep in his throat, disguising it as a cough. He stalled me, catching my hand in his, his thumb stroking over my skin, the coolness of him like a sweet breeze on a stifling day.

I shivered, the heat in my body roaring back to life. I wanted to climb into his lap, taste his magic, feel the cold stone of his body. His eyes turned molten as his fingers tightened. I willed my feet to keep moving, aiming for the chair, pulling myself from his grasp. I heard him exhale through his nose in frustration.

Simon came in from the dining room, pushing it open with his foot as he carried a tray with fresh coffees and teas. He passed me a cappuccino along with a bottle of cinnamon and stalled, his nose slightly twitching. His face broke into a grin. "Your scent is amazing, Mori. New soap?"

I heavily dusted my coffee. "Something like that." Fate spared me from further comment as Jelly and Mako walked in, drawing Simon's keen nose away as he delivered coffees. They shared a couch, and Jelly sat forward after her first sip, about to speak. I stopped her. "We should wait for Roan." I was proud of myself for not blushing as I sounded his name on my tongue. The man himself strode into the room a minute later and my mouth dropped open.

His wet hair hung free, released from its warrior braid,

falling well past his shoulders in a dark wave. He had a spring in his step as he crossed to the tray, grabbed a coffee and sat in the chair next to mine. I couldn't tear my eyes from him, nor shut my jaw.

Jelly laughed at my expression. "New look, Roan? It suits you."

Roan winked at her and turned to face me. He'd shaved off his beard, making him look years younger, almost boyish, and certainly fresh. He was ruggedly handsome. His jaw was broad, and a small dell sat square in his chin. He smiled, and I stopped breathing at the sight of his dimples. They'd been hiding beneath all that scruff. He roughed a hand over the smooth skin self-consciously. "Time for a change, that's all." My fingers tightened on my mug, the heat of it almost burning me.

Roan's chuckle rasped through my mind. *Breathe lass. It's just skin.*

I inhaled a deep breath, forcing myself to look away. "Mew disappeared after you all left." Everyone's eyes swung to me in shock.

Mako waved it away. "He does that sometimes. Nothing to worry about. Anna? Did you figure out his riddle?" I frowned at Mako, wanting to press Mew's vanishing, but he shot me a look that said to be quiet. Jelly glanced at me apologetically. I could read her face, basically saying, he's stressed, let him carry the room. She looked away, but something in my expression triggered her. She'd caught me eyeing Roan. Her eyebrow shot up quizzically. I shook my head a bit, scowling.

Richard floated his mug of tea to the table and sat back, crossing an ankle over one knee. "The clue was the split bridge where truce breakers die. He's talking about Tower Bridge. It's a drawbridge on the north bank of the Thames, beyond the Eye." His eyes scanned the room as he finished in a hushed voice. "She's at the Traitor's gate."

Anna piped in. "Sundidarta, the Soul Seeker, behaves like a ghost. She is translucent, thus the pale hand. She only becomes visible if you have something she wants." Her eyes swung to Jelly. "And I can only imagine the brand is your Fae mark on your back. That is my first guess. The sun is the symbol that's at the top of your mark. But I'm not sure how you'll get protection, or what that means."

I licked at the cinnamon staining my lips, stealing glances at Roan's profile as he sat forward, listening intently. I ogled the tattoo on the front of his neck. It was a skull on butterfly wings that shifted as he swallowed his coffee. When he spoke, it moved with his throat as if taking flight. He said, "The sun? Symbol of light but also gold, life, vitality. The Self."

I couldn't stop staring; couldn't wait to ask him what his tattoo meant. He was mesmerizing, so handsome, so… He snapped in my head. *Lass, pay attention!*

The only tell was me sitting up taller. I kept my face neutral. I cleared my throat. "We need to bring in the information from your ritual. They're tied together. I'm sure of it. One twin told you to find liquid gold."

Roan rubbed his large hand on his fresh jaw, nodding, making my thighs clench together. He spun his head to me, catching me staring at him like a letch. "Keep going, lass. Two pet names. What do ye reckon?"

I blinked myself out of my stupor. "Well, there's Jelly, obviously. What other nickname do you guys use? Maybe something between you?"

Mako frowned, rushing a hand through his hair. "Just 'savage queen.'"

Simon grinned. "Seriously? Not even 'babe' or 'sweetie' or 'honey?'"

Mako laughed. "No. She's only ever been my savage queen."

Something tripped in my head. It slid from my mind as

Roan swallowed more coffee, distracting me from any kind of thought. He turned his head, brows furrowed. "Pull it together, Mori. We need ye to focus."

I hissed over my coffee and walked to the fire on shaky legs, needing to get away from him. I set my mug on the mantle, speaking out loud. "Jelly. Sun. Liquid gold. Savage queen. Mako plus Jelly." I puzzled over the words, unable to find a clear link. I shook my head. "I can't grasp it. Not yet."

Jelly said, "Okay, we'll get there. So, where is this traitor's gate?"

Richard answered in a matter-of-fact voice. "In London."

Jelly's coffee slipped from her fingers, splashing on the rug at her feet. Her face was ashen. "London? I can't go to London! All those humans! I…I just can't!" She ran from the room, twisting from Mako's outstretched hands. I chased after her.

SEVENTEEN

JELLY

Terror nipped at my heels as I ran outside. Nipped was the wrong word. It chased me like a starving tiger, snapping at my calves, causing me to stumble as I crashed into the oak tree and slid down, hyperventilating from the sense of impending doom.

Mori swung around the trunk an instant later, panting. "Jelly, what happened just now?" I rocked my head from side to side, fear stealing my voice. She collapsed next to me and hung her head between her knees. "Gods, I hate sprinting." When she looked up, her hazel eyes dripped with concern and confusion.

I gripped her hand. "Millions of humans, Mori. Millions! I can't. I just can't. We have to find another way. Draw the Seeker here. Or ask Mew to go. Maybe Mako. He can act on my behalf because he's my mate. Yes, that would work. He can go in my place."

Mori looked down at the ground. "I don't think he can, Jelly. This is your mission. Your missing piece. No one can take your place. You don't have a choice."

Mako's voice sounded around the tree. "She's right." He stepped into our sight, his lips tight in a frown. "In this case, you don't have a choice."

I growled in my throat. "You swore to me I always had a choice with my life!" I glared as my mate shifted his stance wider, cementing his position on this. Shit. I changed tack. I pleaded. "You don't understand. I lost it in the superstore. London is huge! And I'll be all alone! I'll blow up a castle or something!"

Mori snapped her hand out of mine, crossing her arms. "You won't be going alone. We're coming with you. Me, Mako… and Roan." Her breath hitched as she said his name. Her cheeks turned pink. She was hiding something.

I grabbed at it. "Why are you blushing? What happened with Roan?"

More blood rushed up her face. "Don't change the subject."

"Did you…?" I waved a finger at her crotch.

She steamed and slapped at my finger. "What's happening to me isn't the issue. I'm dealing with it."

"What is it? Was he no good? Talk to me, tell me everything." I leaned closer, scanning her hazel eyes, which were hard and narrowed as she guarded herself.

She stuck her nail in her teeth before yanking it back down. "Stop changing the subject. Worry about you." She looked off into the distance. Something was different. She was radiating heat, practically steaming with it.

"Mori, you can tell me."

She spun on me. "Stop it! Be grateful we aren't going to Tokyo! It has over thirty-seven million people. London has less than ten. I know because I read a book on human statistics."

My stomach dropped out. Ten million humans. "I really can't do this. Please don't make me go. Please. There's no way." I hated the whine in my voice, but I was terrified.

Disgusted, Mori jumped to her feet, venom in her tone. "Where is my warrior friend who faces her fear with her chest proud and chin high? The Shaman would be embarrassed for you. My father as well. Mako, she's all yours. I don't have the patience for this shit."

I stared at her with my jaw loose as she stomped away. She'd never turned her back on me. Not once. Something was wrong with Roan. She'd stared at him earlier like a panting hyena while darting furtive glances at Branko. She was on edge and didn't want to admit it. I couldn't blame her. I didn't want to face my life either.

Mako lowered and took her place at my side. His voice was stern. "Jelly, you can do this. You have to."

Guilt washed through me. "What if I explode? What if I see this writhing mass of humanity and freak out?"

"I'll be with you. Every step, I'll be there. We won't go out when it's busy. We'll stick to the back streets. You can do this." His jaw clenched, and he struggled to keep his voice smooth and encouraging.

Fear snaked its way up my spine. "Mako…There's no one to cover for me if I mess up. I had Nesta before."

Mako's eyes narrowed as his tenuous grip on his temper snapped. "Are you serious right now?" He stood, stepping away, seething. "My mother covered for you the first time, doctoring the video of the explosion!" He gave me his back, his hand running through his hair, gripping it in frustration. He spun around with wild eyes, slamming his fist on his chest as his voice cracked. "Jelly, you have me! I should be enough! You can't be selfish about this! Not this time!"

I sprang to my feet, meeting him toe-to-toe. "Selfish? This time? Are you kidding me? Once again, this gets thrust on me. You're right, I can't turn it down, because your brother's life is at stake. And the Earth's sanity! We have to stop your sick bloodline from hurting anyone else!"

"My sick…? Do not lump my father with them! You know him!"

I snorted and threw my hands over my head. "Do I? Do you? You only just found out!" I poked myself in the chest. "Through me!" My voice dropped into a tight growl. "I have no control over my magic. I have to meet a Seeker because the Surfecti dislodged a piece of my soul." My voice rose in a crescendo of anger. "Me, Mako! It's always me! I'm the one! I have to go to the Hellhole! Why? Because Leoht sits at *my* fucking neck! I never asked for any of this! None of it!"

He stepped back, his voice bitterly cold. "I see. Your life would be easier without me."

I hung my head, sliding my hands over my ears in frustration, so overwhelmed by everything I had to manage. "I didn't say that."

Mako was an iceberg, floating away from me, drawing back his emotions. "Yes. You did." He turned on his heel and walked away. I slammed the back of my head against the mighty oak and slid down, wrapping my arms around my knees.

"I thought they'd never leave." First came the voice, then the cat. Her tone was dry. "It must be so difficult, having such loyal people on your side. I can't imagine how you tolerate it."

I groaned and pressed my skull against the tree. "Icy, go away. I can't do another vision. Not now. I've already done two, and it's not even noon."

"I have secured a rare opportunity, and we must not waste it. Make me purr." She climbed into my lap on unsteady feet. She curled into a ball, blinking. I sucked my teeth in a scowl. She rolled her ice-blue eyes. "Trust me, Jelly. You need this one." I stroked her fur, and her throat vibrated, shooting us down a white tunnel. We arrived inside a chamber lined with thick granite blocks. Oil lamps flickered in holders, releasing wisps of black smoke. The air was musty with a hint of frankincense.

A woman bent over a stone slab table. She had an instrument in her hand, the thin loops making a rattling noise. Icy announced our arrival in a steady voice. "Greetings, Goddess. You honor us with your summoning."

I had enough experience with goddesses to follow protocol. I bowed my head and waited to be spoken to. Her voice lilted. "Icy. Jelly. Greetings." I raised my head as she turned and screeched, jolting backward so fast I lost my footing on the slick floor and crashed on my tailbone. She had a cat's head on a woman's body. The goddess smiled. "Yes, yes, happens all the time." She blinked slowly, and I stared at her slitted pupils. Her whiskers twitched in amusement. "I am Bastet. I am the eye of Ra." I glanced at Icy, who looked at me with contempt. I scrambled back on my feet and bowed again. She tipped her head. "Are you familiar with me?"

"No, Goddess, I am not, and please forgive my reaction to your glorious face." She waved a graceful hand in the air, dismissing my blundering trip to the floor.

"Ra is the sun god. I am his daughter, most often known for my destructive nature." She stepped toward me, the movement feline and graceful. "Not always deserved." Her triangular nose wrinkled in distaste. "The humans are miffed I slaughtered all those people. It was so long ago! Never mind. Ancient history." Her ears flickered toward me. "I understand from my emissary that you need protection and information on an impending journey." Icy bowed her small white head in reverence as the goddess referred to her. "Tell me everything, so I may best help you."

Icy whispered over her whiskers. "Everything, Jelly."

I explained my complicated dilemma with the extra magic, the marking, Kokuro's claiming, Terrun's defeat, and the most recent dream of the Hellhole, the ritual, and yellow, ending with my primary fear. Embarrassed for myself, I told the truth. "They say Sundidarta is in a city of humans, millions of them, and I'm frightened. I have to meet her at a bridge that's popular with tourists. Tower Bridge. I don't have the best record when dealing with humanity. I'd rather not go at all."

Her lips drew back in a snarl. Internally, I groaned. I'd blown it. Somehow I'd ruined this sacred visit, not even knowing why we were here. Slitted eyes blinked at me slowly. "Let me see your mark from Kokuro." I pulled my shirt over my head, holding my hair up. My brain had a wonderful debate, asking how stupid I was to give my back to a strange goddess. I ignored it, trusting Icy. She traced the design softly. "I see, Icy. I see why you brought her to me. Yes, I will grant my protection." A sharp prick stung my back. "Turn around."

She licked a finger, purring a rough noise. "Your soul is delicious. She will not want to return it." I stood before her, naked from the waist up. Bastet trailed two fingers from my forehead down my body. When she reached the spot above my navel, she lightly growled. "This is where you're empty. Poor child. So hollow." She stepped back. "Do not argue with the Seeker. She will rile your anger. She will provoke you to where you wish to sever her head from her spine." I swallowed. That could be an issue for me. "Stay calm and ask for a tahwil. Do not leave without it. You will need it for your task."

My forehead creased in confusion. "A tahwil? What is that?"

"Hard to say. It is different for everyone."

I dipped my head in quick gratitude. "We have a gift for the Soul Seeker. I thought that was enough for her to return my lost piece."

Bastet's lip curled up on one side, exposing her long canine. "The gift is only to gain her attention. She holds your soul piece for three moons. Should you fail in your mission, it will be hers forever. But if you succeed, it will return to you."

"Three months? But the ritual happened ages ago." My pulse galloped. I was running out of time. "So she's not a Seeker as in she finds it for me? I thought that was her purpose."

Her eyes narrowed. "No. She seeks missing pieces to consume for herself. She has been alive for centuries. It's how she still survives, feeding off the disconnection of souls. She lives in the filth of the shadows. I have granted you protection from the worst of her."

I bowed and pulled on my shirt. "Why are you helping me?"

Bastet purred a laugh. "I have a soft spot for strong women. Icy told me about your dilemma, and I wanted to help. Remember, a tahwil, and do not succumb to rage. Best of luck, Warrior Jelly." She turned and sauntered away, dismissing us. Icy rubbed against my legs, and we vanished in a flash of bright light.

I gasped in a breath at the foot of the oak tree. Icy stretched every limb and stepped off my lap. I rubbed my eyes, dropping my hands in my lap. "Thank you, Icy. I wouldn't have known all of that." I ran my fingers through my hair. "I'm so far out of my depth."

Icy chuckled and stretched her butt in the air before marching off. She paused to look over her shoulder. "Coming, Jelly?"

I thought of Mako and Mori, and of how disappointed they were. I had to make amends. My feet plodded toward the large mansion, but voices from inside hastened my stride. Simmi and Mako were yelling, then Sebastian roared a response. He was awake, and it was getting heated. I ran. I whipped through the doorway and froze. Mako, Simmi, and Sebastian were in Fae form, lips drawn back to show sharp teeth. Simmi looked crazed, and far larger than I would have expected.

"How could you keep this from us?" Simmi shrieked the words, her voice cracking with anger and betrayal.

Mako's voice was pure fury. "You lied to us!"

Sophia stood in the middle, buffering, pleading with them all to calm down. I ran to her side, pushing my spine close to hers, facing Simmi and Mako. "Hey, hey, take a breath." I spoke as soothingly as possible. The Fae inside me wanted to burst out, riled by the rush of furious magic in the air. Anna had everyone else behind a shield by the wall of books, letting the Fields family duke it out alone. Smart. I scanned my mate and his sister. No blood. That was good. "Sophia, turn with me. Talk to your kids. Talk them down. I've got Sebastian."

Sebastian's chest heaved as he struggled to control himself. His voice strained from the effort as he spoke to me. "I had to keep them safe! Can you fathom what Terrun is capable of? What he'd do to my children, specifically? He kidnapped Simmi and bled her! And now Vingor has Leif! In the fucking Hellhole!"

I lifted my hands slowly. "I do, Sebastian. I know exactly what Terrun would do. Vingor, too. Leoht spoke to me after you collapsed. She told me her story. She is so grateful to you, Sebastian. You saved her life."

"Not enough! Too many have died!" He stabbed his clawed finger into his chest, tearing his shirt and his skin. So much for no blood. "My parents! My parents allow it! They turn their backs on their people and let weaker Fae suffer because of some fucking by-law! He's the KING! He should do better!"

He shouted over my head, jabbing his reddened claw at his children. "You think I deceived you? I protected you! I told you to avoid that cave! I told you repeatedly!" He bent over, his hands on his knees, his body shaking. "And you ignored me. My son, my firstborn. Trapped in the Hellhole." He stood again, raging, his claws rigid at his sides. "The Hellhole!!!"

Familiar with anger and anguish, my worries about my mission disappeared on seeing and hearing his raw pain. He'd been so kind to me. He'd given everything to save Leoht. I slid my fingers to the pearl. *We're going to London, aren't we?* The pearl pulsed once at my throat. I stepped closer, lowering my voice. "Sebastian, I ran out of here scared, but I'm going to London. Understand? I'm going to get my soul piece. I'm doing it. And then we can get Leif."

He stared at my face, my seriousness, my commitment. With a tremor, he released his claws and absorbed his Fae magic, his ears smoothing and rounding as his body slightly diminished in size. He sagged forward. I caught him, bending under his heavy weight. His arms came up around me and he clenched me close. "Jelly, I would do it for you if I could. But I can't go near the Hellhole. They would tear me to pieces down there." I swallowed, thinking he was shit at giving pep talks.

He suddenly pulled away, puzzled, his hand between my shoulder blades. "What did you do? Where did you go?"

"What do you mean?"

His voice was urgent and awed. "Jelly, I need to see your back. Now." The tremble in his voice caused Mako to push past Sophia to be at my side. Simmi stopped yelling. They dropped their Fae magic.

"Okay. Pull up my shirt." I spun and gave him my spine.

He sucked in a gasp, his finger gently prodding between my shoulder blades. "Does that hurt?"

I looked over my shoulder with a frown. "It's a little tender. What's there? What do you see?"

Mako squinted at my skin and moved to my front. He cupped my face in his hands, searching my eyes, as if looking for extra marking or lines. Sebastian called over to the Surfecti behind the shield. "Anna, Richard, Roan, come see this." They gathered beside him quickly. Sebastian said, "Here, look from this angle. See the shimmer? Like a sheen?"

Anna gasped at whatever was on my back. "It's the Udjat!"

"What does it do?" I twisted, although it was impossible for me to see the mark. All of them looked confused.

Roan rubbed his hand on his smooth chin, pensive. "Protection from evil. Where did you get that, lass? I don't remember it being there before."

Soon, everyone was clamoring to see. Sebastian led me

under a light so this new symbol would show better. He poked his head around to look me in the eye. "It lies in the middle of the sun, Jelly, just as Anna predicted from Mew's riddle. Who marked you?" He lowered my shirt, turning me by the shoulders.

"Um, Goddess Bastet? Icy took me to see her."

Anna paled, swooning. Richard hustled her into a chair.

Roan glared at me, disbelieving. "Bastet? Ye met the avenging daughter of Ra?" His voice started softly and ended in a roar, practically making my hair fly back. "Where is that fookin' cat? Icy! ICY!" He stormed away, yelling for her.

I gulped. "Why? What's the matter?" Roan's great rush of rage confused me.

Mori stepped forward. She lifted her fingers to reassure me, but dropped them, remembering she was angry with me. "She's called the Lady of Slaughter. She's murdered thousands. But supposedly, she has a softer side, protecting women in particular. Her power also lies in healing. Icy needs to explain why she took you to her."

"Seems our answers are forthcoming," said Branko, his eyes glinting with mischief. His shifter ears allowed him better hearing, but it didn't take long for the cacophony to reach mine as Icy howled at Roan while he bellowed back. I bit my knuckle so I wouldn't laugh.

"Put yer damned claws back in yer feet, ye fookin' menace!"

"Release me, you rogue! Bastard! Unhand me now, filthy brute! Treating me like I'm a common house cat! How dare you! How dare you carry me like this!"

Mori grinned at me, our argument momentarily forgotten. "She's pissed. I'm not sure what you're hearing, but she's yowling and hissing and growling."

I giggled. "She's demanding he release her. She called him a brute and a bastard."

Roan marched into the room, holding Icy by the scruff of

her neck as she flung her limbs in every direction, blood on her sharp claws, trying to catch hold of Roan's skin. She'd managed one swipe, four telltale red lines oozing on his forearm. He held her aloft with sharp disdain. She finally relented and stopped struggling. Roan's voice was a ruthless command. "Tell us why ye took Jelly to the fookin' goddess of war!"

"Put me down and I will." Icy's ears flattened as she sniffed, looking down on Roan.

I translated. Roan snorted, staring at her venomously. "Not bloody likely. Ye'll run off again."

Sebastian offered to hold her, and Icy contemplated before nodding at him. "Fine." He took her gently and sat with her on his lap. She licked down her fur indigently, making us wait, her tail vigorously swatting the air back and forth. Finally, with a huff, she settled. "My mistress gave Jelly extraordinary insider information about the Soul Seeker." She hissed at Roan. "You should be thanking me!"

Sebastian translated her meows for the non-Fae in the room. Icy continued. "My mistress knows the Soul Seeker's intentions. You all believe Sundidarta helps people retrieve their soul pieces. She doesn't. She seeks them so she can eat them herself and gain immortality, and Goddess Bastet gave Jelly her protection for a small drop of her blood."

Mori leaned in. "Why? Is there some pact with the devil we don't know about?"

Icy's tail lashed the air. "The Goddess defends women and is the guardian of both joy and war. Ancient Egyptians worshiped her with music, dancing, celebration, and sex. She wanted to taste a Mers, a creature who recharges magic through intimacy. And Jelly, with all her extra strains, was a curiosity to her. Roan, you only acknowledge the dangerous and vengeful side of Bastet. But I, her faithful servant, saw an opportunity to help Jelly. Jelly told her story. Bastet saw Mother Kokuro's mark on her back and helped her. Jelly would have met Sundidarta without knowing what to ask for. It would have been catastrophic."

Roan looked chastised, realizing the small cat had likely saved my life. "I apologize, Seer Cat. Ye did a good thing by taking Jelly to yer goddess." He dipped his head at her with his hand on his heart. She tipped up her chin in acknowledgment, then flicked her head away as if the sight of him disgusted her. He spun to me. "Jelly, what is this information?"

"She told me to ask for a tahwil. The Seeker will set a task, and she'll be vague. I need to complete the task in order to get my piece back. Oh, and she said I couldn't lose my temper." I wrung my fingers together while biting my lip. "Apparently, Sundidarta will goad me, and I mustn't react."

Mori groaned beside me. "A tahwil is something for transformation. And not lose your temper if someone's provoking it? No offense, Jelly, but you're screwed."

EIGHTEEN

MEW

A snarl of traffic clogged the bridge, black cabs idling among red buses while bicycles and motorcycles whipped down the center. Commuters traveled along the walkways on the sides, inhaling the thick fumes under umbrellas. I joined the somber parade, making myself invisible, keeping my sights on the tower. Remaining out of view of the Yeomen Warders, the Beefeaters, was easy for me, but wouldn't be for Jelly. I frowned. I'd need to address that.

I jogged down the stairs and headed for the ancient gate, lifting my hand to call Merlina, as her lightly clipped wings allowed her to travel beyond the grounds. The recent Ravenmaster gave the ravens more freedom, and Merlina frequently visited outside the Tower walls. She came to me immediately, her intelligent eyes sizing me up. She spoke in a rasping croak. "I haven't seen your kind in a while. What brings you to my castle?"

"I wish to give the Soul Seeker a gift in return for an audience with her."

Merlina flapped out her wings before tucking them in. "For you?"

"No. For a warrior mermaid named Jelly."

Merlina laughed, the sound grating my ears. "A mermaid? In London? How so?"

"The Mother claimed her, allowing her to walk on two legs." No sense lying. The Soul Seeker would know who Jelly was.

The raven's eyes narrowed as she tilted her head. "Kokuro?"

I nodded. "Kokuro."

Merlina snapped her sharp beak. "Come with me." I followed her as she took flight and glided for Traitor's gate, making a rucking noise in her throat. Clutched in my hand was a long, shimmering white feather, one of my younger ones with fewer secrets. Sundidarta would find it worthy, as I did not part with this lightly. Merlina hopped on the lush grass, inclining her head toward the innocuous gate made of wooden lattice, where countless people had passed through to their deaths.

"Soul Seeker! You have a visitor!" Melina flapped out her wings as she shouted.

I shivered in the rain. Not from cold, but from ghosts. They were everywhere. One of them saw me and made a beeline in my direction. Queen Anne Boleyn sidled to my side, cradling her head in the nook of her elbow. "Your Highness," I said through tight lips as I forced myself to look down at her face. Her lips turned down, her eyes meeting mine as I bent to one knee in the damp.

A pearl necklace barely clung below the smooth slice of her neck stump. As a small favor, Anne's vile husband King Henry had granted her the mercy of dying at the hands of a swordsman who could strike a clean cut rather than the brutish swing of the executioner's axe, often needing several hits to sever the spine.

She scoffed. "No one calls me that anymore. I'm a traitor, remember? Why are you here? It's not possible for you to be missing your soul. Aren't you supposed to be flapping around singing praises? On whose behalf do you visit?" I was under no obligation to answer, but I'd liked this queen, betrayed by her own lady-in-waiting and cheating husband. "Tell me who needs their soul."

I stared into her miserable brown eyes. "Your majesty, a Mers woman, a Warrior, had a piece jolted from her soul during a ritual. I am here to secure an appointment."

She snorted. "A girl as a warrior? Times have changed, I see. This pleases us, me. God knows there was no place for women in my day beyond making heirs." A hand smoothed back the hair on her unattached head. "Well, a pleasant day to you. I hope you get what you came for."

"Thank you, Your Highness. Pleasant day." I fully exhaled, praying that no other spirits would visit me. This place gave me the collywobbles. As the ghost drifted off, I kept my eyes on the gate. Oozing up from the ground, Sundidarta appeared. I clenched my jaw and stood.

She was disgusting. Her skin clung to her bones in a series of patchwork shades, some not human. A dragon scale here, a thatch of fur there. Greasy hair clung to her scalp, multi-colored with clashing textures, as if she couldn't decide what to choose. She held out her pale hand, the hue somewhat green, like an old bruise that never healed. "What have you brought me?"

"A feather of knowledge, Soul Seeker. I come for a friend. She is the one missing a piece of her soul."

"Hmph. Well, if you're the one visiting, she must be important. Is it the mermaid's piece I found in the ether?"

"Yes." I swallowed, hating this abomination with every bone in my body. "Scyphozoa Vetula."

Sundidarta grimaced, stretching her skin at an angle. She had sewn the patchwork skin of her face too tight. "Huh. That's too bad. She's so tasty, and it's such a sizeable chunk." Anger flared in my chest, knowing she'd already nibbled Jelly's soul. I controlled my expression, despite wanting to reprimand her. She groused at the look on my face. "Oh, I just licked it, nothing more. I was hoping to keep it. It's not often I find something so powerful. But knowledge is also quite the prize. Let me see your gift."

I kept my voice calm. "No. Not until you agree to meet with her."

She tapped torn nails on her puffed lips, too large for her face, and clearly not her own. Finally, she tossed her hand in the air. "Fine. I will see this Scyphozoa. Tomorrow at noon."

I balked. "Tomorrow at noon? A nighttime visit is preferable when there are fewer humans."

She hacked a clogged laugh. "Noon tomorrow, or never. Her choice. Now, the feather." Her cloudy mud eyes stared at me greedily as her palm stretched out, a jagged line of scarring down the center. The scent of rot rolled off of her.

Swallowing bile, I set it delicately in her hand, careful not to touch her strange flesh. She thrust it between her fish lips and chewed noisily with her mouth open, crunching on the spine of my offering. Spit sprayed from her mouth. "Oh, my! That is delicious! I never knew that about the Mayans."

She cackled as I held my expression blank, not giving away the trepidation in my heart. She couldn't use the knowledge in the feather for much, but I hated to offer her any of my accumulated wisdom. It rubbed me wrong to give this horror anything. She leered at me. "I will set the mermaid an impossible task. She won't win despite having powerful allies. I look forward to my feast of fishy soul. Ta ta!"

I watched as the green water around the gate swallowed her whole, her shrill laughter the last of her to fade. I shook my body from head to toe to rid any clinging energy she may have sent toward me. With a snap of my fingers, I too disappeared, returning to coven headquarters to deliver the news. I shimmered into my body in the pantry, hoping to arrive unannounced. Unfortunately for her, Veda was on a ladder, rearranging the mason jars of pickled vegetables. She screamed, jerking the ladder and flinging a bottle of beets in the air as she caught her balance on the tall shelf. I caught the beets in one hand, steadying the ladder with the other.

"Great One! You gave me such a fright!" She clasped a hand to her chest, trembling from the shock I'd given her.

"I'm so sorry, Veda. I thought I could sneak in. But I was hoping to see you. Sundidarta accepted the feather. Your idea was spot on."

Veda carefully descended the ladder, clutching a jar of pickled green beans. With a reverent bow, she took the beets and tipped her head toward the kitchen, indicating I should follow her. "I will give you the good news first. Mori, the redhead, has begun untangling her Svadhishthana. Now, the bad news. There was fighting. Sebastian woke and told his children his true origin."

I frowned. She nodded, dropping her voice. "They are upset. Jelly ran away, screaming that she couldn't go to London, but she's come around. She will go. I eavesdropped behind the dining-room door, and the Goddess Bastet marked Jelly with the Eye of Ra. They are saying the goddess might have claimed her to give her protection. What does this mean, Great One?" She shook her head. "Mew?"

I blinked at her, rubbing my hand on the back of my smooth skull. "All of this just happened? I wasn't gone that long." I lifted a finger. "Hold on please, Veda." I reached out with my mind.

Boss? It's Bartholomew.

Did the Seeker accept the feather?

Yes, ma'am, she did. She's agreed to see Jelly tomorrow at noon.

Noon? That's unfortunate.

I sighed. *Intentional. She knows London will rattle Jelly. She wants to keep the mermaid's soul piece. She says it's tasty.* I braced myself for her wrath. It wasn't from my actions, but I would be the recipient.

A vice grip clamped around my head as she bellowed her response. *She tasted it???*

Tears squeezed out of my eyes. *Boss? Turn it down, please. She said she licked it.*

Revolting creature. She plans to force Jelly into the thick of humanity, then. Can you prepare her in time?

I will do my best, ma'am. I will start right now. There's one other thing. Another goddess got involved. Bastet marked Jelly with the Udjat.

Bastet? Why would she claim her? They're all piling into this drama. First Kelbazi, then Kokuro, now Bastet. Well, I suppose she had her reasons. Has the youngest manifested her powers yet?

I scratched my head. *Who? Simmi?*

Her eye roll was in her voice. *Yes, Simmi. She has Leoht's power strumming through her blood. It should have showed up by now. Watch her.*

Yes, ma'am. I exhaled with the weight of the world on my shoulders. Good thing they were broad. I turned to Veda, but she had closed her eyes, her bindi spinning until it shot off great sparks of light. She swayed on her feet from the force of it. I held a steadying hand on her shoulder until the vision was complete.

She stared at me in shock. "Oh, Mew! I must assemble crystals for her journey! My guides have said it may not be enough, but I have to try!" She stared at her half-assembled tray to present for lunch, wrung her hands in her sari, and scattered from the kitchen, muttering that we could feed ourselves.

I pushed open the door to the smaller study, planning to gather my thoughts alone before seeing everyone in the library. Instead, I found Mori scowling, flipping through an old tome on Surfecti magic. She looked up and relief spilled across her face. "Good. You're back. Although you scared the shit out of me when you vanished like that. Where did you go? Can you tell me?"

I smiled and shook my head. The boss had sent me for a time-out after giving them the information for Tower Bridge. I thought I'd spoken in enough of a riddle to avoid her wrath, but I'd been mistaken.

She pointed to the book, her voice sarcastic. "There's no mention of a Mers with Surfecti forced fusion combined with oyster Fae magic, topped off by the frickin' cherry of a feline goddess's touch. I just can't imagine why not."

I chuckled. "You won't find anything in books. To start off, the forced fusion was dark magic, even though Jelly agreed to do it. Her missing soul piece must have been the price."

Mori nodded sagely. "There's always a price. Jared, the librarian in the village, mentioned that." She shrugged. "She still would have done it. She had to." She closed the cracked leather cover of the book, carefully setting it back in its spot on the bookshelf. She dusted off her palms, scanning the spines of others.

"Mori. We're in uncharted waters. We have to work from instinct. Have you figured out the hints the twin dropped?"

Mori frowned. "The liquid gold? No." She tipped her head, squinting her eyes at me. "But I'd rather bounce it off one person rather than the entire group. They tend to take off on tangents. Sit with me?"

"Of course."

She stuck her thumbnail in her mouth. I'd never seen her tear it, just bite it. She spoke her thoughts out loud. "Find liquid gold. Two pet names. You plus her. Okay, two pet names. We have a savage queen and Jelly. Queen Savage, queen Jelly. Liquid gold, queen Jelly." She stood and paced, saying the same words over and over. She squinted at me suspiciously.

I ground my teeth together. I couldn't give any direct hints. Not even one. I was pushing my luck with the boss. Mori spun, tromping over the same span of carpet. I glared at Mori, making her pause, and enunciated my words slowly, capturing her attention. "Mori? Would you like me to light a fire?" I winced as a flicker of pain met the back of my eyeballs.

She frowned, dismissing me offhand. "No, I'm already too hot. Something's wrong with my internal thermostat." She tripped as her hazel eyes flew open. She nodded enthusiastically. "On second thought, yes, light a fire. I'd very much like to be warmer." She stared at me, and we slowly nodded together. I stacked a small pile of kindling in the hearth and lit it, holding several sticks in my hand.

She said, "Queen savage." I tossed a small stick into the fire. "Queen Jelly." I pushed the sticks around a little. She chewed on her nail, resuming her trek across the carpet. She tried a different approach. "Jelly." I threw the stick in, grinning through the pressure in my skull. "Something Jelly." Another stick.

She paused, the connections sliding into place. "Something to do with Mako and Jelly." Another stick on the flickering blaze. "Mako doesn't have a nickname. He's connected to whales." She watched as I sat as still as stone. "Fuck." Instead of pacing, she rocked side to side, weighting one foot at a time, her eyes glued to my every move. "Mako. Mako. Mako. Fae."

I flicked on a larger stick, trying to hold in my gasp as the lightning in my head shot to my ears, ringing them. She noticed the difference in my choice of kindling, making the fire grow warmer. "Fae. Prince. Future King. Royalty." With each word, she paused, waiting for what I would do. When she spoke the last word, I took a stick and broke it in half. Would she get the hint?

She did. "Shorter. Royal?" I reached over and tossed a log onto the fire, sparks flying up as the damp wood popped and smoked. "Royal Jelly?" I smugly put another log on the fire, my jaw clenching as the boss zapped me, but I wasn't bleeding, so she was allowing this. Mori nodded, her eyes excited as she clenched and released her fists. "Royal Jelly. Jelly is going to be queen of the Fae?"

I suppressed the urge to groan, crossing my thick arms over my chest. Mori's eyes darted back and forth as her forehead creased in concentration. "Royal Jelly. Royal Jelly. Liquid gold, royal jelly…" Her mouth opened wide as the penny dropped, and she spewed the words in a rush. "Royal Jelly is the liquid gold that's fed to queen bees! The bees are the key to retrieving her piece!"

I swept her into my arms, spinning her as she laughed maniacally. She squealed with elation. "I got it! Put me down! We have to tell them!" She grabbed my hand and yanked me with more strength than she'd ever shown in our sparring. Clearly, when her brain was lit up, it transferred into her muscles. She flew across the foyer, feet barely touching the ground, and flung open the library doors, startling everyone in the room. "Queen bees eat royal jelly! Mako plus Jelly. Royal jelly! Liquid gold! The bees! Jelly needs to go to the bees!"

Roan was the first to react, crossing the floor with great strides. He slid a hand to the back of her neck and gripped her tight, his eyes glowing, fire and magic crackling at the surface of his skin. Ah. That's who had released Mori's frustrations. She grabbed his shirt in her fists, her head flung back as she smiled at him. He was on the edge of kissing the hell out of her, but he held back, letting his fingers fall from her tresses, turning to stand at her side, his hand possessively encircling her waist as if he wanted to show her off as his.

"She's fookin' brilliant. She is," he said with great pride. He nodded to a shocked Jelly. "That must be yer task, Jelly, the reason ye need a tahwil. The Seeker is sending ye to a hive for some reason."

Richard sat forward, his face somber and full of warning. "Jelly, you mustn't tell the Seeker you've already figured it out, or she will set a different task. The twin gave you that information to help you. Don't squander it."

Mako pressed his lips to Jelly's. She reeled from the magic he shot into her. He said, "Simple. See the Seeker. Get the prize and get out." He turned to me. "Can we go at night? When the city is quiet?"

I frowned and rubbed my face, wondering how I was about to deliver this news without throwing Jelly into chaos. No way around it. We didn't have time. "Jelly, she wants to rattle you. She's set the meeting for tomorrow at noon."

Rather than slip into rage as I expected, she slid into despair, which seemed worse. Her shoulders rolled forward as she caved in on herself, hands shaking as they braced on her thighs. Her head hung down as she struggled to breathe, her voice ragged. "Noon. Tomorrow. Ten million humans." Mako pulled up her face in his hands, making her look at him.

He growled at her fear. "You are the savage queen. You can do this. You can do anything." He glanced at me. "And we'll be there, right Mew?"

I replied with as much confidence as I could muster. "We will be near, as close as we can be, but we cannot attend the meeting."

Anna sat up with a jolt. "Noon! That's why Bastet marked you! She is the daughter of the sun, strongest at high noon! That's why she gave you the Udjat." She waved a hand imperiously. "See? Nothing to worry about." Everyone nodded, fooling themselves with false confidence.

Branko shook his head slowly. His voice was like gravel. "I disagree. She will have the cat goddess's sun protection, yes, but it does not shield her from herself." He gave Jelly a look of apology.

"Your magic is still tumultuous, and Mako cannot be at your side." He sat his chin on his fist as he leaned forward. "How can you keep your anger restrained while being taunted by the Seeker?"

Veda flew into the room, panting. "I have something to help." She held up a strand of shimmering, multicolored crystals. "I haven't done the spell casting on it yet, but I will. These are stones for anger management. Amethyst, Rose Quartz, Moonstone, Peridot, Smoky Quartz, and I added the protection stones, Hematite and Kyanite. We'll need to put it on your body somewhere the Seeker won't see." She raced across the room to Jelly, waving her hands to have her stand. "Up, Jelly. Up."

Veda's bindi spun slowly. Mako noticed. "Are you getting help from your guides?"

She did her half-nod, half-shake, her sculpted eyebrows drawn together in concentration. She wrapped the strand around Jelly's waist, seeing how far down it hung. "It will need to be longer." She raised her eyes to Jelly's skeptical face. Her head bobbled as her bindi spun faster. She spoke out loud to her guides. "Yes, yes, I can sense that. Yes, of course, I agree." She stepped back with a beatific smile. "I will return." With that, she ran from the room.

Simon paced, burning off his nerves. "I'm with Branko. This doesn't sit right. What do we do about the humans? Tower Bridge is teeming with tourists, and the day-to-day traffic of Londoners. They'll be on their lunch breaks."

Richard frowned as he tapped on his tablet. "The forecast says tomorrow will be a rare sunny day. People flock outside when that happens."

Jelly paled. "Guaranteeing they'll swamp me." She bit down on her lip. "She's intentionally putting me on the back foot!"

Sebastian said, "That's because she doesn't want you to have your piece back. She wants to keep it."

Jelly rose to her feet, her fists on her hips. "Well, she can't have it! I need it back!" She spun to me. "Mew? What can you do?"

I stared at Roan with a lifted eyebrow. Roan cleared his throat. "Jelly, I need to teach ye to shield." He glanced at Mori and Mako. "All of ye. Humans have nonstop chatter in their minds, over and over, thinking of their worries, their hopes, their futures, their mortgages, their lovers, their children, their jobs…it's incessant and it will make ye go mad. Ye can't have ten million in yer head. Believe me, ye'll jump off the bridge to be free of it."

Mori frowned at him. "Why don't we hear everyone here?" She tipped her head at Branko. "For example, he's scowling, and I can guess that he's worried, but there's no sound of his thoughts." I could both hear and see them, as strongly as if he had them flashing in neon lights. He was nervous for Jelly, longing for Mori, and terribly, terribly jealous of Roan, but too honorable to cut it. In his mind, she had already chosen Roan, icing him out. Oh, Branko. He was so wrong.

Roan answered. "They have magic to shield them. It's one of the first things we learn when we're young. The three of ye willingly wanted me to teach ye, so yer minds were open to me. Now, I need to teach ye to block. Jelly especially. Let's go, lass. Clock's ticking."

I stepped forward, rubbing both hands over my smooth head, worried, but trying to hide it. "I'll help. As much as I can. Let's go outside."

NINETEEN

MAKO

We'd been at it for hours. Every instinct in my body urged me to protect my mate as she struggled, and yet, I also wanted to yell at her to work harder. We were talking to Jelly's mind simultaneously, and she couldn't block us out.

I kept my voice as soothing as possible. *Just tune us out, Jelly. Concentrate on building a wall.* Internally, I was a riot of frustration. She needed this piece of the puzzle to rescue Leif, and she was getting angry with herself. I had to keep my temper in check so I didn't set her off.

Mori muttered the same words on repeat. *Cinnamon, nutmeg, allspice, ginger, cloves. Cinnamon, nutmeg, allspice, ginger, cloves.* I imagined a stereo volume and turned the dial to the left, muting her. That left Roan, who shouted at Jelly.

Can ye hear my thoughts, lass? Add ten million more! Focus, Jelly! Stop the noise! Ye have tears streamin' out of yer eyes! Block me!

His dialect grew thicker the more he pushed at her. She roared and flung her hands to her head, squeezing her eyes closed. "Shut up, Roan! Shut up!" Roan marched up to her and shook her once by the shoulders so she'd look at him. I growled as he manhandled her and took a step forward, only to be held back by Mew, his arm stalling my stride.

He murmured quietly. "She needs him to teach her. He's meeting fire with fire. Don't interfere."

I glanced at Mori, who walked in a circle, keeping her index, ring finger and thumb pinched together tightly, blocking all of us out, even when we spoke normally. She didn't react when Jelly had shouted. She'd grasped the ability immediately.

Mew said, "Mori is used to controlling her mind. It's a steel trap. Jelly? Not so much. Your mate runs on emotion." He glanced at her, worried. "Especially anger. That's what Roan is trying to tell her. If she'll listen. The Seeker will destroy her." He rubbed his hand over his neck, then his face. "If Jelly loses her temper in even the slightest way, the Seeker will retaliate and Jelly forfeits her soul piece. Sundidarta loves the power she holds, is temperamental, and if she perceives any disdain from Jelly, she will disappear. You'll never get to the Hellhole."

Fear replaced frustration. "Does Jelly know that?"

"Roan just told her."

Jelly stomped away from Roan, sending a shot of turquoise flame into the sky to burn off her irritation. She burst into a sprint away from us. I froze. Only turquoise magic. None of the others had come through. I shouted to Roan. "Did you see that? It was just hers! That's better, right?" Hope flickered in my chest.

He stroked his chin, nodding. "Aye. It is." His eyes swung to Mori, and he concentrated on her. She didn't look up. Roan walked over to us. "See if ye can break through."

I called to Mori in my mind. *Mori? It's Mako. Stop pacing and come over here.* She kept her eyes on the ground, oblivious to my attempts. "Nothing. She's great at this."

Roan grinned. "Aye, she is. Unlike yer mate." He called her name in a deeper voice, vibrating with magic. "Mori, come over, lass. Ye can drop yer fingers."

Her face snapped up when she Roan spoke to her. She sagged with relief, shaking out her hand. "Oh, thank goddess. I'm exhausted." She walked to us and looked around in confusion. "Where's Jelly?"

"She ran off." Roan sighed and scratched at his chin. "But before she did, she sent her magic to the sky. Just hers."

Mori beamed with excitement. "That's fantastic! She was focused enough to just pull hers!" She read our glum faces and her bright smile faded. "She couldn't block us out, could she?" She scratched at her head, thinking. "Hey Roan, is there a way to just talk to Jelly without you and Mako listening in?" Both he and I raised our eyebrows. She snorted good-naturedly. "Just tell me."

Roan swept up her hand, pinking her cheeks with the contact. He tucked her fingers into place, the middle and ring held down by the thumb, pinky extended high, index relaxed. "That's for calling Jelly. If ye do it with just the index up, that's yers. Both pinky and index up are Mako. If both are down, that's me. If ye speak to her, we'll pick up Jelly's reply, as she can't yet block us."

Mori closed her eyes. Jelly's voice rang through my head. *Tell Roan he can shove it!*

I asked Mori to uncurl her fingers so I could try. I wrapped up my fingers for Jelly's signal, calling her mentally. I kept a touch of humor in my voice to coax her. *Savage queen, come back. You'll get it, but you need to keep trying.*

You can shove it too, mate of mine. Why is this so hard for me?

I clenched my jaw at the petulance in her voice. *Jelly, the focus you've learned is helpful. When you shot off your magic in the sky, it was only yours. No other colors came through. Did you notice?*

There was a pause. Then a soft reply. *No, I didn't.*

Roan says it's good. You were concentrating on the mind magic, and your personal fire was stronger as a result.

Her voice turned to a scowl. *I'm useless at blocking. I'm going to lose my mind and jump off the bridge. I'm absolutely certain of it.*

Come back. We need to keep practicing.

Her reply was surly. *Fine.*

I roughed my hands through my hair, yanking at the roots. I needed to keep my patience. She couldn't flake out and refuse to go. She had to get this under control. Roan stalled my pacing, speaking to me privately. *Mako, what's got ye so het up? Is it from seeing Leif?*

I took him by the shoulder, moving away from Mori and Mew. I sighed heavily. "Leif is furious, Roan. You heard him. I don't know if he'll ever forgive me. He's lost so much time. If Jelly can't do this, and we can't get Leif, I won't be able to live with myself. I swear on the gods, I will not survive this. Certainly my relationship with Jelly won't, fated mates or not." I bit down at the thought of losing my brother and my mate. Roan scuffed at the ground with his shoe, eyes down.

I jerked my head at Roan, moving back toward the other two. "What can we do to help her succeed?"

He rubbed his smooth chin, something Mori watched with rapt attention. He turned to Mew. "Thoughts?"

I noticed Mori stood away from Roan, eyeing him cautiously, yet hungrily. I wrapped my fingers under my thumb, lifting the index finger. *Mori? Do I have you?* Her eyes snapped to mine. I held up a finger on my free hand, silently asking her to wait. *Roan, turn and look at me.* He stayed engrossed in his quiet conversation with Mew.

I focused on Mori. *I's just us. Why aren't you teasing Roan? You're normally cracking jokes and flirting with him. Did something happen between you two? I noticed you fobbed off Jelly and didn't answer her question. Is everything okay with him? We need you focused tomorrow. No distractions.*

Her freckles scrunched together as she scowled at me. She

huffed impatiently before answering, putting both her index and pinky fingers up. *He restored me, okay? I got overwhelmed after Mew disappeared and I was shaking all over, and he helped me. It meant nothing! Nothing!* She shrieked the last word.

Whoa, Mori. Sorry. I simply noticed your vibe was different. No judgment from me. I think it's a good thing.

IT'S NOT!

Her face flushed as she stomped her foot, whirling when Roan came up behind her and gently lay his hand on her back, concern on his face. "Ye all right, lass?"

"Clearly not!" She stormed in the direction Jelly had gone, meeting her halfway as my mate jogged toward us. They carried out a conversation with plenty of gesturing from Mori. She waved her hands in the air, pointed at Roan, and covered her face. She then threw them out wide in exaggerated exasperation.

Roan, Mew, and I watched silently. Roan groaned, his voice aching. "Ah, fook. She regrets it. She fookin' regrets it. Gods damn it."

Mew patted his shoulder. "No. She doesn't. She regrets she liked it so much. That's passion right there. That's a woman who wants more. Word of advice? Let her lead." When they looked in our direction, we pivoted our heads, clearing our throats and muttering nonsense, pretending as if we hadn't been watching.

They approached us. From behind Mori's back, Jelly gave Roan a wicked grin, two thumbs up, and a big wink, causing me to bite on my responding smile. Roan fought back a grin of his own. He put his hands on his hips. "Jelly, it's working, lass. Ye have to trust me on this. Mew knows how to help ye get a handle on yer anger. That's what making ye falter."

Mew stepped forward. "Sit with me, here. Cross your legs and put your hands on your knees, palms up. This is almost ridiculously simple, but that's where the beauty lies. I should have taught you this earlier. I overlooked it."

Jelly looked at him suspiciously while lowering to the ground. "What are we doing?"

"Calming your emotions." Mew inhaled deeply through his nose, encouraging Jelly to copy him. "Slow your exhale so it's twice as long as your inhale. That's right. Good. Now, close your eyes. Keep breathing like that. I will chant a single word repeatedly. Let it flow over you. Ideally, let it flow into you. Here we go."

He fully inflated his lungs and released a sound that sent chills across my skin. Mori swayed on her feet and Roan closed his eyes, absorbing the vibration of Mew's deep voice. Jelly relaxed her shoulders, which had been tight to her ears. Her lips parted as she softly sighed her exhalations. Something in Mew's voice melted my hard edges, calming me from my frenetic thoughts.

Mew stopped chanting. We were silent, reverent, listening to the wind in oaks, the chatter of birds, and the distinct hammering of a woodpecker in the distance. Mew's soft voice carried in the breeze. "You can open your eyes now, Jelly."

As always, I fell into the swirl of turquoise as she trained them on me. Her voice was soft. "That was beautiful. I'm so relaxed. Roan? I'm ready to try again."

"All right, lass," he said. "Mori, Mako, talk gently. None of us shout. Let's ease into it. Jelly, pinch yer index and ring fingers to yer thumb. Now block us."

I crooned a silly song while Mori recited the periodic table. Roan spoke of a place he loved when he was young, with rolling green hills, a cloudy gray sky, and dots of white bleating mournfully while they grazed. Jelly remained still. After a while, she opened her eyes. "Did you start yet?" She blinked rapidly before breaking into a wide smile. "Seriously? You were talking to me?"

I dropped to my knees and hugged her ferociously. We were one step closer to Leif. I held her face in my hands. "I knew you could do it! Mew? How does she do it independently?"

He smiled. "Same as I did. Just repeat the sound in your mind."

She giggled. "I can't believe it's that easy." She chewed on her lip, her doubt resurfacing. "But that was just the three of you talking. We're talking about a city full of humans."

Mew crouched down in a squat. "You can do this, Jelly." When she frowned, he lifted her chin in his fingers. "You have to."

She nodded over a tight swallow. "Okay. Let's go back inside. I'm famished."

As Roan, Mew, and Mori walked off, I held Jelly back. I stroked her cheek with my hand. Her smile grew wider. "You look like you want to eat me. What's up?"

I tugged her closer, one hand in her hair, the other around her back. When our lips met, I pushed magic into her. She accepted it fully, soaking in it. I flooded the cobalt line in her, needing it to wrap her in strength. She broke the kiss, leaning back from my lips. "Whoa, Mako. Why are you giving me so much? What's wrong?" She stiffened in my arms, her voice cold. "Do you think I'm going to fuck it up?"

Damn it. She'd seen through me. "Jelly, I'm fortifying you. I'm giving you everything that I am, so you have more strength. Stop being so suspicious." But my words didn't reflect my energy. I was tense, the ease of Mew's chanting slipping away.

Jelly stepped back and crossed her arms. "You don't think I can do it."

I rubbed my forehead with my fingers. "So much can go wrong. I can't stop thinking about Leif and worrying that my uncles…" I tripped over the word. "That my uncles are hunting him."

Mori's voice burst into our heads. *You need to eat. Come inside.*

Jelly put her hands on her hips. "Mako. I get it. We're all

scared that I'll mess up and lose everything. But your fear doesn't help me, okay? We've been through this a thousand damned times." She spun and marched away. I followed behind, my heart pounding like it would explode from stress. I couldn't silence the doubting voice inside. I'd never forgive her if she failed.

Jelly ate silently, perched on the cream-colored sofa, bouncing her knee with nervous energy. The room was quiet. We'd called a truce from thinking to refuel. Jelly licked her fingers, the red juice of the pickled beets staining them. I cleared my throat, drawing everyone's attention. "So, how do we do this? Do we teleport straight to the gate?"

Anna set her plate on the table next to her and dabbed at her lips with the linen napkin, carefully folding it and placing it on the plate. "No. Unfortunately, we can't. I can't just drop you in the middle of the humans. We'll go to a secure location. You'll travel from there."

My heart gripped in my chest as Jelly stilled beside me. I'd hoped we could pop in and out on the tower grounds. Gray and I had roamed the streets of London, and I was familiar with the city. It was massive, foreign, and Jelly would undoubtedly panic from the crowds. I kept the waver from my voice, projecting strength. "Are you taking us to Soho like usual, or can we get closer?"

Anna pursed her lips. "I've spoken to the London Coven, and they have a location in Borough Market where I can drop you. It's a fifteen-minute walk to the Tower from there, less than a mile. Just cross London Bridge and go right. It's the closest I can get you."

Jelly audibly swallowed her nerves beside me. She wasn't able to keep the tremor from her voice. "Okay. Less than a mile. I can do that. Then we leave from the same location?"

Anna nodded. "That's right. Mako, Mori, and Roan will go with Jelly. Mew will meet you at the tower. Simon, Branko,

Richard, and I will come as backup. As soon as I drop you off, I will return for them. We will approach on the north bank."

Jelly's knee bounced. "Backup? For what? In case I do something stupid?"

Richard soothed her. "No one thinks you'll do something stupid, Jelly. We will be there in case you need us. That's all."

I stroked my hand on her thigh reassuringly, settling the bouncing while hiding my own internal worry. I had to stay strong, be the man, be the mate she deserved. I hadn't realized how frightened she was, and I needed to be her support, pushing my own worries to the side. Everything hinged on Jelly keeping her cool. I shoved my brother's face from my mind.

My dad leaned forward, catching Jelly's eye. "Jelly, we need you to focus on the Seeker and nothing else. Your mission is to get the tahwil and the riddle, period. You'll need every ounce of your magic when meeting her." He glanced at me, giving me a look of warning to stay calm before he met Jelly's gaze again. "With my curse lifted, there is the possibility my brothers have a network of spies. The Seeker may be in cahoots with them. If they can stop you from reclaiming your soul piece, she gets to keep it."

Jelly vibrated with anger at the thought, her thigh tensing and resuming its bouncing. Whispers broke out as people discussed what this meant. Veda entered the library, skirting around the wainscoting. I saw Mew look at her questioningly, and she answered with sparkling eyes and a wide smile. Mew's deep voice stilled our chatter. "Veda has brought something to help."

She held the strand of crystals, flashing and catching the light. It was twice as long. She walked confidently to Jelly and motioned for her to stand, wrapping it around her waist, stepping back to check it hung as she wanted. She fiddled it slightly, readjusting the clasp so the chain was right at her natural waist, the long end draping down to her pubic bone. She said, "I blessed it, charging the stones to full power. It will help you withstand your inclination to argue, and the black ones will repel her if she tries to touch you. It's an extra layer on top of Bastet's blessing. I understand Mew gave you a chant?" She nodded eagerly at Jelly.

Jelly said, "Um…"

Veda giggled and shook her head. "No, it's OM, the sacred sound of creation. Simply keep it humming in the back of your mind as you meet with Sundidarta." She scanned the room, her eyes alighting on me. "Or perhaps Mako can throw his voice into her head from a distance?" She turned to Mew. "Can he do that?"

Mew roughed his palm on his neck, his tell that he was thinking hard. "I don't see why not. Jelly has to meet with her alone, but there was no mention of mind interference. The three of you can chant OM from the bridge, unless, Jelly, you think it will distract you?"

Jelly shrugged. "Why don't we try now? See if you can anger me while Mako, Mori, and Roan chant?"

Veda chirped, clapping her hands once. "Excellent. Let's see what happens." She removed the chain. "We'll keep this at full power, shall we?" Jelly paled and stammered that she needed a moment, leaving the room. I watched her go with a mixture of anxiety and impatience.

Veda studied me and pressed her thumb on my forehead. She leaned close, a whiff of cardamom on her breath. A spear of light flashed behind my eyes. I faltered, feeling exposed and raw, and drew back. She dropped her lips to my ear. "She is too proud to admit how much she needs you. Temper your frustration, Mako. She is doing the best she can, and she is frightened of disappointing you. At present, your love is conditional, and she senses her mate, who should devote himself to her fully, is doubtful. You are skeptical. But you are the key to her success. It is a heavy burden, but you must believe in her with your entire heart, or she *will* fail."

TWENTY

JELLY

The sound of their chanting hit me like a tsunami, carrying me away. I blinked in the dark span of my mind. A light from above filled a circle around me, and Leoht stood in front of me. I stared at her. "Now, Leoht? We're in the middle of something."

She leaned down to look me in the eye, her pink pupil mesmerizing. "The chanting makes it easier for us to meet. You can do this. I believe in you."

I inhaled sharply as my brain reengaged with the room. The reverberation of three voices chanting in my head pulled me into a trance-like state. I could barely focus on the sharp, feminine voice before me. I opened my mouth to reply, but no words came out.

Mew spoke, the deep sound distant in my head. "Turn it down a little." They became a background hum as opposed to a roaring river.

"That's better," I said.

Anna's voice scathed my ears, full of contempt. "Look at you! So smug, sitting there thinking you've got a handle on this.

Slipping back into old patterns, I see, so full of yourself. You're an arrogant child, Jelly. A selfish, arrogant—"

I chuckled, seeing right through it. "Nice try, Anna. You love me with every stiff fiber of your being. Those words don't work anymore."

Richard's voice was gentle, but his words were brutal. "Countless Fae are being bled as we speak, tortured beyond comprehension." That pricked my anger. He continued smoothly. "And the Earth screams in pain as the humans blithely toss their rubbish in her face." I clenched my teeth as he crooned. "She is dying. The turtles choke, the whales starve…so much pain." I inhaled through my nose and exhaled, my temper crawling up my spine. "That's not the worst of it, either. Poisoned rivers flow to the sea, mutating the sea life, destroying the water. It's over, Jelly. Everything is dying, and you, poor, helpless you, can do nothing to stop it."

"Like fuck I can't!" The chanting fell silent, snuffed out as my eyes snapped open, wild rage flowing freely. It froze and vanished as Gray patted flames from his father, leaving scorch marks on his white shirt. "Oh, Richard, I'm sorry!" My fang snagged on my lip, tearing it. I swiped at my ear. Pointed. I pulled in my magic and sagged in the chair, sucking my lip in for healing.

"Hmm." Mew hummed with a grim face. "That didn't go according to plan. What happened to the chanting? Was it helping?"

I poked at my lip. It had healed. Miraculous. Must be Bastet's Udjat. "It was. It definitely was, but Richard brought up so many horrible images. I feel their pain, the Earth's pain. It makes me want to burn the humans to the ground." The pearl buzzed at my throat. "Leoht wants to speak to me. Hang on a sec."

Her voice leaned more toward bells than bass as she spoke. *I will shield your mind when you meet the Soul Seeker and counteract whatever images she uses for manipulation. She will not get past me. I will help you keep your temper. Do not be afraid.*

I chewed on my lip. "Leoht says she'll help me stay calm. Between her, the chanting, and the twisted fingers, I feel almost confident. Almost."

Veda approached confidently. "And the crystals will help. You have so much support, Jelly. You are not alone." She tilted her head from side to side, her bindi spinning slowly. "You must rest now. Please, my guides insist. Do not disobey."

Mew cleared his throat. "She's right. I have to go. I will see you near the Tower."

I gulped. "You're leaving?"

He wrapped me in a hug. "You can do this. I will meet you at noon tomorrow."

I squared my shoulders and turned to Mako. He stood, taking me by the hand, silently leading me upstairs to our bedroom, closing the door with a click. I tugged off my clothes and slipped under the sheets. I cut him a sideways look. "Mako, no sex. Just sleep."

He climbed beside me, his warm body close as he wrapped his arms around me, pulling me back to press against his chest. His throat rumbled with a soft laugh. I'd missed that sound. Suspicious, I rolled over to face him, but couldn't find deceit in his face. He kissed me softly, giving just a whisper of magic, gentle and loving. I snuggling into his chest, and put my hand on his heart, the Hai Matau resting on my fingers. I drifted off, thinking about Leif.

Somewhere in a dream, there were muffled voices, just a general generic hum. The words became crisper, the emotions clearer, primarily desperation. They pleaded for help. The pearl gave two frantic pulses, briefly paused, two pulses, pause, two more... Leoht was silently screaming the word no. The dream jolted into clarity. I was in a vast cavern, a massive area lined with rows of narrow shelving with barely five inches between each one. From the floor to the high ceiling, vials upon vials of multicolored liquid sat on the shelves, each labeled meticulously with a small white tag.

I swung around, tiptoeing toward the frightened, quivering voices, and entered another cave. I gaped at what was before me. I saw three bodies, strapped into reclining chairs, with heavy-gauge needles for maximum flow plunged into both arms. Tubing snaked along the floor, collecting liquid into small bottles. Someone was moving to the side of one person in a stealthy crouch. His voice was tight. "Hold still. This will sting."

I gasped, barely a noise, and the stranger leaped in my direction, canines bared, knife high, ready to slash at my flesh. I held up my hands. I recognized him immediately, but he'd never seen my face. "Leif! It's Jelly! Mako's mate!"

"Prove it." His eye darted toward the door before narrowing back on me, knife still clutched in a tight grip.

I spoke as quickly and quietly as I could. I held up my index finger. "It's the mate's mark. Cobalt blue. The same as his eyes and tail, and the hue of his magic, which acts like water. He can manipulate liquid, holding it still." Leif's lips curled back. I rushed for something more personal. "Mako has a chipped front tooth from when he dove off a cliff and it was too shallow. He hit his face on a rock in the sand. He was five. He wears a jade orca. He just put it on again."

The hand holding the knife slowly lowered. He nodded once. "Since you're here. Help me free them. Hurry." I hustled to undo the straps while Leif gently eased the needles from their arms. I noticed that not all the blood was red. One creature, rake thin with green skin and enormous gold eyes, bled blue. Another's blood was yellow and thin, and I would have mistaken it for urine had I not seen it drip from her arm.

My voice was sparse. "How am I here?" He paused, staring at me for a long moment, and then shook his head.

We helped them sit up. Leif's expression was urgent. "Vingor is bleeding more of them. More bodies, doubling needles. I haven't been able to save them all."

I tried to keep the desperation out of my voice. "Leif, we're coming. Soon, I swear." He turned to move, but I stilled him, my hand gripping his forearm. He stared at where our skin met. I slowly drew my hand back and swallowed. Brother or not, he was a wild Fae, and I had just touched him uninvited.

He cocked his head, hearing something. "Go. The guards will be here soon. Go!" He gathered the freed creatures into his arms, swinging one on his back. At the dark entrance, he looked left, then right, and sprinted away, his footsteps fading to nothing. I ran after him, peering beyond the opening into a pitch-black tunnel. Go where?

Voices echoed closer, deeper and snarling, like they were arguing. My heart froze. This wasn't a vision where I was observing. I was here. The pearl pounded at my throat in horror. I shouted for her. *Leoht! What do I do? Where do I go?*

Her shriek was piercing. *HIDE!*

On light feet, I sprang back to the cavern of bottles. Automatic lights, activated by my movement, flicked on, casting the cave in an eerie red glow. In the far back right corner, wooden crates stacked into a tower, partially covered by a pile of sacks. Up high, I saw an opening, but I didn't have time to climb, nor did I know where it led. I slipped between the crates, pulling the rough material over my head as the first voice shouted.

"Where are the prisoners? Fucking Ghostfish! He's done it again! Vingor will have our damned heads!"

Another voice scowled. "I wanted a taste of that blue blood."

Someone else said, "I told you we shouldn't have left. But you wanted to chase that voice. Check the dispensary. The lights are on. Maybe he's in there." I curled into the tightest ball I could manage. I held my breath, praying to the Goddesses and Mother Kokuro to protect me. My heart was pounding out of my chest. Leoht wailed in my head in a foreign language, her tone hysterical. I gripped the pearl tighter to still her frantic pulsing, petrified she was signaling the Fae somehow.

Mako's voice rang through my head, panic-stricken. *Jelly, where are you? I can't wake you up!*

I clenched my teeth as the heavy feet drew near. I was ready to take the biggest breath possible and scream, praying my magic worked in here, praying it worked at all. The footsteps stopped, as did my heart. He was mere inches from me. He ran away when the other guard shouted, spotting traces of blood leading to the right.

I screeched at Mako. *I'm in the Hellhole!* I was suffocating, as I didn't dare breathe. I couldn't. My sight went dark, darker than the cave I hid in, and a rushing sensation skated my skin. Leoht howled in terror, telling me to run, to flee. Maddened by Leoht's shrill voice, I screamed.

Turquoise magic shot out of me, engulfing the man above me, his lips pressed to mine. He didn't falter, but bathed in my fire. "Pull it in, Jelly. You're back." I screamed again, the vision too close to the surface, Leoht's panic commanding my voice. Mako gripped my face. "Jelly! Look at me! You're home. You're safe." I reached for his hands, warm to the touch, his hair falling forward and brushing my skin. He was real.

I burst into tears, sobbing so loudly I choked. "Mako! Oh, my gods, Mako! I saw him, I saw Leif!"

Mako's eyes flew wide. "What? What do you mean you saw him? You went into a vision?"

"No. I was there! I touched him. He's rescuing Fae, freeing them. Leoht kept throbbing and pulsing and shrieking in my head, and I almost got caught by the guards! They were right there, right on top of us." Mako kissed me again, softly peppering my cheeks, lips, and forehead. I pushed him back, sick to my stomach, the adrenaline still pumping through my body.

"It's okay, Jelly. Here, drink some water."

I closed my eyes, fearful to see what destruction my scream and my magic had done to the room. Last time I'd lost control in a vision, I'd obliterated it, smashing it to pieces, hurting people. But this wasn't a dream or a vision; it was far worse. Mako helped me sit up. I blinked. Everything was in pristine order.

Mako chuckled. "I've been practicing shielding. I'm mated to an exploding woman. I contained it."

I gripped his arms, my nails digging in. "Mako, how did I visit the Hellhole? I was there, physically there. I helped unstrap the bleeding Fae." My heart flipped over, squeezing with delayed shock.

He shook his head. "You were thrashing in your sleep. You had my Hai Matau clutched in your fingers, and I couldn't pry them off. I tried, thinking that's what had you trapped there."

"I was clutching the pearl in the Hellhole. Then you kissed me."

He nodded. "Then I kissed you. I called to you through the mate bond, hoping my magic would lead you back to me. I shouted for Roan and Mori right before you burst into flame." At those words, the door to our room flung open so fast it hit the wall and reverberated. I pulled up the covers reflexively.

Mori doubled over and heaved for breath. "Oh my gods, you're okay. We were outside, practicing with my magic." She waved at the window. "Ran as fast as we could."

Roan controlled his panting, his face mingled with anxiety and alarm. "Mako! What did ye mean she's stuck in the Hellhole? Was it a vision? Fookin' hell, Mako! Ye scared the bejeezus out of me. Jelly, what happened?"

My eyes were like saucers. "I was there, Roan. In there with Leif."

Mori looked up. "You had a vision?"

"No. I was in there. Physically in there." My stomach lurched.

Mori's eyes flew wide. She hauled on Roan's sleeve, tugging violently. "How is that possible?"

He moved at her distress, putting his arm around her shoulders and roughly stroking to ward away her fear. "I don't know, lass. But we need to find out. Get dressed."

We yanked on our clothes and rushed to the library, finding only Anna. She reclined on the sofa, a red cushion under her knees, a forest green one behind her head. She put down her book as we raced in. I told her what happened. The book fell to the floor with a thump. She held up her hand. "Slow down, Jelly. You saw Leif rescuing Fae in a vision?"

"No, that's what I'm saying. I was there! And here! I was sleeping, touching the Hai Matau, and I was there, unstrapping captured Fae."

Her forehead lined with confusion. "And Leoht? Was she in Fae form?"

"No. She stayed as the pearl. But she was terrified. She kept pulsing the pearl over and over and screaming. When the guard was on top of us, just about to find us, she was shrieking. I couldn't calm her. I couldn't stop her from screaming."

Anna paced, something I hadn't seen her do before. She tucked her hair behind her ear and stopped to spin toward us. "What happened right before you fell asleep?"

"Mako kissed me."

"Were you touching the orca's tail?"

I nodded. "That's right."

There was an urgency in her voice. "What were your thoughts before you fell asleep?"

My eyebrows drew together as I remembered. "Leif. I was worrying about succeeding with the Seeker, and that if I messed it up, we'd never get him back."

Anna pulled open a drawer on a side table, retrieving a vivid green tonic. "Drink this. It's for nerves." It was sour and sharp, but went immediately to work settling me. Her pale blue eyes glittered as she watched me.

I frowned. "I'm not sure what you're looking for by staring at me, but Leoht was terrified. She didn't want to be there. However it happened, it was an accident."

Anna said, "Bilocation. I'm not entirely sure how it works, whether it was you with your multiple strains of magic, or Leoht as Fae, or a combination of the two. I'll need to research it. How did you get back?"

I sat forward and blew out a breath, ruffling my hair. "Mako dragged me through the mate bond."

Mako nodded solemnly. "I could sense her terror, and I kissed her, dumping my magic into her while calling for her in my mind. She came back in a ball of blue flame." Anna paled, and Mako grinned. "I shielded the room."

Anna turned to me with a frown. "Definitely no falling asleep touching his necklace. We can't lose you Jelly."

"Understood." I nodded as an icy drip of fear clung to my chest. Bilocation. One more hoop in the circus of my life. I slumped onto the sofa, biting my cheek hard enough to break the skin, the metallic taste of my blood soothing. I realized I hadn't done that in a while. Once upon a time, before Mako, I chewed on my mouth constantly.

My brain rolled from the challenges ahead of us. One step at a time.

I reached for the pearl, holding it carefully in my fingers. *Leoht? Are you okay? Leoht? Are you there?*

No answer.

The pearl was cold and silent.

TWENTY-ONE

MORI

Jelly looked panicked as she held her pearl. She kept it contained, but I could tell she was upset by the way she stumbled across the floor. Several times, she closed her eyes, then squinted as if in pain, her lips pressed tightly together. She exhaled and gave me a fearful look. "Leoht's not answering me. I wanted to ask her how she made that happen."

Anna had just picked up her tea and sloshed it on her hand as she reacted to Jelly's words. Hissing, she flicked her fingers. "Where is she?"

Jelly's eyes were frantic. "I have no idea."

Roan sat up straighter. "Jelly, ye went to the Hellhole. Leoht's probably got PTSD. Post-traumatic stress disorder. Shell shock. Ye can't think straight when yer in that space. It was accidental, but ye visited the place where they tortured her." He shook his head sadly. "She'll need time to recover."

Jelly's shoulders tightened, and she slammed her arms around herself as she trembled, pacing in a small circle. Her voice rose, hysterical. "I need her for the Seeker! I can't go without her! She's meant to be with me! She said she would go with me and shield me. Everything hinges on this meeting. She's never left before. Never! How could she disappear now?"

Anna frowned and slipped out of the room, leaving her tea. Jelly's eyes filled with tears as her knees gave out when she tripped. My blood froze. This wasn't normal for her. Mako swooped in to catch her, wrapping her in his arms. He kept his tone level, confident. "She'll come back by tomorrow. She knows how important this is."

Jelly curled into his chest, fisting his shirt, and sobbed. Worry seized my forehead, creasing it deeply enough to leave wrinkles. Jelly didn't give into tears. She usually spun her fear into anger. Roan watched Jelly's meltdown cautiously, his thick hand stroking across his chin. He let out a puff of an exhale, defeated.

He rose from his chair and crossed to me. His voice was soft. "Ye can't do anything, lass." He tipped his head at Jelly and Mako. "Right now, her mate is the only one who can help her." He held out his hand. "Come with me. I want to show ye something."

I gripped his outstretched fingers, grateful for the distraction. I loathed being helpless. He headed out the side door, stepping onto the grass. I dropped his hand and motioned at my pile of dirt I'd dug up. "Should I put that back?"

"Later. Ye can put it to rights later. I need to take ye somewhere." I quirked up an eyebrow, making him chuckle. "Ye'll like it, lass. Quickly, now. Before the sun drops." We walked for about twenty minutes, both of us quiet, lost in our thoughts. We stopped at the bottom of a knoll. He gestured for me to climb first. I scrambled up the grassy side, and when I reached the top, my breath came out on a sigh. Roan came up beside me. "Beautiful, isn't it?"

"Gorgeous." A meadow of wildflowers stretched far into the distance. The small heads of the flowers bounced on the light breeze. Bees and butterflies flitted amongst the blossoms, gathering dinner. To the left was a large pond edged in tall grasses.

The surface rippled from the multiple birds who bathed, swam, and drank. It was an oasis amid our storm, just nature being herself, beautiful and undisturbed. The tension in my body released on a sigh.

Roan moved behind me, his arm outstretched over my shoulder, pointing to different birds. "That one there? The orange and blue one? Kingfisher. And that lot all clustered together? Mallards. The ones with the green heads are the males. Strange anatomy on those ducks. The males have a corkscrew-shaped willy."

"Willy? As in penis?" Surely he was kidding.

He grinned, his smooth cheek grazing mine. "Aye, it's true. And the lady duck's bits are also corkscrew, but turning in the opposite direction. If she squeezes herself, she blocks him."

"That's an insane rendering of cockblocker." I snorted at the image of a lady duck saying no.

His chin jerked up. "Ach! Brilliant!" He turned me, pointing to two large white birds on approach, flapping their wings back as they gracefully landed. "Mute swans. They've been together for years. They mate for life." I swallowed thickly, watching the swans bend their necks and nuzzle each other. Mates. Roan's voice hitched up with excitement. "Look! Over there, a Grey Heron."

I giggled. "He's walking on sticks!"

Roan laughed, his skin brushing against mine, the deep sound of his laughter sending a shockwave through my body. His body heat consumed my back. Roan murmured in my ear. "The New Forest is a nirvana for birds. Many rare species were on the brink of extinction. They came here and thrived."

I slowly turned to face him, so near his breath stroked my cheek. He didn't step away. "Because of the Coven?"

"Aye, some. They're protected here. No free roaming dogs, no cats. Icy's too spoiled to hunt." I smiled at the joy in his voice.

His eyes dropped to my mouth. He kept talking while staring, his voice deepening. "Just peace. Like it should be."

"Thank you for bringing me here, Roan. I needed this reminder of the beauty in the world."

Roan gazed at me with soul-affirming affection, making my breath catch. Behind him, the sky was yawning, streaks of red and orange stretching out as the sun slipped to slumber. His voice was soft, reverent. "The light on yer skin. Yer hair. It's glorious." His mouth lowered slowly toward mine. My heart raced with anticipation. "Caught up in flames like a woman on fire."

My lips parted in shock at his words. He took as an invitation and kissed me, hungry for my taste. His hand splayed on my back, tugging me against him, and I wanted to melt into the sensation of his hard muscles pressing against my body, but my brain cranked into overdrive with a jolt. My mind flashed to a memory, the one I'd been trying to grasp for ages.

"Roan..." I pushed my hands to his chest to give myself space.

Bermuda. Fae-Mers Seer. Prediction. The Seer had smiled at me, saying I should expect someone in my life, someone who would journey with us as we mended the magic of the world. She'd said, 'He will make himself known, Fire Maiden.' Then her eyes had shifted colors, something they did with each blink. In that split second, they were green, identical to the ones now watching me cautiously.

He grumbled. "Yer not kissing me back, lass. Don't ye like it?"

My head swung from side to side. Realization slapped me in the face, and my heart seized and shattered into pieces. "Roan, I can't do this." I turned, almost rolling an ankle in my haste to flee down the knoll. I took off at a sprint. My legs were no match for his, despite being muscular from hours of training. He grabbed me around the waist, spinning me to look at him.

"Mori, what just happened? Why are ye running like yer pants have caught fire?" He searched my face for an explanation. My pants were definitely on fire. His hands were scalding hot on my waist.

My mind raced, frantic. *I can't fall for you! I can't fall for you!*

His hands gripped tighter. "Why are ye saying that?" His voice sounded hurt.

"Stop!"

"Yer screaming it in yer head! Why?"

"I'm sorry if I gave you the wrong impression. Please. I'm sorry!" I yanked free of his grasp, stumbling backward, panting. He let me go, confusion in his gorgeous green eyes. "I can't, Roan. I just can't." He slowly crossed his arms, protecting his heart. He widened his feet, grounding himself as I staggered, my head on a swivel.

His voice was gentle in my mind. *Stop, lass. Stop and look at me.* The sky behind him was lit with the fire of the setting sun, causing my breath to stutter at the image. His face was a juxtaposition to his stern stance. It was open and warm. *I am a patient man, Goldilocks. No one will make ye burn like I do.* The caress of his words and his tone caused my belly to explode in flames.

I spun and sprinted away, folding my fingers into the strange knot, screaming for Jelly. She met me in the kitchen, pulling me to the small alcove and holding me while I gulped for breath. She still looked unsteady, and I hated to pile more on her plate, but I was freaking out. I crammed my panic into a small cage in my chest, hiccuping as I tried to express my rampant thoughts. "He called me a woman on fire." When she didn't immediately piece it together, I stomped my foot. "A woman on fire!"

She scanned my face in confusion until it hit her, her eyes flying wide. "He did? But that's what—"

"Samara said. Although she called me Fire Maiden, but I'm pretty sure semantics aren't important."

"How did he know? Did you tell him about the prophecy? I thought that was only for us. I haven't told anyone. At least, I don't think I did." She rubbed her hands up and down my arms.

Two tears of alarm and confusion slipped from my eyes. "Then he called me Goldilocks. Who is Goldilocks?"

Jelly wiped my cheeks with the heel of her hand. "I don't know. But dear goddess. Why now, of all times?"

"I know! I told him I can't fall for him."

Jelly pulled back, her voice soft. "Why not?"

"Because I want to fool around with Branko, too! And maybe Gray, or someone, or everyone! I'm not meant to be mated. I'm not meant to have one great love. But what if he thinks we are? What if he gets needy and clingy and I end up hating him for it? Besides, you and Mako argue all the time, and I don't have the emotional capacity for that."

"I think arguing comes with the territory, Mori. Compromise is part of love." Jelly crossed her arms with a small smile on her face.

I countered. "Anna and Richard. They never fight."

Jelly laughed. "I'll bet Anna spits fire in private. They just put up a unified front because they're British."

I took a deep, deep breath and exhaled through pursed lips. I needed my wits about me. I ran my shaky fingers over my hair. "What do I do now?"

"About Roan?"

"Yes! About Roan!"

Jelly's lips tightened into a downturn. "Gods, Mori. I need you both tomorrow. I need you to work with him. Can you do that? Can you pull it together?" I stepped out of the alcove, nodding, unable to say it out loud. I couldn't seed doubt in her mind, although mine was overflowing. I turned for a glass of water and shrieked. Veda was standing right in front of me, her bindi spinning wildly.

She held her hands out in front of her, waving them at my chest. "Oh, Mori! Your Anahata! It's splintered! What happened? Before it was too dull, but now it's flashing in shards of green like it's shattered." Her bindi spun, and she recoiled, clutching her throat, receiving some kind of message. "You…you denied his love? No, no! You must not reject such a gift!"

I gritted my teeth, wanting to tell her to mind her own business, but she looked too stricken for me to be rude. "I don't have time for love, Veda. We have too much going on."

Her face lost its horror, and she leaned close. "You don't understand. It strengthens you. Makes you more resilient." Her brown eyes lost focus, and she muttered to herself. "Yes, I can see it. To heaven and earth." She blinked twice. "You are frightfully ungrounded. That's why you struggle. You dream of a different life. I have something to help you. Wait here, please." She dashed away. I turned to Jelly, who was frowning.

She said, "It's spooky how well she can read you." Her eyes narrowed. "What did she mean? Do you even want to be here? With me?" I opened my mouth to answer with an automatic yes, but the word stuck like dry toast. She noticed my hesitation. "Do you stay because of what the Seer said?"

I swallowed over a lump in my throat and confessed. "I planned to go with Roan to meet different Surfecti, to have a purpose all my own." Jelly blinked in shock. "I tried to tell you." I spun my fingers in her direction. "But you always have something going on. Or going wrong. I didn't want to throw you. But shit, now I have. I can see it in your face. I planned that after we got Leif, I would leave with Roan, but now I'm torn. Worse than torn, I'm shredded."

Jelly's jaw was slack, her voice broken. "Mori. You should have tried harder to tell me. Sat on me or something. You know I support your dreams."

"I'm the faithful companion, Jelly. That's what Samara said. I'm second fiddle."

Jelly groaned and slapped her hands to her face. "Mori, we've been over this. You're not second to anyone. You're my sister."

"Sisters step aside for fated mates." Every ounce of energy drained from my bones as the words hung in the air.

Jelly's lip trembled. She bit back her tears. "I'm sorry, Mori. I never meant for this to happen."

I held open my arms. "Me neither." We hugged tightly, finally acknowledging that our lives were different. We could never go back. We both held our breath so we couldn't cry, but our bodies trembled all the same. Simultaneously, we stepped away, our faces contorted and twisting, which eventually made us laugh. Better than tears.

Veda came through the door, rescuing us from falling into small pieces. "I have…oh! Oh…" She made a tutting noise and gathered us into her arms, filling my nose with cardamom and chamomile. "Life is so painful." Jelly and I started giggling as we caught eyes with each other, squished against the neck of this odd witch. She let us go and smiled. "See? All better. Now, Mori, I have something for you." I glanced at Jelly nervously. She just shrugged.

Veda held out two bracelets, the crystals a brilliant green. I balked. Veda grinned. "It's not what you think. This is not to attract the bear." I gaped at her, my eyebrows raising up. "Oh, he's clearly a bear. It surprised me he wasn't a Shifter. I expected a grizzly any second with all that growling he does. Grr grr grr." She swiped out her hand, her fingers mimicking claws.

Jelly burst into gales of laughter. I slapped my palms to my blushing face. Veda bobbled her head with a wide grin. "Hold out your hands, Mori. This is Green Tourmaline, also called Verdelite. It connects your heart to the world beneath your feet while reaching for the heavens above, making a clear channel for energy. It enhances courage, stamina and vitality. It will connect you to all of Earth's creatures. It has a high vibration, this crystal, and it will repair the damage to your Anahata."

I tucked my hands to my chest, curled like a squirrel guarding a nut. She tugged on them. I shook my head. "I don't want it, Veda. I don't want my anaconda repaired."

"Anahata."

I rolled my eyes impatiently. "Whatever."

Her bindi spun, hypnotizing me. My eyes tracked it until it went so fast it blurred. An image projected into my mind of me: bitter, alone, angry, so angry, yet painfully sad. It morphed into a picture of me laughing until my ribs ached. Her bindi stopped spinning, and I blinked, swaying on my feet, completely disoriented. She gave me a hard stare.

I cleared my throat. "Were those my choices?"

She nodded soberly. "This is for you. Your Anahata." She dropped her voice, looking around as if we had spies. "You cannot give away something that is broken."

I sulked and crossed my arms. "I'm not giving anything away."

She shook her head sadly. "But it means you also cannot receive. Wear the bracelets, Mori, for one month. See what changes in you." I looked at Jelly for help.

She shrugged again, one eyebrow raised. "Tomorrow, a chain of multiple crystals the length of my body will defend me from a creature who wants to eat my soul. What's a couple of bracelets?"

Icy strolled into the kitchen, blinking her pale blue eyes. A shiver of energy went through me as Veda clasped the first bracelet. Icy sat down, watching Veda while chatting with Jelly. "Meow murrr purpmow meeow." Jelly's head bobbed at whatever she was saying. Veda slid the clasp of the second bracelet closed and I rocked back on my heels, understanding the cat as she finished her sentence. "About her heart."

I backpedaled away from her, tripping over my feet. "What did you just say?"

Icy stared at me before her whiskers squinted up. "Did you understand that?" She turned to Veda. "Those are powerful." Jelly translated for Veda, who beamed from the praise.

I sank to the floor, overcome. Icy marched up to me and stared deep into my eyes. "I was saying that it's as obvious as the nose on my face that you suffer from scaredicatitis. It's time you did something about your heart."

My mouth opened indignantly. "Scaredicatitis? Scaredy cat? Me? I'm a warrior, Icy."

She licked her side in a frenzy, as if something had pinched her. She paused mid-lick and snorted. "Oh, please. I've seen your file. Like a fruit fly, flitting from merman to mermaid to merman again, never allowing your heart to become attached."

Speechless, all I could do was gawk at her. I recovered, finding my tongue. "My file? What does that mean?"

She shrugged a white shoulder. "Everyone has a file. I looked into yours once I received a snapshot of your larger purpose." She gave me an intimidating stare, no small feat from such a diminutive creature. "You need those bracelets. You shut down ages ago." Her eyes rolled up in her head as if tracking her memories. "Oh, yes, with Blythe."

"Blythe?" My cheeks reddened. I'd lost my virginity with Blythe. I'd fancied him something fierce, but he only saw me as a quick lay. I'd waited for him, cajoled him into taking me for my first time, creating this wild fantasy of how we'd fall hopelessly in love, make babies, live together forever, even finding each other in the afterlife. What a fool I'd been. He hadn't even kissed me goodbye afterward, simply thanking me, *thanking me*, as if all we'd done was a quick swap of magic. I was so humiliated

I buried the hurt in my heart, never telling a soul how shattered I was, not even Jelly.

Icy nodded. "You assumed that was how all relationships worked. You never tried otherwise. You simply shut down." She lifted a foot and groomed it.

Jelly sat on the floor next to me, equally dumbfounded as we stared at the fluffy Seer, forever trying to tame her fur with her pink tongue. Jelly stroked a hesitant finger over the green crystals. "Mori's file mentioned Blythe?" She turned her head to catch my eyes. "You said he was a terrible lover. You said you dumped him."

"He certainly wasn't good. He was too fast and a sloppy kisser." I shuddered at the memory. Kissing Blythe was like having an eel loose in my mouth. Reality had not lived up to the fantasy.

Icy sighed. "But you were infatuated with him. You wanted to take it further, and when he didn't, you slammed down a gate in your heart, becoming a user, vowing never to be used again." She lifted a paw and waved it toward my chest. "Thereby, shutting down your heart center." I opened my mouth to protest.

She continued. "You are a warrior, and a damned fine one, and that requires steady recharging. You use others to get what you need when you need it, and you move on. There's no shame in that, Mori, but it's had lasting repercussions. It hardened your heart, and something broke free." Her whiskers twitched. "And you have that crazy ball of fire in your belly." She tipped her head. "I can't see what it means yet."

She stood up and shook her body, talking over her shoulder as she stalked away. "Ask Roan to teach you how to block out the animals. You'll go mad as a box of crackers otherwise."

I smoothed the crystals with my fingers.

Ask Roan. Great. Just peachy.

TWENTY-TWO

JELLY

Under the moonlight, on a blanket from our bed, Mako dragged my hips at the perfect tempo, building me into a storming crescendo that swallowed my thoughts and words with a joined moan. I rolled off and lay next to him, panting. His smile looked forced, as if we'd made love for a purpose rather than pleasure, and I suppose we had. I needed to be at top power tomorrow. We both did.

He turned on his side, pulling the blanket with him to fold us together like a panini. He cocked his head in his hand, propped up on his elbow. I faced him, tracing my fingers along his jawbone. "Mako, who is Goldilocks?"

He barked a startled laugh. "Need a bedtime story?" When he saw I was serious, he looked puzzled. "It's an old fairytale. A girl breaks into a house with three bears. She tastes their porridge, sits in their chairs, and then lays in their beds. She tries each one, finding the smallest bear's items the most preferable. All of his things are just right." He smoothed my hair from my forehead. "Why do you ask?"

"Three bears? Promise you won't say anything?"

"Of course not."

"It's Mori. Roan called her Fire Maiden, not exactly, but

close enough, and she freaked out and ran away, and then he called her Goldilocks. Remember? Samara?" He shook his head, a blank look on his face. I rolled my eyes at him. "In her prophecy? You, me, and Mori, and another. Samara wouldn't tell her who, but that he'd make himself known. And then Samara called her Fire Maiden." Mako's eyes moved back and forth as he sifted through his memories.

He blinked as it came back to him. "Then why would he call her Goldi - oh!" He burst into laughter. "Roan's telling her to try other porridges." It was my turn to look confused. He tickled me, making me squirm against him. "Go taste other men. He's confident she will come back to him because he's just right for her."

"Do you think he's her fated mate?"

Mako's face turned serious. "Do you?"

I lifted one shoulder. "She doesn't want him to be." I folded in my fingers. *Mori? I found out who Goldilocks is.*

So did I. I asked Gray. Why are you talking to me? You're supposed to be rolling around in the moonlight, getting charged up for tomorrow.

We did. We're done.

She snorted. *That was quick.*

I laughed, making Mako's lips curl up as he watched me. *Where are you?*

The library.

Don't leave. I'll be there soon.

I dropped the hold and slid my hand into Mako's disheveled hair, messed with my fingers during our passions. We rolled onto our backs to look up at the sky. The Northern Lights dipped and swirled above us. I tried to read a pattern in the dance, a sign of some sort, but they swept through the clear sky in no discernable message, sometimes growing stronger, then fading back, the colors shifting from green to blue, then violet. Mako watched silently next to me.

I sighed loudly. "I'm trying to find a secret message."

"Me too. Can't see anything peculiar, but it's beautiful."

We snuggled a little longer until the cold of the ground seeped through our thin blanket. I said, "Mori's in the library. I'm going to hang out with her for a little bit. Want to come?"

"No, I need to sleep. I want to be fresh for tomorrow." He said the words causally, almost too lax, as if suggesting I should follow suit. He flung off the blanket, the cool night air immediately causing goosebumps on my skin. I wrestled into my clothes while he pulled up his pants.

Dread pooled in my belly at the thought of meeting the Seeker. "Mako, tomorrow…"

"Is tomorrow. And we will be fine. Come on, it's freezing out here." He would not entertain my fear, wrapping his arm around me as we walked back to the house. He was being suspiciously patient. I scanned his face, noting his tight smile, but he kept his hands from pulling his hair, his normal response to frustration. He tugged me along, and we split off in the foyer with a quick kiss, him heading upstairs while I turned for the library.

The cream curtains blocked out the night sky, a fire puttering merrily in the hearth. Mori was curled into her favorite chair, the worn velvet wingback, holding a massive book in her hands, undoubtedly reading something complicated. She looked up as I entered and showed me the cover. I laughed. She was reading fairytales.

She closed it and said, "Every story has a moral lesson. There's always a conflict that comes to a suitable resolution. In my opinion, they're brainwashing children, and they are not light, fanciful stories. The original tale of the little mermaid is dark as fuck. A witch cuts out her tongue so she can walk on land, and then she falls for a prince, but can't tell him, and he marries someone else and she dies."

I frowned. I'd been voiceless. All the mermaids in our clan

were voiceless, forced to the surface on Procreation Missions. Mori nodded sagely. "You're thinking of the missions, aren't you?" She sighed and flipped the book open again. "And then, there's Goldilocks with her three bears, although she shouldn't have chosen the smallest. That was stupid."

I coughed out a laugh. "What will you do with yours?"

She looked up. "Roan?" She shrugged nonchalantly. "Lay in different beds, I suppose." Her jaw clenched. I settled into the chair beside hers; the leather warmed from the fire. I smiled to myself as she launched her thoughts into the quiet space. "I'll start with Branko. He's more my type over Simon, and anyway, I think Simmi likes Simon. Gods, how confusing are their names? And we're not sure about Gray. Remember? Mako said he prefers men, so that leaves Branko." She nodded her head resolutely, as if persuading herself. "Once you've met with the Seeker and we have a moment to breathe, I'll seduce Branko."

"Sounds like a solid plan. And you won't have to work very hard. He likes you. He follows you with his eyes."

She frowned and crossed her arms. "Stupid. It's a stupid plan." She spun in the chair, tucking up her legs to face me, stuffing the book behind her. "Roan's a great kisser. He's a good man." My eyebrows raised. She lobbed a hand in the air. "And then he takes me to see the birds in the pond at the far end of the property to distract me from our worries, and it was beautiful, and we were laughing, and then he kind of called me Fire Maiden and I flipped out. Stupid, infuriating man."

I chewed on my lip. "You need him to teach you to block the animals and the birds. Box of crackers, remember?"

She scowled. "I know. It's relentless. The house has mice. Thankfully, they've all gone to bed or to nest or whatever."

I said, "You should call him."

She jerked her chin at me. "You do it."

I folded my fingers, leaving the index and pinkie slack. *Roan? Are you up?*

Aye, lass. Is there a problem?

Mori can hear animals talk. Veda gave her bracelets. Icy told her she needed you to teach her how to block their voices or she'll go nuts.

He cleared his throat, humor in his voice. *I'll be down shortly.* I dropped my fingers and gave Mori a lopsided grin. She was practically falling out of the chair, leaning toward me.

I said, "He's coming. He was laughing about you understanding animals."

"Or that I need him. Damn it!" She flounced back in her seat, thumbnail in her teeth, both feet tapping the floor in irritation. Roan strolled into the room, his eyes immediately searching for her. A tiny sigh escaped her as their eyes met.

"Ye have a wee problem, lass. How can I help ye?"

I rose from my chair to leave. "I should go."

Mori's voice was sharp. "No. Stay." I sat back down, keeping my face neutral. She didn't want to be alone with him. It wasn't from fear, but from desire. She turned to Roan, holding up her arms. "Veda gave me these bracelets, and then I heard Icy." She huffed out a breath of impatience. "I don't want to go to London and listen to the pigeons squabble."

Roan's eyebrows pressed down as he approached her, staring at the crystals. He crouched in front of her, settling between her legs so fast she didn't have time to draw them up without kicking him in the teeth. She blushed a furious shade of red. If he noticed, he didn't comment, muttering out loud. "Why would she give ye just green tourmaline? I would have picked watermelon for the balance between yer heart and root. She connected ye to all of it. All right then. I can see her reasoning."

Mori, grumpy, made a snorting noise, annoyed that he knew about the metaphysical properties of stones than she did.

He picked up her hand and pressed her fingers into a pattern. He glanced up and grinned at her blush and pout. "Don't fret, lass. This one is easy." He folded her index and middle finger down, crossing her thumb over them. Then he positioned her pinky in front of her ring finger. "Got it? This will block out the creatures."

She nodded, mute as he stared at her, reading so much on her face. Want. Confusion. Trepidation. He stood and stepped back. She found her voice. It came out a bit rough. "So I wander around London with my fingers wrapped up like a pretzel? What about the humans?"

He frowned. "Aye. Later, I'll teach ye how to do it without the hand gesture. For now, this is it. That'll block everyone, pigeons included." He blew out a breath and looked at us both apologetically. "I wanted to teach ye hands-free before a mission, but ye need to feel through the magic for at least a week before I can. The fates had other plans."

Mori grumbled into the air. "Fookin' fates."

Roan's green eyes sparkled with mischief. "Was that all ye needed, lass? Or can I help ye another way?" He couldn't keep the teasing out of his voice if he tried.

She squirmed and scowled at him. "That was all. Good night, Roan."

He chuckled. "Get some sleep. Both of ye. Ye need to be fresh tomorrow." He winked at us and strolled from the room.

Mori's head dropped forward. "He's impossible."

I grinned. "He's nice to you. Sweet on you."

She rolled her eyes. "Like I said, he's impossible."

I stood and held out my hand. "Come on, let's go to bed."

"Why couldn't he keep it casual?" Her face was a freckled sulk as she nibbled her nail.

I stared at her. "Mori, he's innocent in this. He said the sun looked pretty on your skin and hair. You freaked out because of the prophecy. Have you told him? Explained it?"

She scowled. "No. I didn't don't want him to go into a tangent about fate. Fuck that."

I took her by her free hand and pulled her from her chair. I left her at her door, still grumbling, and snuggled in next to Mako, careful not to touch his chest or his Hai Matau, and fell into a deep sleep, no visions or nightmares disturbing me.

I woke early, as did Mako. We entered the dining room, finding everyone there except Mori. Sebastian and Sophia nodded to me, smiling tight, nervous smiles. Branko was stern, pushing eggs around his plate. Simmi and Simon were sitting close together, whispering. Simon saw us and left to make our coffees, his new passion. Roan ate with vigor, ignoring everyone as he fueled. Gray sipped a coffee, murmuring with his parents.

A cranky Mori stumbled into the room, her fingers knotted together. She groused at us. "Crack of dawn, nattering about juicy worms. Gross." She waved her tangled hand. "Birds. A whole flock of them giving each other directions about where to find breakfast. And then I had to listen to them discuss the weather. Will it rain? Where will we wait if it does? Has Tinky learned to fly in the rain? Her wings are still frail. Tinky. There's a baby bird named Tinky. Goddess, help me."

She rubbed her eye with the back of her hand. "I couldn't get the position right for ages. My pinkie kept slipping. And then, once I did, I fell back asleep and my fingers relaxed, bringing all the voices right back. Woodpeckers are the worst. Drilling and drilling, screaming to each other about grubs."

Simon stepped from the kitchen with a tray of coffees, cheerful as he placed a mug in front of her, the foam dusted with extra cinnamon. He'd brought the bottle and set it in front of her. "Figured that was you. Whatcha doin' with your fingers?"

"Blocking out birds." She popped the top on the spice and dusted, frowned, and dusted some more.

"Huh," he said, "Okay. Want to fill me in?" He lifted his fresh coffee to his lips and took a sip.

She growled into her mug. "Veda gave me crystal bracelets to satisfy my anaconda."

Simon choked, holding his coffee away from him to keep from dumping it on himself. There was a beat of full silence. Then the men burst into laughter. Simon wheezed and cleared his throat, grinning from ear to ear. "I'm pretty sure she didn't."

Mori spun to glare at him. "Why is that funny?"

I took a large sip of my cappuccino, wondering myself why the men had erupted. Branko rested his chin on his hand, his elbow on the table, gazing at Mori affectionately. "Anaconda is slang for an exceptionally enormous penis."

I inhaled coffee and spluttered, bending over, trying to breathe through the burn. Mako whacked my back. Hysteria bubbled in my throat, and I joined in the laughter, cackling as I tried to clear the coffee from my airway. Mori shouted above the din. "Fine! I'm not familiar with that, um, term." Her voice dropped to a quiet mutter. "My heart center. They connect me to the collective energy to heal my heart."

Everyone stopped laughing. She stuck a piece of buttered toast in her mouth to prevent herself from saying more. Richard set down his tea, still smiling, and said, "We needed that laugh. Thank you, Mori."

She waved her bread, butter slipping over the side to coat her finger. "Don't mention it." Her eyes slid to Simon as he sat beside Simmi. Simmi's eyes sparkled at him in delight. He kissed her temple, nudging her with his nose. Mori sucked her teeth irritably, but eyed Branko hungrily as she bit through her toast. He kept catching her glances, a smoldering look on his face. Over breakfast, we talked about everything except today's mission, Simon telling jokes to lighten the tension, many of them about snakes.

Eventually, Anna dabbed her mouth with her napkin. "Shall we go over the plan one more time?" Immediately sobering, we all nodded. "I take Jelly's crew to the Borough Market witches. They walk to the Traitor's gate. Mew will meet them there. Then, I take the rest of us to approach Tower Bridge from the north. If for some reason you need us there faster, Roan, you reach out to my mind. Jelly goes in, gets what she needs, and leaves."

She stood, picking up her plate. She'd pulled her hair into a severe bun, with more pins than usual, and dressed head to toe in black. "We will not tarry in the city. Wear black. It will help you blend in. Jelly, hide your hair." She frowned at my face. "Your eyebrows are dark blue, but close enough to black to pass. Don't use glamor to hide the color. In London, they won't be too out of place. Wear boots you can run in, and a jacket that hides your crystals." She paused for a long breath. "Do not use magic in front of the humans. Clear?" We all nodded. "I'm going to the market now to see where we're landing. We leave in two hours."

I froze. It was happening. Mako slid his hand into mine under the table. Anna walked toward the swinging door to the kitchen. I stalled her. "Anna? I want to be armed. Can I use glamor to hide my knives?"

She frowned. "It's a small amount of magic, so yes, I will allow it. But remember, magic attracts magic, and we need to be discreet. There's the possibility that Vingor expects us, especially if he's working with the Seeker." She pushed through the door, butterflies taking residence in my stomach.

Roan slid back his chair. "Mori, I made something for ye." She looked up suspiciously. He reached for a dark bundle behind him. "I stole yer trousers and reinforced the pockets down the thighs. For yer stars. Ye can't wear a strap of them on the city streets." She blinked at him in surprise, her lips parting.

"That's incredibly thoughtful, Roan." She licked butter from her fingers before taking the pants and inspecting them. Her face broke into a smile. She reached forward with her other hand to stroke the fabric. "These are incredible! You double lined the pockets with…" She immediately scowled, yelling at the birds through the window. "No one cares! No one!"

Roan chuckled as she wrapped up her fingers to block out the voices. Mori tipped her head at Roan, beaming. "Thank you, Roan. I love them." I caught the quick flash on Branko's face, something like regret or annoyance.

"Yer welcome, lass." He cleared empty plates from the table, pushing through to the kitchen. As the door swung clear, Veda came out. She held up the long strand of multicolored crystals. Chunks of black stones swung from the end. I raised an eyebrow.

She bobbled her head. "More Black Tourmaline. My guides said you needed additional protection. It will sit right at your waist, as close to Manipura as possible. That's where you're weakest. I initially thought it needed to hang down, but they assured me it's better this way. Stand, please. I'd like to read you as best as I can with you wearing it."

I willed myself to stay calm as she wrapped the crystals around my waist, securing the black stones to sit tightly above my belly button. Instantly, the chain's power filled me. "Wow. That's strong."

"It is. Remember, keep your temper. These will help." She stepped back, her bindi spinning slowly. She nodded. "It is good. Very good." She patted my cheek kindly. "Safe journey, Jelly." She bustled back into the kitchen. Everyone made their excuses and pushed away from the table, Branko lingering the longest until turning with a scowl, swallowing whatever he wanted to say. Mako, Mori, and I sat in silence. Roan reentered and sat across from Mori.

His voice was stern. "We walk from the market over the

river across London Bridge, turn right, and head to the Tower of London, where we split, leaving Jelly with Mew. The three of us carry on to Tower Bridge. We watch Jelly while she's at the gate and sing to her. Mori, ye'll need to keep yer fingers tied up against the birds."

Mori lifted her knotted hand. "But I can still chant?"

He nodded. "Ye can chant. The hand positioning is for blocking." He rubbed a hand along his freshly shaved chin before sliding it to the back of his neck, under his braid. "Mew will take Jelly to Traitor's Gate. Once she's done with Sundidarta, she meets us on Tower Bridge and we head back to the market on the north bank. Right?" He stood, his hands splayed on the table, his voice deadly serious. "In and out. Nice and quick."

Mori's face twisted into a grin. "That is *so not* what she said." He blinked at her in surprise, his smile widening until his dimples showed. I giggled. With a chuckle, he left.

I ribbed her with my elbow. "Flirting again?"

She shrugged. "I'm nervous. I always flirt when I'm nervous." We all stood. Mako went to the library to look something up, and I returned to our room and plonked in the comfortable chair in the corner. I held the pearl in my fingers. I hadn't told anyone Leoht was still missing. Remarkably, no one had asked.

Leoht? Leoht, we're going to London soon. Leoht? I really need you. Leoht? Panic turned my breakfast to stones in my stomach. Where was she? I shook myself, steeling my spine, and began chanting the sound of the universe in my mind, hoping it might take me to her. It did. I found her curled into a tight ball, resting on pale silk, nestled inside her mother's shell. She didn't acknowledge me at all.

A voice sounded around me, sighing sadly. *She hasn't moved. I did not expect you to journey to the Hellhole through Mako's amulet. I am doing my best to draw her out of herself, but she is stricken. Go, Jelly. Leave us.*

Fear gripped me. "But I need her for the Seeker. She said she would help me keep my temper, show me the bright side of life when Sundidarta tries to make me angry. Leoht? Leoht, please. I need you. I can't keep my temper on a good day, and this is critical to getting Leif, to getting my soul back. LEOHT!"

She didn't stir, not even a twitch that she'd heard me shout. It was as if she were dead.

Mother Kokuro's voice was soft. *She cannot go. You must do this without her.*

I came back to myself, blood in my mouth. I'd bitten myself in the vision. Mako was kneeling in front of me, gently shaking me. "Jelly, it's time."

"What? I was only gone a minute…" The realization hit me. "I went to Mother Kokuro. Fae time." I swallowed. "Leoht…she's stuck. She's not coming." My eyes filled with anxious tears. I depended on her strength. Too much, it appeared.

Mako pulled me into his arms, flooding me with magic through his kiss. He grabbed my chin with his fingers. "You can do this, savage queen. We'll be close. Everyone will be close. We've got you. Okay? Don't tell the others. It will only worry them." His cobalt eyes scanned mine, projecting a resilience I didn't feel.

I swallowed my fear. We had to go. "Okay." I dressed all in black and pinned my hair up. I tucked my dark jeans into tall boots, the soles sturdy, with no heel. Mako pulled the black beanie onto my head, tucking in wayward blue strands to hide its bright color. "Isn't it weird I'm wearing boots on a sunny day? Won't that make me stand out?"

He kissed me again, magic streaming through my blood. "In London? No. You'll be fine."

We held hands in the foyer, Anna's voice brisk. "There is a tent behind a stall for French cheeses called The Friendly Fromage. Jelly, are you ready? You have your crystal belt?" I lifted the hem of my jacket to show her. She looked at my hips. "Glamor your knives now, before we leave." I shimmered a tiny drop of my magic against the pale leather holster, turning it invisible. With nerves gripping my belly, we disappeared.

TWENTY-THREE

JELLY

The roar of human thought overwhelmed me. I fell to my knees, desperately wrapping my fingers together until only the sounds of people chatting in normal tones came through. I shook my head to dislodge the assault. "Oh, gods. That was awful." Mori trembled beside me, silent as she wrapped up her fingers in the special knot.

Once secured, she groaned. "There are a lot of pigeons in here. Rats too, but they're hiding."

Mako peeked through the tent flap to scan the area. He held open the canvas. "All clear." Anna squeezed my shoulder and vanished. We stepped out of the tent into a vast open space teeming with humans carrying bright shopping bags, haggling over prices.

The witch manning the table wished us luck. "Blessed be."

I faltered at the mass confusion of humanity. Mako wrapped his arm around my waist. "Just walk. I'm right here."

"Mako." I gasped his name through tight breaths, sweat breaking out in a cold blanket over my body. "It's too much."

Roan cursed under his breath. "Of course, it's fookin' Saturday. Busiest day of the week. Fookin' Seeker. Come on, lass, I have yer back. My hand's on yer shoulder. I've got ye. Mori, next to me. Put yer arm through mine. Don't let go."

People scattered out of our way as we marched between the cheese stalls, our pace purposeful. We broke out of the crowds into a deserted stone alleyway. Mako stopped, and I sagged against the wall, hyperventilating.

He placed a cool hand on my cheek. "You're white as a sheet. Deep breaths, Jelly. We'll go through the next section, then we're out on the street." He kissed me, bolstering me.

Roan checked around the corner before motioning us forward. "Less than a mile, lass. Ye can do this." We pushed off again, this time into an even busier area, fruits and vegetables piled high on wooden carts and tables. I kept my eyes on the ground, trusting Mako to guide me. My eyes scanned over to a crate of fruit, displayed beautifully, a stack of purple balls. I froze on the spot, causing Roan and Mori to bump into me. Roan growled in my ear. "Keep moving, Jelly."

I hissed through my teeth. "That's the fruit! From my dream! Mako! When I set you on fire!" My voice rose in a hysterical squeal, my shoulders bunching as I swung my head back and forth. "That's the fruit!"

Roan clapped a hand on my mouth. He let it drop when I settled. "Ten o'clock, black suit. Keep yer face down, Jelly. No sudden movements, no magic. Just keep walking. I've got eyes on him." He tugged my hat down more, his heavy hand on my shoulder, guiding me forward. I stumbled, but Mako's arm around my waist kept me lifted and moving. A twang at my navel tripped me.

"The crystal just pulsed!" I clenched my teeth against the spark of magic reverberating through my guts. I hissed under my breath. "Eators, Roan. It has to be. That's who was in the dream. A human with red eyes. Vingor or Terrun sent Eators to hunt us!"

Roan's voice was deep in my ear, his body right up against me. "Yes, they're changed humans. I can sense their magic. Two more joined him. They're keeping back, but they've caught our trail. Keep moving. We can go faster once we hit London Bridge." My heart galloped inside my chest, drying my mouth like the desert. My left hand clenched in the finger hold, woven through Mako's stiff arm. I slid my right hand to the knuck at my side, ready to draw it if necessary.

We left the market and piled onto the street. It was chaotic with buses and taxis and cars and people. Oh Gods, so many humans. Mako yanked me to make my feet work as he muscled through the throng, dragging me beside him. I looked over my shoulder. Three tall men followed us. They had red eyes. Otherwise, they were nondescript. I swung my face forward and picked up the pace. Mako was right at my side. Tourists and shoppers packed the walkway, and I clung to Mako as he weaved through them.

Roan was not as delicate, pushing people clear. They squawked in automatic outrage, but quickly swallowed it when met with a thundering wall of muscle. He held Mori around the waist, almost carrying her as her toes pushed off the sidewalk. He snarled at us. "I have to delay them. Get to the end and turn right. When I say 'now,' I want ye to run."

Mori argued with a hissing noise. "Absolutely not! We're not leaving you to face three Eators alone with no magic!" Roan ignored her, shoving her to Mako's other side.

He spun away with a shout. "Now!"

The roar of his voice acted like a starter's gun, and I broke away from Mako in a full sprint, running on the edge of the road when the traffic eased between lights. We reached the end of the bridge and turned to glance back. Mako and Mori stopped as well, watching as Roan punched and kicked the men in suits.

One of them broke off and took chase after us, his red eyes glowing as he marked me.

Mako grabbed my arm. "Go!" He steered us across the busy road, holding up his hand as we raced into traffic. Horns blared, people shouted, and all I could do was run.

Mori huffed as she kept right at my side. She pointed in the distance with her free hand. "There! There's the tower!" A strange song of bells rang out through the air. "What was that?"

Mako answered while continually checking over his shoulder. "Big Ben. We have fifteen minutes until noon. Can you keep running? I'm going to stall him. Just get to the Seeker. Hide near the gate. Mew will find you! The bells will toll again at noon. Roan and I will meet you there!"

His hand was heavy on my hip as he drove me forward. I reached for him with my hands outstretched, immediately assaulted by human thoughts, rushing at me like a tidal wave, and I crumpled and fell to the ground, clutching my ears. Mori folded my fingers, gritting through the voices in her head. The thoughts ceased, replaced by Mori's tense voice as she trembled to put her fingers back into position. "Get up, Jelly! Get the fuck up!"

Mako bounced on his toes as he faced the man in the suit, running at full stride. I pushed to my feet with one hand as the Eator grabbed Mako in a headlock, moving so fast he blurred. Mako's arm swung backward and wrenched up. The Eator stiffened, let go of Mako, and collapsed to his knees, holding his stomach. When he pulled his hands away, they were crimson mixed with black.

He looked up and snarled, fangs popping out of his bland face as he lifted a trembling hand to strike magic at Mako. Mako jumped to the side and a throwing star buried itself in the Eator's throat. It fell with a jerk from the force. I snapped my head to Mori, her lips drawn back in a satisfied sneer, and swung it back to see Mako yank out the bloody weapon and leap to his feet.

Mako pounded the pavement, frantically waving at us to keep running. Mori squealed with relief. "Roan is right behind him! Go, Jelly, go!" She yanked on my arm and we sped down the sidewalk, thankfully less crowded than the bridge, but it thickened again as we reached the Tower, tourists milling about, laden with souvenirs, and wearing fake crowns. We slipped into an alley behind a pub, the stench of rancid fryer fat making me gag.

Roan swung around the corner just after us, his eye and lip bloodied, a great tear in his shirt. He leaned over, bracing on his thighs, and caught his breath. He eyed us up and down, checking for injuries. Mako wiped the star on a piece of old newspaper and handed it to Mori, repeating with the stiletto, groping with his fingers for my invisible holster, sliding it back into place. I blinked at him in shock. "I didn't even feel you take it."

My lungs had recovered, only my heart was in my throat as I glanced around the corner of the building to look for the gate. Mew shimmered into shape in front of me, making me squeal and jump back.

Mori almost throat punched him, her fist colliding with Roan's wide palm. "Steady now, lass," he said through a soft chuckle.

Mew rolled his shoulders. His voice was calm. "Jelly, I will get you into position and leave a shield around you, blocking you from the humans. Only those with magic can see you. I can't hide you fully because we need to focus on you. Roan, Mori, and Mako, get to the bridge. When I raise my hand, start chanting. Sundidarta may not allow me to stay, but you'll be fine. I have faith. The rest of you, go. Now."

I spun to Mako, gripping him by the face. "I love you." He echoed my words, planting a blistering fast kiss on my lips. Mori squeezed my shoulder and chased after Mako toward the bridge.

Roan nodded to me. "Ye got this, lass. In and out." I swallowed, confirming with a sharp nod, keeping my eyes on the gate as Roan ran past it on the sidewalk. I readjusted the crystal belt with one hand. A few minutes later, faintly, the bells tolled a short song of four pieces. Then, the solitary sound of a gong repeating.

Mew said, "Here we go. No talking as we pass the guards. Get the tahwil, and no anger." He wove his fingers between the ones on my free hand and moved out of the shadows. No one glanced at us. We walked straight past a man with a giant, whiskered mustache, resplendent in a uniform of a long navy tunic edged in red, a matching hat jammed over his heavy brow. An embroidered red crown covered his heart, and underneath was a C cradling an R. A row of small ribbons with medals pinned to his chest, symbols of his lifelong military service.

We reached the gate, and Mew jerked his chin for my eyes to follow. Mako lifted a hand from the bridge, standing on the walkway where a blue arch met the pavement. Mori's red curls caught the sun while Roan scanned the surrounding area. Mew stiffened, bowing his head to the empty air. "Your Highness, I mustn't chat. Not today." I frowned. He must be seeing things I couldn't. An enormous raven landed in front of us, cocking its head, staring at me with a suspicious, glistening black eye.

Its voice was a raw sound, but feminine. "You must step away from the girl before I summon the Soul Seeker. Over there. You can wait over there."

Mew murmured in my ear. "We're all here." He raised his hand and walked about twenty feet away. My head filled with the sound of Mako, Mori, and Roan chanting. I tried one last time. *Leoht? Leoht!*

Not a peep or a pulse. I was alone in front of the gate on a patch of dead grass, hidden by Mew from all except those with magic. The gate was nothing special, a weathered wooden structure, but the castle loomed over me, the gray stone cold and forbidding. I shivered despite the sun and my leather jacket.

I inhaled steadily, exhaling fully, repeating the pattern, letting the chanting calm me as I waited for Sundidarta, my nerves and teeth on edge. I smelled her before I saw her, like rotting garbage, a septic filth that made me want to retch. I hissed in a breath between my teeth, clenching my free fist, the one twisted in protection shoved in the pocket of my zipped jacket. The stones at my stomach throbbed. She took her form achingly slowly, relishing in my ever tightening posture. I swallowed the cry of disgust that crept up my throat as she came into clarity.

Muddy brown eyes looked me over leisurely as she picked at her yellow teeth with a sliver of bone. My jaw clenched reflexively. Her skin hung in a patchwork of strange angles, none of the stitching tidy. She was a monster, repugnant, and she cackled as I fought to keep my breathing shallow.

She flicked her eyes to the side, staring at Mew. "Leave, or this meeting ends before it starts." Mew frowned and disappeared. With a snort, she looked me up and down. "So. You are the mermaid missing a piece of her soul." Her voice sent nails down my spine.

"Correct. I need a tahwil." Her eyes narrowed as she swept stringy hair from her face with a pale green hand. "Please." I added the pleasantry tightly, not entirely sure of the protocol.

She sneered, stretching the skin on one side of her face, pulling it until it threatened to break free. "You dare come to me with demands? Who do you think you are, girl? This is how much I value your request." She took a step toward me. I stepped back. She yacked and spat at my feet, a glob of yellow phlegm sticking to my boots. I looked down slowly, unimpressed, and gave her a blank stare as I leveled my gaze at her again.

I repeated my request coolly. "A tahwil, please, Sundidarta."

She picked at her teeth, trying to act nonchalant, but I'd thrown her. She narrowed her cloudy eyes. "Who told you to ask for that?"

"Lucky guess." I replied to her casually, focusing on the chanting in my mind. She shimmered ever so slightly, oily shadows creeping off of her, brushing on my skin, seeking purchase. The space between my shoulder blades flared with heat, and the crystal at my belly throbbed, pushing into my flesh. A couple near us spoke softly, although in their minds, they were yelling. I tightened my fingers in my pocket.

Roan's voice crept through my mind. *In and out, lass.*

"Now, this is curious." Her voice slithered against me. "You have help."

"So do you." I almost snapped my retort, controlling my voice at the last second. "Three men in suits with glowing red eyes jumped us. How could they possibly have known where we'd be?"

She chuckled, the noise like marbles in a box. "Gutted one, did you? I can smell his blood and shit on your hidden blade. No loss. Plenty more where he came from. Plenty more to tear all your loved ones to pieces." I didn't react with my voice, but I bit down on my cheek. She sniggered. "Oh my. There's a sore spot. Shall I poke it some more?"

I swallowed blood. "Stop stalling, Seeker. I have places to be."

She flicked the bone to the side, drawling. "Indeed. Indeed, you do. And very little time. First, you must solve my riddle. Then complete the task. Considering what I'm about to propose, you'll be close to the wire. Close indeed. You may not recover your soul. I may get to eat it."

She laughed again, mucus rattling in her foul body. She hacked up another glob of goo, rolling it on her tongue, showing it to me before chewing on it. Her inflated lips worked together, and she propelled it through the air, almost striking my face. I twisted just in time. This fucking bitch.

My blood heated. I fisted and released my free hand, fisting again, and the chanting in my head grew louder, everyone on the bridge knowing my tell. My jaw clenched as I wrangled my temper, wanting to rip out my knuck and tear at the threads holding this vile creature together until she lay in a heap on the grass. The chain of crystals heated, almost scalding. "The tahwil, Seeker. That and my task." My voice was cold stone.

She sighed dramatically. "Ugh. So boring. I hoped to see this notorious temper. Very well." She fished through the pockets of her darkly stained coat, retrieving a tiny, tarnished silver cube in a cage on a chain. She swung it before me. "To retrieve your lost piece, you must abandon yourself to three queens. If rewarded with a drop of liquid gold, your soul will be restored." Her nasty face soured further. She dangled the amulet on a ragged finger, taunting me, waiting for my reaction.

I drew on my Seduction classes, acting the part of a bewildered fawn. I needed her to believe I was utterly helpless. I creased my brow as if confused, using a heartbroken voice. "What is that supposed to mean? That's not a riddle. That's impossible." I bit down on my lip, looking at her imploringly, pretending to take the wrong track. "There are so many queens. Denmark, Spain, Jordan, Bhutan. And you want me to see three? In such a short time?" I raised my voice to near hysteria. "Abandon myself? What does that even mean? And a drop of gold? Do they have smelters? How much time do I have?"

She shrieked with delight at my dismay, certain I would fail. She cackled, phlegm gurgling with the noise. "Three moons since you lost it, so not enough time at all. Best hurry." She threw the small cube at my face. I caught it, surprised at its weight. "Tick Tock, little fish." I boiled inside, clenching my teeth together. Those were the exact words the demented Fae Prince had used. It confirmed she was working with Terrun.

Her eyes flashed with glee as she judged my reaction. She lilted in a singsong voice. "Time is running out for you, little mermaid. You're damned to be broken forever. Poor little thing.

All alone. Forever alone. No parents. Dead, dead, dead. All dead." She laughed, the sound of more phlegm in her throat. "I was told about your father. Shame. Drowned, drowned, drowned. He must have struggled to get so tangled in the net."

Fury rose in my body. My brain chanted kill-kill-kill. I snapped at my cheek for control. I was desperate to slash at her throat. I could do it. She was old, and I was fast. I could end her right now. My fingers eased toward my right hip, but Roan's voice filled my head. *Get yer hand away from that blade! Get out of there! Ah fook! Run, lass! Back the other way!*

The fear in his voice shocked me from my vicious thoughts. *What? Why? I'm supposed to meet you on the bridge!*

Eators! His shout iced my blood. The Seeker had been stalling me.

I swung my head to the right. There was no sign of Mew. Four men in suits raced in my direction from the bottom of the bridge, blocking off my intended escape route. The Seeker hissed, lunging for my face with her jagged nails, her thick lips curling back from her rotting teeth. Mori screeched in my head. *NOW!*

I thought she was echoing Roan when an enormous flock of pigeons descended on the Seeker, battering her with their wings and beaks. I spun to run the way I'd come, but three more Eators sprinted down the path, red eyes glowing, serrated teeth in human faces.

Mori yelled in a frantic shout. *Jump in the river and swim across! We'll meet you on the other side!*

I sprinted to the embankment along the dark water. The river looked horrible and smelled worse. Glancing over my shoulder, the seven Eators closed in. I scrambled up with both hands contorted, intending to run the narrow wall to the bridge. My feet were quick and light, and I pretended I was on the balance beam back at the gym, with safety nets to catch me if I stumbled. A bolt of magic skimmed past my face. I wheeled my arms, bending my spine backward as another Eator shot magic from his palm, narrowly missing me.

The water looked dire, a brown stripe of murk, but I wouldn't make it to safety through running. Swimming was my best chance. I leaped off, fisting the amulet. Sundidarta shrieked with fury behind me, screaming at the Eators to catch me. A bolt of magic hit my back, and the chain of crystals around my waist exploded in a rainbow of light. People on the bridge pointed and shouted as they saw me. Mew's illusionary magic was gone.

I dove into the Thames River, changing to my tail on impact. The water was dank, cold, and coated my tongue with engine grease. I kicked my tail hard, fighting strong currents that threatened to sweep me away, swimming close to the bottom as boats roared overhead. Just below me, a human skull silently screamed, the rest of its body further away, trapped in twisted metal, half buried in the river's silt. More wreckage of forgotten engines and garbage scraped my skin. The noise from the boats was terrifying, and in the dark water, I couldn't judge how close they were. My nose filled with the smell of ancient rot.

Roan's voice found me in the icy depths. He was panting. *Ahead of ye, ye'll see the foot of the bridge. Go there. Be quick, Jelly.*

My tail muscles ached. I screamed back to Roan. *I'm swimming blind! The currents are insane! And I'm coming out naked!*

Got ye covered, lass. Swim!

I needed to get my bearings. I popped up, thinking I was between boats, and almost got nicked by a propeller. Not far. I dove deep again, cursing the brutal drag of the current, pushing for the riverbank. When I surfaced, my eyes were wild with fright and disgust. I thought the ocean was bad. This river was worse, so much worse.

Strong arms lifted me as I choked, spitting to clear the grease from my tongue. My left hand cramped from holding my fingers so tightly, the amulet clamped in my right hand. I shifted to legs. "Put your hands through, Jelly. Let's go, let's go!" Mori urged me to move, bundling me into a coat that stank of stale urine.

I shivered with cold on the muddy walkway at the bottom of the riverbank. Low tide. I was lucky that a boat hadn't decapitated me. Mori rammed a ratty beanie over my head, tucking in my hair frantically. Roan swooped me up in his arms, racing up slippery steps. Mako sagged with relief when he saw me. He moved to kiss me, but I stopped him.

"Don't! You don't want this on your lips. But take this. I don't have safe pockets." There was no way in hell was I sticking my hand in this coat. I handed him the cube, a centimeter in size. He stuffed it away, scanning my face. With a nod, he tipped his head away from the river.

"Let's move. Roan, follow me." People eating sandwiches packed the green lawn. Crowds with pints of beer spilled out of the pubs, soaking in the sun. Mako hustled us away from the promenade, taking to the street, which was relatively empty. We crossed through an alley, running up and over a narrow covered bridge that spanned multiple train tracks.

Roan gagged. "Gods, girl, ye stink!"

Mori whimpered as we ran. "I'm sorry, Jelly. It's all I could find. We just stole someone's only possessions."

Roan turned his head to the side. "The coat is the least of it. It's yer skin and yer hair."

"It's nasty." My words slurred through chattering teeth, the shock of it all taking hold of me.

"Ye were fookin' brilliant, lass, holding yer temper like that. And we suspected the old hag would try something dodgy. It was Mori's idea to send the birds. She told them the Seeker had pockets full of bread." He chuckled and gestured with his head toward Mori. "So fookin' smart."

I tried to smile, but failed. "Did the Eators follow you?"

Roan said, "Anna's lot has them. I yelled for her when I saw them, and she transported everyone, hiding them in a shield. Using a fookload of magic, she is. They chased us over the bridge. Last I saw, Branko had one on the ground, punching it with a stone fist."

Mako held up his hand so we could catch our breath, tucking us in a wide doorway to an office building, deserted, as it was the weekend. His fingers trembled as he touched my cheek. "You scared the piss out of me, savage queen."

I hacked a weak cough. "All over this coat. Please, can we hurry? I can't stand the smell of myself."

He nodded. "This is a back way to the cheeses."

Keeping to the edges, everyone watched for red eyes wearing suits, but all we saw were the faces of people enjoying the fresh food, chatting merrily. A woman appeared out of nowhere, making Mori squeal and grab for her stars. The woman hushed her. "Be at peace. Anna sent me. We've been watching for you. Come."

She led us through a cluster of crates, waving her hand down so that we would stay low. Roan crept forward, holding his breath as his face came closer to my body. She held open a white flap, the back way into the tent.

Anna recoiled and pinched her nose. "Dear Gods, you're revolting." I noticed her hair had escaped from its pins, and she had an ugly bruise on one cheek. Her clothing was dusty and ripped in places. She looked exhausted.

Mako held out his arms for me, and Roan moved close to pass me over. "I can stand up. Honest." He lowered me down, and Mako held me tightly around the waist, turning his nose away from me.

Anna said, "On the count of three, release your fingers and grab each other's hands. You'll have a second of chaotic human thought, and then we'll be gone." She turned to the witch and put her hand on her chest. "Thank you, Gerry, and blessed be."

The woman smiled, returning the gesture. "And to you, Anna. Take care." When Anna said three, I wrenched open my spasming hand, reaching for Mako as the deluge of human worries attacked my brain. And then, blessed silence, and we were gone.

TWENTY-FOUR

JELLY

I took a long bath to recover from my impromptu swim in the river. After meeting the Soul Seeker and her manipulative magic, dodging Eators and swimming across the Thames, I was drained. Anna and the others were downstairs, puzzling over the small metal amulet.

Mori pushed the door open, holding a plate of ginger cookies. She plopped on the bed next to me, merrily chomping into one, brushing the crumbs on the floor. She swallowed before she finished chewing properly, as though she couldn't wait to tell me a secret. She leaned in close, her eyes flashing with excitement.

"I tried to seduce Gray. He's totally into guys, and said as much, but not before he toyed with me. He blocked me with no effort, the gold in his eyes flashing as he turned my seduction back on me. He's good. Fantastic even. He turned me into a damned puddle. I was roasting after talking to him, so I found Branko and kissed him. So hot. I mean, literally cold, like, cold lips, but a hot, hot kiss."

I blinked my eyes wide as she crammed the rest of the cookie in her mouth, nodding enthusiastically. She hastily swallowed that mouthful as well. "I was tired after summoning those pigeons, and Roan offered to help me, but he looked worn out, so I didn't want to sap his magic. We got back here, and Gray was the first one I found, but like I said, he just spun me into a ball of fire with no relief. Branko was vibrating from fighting, so I dragged him into the study, asking him to top up my magic, helping him release his."

She shuddered with delight. "So hot. Cold. Whatever. You know what I mean. Gods, it was so intense. His kiss was consuming. There was no other world except me. At least, that's how it felt. All he wanted was me, his arms gripping me so tightly. His tongue is also cold, not that you asked, but I haven't let you speak yet. It's like we're the yin to the yang, me so fucking hot lately, and he's the perfect balm. I want more. I want all of it. I will make it happen." She shivered again, gleefully biting into another cookie, waiting for my reaction.

Too preoccupied with my own worries to give her exploits the attention she craved, I nibbled on the edge of a cookie. "I have to abandon myself to three queens. So I have to lose everything I am, or at least, that's what I imagine. Those were Sundidarta's words. The Seeker didn't tell me how the transformation box works. Did Anna figure it out?"

Her smile collapsed, crestfallen. I ignored it. She scowled at me. "Did you hear anything I just said?"

I waved through the air. "You tried to seduce Gray and ended up kissing Branko. Now, what about the box?"

She crossed her arms, angry that I wasn't more interested in her exploits. On a huff, she said, "Branko knew what it was."

"Branko?"

She grinned, happy to be back on her current favorite topic. "He says it's a zavodila. It will only open with goodwill, a pure heart. You can't manipulate it or be aggressive. You just allow the transformation to happen." She scooted closer. "He was adorable as he explained it, his eyes lighting up, saying he'd seen an amulet like it before. Someone inspirational wore it. Someone he treasured." Her face became more animated. "He leaned in real close and breathed over me as he spoke and little icicles formed on my eyelashes and I can't help but wonder what his—"

"Mori! Focus! I don't have time for your damned fantasies right now." My voice came out sharper than intended.

She drew back, taking her excitement with her. She stood abruptly, leaving her unfinished cookie on the plate, and brushed her hands together as best she could around the knot she still had to make with the fingers of her left hand. "I see you're all back to your normal self. That means you're ready to go do your thing." She snipped the words, marching for the door.

"Mori, I'm sorry." My apology fell on deaf ears. When the door slammed shut, I fell back on the pillows. I was a terrible friend. Not a great lover, either, it seemed. Mako left in stony silence an hour before. We'd fought over him wanting to visit Leif through a vision before I started my task, with me outright refusing, protecting Leoht. He said I should force her out of hiding. I told him to go to hell. He'd left angry, saying I was self-absorbed and selfish and didn't appreciate the needs of others.

I was back to pissing off everyone I cared about.

A great sigh came from beneath me. I hung my face over the side to find the source. Icy opened one eye and stared at me balefully before yawning. She said, "Jelly, Jelly, Jelly. It's always about Jelly. Jelly needs this, and Jelly needs that, and you expect everyone to trail after you like minions."

I scowled upside down, the blood rushing to my head. "I didn't ask for this, Icy."

She stretched, all four paws reaching in different directions. Shaking herself, she marched out from under the bed. Her tail lashed the air. "Victim card? Please. I didn't ask for this either. You're needed downstairs."

A second later, Roan called my name. I glared at Icy. "Coming, Roan!"

"Lift me onto the bed. I want to sleep on your pillow. See if I can pick up any residual dreams." She eyed my throat and the dormant pearl. "See if I can convince her to return." I did as she asked and scowled as she proceeded to groom, her butt scooting on my pillowcase.

"Gross, Icy." I rushed down the stairs, clinging to the handrail for balance.

I propped my elbow on the arm of the cream sofa, sharing it with Roan. Mako sat surly in his own chair. Roan stared at Mori as she paced in front of the swept fireplace, empty and cold, as it was a sunny day. Branko stretched out his long legs, looking the most relaxed I'd ever seen, following Mori with a look of satisfaction. Anna held up the chain, the box swinging gently. "We're uncertain how long it will take to complete your quest once you transform."

Richard sat forward. "I heard you threw the Seeker off your trail, mentioning human queens. Nicely done, Jelly. All of it. You did very well. We've been mulling over your task. You need to receive royal jelly from a queen, but you have to meet three. Therefore, we can only assume you need to actually become a bee, not just meet them."

The blood drained from my face. "Say what now? How would I do that?"

Richard continued. "Through the amulet. You are to abandon yourself, thus, lose your form, your identity. You must gain the Queen's trust. She won't just give you her most valuable food. The Seeker said the word 'rewarded,' meaning that you will have to prove your worth to her."

He ignored my shocked face, continuing his supposition. "Pollinators are the world's unsung heroes. They dedicate their brief lives to the hive, to each other, knowing that time is precious. There's a small window of opportunity. They harvest food for the winter, even though they may not live to see it. They survive in an extraordinarily structured society. We believe you must become one of them."

I tugged the cold pearl back and forth along the chain. "For how long?"

Anna answered succinctly. "As long as it takes to get your drop of liquid gold."

I looked over at Mori, still pacing, not meeting my eye. Mako wouldn't look at me either. I scanned over the room. Only some of us remained, the others needing to get back to their lives. Simmi and Simon were gone. They'd left for the Fields' home as soon as we came back. She wanted to return to work, and he needed to visit a wolf pack in Oregon. Gray departed earlier for Brussels to attend a global conference on environmental law. Sophia and Sebastian planned to a visit to an old friend. They would leave once I transformed.

My eyes settled on Roan, who now watched Branko watch Mori as she paced. He tugged on the back of his neck, his scowl clear, especially when Mori fanned her face after taking a long drink of a casual Branko. Sebastian broke me from my trance. "Jelly, you are Fae. Talk to the bees, explain your situation, and ask for an audience with the Queen. The Seeker did not specify a particular Queen, and the Coven keeps bees. Start here where it's safe."

"Where are they?" I hadn't seen any boxes of bees.

Mori answered quietly. "Near the pond." She resolutely stared at the fire, avoiding my eyes.

Anna nodded. "Bees prefer an open meadow, ideally with a wetland nearby. We keep seven hives."

Richard beamed. "Auspicious number. Magical." His smile fell. "But I'd prefer to say that we host bees. We do not keep them. They are not our pets, nor are they are slaves." He saw my confusion and explained. "Honeybees fall under the classification of livestock, and many unscrupulous keepers abuse them, driving them far from their homes to pollinate crops. It is disorienting, being trucked from farm to farm, and many die." He shook his head sadly. "Not to mention, excessive beekeeping puts pressure on our endangered bees, our wild bees, competing for food and spreading diseases not naturally found in their habitat."

Richard kept speaking, lost in a tangent. "Then, add in pesticides, neonicotinoids in particular, and the bees suffer problems with flight and navigation, and reduced taste sensitivity, meaning they skip nourishing flowers. Neonicotinoids impede the learning of new tasks, all of which impact foraging ability and hive productivity. They especially harm the bees that are ground-dwellers."

He sagged in his chair, weighed by his facts. "Pesticides make them more susceptible to parasites and viruses. Prolonged exposure to makes it harder for bees to groom themselves and each other. It's tragic, and unnecessary." He cleared his throat roughly. "We don't use pesticides. They live long lives here."

Anna patted his hand, knowing the topic upset him. She turned to me. "As it is summer, the bees will live for two to six weeks."

"Two to six *weeks*?" I echoed in shock. "That's hardly anything! Barely a life!"

She smoothed over her hair. "Queens live roughly five years. Worker bees will live for twenty weeks over the winter. That's when they rest, and it is safe in the hive, assuming they have enough food. We top them up if they're running low." She leaned forward. "Jelly, bees live arduous lives. Foraging exposes them to environmental hazards, predation, and dehydration. They lose a tremendous amount of nutrients while working. Many new bees do not survive their initial foraging flights."

I said, "All of this is interesting, truly, but how does it help me?" As soon as the words left my mouth, I wanted to take them back, hearing Icy's remonstrations in my head about being narcissistic. Mori clearly agreed with the cat, as she scoffed and rolled her eyes. I bit back the wretched sensation of being a diva and waited for someone to answer.

Richard, patient, kind Richard, held my gaze, his voice gently reprimanding. "You must abandon yourself, Jelly. Your Self. You."

Mori snapped out. "In other words, get over yourself. Everything's on hold. We're all waiting for you to figure this out, and we can't do anything about Leif until you do." Mako grunted in agreement.

I sat back as if she had slapped me. I looked over at Mako. My lover's face was a thundercloud. I swallowed my hurt. "Mako, a word in private, please?"

He stood without looking at me and pushed through the door to the dining room, turning to face me with a tight jaw. I chewed on the inside of my lip. He stayed silent. I broke the tension between us. "I can't leave, thinking you're angry with me. You've got to understand why I won't risk Leoht. She's been through enough." I raised my face, scanning his.

He closed his eyes, breathing in through his nose. His voice was gruff, fighting to hold the emotion from his voice. "Been through enough? Kind of like Leif? Except fifteen years for him." He snorted, controlling his temper as he opened his eyes, his stare burning into me. "I will always love you, Jelly, but I am furious. You're denying me the chance to see Leif, and I have so much to apologize for, something I'd like to do sooner rather than later. If you don't succeed, this is all for nothing, and he's stuck, possibly forever. Do you understand my position? Can you find it in *your* heart to appreciate my point of view and why I'm upset?"

I swallowed over the lump in my throat. His disappointment crushed me. I could barely speak. "I'm sorry I won't do a vision. Maybe you can try on your own."

He laughed once, a sharp sound devoid of humor. It cut. "On my own? Don't you get it? I need you for the Hellhole. I need Leoht. And you're letting her wallow."

Anger flared. "I don't control her, Mako!"

He seized my face in his hands, his eyes burning hot. "You bonded with her, and we need her. Get her to come back, Jelly. You're the only one who can. Get the royal jelly so we can get Leif. That's all I'm asking of you." He dropped his hands and pushed into the kitchen, leaving me hollow. I'd assumed he would kiss me, even though angry, offering his magic or at least good luck.

I allowed myself a sob, just one, and then bit on my cheek hard enough to spill blood. I wiped my face and returned to the library. I had to get out of here. Standing before our remaining crew, I spoke with a confidence that wasn't real. "I'm ready."

Sophia read my bluster and crossed the room to hug me, wrapping me in her strong arms. "Be safe, my daughter." I nodded against her neck, my breath hitching. She squeezed tighter, waiting for me to get a hold of myself. I squeezed back, and she released me, cupping my cheek in her hand. Without another word, she turned, Sebastian taking her place.

I wanted to break down and cry. Mori and Mako were angry, but this was who I was, how I'd always been. Sebastian sensed it all and soothed a hand down my back, lifting my distress with his magic.

"Shh, Jelly. Do you want me to join you? I can lie in the flowers until the bees arrive."

"Yes, please." I held my breath to keep from breaking. I desperately wanted Mako to go with me, but realized he wouldn't. He hadn't returned to the room. Sebastian ran his hand up and down, pulling the sadness from my energy. My voice was hoarse. "Can we go now? I can't stand the waiting." He patted my shoulder and went to have a quiet word with Anna. I kept my back to the room, fighting for courage. I'd never been this wobbly before. Usually, I faced my challenges head on. Understanding dawned on me, and I lifted the pearl in my fingers, begging.

Leoht, I'm about to transform into a bee. I could really use a friend with me.

No reaction. No reply. I dropped it, sorrow engulfing me. I raised my fingers to my temples. *Synchi? It's Jelly. Are you there?* No response. I tried again. *Synchi! I need you!* Seconds crept into years while I waited. Then I became alarmed. I spun to Mori. "Can you contact the Shaman through the mirror while I'm gone? Explain what's happening? I just tried, and she's not answering."

Mori's face paled, her freckles standing out in stark relief. "She didn't answer you? That's not like her."

"It's not. But I have to go. The longer I hang around, the less time I have inside the hive." Mori scowled, having an internal debate, and then crossed the room at top speed, flinging her arms around me. My soul heaved in a sigh of relief as she hugged me.

She murmured in my hair. "You're an asshole, but you're my sister. I love you. Be safe."

"I love you too. Keep an eye on Mako for me. He's so angry with me. Just watch over him for me. Please."

"I will." She stepped back and punched me in the arm. "That's for earlier, you self-absorbed ass." She grinned at my shocked expression. I rubbed my arm and looked over at Roan, whose shoulders were shaking as he silently laughed. Branko's lips twitched.

"Roan? Can I talk to you when I'm a bee?"

"I don't know, lass. We can try, but I don't think ye should allow any distractions. Focus on yer task."

Sebastian approached, balancing the small cube on his palm. "It's heavy. Tungsten if I had to guess. It's one of the toughest things found in nature, almost impossible to melt. It's a curious trinket for transformation. A lot of energy in a tiny package." He held it out for me, swaying on its chain. I took it cautiously, unsure of what to do with it. It hung on a chain, so I assumed I'd wear it.

I looked around one last time for Mako. Surely he would come see me off. He was nowhere in sight. I clenched my jaw and pushed through the side door. The others followed behind in a small procession, similar to a funeral parade. Somber, hushed voices muttered behind me and Sebastian, too soft for me to understand, but they were worried. I paused at the top of the knoll. It was beautiful.

I breathed out, turning to everyone. "Here's goes nothing." I hastened down the other side with Sebastian, into the wildflowers, mentally apologizing to the flowers I crushed beneath my heels. We walked toward the weathered white boxes on sturdy frames, bees zipping in and out of them.

Sebastian turned me to face him. His face was kind. "You can't control the magic inside you, but that's beside the point. Remember that you *have* magic inside of you. You are magic." He kissed my cheek. "I'll wait with you."

"Thank you, Sebastian. Tell Mako I love him. He walked away from me before I could say it."

Sebastian looked pained. "He's so caught up in Leif…" He shook his head. "But he shouldn't abandon his mate when she undertakes such an enormous task."

"We argued about Leif. And Leoht. She's still hiding."

Sebastian's lips pressed together. We lay in the flowers, with him stretching his tall body beside me and grabbing my hand. We stared at puffy clouds drifting over a blue background. His voice was soft, remote. "Terrun betrayed Leoht. Used her, almost killed her. The vial around his neck? That was Leoht's blood."

He growled in his throat. "I haven't told Simmi, but the moment we rescued her I knew he'd forced her to drink Leoht's blood. I sensed her presence in my daughter. It made Simmi more powerful, and it's had a residual effect. Simmi hasn't admitted it, but it changed her." He turned his head to look at me, anguish in his eyes. "Leoht almost didn't survive the Hellhole. To be thrust there in a vision without preparation…I'm not surprised she's still hiding. But keep talking to her. That's the best thing you can do for trauma victims. Tell her she's not alone."

I squeezed his hand. "Thank you, Sebastian. That's good advice." I took a deep breath. "Okay. I'm putting this around my neck. Wish me luck."

"Good luck, Jelly. I'm right here." I slipped the chain over my neck and lay back down, my heart beating against my ribs in anticipation. Nothing happened. I was about to comment when a bee approached, keeping a distance.

It spoke in an authoritative female voice. "Who are you? What is your purpose here?" Shocked by the strength of the sound coming from such a tiny body, my tongue fumbled as I sat up. I couldn't see a mouth, just a small and seemingly angry insect.

"I, uh, I'm Jelly. I need…I seek an audience with your queen."

The bee flew in a wide arc before returning. "Come with me."

"How?"

The bee tipped to the side, sarcasm in her voice. "Try your legs."

Sebastian and I stood. He hugged me without speaking and turned for the knoll. I followed his steps with my eyes, shading them to scan the group. Mako still hadn't joined them. I tugged my sad heart back into place. Mori gave me a Mers salute, her fist to her chest, which I returned, and spun on my heel toward the hives, following my guide. I stopped in front of the white box, unsure of what to do next. The bee said, "Kneel." She zipped away when I did as instructed.

The tungsten cube hung low on my chest, right over my heart. It thrummed with a steady beat, and my vision abruptly changed. The bees at the entrance, who at first appeared to be plain insects, morphed into sentries with crossed swords. I resisted the urge to gawk. The bee on the left spoke sharply. "State your business!" Her voice was pure power.

I bowed my head, thinking it wouldn't hurt to be humble, even though I was a giant comparatively. "My name is Scyphozoa Vetula, but please, call me Jelly. I am a mermaid, claimed as a Fae by Mother Kokuro. I am missing a piece of my soul, knocked from me during a ritual with the Surfecti, and Sundidarta, the Soul Seeker, assigned me a task. To complete it, and retrieve my soul, I must see your queen." I raised my head. The bee whispered to another behind it. It took flight deeper inside the hive.

I stayed on my knees, studying the soldiers. Their antennae flexed, as if smelling the air, or me. They stood on their hind legs, leaving four free, two of which held the swords aloft, a menacing gesture, even though I loomed over them. The one on the right studied me coldly. I kept my eye on the stinger at the end of her body. It looked wickedly sharp and barbed; the nuances highlighted by my strange new vision. More bees bearing weapons crawled closer to investigate, twitchy. The bee from before returned, whispering to the guard. She nodded once, never breaking eye contact with me. She issued a command. "Change."

The cube exploded over my chest, washing me in a golden flash of light, and I squeaked as the hive entrance slipped from my view and the grass blades became bigger, towering like trees above me. The world burst into colors I'd never experienced, everything so vivid it almost hurt. The flower above my head wavered in patterns that hadn't been there before.

I reached to wipe at my eyes and squealed when I found a segmented leg covered in comb-like hairs. "Bring her up," the guard bee said from high above me. I squeaked again as four bees came from behind and lifted me beneath my legs, setting me on the shelf at the entrance to the hive before zipping away.

I tried to speak, but it came out garbled. The sentry on the left chuckled. "Give it a minute. You have mandibles and a proboscis now. Speech is the last thing to settle." I glanced down at my body, split into three segments. I experimented and fluttered my wings, almost falling backward from the shelf, a squawking noise escaping me. One guard grabbed me and hauled me back down. "You're not ready to fly yet. Keep those still."

I panted through my strange mouth, trying to catch my breath from my fright. Everything was going dark from lack of oxygen. The other guard laughed. "Look, she's trying to breathe through her mouth. You don't have lungs, so stop that before you pass out. Breathe through your abdomen. Along the sides. You have small holes. Force the air through those." I imagined breathing into my belly, and my sparkling vision restored to normal. I twisted to look at these holes, then grabbed for my neck with my strange hand, or foot. The pearl was there, but tiny, the size of a grain of sand.

The guard smirked at the other. "Wait for it…"

I yawned open my strange jaw and cleared my throat. An exquisite bouquet of scent hit my face, and I swept up my foot to pat it. I found my voice with a shout. "I'm smelling with my head! Where's my nose?" Engulfed in Mother Nature's perfumery, every flower's scent was overwhelmingly gorgeous. That combined with the colors made me want to weep from the beauty.

The guard explained. "You have sensilla, thin hairs with

olfactory receptors, lining your antenna. Hot tip: if you smell bananas, it's an alarm pheromone released by someone giving a sting, alerting us there's a threat nearby. Return immediately to the hive. And to get it over with, no, you don't have ears. Hairs on your body collect vibrations in the air, specifically on what you would call your knees." I waved my antennae through the breeze, as if sticking my face in a rose, soaking in the glorious fragrances.

The guard gestured to the bee behind her, who eyed me with kind curiosity. She introduced her. "This is Manda. She will take you to Queen Isabella. She'll explain everything. Well, as much as you need for now." The two sentries stood back, uncrossing their swords, and I crept forward on six unsteady legs, wings tucked in tight, following Manda obediently.

TWENTY-FIVE

JELLY

Manda paused at a wall of pale honeycomb, lightly brushed with bronze and gold. "Queen Isabella is an older queen, almost three years, Earth time. She's extremely busy, so we won't stay long."

"Earth time? Is this like a Fae dimension? Does time work differently here?"

She flinched her mandible in what I supposed was a smile based on the warmth in her voice. "You'll find the activity of the hive means the day stretches long. I can't say if we're like the Fae. Now, protocol. Bow when you meet the queen, and wait for her to tell you to rise." She looked me up and down. "You bend your front legs and rest your chin on the ground. It will be darker in there at first, but your ocellus will quickly adjust."

"Ocellus?"

"The three eyes on your head." She tapped on seven hexagonal shapes in the wall in a pattern, and a hidden door swung open, revealing a large chamber of gold, smelling like a warm beeswax candle. She tipped her head for me to step through, and I did, waiting in the entrance, my five eyes adapting to the change in light. The large door closed behind us with a sucking sound. I glanced back, shocked to find no seal.

I should have been worried. I should have paid better attention to the combination she used to unlock the door, but I was so awed by my current form and surroundings that my mandible hung open. Manda led me along the glistening floor, covered with a substance that seemed to swirl under my six feet. Several bees lined the path. Manda nodded to them. "Those are the Queen's ladies-in-waiting. They attend to her needs, dressing her, feeding her, grooming her."

We approached Queen Isabella. She wore robes of gold and black, wings dipped in silver, a heavy crown pressed on her elegant brow. The gold circlet featured spires tipped with what seemed tiny diamonds. Her head cantered ever so slightly to the side, her eyes curious. Her throne fit her body, more like a chair with a slim pulpit. She rested her front legs on top, looking down on me imperiously as I dipped into a bow. She was larger than even the guards, who seemed to dwarf Manda. Her abdomen was longer and her stinger curved, also more prominent than the other bees I'd seen, but it had fewer and shorter barbs.

Manda announced me. "Your Majesty, I present Scyphozoa Vetula, mermaid turned Fae. She says to call her Jelly." I pressed myself deeper into the floor, practically licking it.

"Rise, Jelly." Her voice was kind. I could have cried with relief if I thought these eyes would allow it. "Anna told me to expect you. What brings you to our home?"

I explained my position, including my time constraints, and hoped against hope she would just give me a drop of royal jelly and send me merrily on my way. Instead, she frowned. "I see. Hmm." Disappointment shaded her voice.

Internally I sagged, but kept my voice steady. "Your Majesty?" I stressed again that my mission was urgent. "I must complete my task as quickly as I can. Many lives depend on me."

She crossed her front legs on the pulpit. "The Seeker said to abandon yourself. While you have transformed your body with the amulet, you haven't shed your way of moving through the world. Therefore, I cannot reward you yet."

"What would you have me do?"

"Learn our ways. Manda, take her through the hive. Show her around, let her see." Queen Isabella blinked at me kindly. "Two other queens have agreed to meet you. Both hives are undergoing significant change, and will help you understand the larger picture. Come back to me after seeing them and tell me what you've learned, and I will decide if you shall receive your reward."

She turned to the bee beside her, dismissing me. "Please arrange for my lunch to be served. I've only done half of today's work. I have at least another seven hundred eggs to lay, and I'm famished. And can someone else get me today's hive numbers? I can't remember how many eggs to fertilize."

I bowed to her, thanking her as I stepped backward with my head down. Manda led me through a different door. I watched her tap a combination for entry, but it all looked the same to me. I would never remember the pattern she used. As we walked along a narrow corridor, she turned to me with quivering antennae. "Are you wise in the ways of pollinators?"

I shook my head. "I'm sorry to say I'm not. I grew up in the ocean, and the animals, at least corals, reproduce or pollinate through spawners."

"Of course," Manda said. "If you asked a human to name a pollinator, they would first say bee, meaning us, honeybees. But there are wild bees, solitary bees, bumblebees, moths, butterflies, bats, flies, wasps, birds, animals, and beetles, all contributing to the life on the planet, all of us working to keep the system going." She paused, looking at me soberly. "If we die, the Earth dies." She shook her head distractedly. "The stupid humans are wrecking it."

I snorted, instantly warming to Manda. "Aren't they

always? The ocean is disgusting. It's the reason I started this mission up top. I got so angry, I blew up a store, well, part of one, and that set off a chain of events that has led me here, to you. Please, Manda, show me everything as quickly as you can. I must succeed." My thoughts went to Mako's angry face.

The corridor curved, opening to a vast room with rows upon rows of small beds packed to the ceiling. They stacked on top of each other. I was about to ask how a bee would reach the top one without a ladder, but fortunately saved myself the embarrassment of the question as Manda stretched her wings. She said, "This is the worker bees' housing. They come here to rest at sundown." I gaped at the enormous space. Extending so far in the distance, the beds shrank until they looked like tiny doll furniture. Manda chuckled. "We are at full capacity as it's summer. We have about sixty thousand girls in the hive right now."

I stalled, turning to her with my front feet on my bee hips, disbelieving. "Sixty thousand? Sixty thousand in one hive?" My antennae waved around my head, broadcasting my amazement. "And they're all female?"

Manda grinned. "Right now, we're at ninety-eight percent female. The big boys just left for a drone run. You'll understand better when you go to the next hive. The Queen told me your assignment." She tipped her furry head to examine me. "Tricky. Abandoning yourself won't come easily. It's very seductive to become attached to yourself. Change can be difficult."

I paused. "How does the queen know my task?" Manda didn't answer. She'd already walked away, and I scrambled to catch up, slipping on the strange floor. She pointed to a much smaller room, poking her head inside. The beds were larger, and there were fewer of them.

"This is where the drones sleep until they're called to mate." She sighed. "They don't do a damned thing except screw. No architecture, no childcare, no pollen collection."

I frowned. "Just mating? That's their only purpose? That hardly seems fair. To you, I mean, to the female bees. You do all the work and they do nothing?"

One of her antennae flicked. "You misunderstand me. Without them, we'd die. Sometimes, I'm envious, but I'd rather be industrious, contribute to the collective. Mostly, I imagine they're terribly bored." She pulled the door closed, leaving a wisp of glittering smoke.

I looked closer at the shimmer that clung to everything. "What is this stuff we're walking on? It's all over the walls, too."

"The Queen's pheromones. I'm spreading it as we walk. It's part of my job description. Her pheromones announce she is healthy, and if they fade, we prepare for a new queen." She took another turn, quietly opening the door, peeking in, speaking in a hush. "Can we come in?" I peered over her shoulder. The bees inside waved us in, telling us to shut the door quickly.

I gasped and fanned at my face. "It's so warm in here."

Manda kept her voice low. "This is the nursery. We keep it between ninety-three to ninety-seven degrees. The queen lays about fifteen hundred eggs a day, one egg per cell in the brood nest. She can drop over a million eggs in her lifetime. Look, these are from this morning." Rows upon rows of hexagon structures lay horizontally, and in the center of each one, a teeny egg stood on its end, about the size of a half a grain of rice. Manda gestured across the room. The cells were slightly larger. "Those are drone eggs."

"What's the difference?"

Manda said, "If Queen Isabella fertilizes the egg, it will be female. If not, it will be male. We can turn any of the females into queens, but that would only happen if Queen Isabella's pheromones fade. You'll understand more of that later."

"But…fertilize? How? Does a drone follow behind her?"

Manda was patient with me. "Trust me, it will be explained in good time. Learn this hive first."

We wandered further down, where bees were busy working over the cells, rubbing their heads and faces and dropping a custard-like substance into each cell. Manda said, "These eggs are three days old, already curling over. They'll hatch into a tiny grub and the larval stage begins." I peeked in to see. "The nurses in here feed the babies. They are young worker bees, only six to fourteen days old themselves, meaning that's when they emerged. They care for the brood, making the royal jelly for them to eat for a few days to give them the best head start. If we were creating queens, it's all they would eat. We'll wean these babies soon, moving them onto bee bread, a fermented mixture of pollen, nectar, and bee saliva."

"So, what you feed them makes them queens? It's not some sort of selection process?"

She paused, her small foot on my shoulder. "Jelly, you must understand. Each one of us is born with the potential to be queen."

She waved toward the corner, where even smaller bees were cleaning cells. "Those girls are even younger. They emerged two days ago." She grinned as the bees furiously tidied. "We go to work immediately after we leave the cells. You start on cleaning duty, and then become a nurse bee. After that, if you're chosen, you'll become an attendant to the Queen, and spread her pheromones throughout the hive while caring for her."

"Is that what you are?"

"I am. I'm ten days old. I'll leave the Queen's service soon and go into wax production."

I pointed to a large cluster of capped cells. "What are those?"

"Worker babies. The worker larva gets three days of royal jelly, two days of bread, and then we cap the cell. The larva spins a cocoon and develops into a pupa. New workers need twelve days to develop, and drones are fourteen and a half days." She winked. "All in, we go from egg to adult in roughly two weeks."

"That's incredible!"

Manda smiled. "Isn't it? Come. I have more to show you." All around us, bees performed different tasks, working efficiently and without a solitary complaint.

I waved goodbye to the nurse bees and followed, fascinated by the intricate division of labor that kept the hive running. Manda led us into another area, close to the brood nest. I wove my antennae slowly to capture the heavenly scent. Giant mounds of wax were being shaped by industrious bees, overseen by one older one with a bounce in her step, who shouted encouragement. "Put more on that left side, Gloria! Sasha, that's a beautiful cell! Nice work!" She saw us approach and greeted us. "Hey Manda! You're a little early for your rotation, aren't you?"

"I'll be with you in two days. This is Jelly. She's visiting and Queen Isabella asked me to show her around. Jelly, this is Rachel."

Rachel stepped closer, her antennae close to mine. "Hi, Jelly. No offense, but you smell funny. You aren't sick, are you? Can't have a sick bee in the hive."

"No, ma'am, I'm not naturally a bee, so if I'm offputting, it's the magic."

"Magic, huh?" She looked over my shoulder to shout, "Francis! Francis! That's too much! It's going to sag!" She nodded to us. "Excuse me. Nice meeting you, Jam." She buzzed away.

I called after her. "It's Jelly."

Manda laughed. "Don't take it personally. We're only with her for five days."

I watched the workers, wondering where they found raw materials. Manda must have read my confusion. "All bees have four sets of wax glands." She poked me in my belly. "There, between your abdominal segments. Here, let me show you." She flew over to a cell full of honey, dipped in her tongue and took a sip.

"I'll convert this honey into wax." She grunted, then moved her second set of arms around her belly, pulling out a small piece of wax. "And presto! A wax scale. It hardens the second it hits the air." She popped it in her mouth and chewed it between her mandibles until it was soft. She spat it out and patted the malleable wad against a cell wall that looked thin.

I gaped at her. "So you just turned honey into wax? To build your house?"

Manda chuckled. "Bees are amazing."

The bees worked and worked, barely even looking up from their tasks as we moved past them. As quickly as they constructed the cells, worker bees flew in from outside to fill them. We hustled out of their way as they dumped pollen into the cells. Another bee added a touch of honey and stirred them together before mashing the mixture in tightly, filling every space in the cell. Manda nodded. "That will sustain us through the winter. Pollen can go rancid without proper care. That's why we mix it with honey."

I shook my head, not understanding. Manda explained. "Honey doesn't support bacterial life. It's the perfect preservative for the pollen." We moved on and she waved at the wall, crawling with bees who inspected every square millimeter. "They're on the repair crew, patching up the hive with propolis."

Again, I shrugged my shoulders, embarrassed to be so incredibly ignorant about such important creatures. Manda patted me kindly to remove my embarrassment. "It's bee glue, made from plant secretion mixed with honey and spit. Seals up gaps, improving temperature regulation, reducing vibration, and provides protection from pathogens, not to mention parasites and predators. We lay it on really thick before winter to stay warm while we hibernate."

"Predators?" A pang of alarm raced through my segments.

She blew out a breath, her abdomen heaving. "Everything from microscopic mites to gigantic bears threatens bees. Usually, here, we're invaded by spiders and other insects. Over in Asia, the honeybees have to contend with giant hornets." She shivered. "Can you imagine? Awful. Some birds consider us a delicacy as well, plucking us out of thin air."

She swiped over an antenna. "But truthfully, humans are our greatest threat. They overuse pesticides, eat up the wild spaces with urban expansion, and their pollution causes extreme weather changes that affect the flowers. Humans are a far larger problem than the odd skunk."

She tapped a pattern on the wall, and another invisible door swung open. "Hey girls!" She waved her foot in the air. The bees waved back, vigorously fanning the walls with their wings, while other bees came in and dumped water on their backs, dashing back out for more. This work looked exhausting.

Manda said, "They're cooling the hive, directing the hotter air outside so we don't cook to death. It's called fanning. The other girls are the water carriers, keeping the fanners from overheating." She frowned. "I'm not looking forward to this shift."

I was flagging from taking in so much information. Manda noticed. "Here, have a bite to eat." I sipped on honey, which burst with the flavor of flowers and clover. It was the same honey that Anna used in her healing tea. Manda passed me a pellet. "This is bee bread. It's what we eat."

"Gods, that's delicious! I've had the honey before, from Anna. You know Anna?"

Manda sipped her honey, chasing her bite of bread. "Everyone knows Anna. She's very good at telling the bees."

I tipped my head. "I'm not sure what that means."

"Ah. It's an ancient tradition. Good beekeepers treat their hives like extended family members, and tell the bees the news of the household. Richard comes as well to share stories of the wider world. Both of them visit every day without fail."

She winked at me. "Anna told us you were coming. So, the Soul Seeker? Is she as awful as Anna described?"

I shuddered, shivers running down my fuzzy body. "She's disgusting, a vile creature who has pieced herself together from the skin of others. She eats souls to stay alive. She is most definitely awful. And the River Thames is a close second. I had to swim it." She nodded, thinking to herself. We were quiet for a while. I cocked my head at her. "Can I ask you a personal question?"

"Of course."

I wondered how best to phrase it, choosing to go with a blunt approach. "Does it bother you that your brief life is all work?"

She smiled and brushed her legs over her head, cleaning her antennae in the groove on her elbow. She nudged me as I watched her. "Clean your antennae. We identify each other by touching them. Don't be the bee with poor hygiene. To answer your question, no, it doesn't bother me. Our work is important. We live to serve. We live and we die with purpose to a higher good, and in doing so, we ensure the flowers, plants, and fruits keep growing, providing food, shelter, and beauty to all of Earth's creatures. It's humbling to be so small, yet so important."

I sat with that, copying her and washing my face after eating. Living with such a clear purpose must be freeing despite working from dawn till dusk. She smiled, stroking my front leg. "I've enjoyed meeting you, Jelly. I have to hand you over now. I'm not allowed to show you the next part. I'm not ready to take my flight outside the hive yet." She looked up. "Ah, here she is. This is Lisa. You'll shadow her for the rest of the day."

"Wait? Are we going outside? Flying? I mean, I only just got these wings."

Manda patted my face. "You'll be fine. Magic protects you. Jelly, you have your own larger purpose. You're here to learn our ways, and earn back your soul. Go with Lisa. I will see you later. I must go to the Queen." With a nod and a smile, she left.

Lisa rolled her neck, as if stretching. "I have an errand to do. Wait here for me." I sat on the edge of a honeycomb cell, watching the fanners tirelessly move the air currents with their small wings. When one paused to rest, another took her place. It was an endless activity, and it exhausted me just watching it.

In some ways, it reminded me of my life on the reef, ceaselessly working to help the sea life navigate the pollution, always busy, the work never-ending. Except I'd always worked alone.

TWENTY-SIX

JELLY

I must have fallen asleep. Lisa buzzed nearby, waking me. "Hey Jelly, we've got miles to cover, and I found a beautiful cluster of lavender earlier. I'd like to get more."

"Oh, sorry!" I jumped up, swallowing the lump of nerves in my throat, and followed Lisa, my anxiety spiking as the fresh air hit my face. "Lisa, I have no idea what I'm doing. I've never flown before." I flexed my four wings, trying to flap them up and down like a bird and going nowhere fast.

Lisa giggled. "You're magical, so it will come quickly. Flap and rotate at the same time. Use short, choppy strokes, twist, swivel, twist." I followed her example as she showed me, sweeping my wings back and forth. "Your two sets of wings connect with hooks when you fly, so they work together to give you lift. Go a little faster." I hovered up in the air, squealing. She grinned and said, "We beat our wings about two hundred and thirty times a second, so expect to get tired."

I plonked down. "Two hundred and thirty times a second? Are you kidding me? These wings are so delicate."

She laughed at my expression. "Once we become foragers, we'll travel over five hundred miles and work until we die. All the flying wears on our wings. When they get too tattered, we usually just drop from the sky. If you die at the hive, an undertaker bee has to fly you away, and that's simply a waste of resources. I plan to fall into the flowers." She grinned at me. "Look at your face. How did you think it happened?" I merely shook my head. Dying alone seemed so tragic.

Her tone softened. "Jelly, about a thousand of us die every day. It's natural. Now, before we take off, I need to dance."

"Dance? Now? How?"

She waggled her bum. "It's how we communicate where the food is, and if it's high quality. My dance tells the other foragers the lavender is ready. I'll give the coordinates and the distance, in case someone's too tired to make a long journey. We also have a round dance, which I'll do once we reach the lavender, and a shake dance if we need more workers. That one feels silly, shaking my belly back and forth. If you see me pause and make funny movements when we're flying, I'm just dancing. Hover next to me, okay?"

She raced out of the entrance with a running start, launching herself into the air. I copied her and squealed as I initially dropped low, but quickly found my wings, zipping after Lisa with a scream of elation. She did indeed pause several times, dipping to one side more than the other, wiggling her bum in a figure-eight pattern, pointing out our destination. Several bees followed us. We arrived in a thick patch of purple flowers, the colors so vibrant I blinked several times. Lisa noticed.

"Bee eyes are phenomenal. Flowers look like runways to us. Some of them literally map out our flight plan, so we zoom straight to the good stuff. Smart, huh? The flowers make sure they get pollinated. Go hang out on that rose and watch. We won't be the only ones here." She sucked up a flower's nectar with her long, straw-like tongue. She called over. "I'll hold this in my honey stomach. If I get hungry, I can release some of the nectar, but I'll try not to. The hive needs it."

Butterflies flitted around the bees, chatting and catching up on gossip as they sipped from the flowers. Slower, heavier bumblebees came by, one of them begging my pardon as she fumbled around on my rose, almost sending me flying as I slipped on the petal. Her body was furry and covered in yellow pollen. A small zap shot through my body, making me squeak. The bumblebee apologized again. "Sorry, love, it's our nature. We pick up an electrical charge as we fly. It's called scrabbling, and attracts the pollen."

Down on the ground, beetles rummaged around, climbing on the shorter flowers for food, dragging pollen from blossom to blossom. A ladybug nipped up and folded her bright red wings with black polka dots, startling me. She tipped her head. "Oh, excuse me! I didn't know this flower was occupied."

The bumblebee lurched over the vibrant pink rose. She tipped her head at us. "I was just leaving." As she lifted her heavy body on impossibly small wings, the rose petal rebounded and I slid off and shrieked. Under the flower petals, a cluster of pale bugs tore through the delicate flesh of the receptacle. The ladybug hovered beside me and grinned, rubbing her front feet together in glee.

Her voice was wicked. "Aphids. Masses of them." She flew to them, gripping one and ripping into it. She swallowed her mouthful. "I eat about fifty of these little plant suckers a day. This is a feast." I flexed my wings and returned to the upper side of the rose, leaving her to enjoy her meal.

I watched Lisa with fascination as she stuck her proboscis into flower after flower, collecting pollen by default, dusting her face yellow. She swept her head and antennae into small pouches on her hind legs and found me on the rose. "Okay, my baskets are full, and I've got a load of nectar. Time to go back to the hive."

"What are those called?"

She lifted a leg and looked at it. "Technically, corbicula, but we just call them pollen baskets. Ready?" She did a wiggle and a waggle, telling her sisters she was heading back. The return journey took far longer as she was heavy with nectar and pollen. We paused for the guards.

They confirmed we belonged, and we flew until we stopped in an area filled with house bees, young worker bees. Lisa passed the nectar over, mouth to mouth. She rested while the house bees digested the nectar. Lisa said, "They're adding a special enzyme called invertase. It converts the nectar into two simple sugars." She looked at my blank stare and clarified. "It becomes honey."

The nectar went from bee to bee. With each pass, the moisture content reduced, becoming thicker. Once at the right consistency, the final house bee deposited it into an open honeycomb cell. More bees arrived to fan the fresh honey. Lisa said, "They do that night and day to dry it and ripen it. If they don't, the honey will ferment, wasting all of our work. Look, those are ready to be capped." Worker bees scrambled over a row of filled and ripened cells, pulling wax from their bellies, sealing the cell and making it airtight.

"How can you tell when it's ready?"

Lisa shrugged. "We just do. No one can explain it." She winked. "Must be magic. Okay, I need to dump my pollen." She did this herself, dropping it directly in a cell. As the last grain fell off, another bee arrived and stirred in a drop of honey. We repeated this journey to the lavender six more times. We were on our seventh trip when a bee in the distance danced in a different direction. Lisa watched the bee do a waggle dance. "Oop. The lavender's exhausted. We're heading south to a new destination."

We flew and flew until the sun slipped down for the day.

After our dinner of bee bread and honey, I washed my face and antennae, every segment on my body aching with fatigue. Lisa motioned me back to the enormous sleeping area. "You were great! You can bunk next to me. Manda sleeps above you." She led me to one close to the floor.

I climbed into bed after scratching a line in the wax wall next to my bed to keep track of the days as a bee. "I'm exhausted. I can't believe how hard you all work."

She grinned, already pulling her blanket up to her chin. Around us, small snores sounded from sixty thousand beds. "Honey sleep, Jelly."

Honey sleep, not sweet dreams. I'd have to take that home to Mako. A pang of longing accompanied the thought of my mate, an ache of deep love mixed with sorrow. I missed him. I missed everyone. Leoht had remained silent despite my attempts to reach her. Maybe she couldn't speak to me in this form. With a foot on my throat, caressing the pearl, I passed out.

Manda shook me awake in the early dawn, dropping her voice to a whisper. "I've been thinking of you all night. Can you tell me why you're doing all this?"

I rubbed my eyes with my feet. "My mate's brother is trapped in a Fae dimension, and I need to be complete in myself before we can rescue him." I dropped my legs, sighing. "So much is riding on my shoulders, Manda. I just need...I have to succeed. Every day I'm here is one more day that he's there. It's all I can think about."

She frowned. "Focus on your growth, Jelly. Put yourself first."

I sighed. "That's the problem. I'm already too selfish." I added with a sad whisper, "At least, that's what my mate and best friend think."

Manda nodded, running an antenna through her elbow. "But to be whole, to find yourself, you need to be selfish. It's not always a bad thing, but don't lose sight of the bigger picture." She looked at me intensely, as if dropping a hint. "Come on. Lisa's waiting."

I noticed several shallow dishes on pedestals with rocks in them. I wondered aloud what they were. Lisa blinked five eyes in surprise. "Bee baths. You haven't been yet? You'll die without water. I'll leave you with the water girls for a while. See what you can learn from them."

A sassy bee named Sarah took me under her wing. She wasn't a forager yet, and collecting water for the hive was her job. We balanced together on a rock in the dish. She cautioned me. "Don't fall in. If you do, use small surface flaps of your wings and skim back to safety. You can't swim in this body. Must be strange for you, considering you're a mermaid." She laughed. "Don't look so shocked. The hive shares all information. But you can drown in the tiniest of puddles because you breathe through your body. Those little holes on your sides are called spiracles, and if they fill with water, you're done for."

Sarah crept toward the water, waving me forward. "Anna set up the bee baths. The witches refill them daily. Once a week, they clean them. We're so grateful for these baths. Otherwise, we'd have to go to the pond with all the hungry birds." She shuddered her wings at the thought. "We need water to dilute the honey, especially if it crystallizes, and to keep the hive cool, and of course, to feed the babies. It takes lots of water to make royal jelly."

She dipped in her antenna to sample the water first. Satisfied, she stuck her proboscis in and slurped. She motioned me forward with one leg. "It stores in your honey stomach, and once you're full, we'll take it to the hive." I followed her lead, sucking in the water, rich with minerals. Delicious.

We flew back and forth at the high point of the sun. We sprayed the fanners with water, or passed it off to other worker bees assigned to either babies or honey production. They took it from us tongue to tongue. Once the workers ignored us, Sarah waved me over to sit on the rocks. I flexed my wings in the sun, enjoying the warmth. She looked up and grinned as a bee waggled her way toward us. "Lisa's back. More nectar gathering for you."

The days blurred. Each night, I frowned as I etched in another line in the wax by my bed. I needed the royal jelly. How long did I need to labor until I was worthy? We rose before the sun for breakfast, discussing the day's foraging and where to focus our attention. Anyone who wanted to speak spoke. Then, we worked ceaselessly until dusk.

An English summer meant the days stretched long, and because the weather was cooperative, sunny, we easily put in fifteen-hour days. Once the sun set, we would return to the hive and help with processing nectar and pollen, and clean up debris. Younger bees, who still worked in the hive, slept in shorter shifts, tiptoeing in the dark to monitor the temperature of the hive, protect against invaders, and check on the children. Each night, Manda and I talked in hushed voices, our friendship blooming like the surrounding flowers.

One morning I woke, ready to put in my day's work, but Lisa's foot on my shoulder made me pause. She hopped back and forth in excitement. "The Queen has requested you." I wolfed down my breakfast and wiped my face. Maybe she would forgo my need to meet more queens. Maybe she'd give me the drop of liquid gold and I could go home. Lisa escorted me to the throne room, pressed the entry code, and departed.

I walked in on hopeful feet, confident I was soon to be free. My excitement dashed to the floor as Isabella heaved a great sigh at my entrance. She waved away her ladies, leaving me bowing before her. "Rise, Jelly." She stepped down from her giant throne and beckoned me toward a comfortable seating area behind the throne, with furniture made from wax shaped to accommodate a bee's body, cradling me. She gathered her wings around her like a cloak and settled. I sat silently, apprehensive.

She offered me refreshments, and while I sipped honey from a wax goblet, she spoke. "Bees used to be worshiped. The Ancient Egyptians believed the Sun God, Ra, cried us into existence."

I lifted a foot to interrupt her. "Begging your pardon, Your Majesty, but did you say Ra? His daughter, Goddess Bastet, marked me, or clawed me."

She winked one of her enormous eyes. "She did. Honeybees are messengers between Earth and the spirit realm. We have connections to places and people beyond what you can see. Bastet has been very busy. She visited your ocean goddess Kelbazi, the one with the sea snakes as hair. Kelbazi spoke to the salamanders in the Hellhole, who spoke to the twins, who gave you the hint about a drop of gold. Many powers want to ensure your success. Everything depends on it."

My mandible opened and closed. I spluttered. "I wondered how it all happened so smoothly." I dipped my tongue into my honey, not daring to ask for my royal jelly, although every part of me wanted to.

She set down her goblet. "Back to my story. Indigenous cultures still revere us. Our honey, propolis, wax, royal jelly and venom are essential elements in their medicines. They honor us with celebrations." She adjusted her crown. "Many modern humans are unaware of our contribution to their lives. We are responsible for three-quarters of the world's vegetable, fruit, nut, and seed reproduction. Without us, the world would starve, and I can't for the life of me understand why they remain in the dark. Pesticides, particularly glyphosate and neonicotinoids, are killing us."

"Yes, Richard told me about the chemicals. When I went to

the superstore, I passed through the garden center first, and I saw an entire shelf, a massive thing, devoted to pesticides. The labels on the jugs had skulls and crossbones, with 'poison' and 'caution' written capital letters. It's right there on the bottle. I don't understand why they use them, Your Highness. I truly don't."

"They do not understand the sorrow of bees, and all will suffer from their ignorance." She clapped her feet together, and her collection of ladies bustled into the room. Queen Isabella turned to me. "Your work in my hive is done. You must move on to the next." My heart dropped. She called to a young bee standing awkwardly, twisting her front feet together. She must be new. "Chantalle, take Jelly to Lisa. She will escort her to Queen Candice's hive for the next part of her mission."

The queen nodded to me once and turned her back, sweeping across the floor, her handmaidens fussing over her cloak as she left. I wanted to call after her, beg her for the drop of royal jelly, plead for my task to be complete. My wings sagged in resignation.

Chantalle stepped forward, smiling shyly. "Ready?" With a nod, we exited through a different door, leading to a corridor I now recognized. The guards at the entrance barely acknowledged me, despite seeing me day after day. We waited, making idle chitchat until Lisa arrived. Chantalle bowed to both of us and flew back inside.

Lisa waddled toward me. "It's a beautiful day! I understand you're leaving us." I nodded. She said, "Come with me while I dump my pollen." We walked to the pots, her chattering along the way. "Queen Candice leads the hive to the east. She's old, nearly five, and the word on the wind is that her pheromones faded, causing the worker bees to prepare for a successor."

"Meaning the larvae only ate royal jelly, right?"

"That's right. The royal jelly turns on their reproductive

system. The workers fed twenty of them, starting two weeks ago. Only one of them will be queen. I wish I could stay and watch."

I stiffened in alarm. "You won't be there with me?"

Lisa shook her head. "It's not my hive. I'm to deliver you and leave."

"Oh," I said in a small voice. "Okay, then." After cleaning her legs, we made our way to the entrance, and I nodded to the guards. "I guess this is goodbye. Thank you for keeping them safe." The guards pulled back their swords without comment, letting us pass. Lisa did her dance, telling her sisters where she was going, and we flew into the morning sky.

TWENTY-SEVEN

JELLY

Lisa slowed as we approached the next hive, wiggling her body while projecting her voice against the wind. "I am delivering Jelly, the mermaid bee! She's here to see the queen." She didn't fly up to the hive, hovering beside me. Her voice held an edge. "Bye, Jelly. Try not to freak out today, okay? It's brutal, what you will see, but it's just how it is." She turned, waggled, and zoomed away. I landed at the entrance and dipped my head at the guards.

One guard grimaced. "The magical fish bee. We've been expecting you. Picked a hell of a day to show up. Let me get your escort. Wait here." She disappeared inside the hive, and another bee seamlessly took her place, eyeing me up and down. I wrestled back the urge to fidget with my antennae, nervous to meet these new bees, as the energy in this hive was jittery. Bees flitted past, glancing at me suspiciously. The first guard returned, bringing a lady-in-waiting, or so I assumed, until I noticed the sword at her side.

"I'm not a threat," I said, holding up two feet. "I'm just here as an observer."

The guard, my escort, grunted. "Tensions are high today.

We're not taking any chances with strangers." She spun and walked into the hive, pausing with a glance over her shoulder to ensure I followed. "My name is Tabitha. Do not scream and do not interfere. If you do, I will cut you down."

Wow. So unfriendly. I kept my thoughts to myself and bobbed my head in understanding. She ushered me into a space lined with guard bees, alert and shifting on their legs. When I hesitated, she pushed me forward, and took a space against the wall, wondering what we were looking at. Twenty domes filled the center of the area, like peanuts balancing on end. Nurse bees hovered near each one, waiting, wringing their front feet nervously in white aprons. Tabitha leaned over. "It should start soon."

"What's going on?"

"You'll see." Tabitha ground her mandible tightly. She nodded at the hovering bees. "The nurse bees are tired. When feeding new queens, ten thousand of them are on duty until they cap the cells. Until that happens, the larva gets fed roughly every forty seconds. It takes a lot of resources to create a new queen."

"New queen? Is Queen Candice dead?"

Tabitha ignored my question. "Look." She raised a foot, waving at one peanut. "It's starting." Her head swung to the right. "Okay, here we go." I followed her stare, seeing wiggling at the bottom of another oddly shaped cell. It was being cut open from the inside, the movements frantic.

The nearest nurse bee launched into action, helping from the outside. Three more peanuts broke at the bottom. Soon, over half of the cells were trembling, the odd leg poking out while jaws chewed maniacally through the wax. Three more. Then another. All the bees were edgy, shifting, waiting. A strange sound pierced the air, accompanied by the underlying buzz of the bees. It was a piping noise, almost like a duck quacking or tooting. Several more joined the first chirp.

"What's that sound?" I twisted my front feet together, the hairs on my body standing up. The air was thick with suspense.

Tabitha said somberly, "It's a battle cry."

The bottoms of several peanuts swung open, like hinged lids, and the princesses fell to the floor, struggling up on new legs. Some still fought to exit their cells. Then the carnage began. The newly freed bees heaved themselves close, thrusting their stingers into the cells, piercing the wax walls and its occupant. Screams rang out as the sisters fell on the cells with savagery.

Alarmed, I took a step forward, but Tabitha pulled me back to the wall. "Do not interfere!"

I struggled against her sturdy leg. "They're stabbing each other! We have to stop them!"

Tabitha's face was grim. "It's survival of the fittest. A queen bee's stinger is smooth, letting her sting over and over without dying." Suffering shrieks pierced the air. "We call it *principissae homicidium.*"

"Homicide of princesses?" I breathed out, horrified, my body going slack as my bee bread breakfast worked its way up my throat. I turned my face to the wall, wishing I could block out the sound of the screaming. "I can't watch."

Tabitha swung me around and held me in place. "You must witness the sorrow of bees."

I clutched at the tiny pearl at my throat, yelling for Leoht in my head. I wanted a friend with me, desperate for comfort, but she remained absent, leaving me alone in this ghastly experience. Carcasses lay on the floor, and legs hung limply from cells, liquid splashing onto the floor in puddles, the princesses slaughtered in their beds.

Four remained, their chirping cries frenzied as they lunged for each other. Tears streamed down their faces as their stingers ran true. One bee's wing tore off, and she dropped her head in defeat, waiting for the killing blow. They wrestled and stabbed until only one young bee remained, her abdomen heaving as she struggled for breath.

Bees dressed in black arrived, solemnly dragging the bodies away, a clear liquid streaking the floor. I groped for Tabitha, not taking my eyes off the bees. "Is that blood?"

Tabitha squeezed my foot once and released it. "Mortuary bees remove the dead from the hive. They will fly them far away for their final rest." My heart clutched at the waste of life. "Our blood is clear, called hemolymph. We don't have blood vessels like most animals. It circulates freely in our bodies." She cleared her throat, pulling her wings in tight. "This is the worst part." I could hear the tears in her voice as she struggled to hold her composure.

"What? That wasn't awful enough? What could be worse?"

Tabitha's face crumbled moments later, and she lowered herself, bowing her head. I followed suit, but kept my eyes up to see what could outweigh that cruel butchery. An elderly queen entered the chamber, now relieved of the dead bodies of her daughters. The room collectively murmured. "Queen Candice. Thank you, Queen Candice."

She held her chin high, her gold crown faded, the sparkling stones dull, and even I could see she was tired. She smiled at the one remaining princess, who had also kneeled in her mother's presence. She spoke in a calm voice. "I name you Charlotte, queen of the hive. Rise, daughter, and take your destiny. I will not defend myself. My reign is over."

Tabitha's voice broke in her whisper. "Sometimes the old queens fight back. But Candice knows it's her time."

The Queen stepped close to the princess, saying, "So strong. So brave. Stand, Charlotte. Lead the hive well, daughter of mine. Do your mother a kindness, and stab for the heart." Queen Candice kneeled at the feet of the hesitant princess, holding her stare. "Be quick, dear. You have responsibilities now."

Charlotte closed her eyes for a moment, as if begging the heavens for forgiveness. She whipped them open, plunging her stinger into her mother's chest with a tortured shriek. Regicide. Matricide. Murder. I'd seen bad things in my life, terrible things, but nothing compared to this. I spun my head to the side and upchucked the contents of my small stomach. I bit down tears I could not shed. While every bee in the room mourned, none of them cried.

Charlotte pulled her stinger out quickly, lowering to the floor, cradling her mother's head. She whispered to her, and smoothed her antennae with her feet, holding her until the old queen lay still. Charlotte's face was stoic. She settled her mother softly and stepped away, turning her back on the body. One of her acquired ladies-in-waiting gently removed the crown from the former queen.

Mortuary bees quickly collected Candice and flew away. The bee holding the crown approached Charlotte with a bow, lifting it high. Charlotte took it and placed it steadily on her brow, a ripple of gold surrounding her, lighting up the crown till it glowed, hitting us all with her powerful scent. Every bee in the space shouted. "Long live Queen Charlotte!" The guards thumped their front feet to their chests.

Charlotte acknowledged us quietly. "Stand." We did, me on shaky bee knees. She looked at me pointedly. "I understand we have a magical guest." I swallowed as she strolled toward me, her stinger glistening with the blood of her sisters and mother. She tilted her head as she spoke. "Every drop of information regarding this hive passed to me when I killed my mother. Come with me, Jelly. We have much to discuss."

I glanced at Tabitha, who had smoothed her expression as the new queen approached. She nodded to me crisply. I followed the queen, trailing behind her ladies, who wafted Charlotte's pheromones on the walls and the floor, erasing the old queen's existence, save the memories of those who had treasured her.

We entered a throne room, far grander than Isabella's, with wax columns and beams for decoration. I was told to wait. The Queen's ladies rubbed their heads furiously, feeding her royal jelly, while others fussed with her wings and her robes. Eventually, she spoke with an authoritative voice, full of steel. "Leave us." Her eyes swung to me. "Everyone except you."

Her ladies curtsied, "Milady," and "Highness," sweeping from the chamber as fast as their wings could take them.

When the door sucked shut, leaving the two of us in silence, Charlotte burst into tears, causing me to gasp. "Oh! Oh, Your Highness!" I rushed to her and stopped dead, uncertain of what I should do. If she were Mori, I would fling my arms around her. I wasn't sure how to approach a crying queen, but she was literally only a few minutes old and grieving. "How can I help?"

She buried her face in her feet, her crown slightly askew. "There's nothing you can do. I killed them all." She sobbed. "My sisters…my mother." She lifted tear-filled eyes to me. "How is this normal? We're praised for being a cooperative, such a shining example of society, and yet…" She hiccuped through tears. "And yet, it begins with a barbaric act. I murdered them!"

I took a step closer, my voice quiet and aching with empathy. "It was awful, Your Majesty, absolutely terrible. I am so sorry for your loss."

Her breath hitched. "Could you have done that? I started my life with murder."

I swallowed thickly. "It was your duty as queen. Because it was kill or be killed. You had no choice. But that is so often the way of women."

Her breathing settled, her abdomen not pulsing so rapidly. "You sound familiar with this."

I nodded sadly. "I am. Would you like to know more?"

"Please. I would like the distraction."

I told her about the mermaids, our forced Procreation Missions, and the Trident that dictated our lives. I explained the ritual that turned me from Mers to Fae. I spoke of how I'd changed since coming to the surface, and how everything seemed to hinge on my success, leaving me no option but to follow through. I ended with a sad smile. "My mate calls me his savage queen. The world gave me a moniker when I blew up the store. The Queen of the Blue Lagoon." My smile faded. "But he and I left on bad terms. He's angry with me."

"Because you chose yourself?" Her voice lilted with humor, as if my guilt was unjustified. I shrugged a shoulder. She smiled and said, "Oh, goodness. You have a soft heart under that bravado, don't you?" She sighed. "I won't have a mate. I will mate, as in doing the act, with more drones than seems decent, but it's our way. I will have devotion from my hive, but a mate, a single bee who loves me above all else? I won't have that. You're lucky, Jelly."

She sat on her throne for the first time, testing it. She'd recovered from her outpouring of grief, her crown on straight and robes fluffed out. "You've seen the horrendous way we come into power." Her mandible clacked together in resignation. "I want you to witness the further devastation of being Queen Bee." She rose, and I curtsied, making her laugh. "Thank you for the pomp and circumstance, but it's unnecessary between the two of us." She eyed me. "But you will bow when there are others present." She clapped her feet together and her ladies filed in immediately. She ordered them with ease, born to the role. "Dress me for my flight and find a guard to escort Jelly. I want her to watch."

One lady gasped, dropping into a deep bow. "Your Highness, that is highly irregular!"

"But necessary," Queen Charlotte said dismissively. "It is my wish. Make it so."

"Yes, Milady." The bee dipped further before hurrying

away. She returned with Tabitha and another, who introduced herself as Penny, both of them bending before their new queen.

Queen Charlotte said dryly, "It is time for my mating flight. I don't need you all nipping at me to make me go." She turned to my guards. "Keep Jelly away from the drones, but close enough she can see. She must see."

"Ma'am," they said in unison. We left the queen preparing.

I turned to Tabitha as we waited outside. "What's happening now?"

Penny answered. "She is currently a virgin queen. No one in the hive will accept her until she mates. If a queen is reluctant, the bees chase her around until she goes. Queen Charlotte has backbone, wanting to get out there immediately."

Tabitha's voice was proud. "It's a nice day, so no rain delay. I'm happy for her to have a pretty day. It's the only time she'll leave the hive."

"Just this once?"

Tabitha nodded. "Just once in her entire life, unless we grow too large and swarm. Now, a little background. We will escort the queen to a drone den, a congregation area. They are waiting for her. It's far from here." Tabitha frowned. "To avoid accidentally mating one of her brothers."

I blinked, a sour apprehension in my stomach. Tabitha huffed as she read my expression. "Drones come from the other hives. They perfume the air with their pheromones to attract her, but that's mostly for show as they use the same congregation areas year after year. We'll have a lot of strangers there, gathering from two hundred colonies, and there will be about twenty-five thousand individuals waiting for their shot with the queen."

My mandible hit the floor. "Twenty-five thousand? Twenty-five thousand boy bees are going to mate with a virgin queen? She's been alive for less than an hour! Won't that kill her?"

Tabitha chuckled. "No, not all of them. Maybe twenty at most will be successful. They don't have stingers, so they won't hurt her." She looked me in the eye. "Trust me, it hurts them far more than it hurts her." I opened my mouth to ask more, but she shook her head. "You'll see."

The door sucked open and Queen Charlotte swept past us. We dropped our torsos forward. Penny rose from her bow and said, "Here we go." We followed silently, my nerves making my wings vibrate. As we walked the corridors, bees curtsied, wishing their queen good fortune on her flight.

We reached the entrance, and Charlotte turned to me, dropping her voice. "If you're ever fighting with your mate, thinking he's terrible and you hate him, I want you to remember this moment. I want you to remember my life and everything I sacrifice for the hive."

I promised with an enthusiastic and somewhat frightened nod. "I will."

Charlotte said, "The closest drone den is a mile away. Watch my back for birds." She paused, inhaling through her abdomen deeply, antennae tasting the air. She smiled at the sun. "It's a beautiful day to fly."

We launched and followed her as she shot straight for the congregation area, attracted by the smell of the males. At first, I couldn't detect any scent over the perfume of the flowers, but then a heavy musk filled my antennae. I sensed the low buzz of the males as my whole body vibrated, especially my legs. As we approached, thousands of eyes swung toward us, immediately attracted to Charlotte. She flew fast and high, so only the fittest drones could reach her. The chase began. Drones took to the air in a swarm.

The guards held me away from the fray, but close enough to witness. We were high in the air, and thankfully, no wind buffeted my wings. Charlotte flew as hard as she could, challenging them to catch her, circling around close so I could see. The first drone reached her and grabbed her with all six legs, straddling her and wrapping his body around hers. The mating was over in five seconds, ending with a loud pop. The drone screamed and fell to his death.

I cried out to my guards. "What just happened? Was he supposed to do that?"

Tabitha tried a clinical approach. "He, the drone, contracts his abdominal muscles, increasing the pressure of blood in his body, and inflates his… uh, endophallus, shooting his sperm with substantial force."

It seemed Tabitha was uncomfortable with sex. "Endophallus? Penis?"

She nodded with relief. "Precisely. As he transfers his semen, he becomes paralyzed, and flips over backward as he ejaculates."

I frowned. "That's a hell of an orgasm."

Tabitha grimaced. "Literally explosive. His semen blasts through the queen's sting chamber and into an organ where she stores all the sperm she'll ever have. This is it. She'll collect all of it now. The drone's release is so strong it ruptures the endophallus, and the bulb remains inside the queen."

"Wait. His dick blows off?" I couldn't help but screech the words. The drones stared, but quickly turned back to their prize in the sky, chasing Charlotte with renewed vigor.

Tabitha swiped her antenna. "The next drone to reach her will extract the, um, ruptured piece, and do the same thing." As she spoke, another pop quaked the air, followed by an agonizing scream as the drone dropped like a stone, yellow liquid shooting upward from his torn belly. Then another, and another, and another.

I gagged. "I can't…I can't do this. I can't watch this." I covered my eyes with my front feet.

Tabitha yanked them down with a hiss. "You can and you will!" She sounded furious. She turned my chin to face toward the mating. "You will witness this if you wish to have your soul back!"

Tears streamed down my face as drone after drone plummeted to the earth below, sacrificing their lives for the continuation of the species. Charlotte whizzed at speeds that made her blur, ensuring only the fastest could mate her. After the seventeenth drone dropped from the sky, she raced to us. "I'm done. I'm full." She sped away without waiting for a reply, leaving the drone den behind her. They didn't follow, disappointment drooping over their wings.

We flew hard, guarding Charlotte's sides. I yelled to Tabitha. "What happens to the drones who don't mate?"

"They wait for another virgin queen."

We approached the hive entrance, landing on light feet. Charlotte swept into the hive, immediately surrounded by her ladies. I stepped forward, but Penny held me back. I expanded my belly for breath. "And then what? They come home for the winter?"

Tabitha's face crushed down. She cleared her throat, but no words came out. Penny answered me softly. "The boys die. There isn't enough food for them to survive the cold months. They are driven from the hive in the autumn. They will starve or freeze." She shook her head sadly. "The queen creates new drones in the spring." She waved a fuzzy foot in the air. "And we start again."

My mandible dropped open in disbelief. "No! They're born to what, get one shag, which, if they're successful, rips them apart at their genitals? And if they fail, you kick them out?"

Penny spoke quietly. "It is the sorrow of bees."

I exploded. "Oh, stop with that philosophizing bullshit! This is insanity!"

Tabitha narrowed her eyes at me. "We are lucky, Jelly. There are bees who don't have access to clean water and wildflowers. We have plenty to eat, very few predators, and a doting team of humans who care for us. They ensure we survive the winter when we don't have enough food. We live on land without pesticides, with fresh air. You don't get to judge us!"

I dropped my head in shame. "I'm sorry. Of course, you're right. I can't possibly understand."

Tabitha leaned closer, staring with wide eyes. I paid close attention. "But you must, Jelly. You must understand." A messenger came from inside the hive, whispering to my guards. Tabitha and Penny both paled. Tabitha said, "Well, it turns out you won't be visiting the hive to the west. They're currently in a swarm."

I balked. I needed to see three queens. "A swarm? What does that mean?"

Penny sighed. "It means Queen Jaima is looking for a new home. It's a secondary method of reproducing. She'll leave half of her colony behind. They will have fed the larvae for a new queen. Queen Jaima will resettle with the bees she takes with her." She rubbed her antennae distractedly.

Tabitha sighed. "I need a sweet drink after all that. Let's refuel and discuss what to do."

TWENTY-EIGHT

MORI

Jelly had been gone for fifteen days, and yes, I was counting. Was she dead? It could easily happen to a bee. I assumed Mako would feel it if his mate died, and I pestered him daily for updates. So far, so good, at least we hoped.

I spent my days pouring through the books in the study, relishing the vast array of topics, crawling through the Fae folklore to better understand them. Anna had the best selection of reference books I'd ever seen. Jared would faint from the glorious collection.

I trained with Mew, Roan, and Branko at different times of the day, rarely overlapping, as Branko and Roan growled at each other when I took a hit, puffing their chests as if to defend me. Mew was a godsend, always supportive, pushing me harder each day. I could fully relax with him, as nothing sexual had ever colored the waters of our friendship. He encouraged my mind to explore beyond boundaries, dropping tidbits of information I would follow up later in the library.

Branko taught me to fight with swords, polishing up old armor from the basement, as well as an array of daggers he'd uncovered. More often than not, our sparring ended with our bodies clashing together for wild kisses, exhilarated from the physical exertion. The hotter I became, the cooler his skin, and it was a delicious frisson after each session.

Roan worked with the mental side of my magic, and I'd immediately insisted he teach me the hands-free method for shielding from the birds, foxes, deer, frogs, toads, and multiple insects who regaled me with their incessant chatter. I'd almost gone out of my mind one night, yelling at Icy to catch the damned mouse who lived in my baseboards, preaching to me about cheeses.

The technique was brazenly simple, a visualization of a shroud pulling over the mind, anchored with a silver stake. Grateful to have free use of both hands, I'd immediately saluted him with raised middle fingers. He'd tackled me to the ground, kissing the scowl off my face until I squealed. He taught me advanced meditation to silence the chatter in my head, allowing the chaos of information in my brain to sift away into a solitary, useful thread, tying together seemingly unrelated material. He rewarded my efforts with sweet replenishments for my magic.

Anna and I dove into the origins of Surfecti magic, the multiple strains who had allied and who had fallen from favor. Richard took part in these sessions, delighting me with anecdotes, making me laugh and appreciate the Surfecti's rich history. The fallout with the Mers had stung, as I could appreciate both sides, and I mourned for the loss the Mers had suffered from their stubborn refusal to work with those on the surface.

We'd contacted the Shaman through the mirror, and she'd waved off my concerns about the state of the government. The mermaids were still rioting, but they planned to hold an election, something we'd never attempted before. Usually, seats of power passed through bloodlines, but the lack of merbabes made that difficult. She and my father were heading the charge. She told me not to worry; they had everything handled, but I did.

Other than that, I learned to cook, mostly bake, with Veda.

I was obsessed with strong spices, especially cinnamon and cloves. All of it was an adequate distraction, and I tried not to panic that Jelly was taking too long, as any mention of her absence sent Mako into a tailspin.

Icy spent most of her time on my bed, sleeping on my pillow, curled around my head. Every night, I had wild dreams that she'd taken me places. Early this morning, while it was still dark, I'd woken to a deep voice saying, "Soon." I'd thought it was Roan or Branko, but the voice was deeper than theirs, and carried a strange vibration, making me wake feeling nauseous. I'd flicked on the light, finding only the cat there, purring contentedly, making smacking noises as she slept.

Tonight, it was late, well past dinner, and Anna and Richard had retired to bed. Mako had escaped to his room with a giant book on the Fae, and Veda was busy with tomorrow's bread, leaving me, Roan, and Branko sitting aimlessly in the library. I hadn't slept with either of them, only partially replenishing my magic with sultry kisses. They'd come to an uneasy truce, understanding I wasn't choosing one over the other, despite their best efforts to woo me to their individual beds.

I poked at the fire, moaning that I was bored.

Branko grinned at me. "What do you do for fun? On the reef?"

I shrugged. "Do pufferfish and go dancing." I smiled at Branko's confusion. "Pufferfish are a mild sedative. Probably like alcohol. Takes the edge off."

Roan swirled his glass of amber liquid, clinking the large, square ice cube with the motion. "Have ye tried whiskey yet, lass?" He held out his glass. Our fingers touched, and I resisted the urge to linger.

"I've never had alcohol before." I sniffed it and wrinkled my nose. "Smells like dirt."

"Peat, to be more precise. Take a wee sip and hold it on yer tongue." His eyes darkened as he said the last words, and my blood heated, shooting straight to my core before lighting up my traitorous cheeks. I took a tiny, hesitant sip and held it in my mouth, eyes watering, wondering how rude it would be if I spat it in the fire. Roan smiled wickedly. "Swallow it, Mori."

Branko made a purring noise in his throat. I choked it down, burning all the way to my stomach. Or maybe that was the tone of Roan's words and the sound Branko made. I couldn't be sure. I inhaled roughly, trying not to cough. Branko chuckled beside me. I turned to him. "Oh, funny is it? Firewater that smells like donkey ass?" I thrust the glass in his direction. "Here, you take a sip."

Branko's cool fingers did linger, holding mine for much longer than necessary before he took the glass from me. My eyes caught Roan shifting in his seat. Branko said, "I grew up drinking Becherovka. This can't be worse than that." His tongue rolled on the foreign word. I perked up.

"I've read about that! It's the most famous liquor in the Czech Republic." I frowned. "I thought it was for stomach aches. I think there are twenty herbs and spices in it." Spices. Secret spices. Something nudged on the edge of my awareness. "I'd love to try it sometime."

Branko smiled broadly, no longer as rare for him, and every time his lips curled up, my breath caught. He had a beautiful smile. "I will bring some to you the next time I go home." Branko rolled the whiskey on his tongue, parting his lips to breathe over it before swallowing. He said appreciatively, "That is smooth, Roan."

Roan waved a hand. "Have a dram." Branko asked if I'd like one. I scrunched up my freckles and shook my head. He fetched himself a glass, plopped in an ice cube, and poured his own splash, topping up Roan's, the two of them launching into a discussion about oak casks.

Feeling excluded, I went to the bar, fishing through the bottles. I sniffed each one, recoiling from several. I settled on two, both spicy and woody, waving them at the two men. "How do I drink this? Should I mix it with anything? I'm not sure I'll want to savor it, but these two pique my curiosity. This one has something on the bottom." I tipped the bottle to show them the small, white glob. Roan and Branko shared a look of mischief.

Roan said, "That one is tequila, all blue agave. The other is mezcal, made from multiple varieties of the agave plant. It's the one with the worm."

I frowned at the mezcal. "Worm?"

Roan laughed. "Not truly. It's the larva of the red maguey, called the chinicuil or gusano rojo. It becomes a caterpillar and then a moth. That is a wee baby moth in the making."

I looked closer. "Why is it in the liquor?"

Roan shrugged. "Someone thought it would taste good."

Branko said, "If you don't want to savor it, tequila is best taken in shots with salt, followed by biting a slice of lime."

I nodded. "Sounds like how we do pufferfish. Just squirt and swallow." Both of them tightened their bodies in their chairs. Oh, Gods. That didn't come out right. "Okay, who's in? I can't do shots alone. That's just sad."

They chuckled, Branko slowly shaking his head while Roan waved at me to pour three. I found a lime in the small bar fridge under the counter and, at their instruction, cut it into thin wedges. I rummaged around and found a salt shaker. I put the goodies on a tray with a lip, carrying it over to the fire. I set it on the bench and looked at them curiously. "Now what?"

Roan sucked the stretch of skin between his thumb and his index finger into his mouth, holding my gaze while he did it. He sprinkled salt on the wet patch. Branko did the same, his eyes heating as I watched his mouth. My turn.

Green and steel eyes focused on my lips. I might have taken

longer than necessary, heady from the rapt attention. We clinked our glasses together, and I copied the men, licking the salt, tossing the shot in my mouth, following with lime clutched in my teeth. I spluttered over the burn of the liquor. "Goddess, that's terrible!"

Every bone in my body went soft as the tequila rocked through my blood. My incessant thinking slowed to a crawl. I laughed. "Oh. Now, that's good. Way faster than pufferfish. Let's do another!" Roan's lips twitched as he rubbed his hand on his chin at my enthusiasm. His eyes briefly met Branko's and something silent transpired between them. Branko poured three more. The second one hit me hard, and I swayed to my feet, staggering to the stereo.

I squinted, scrolling through the music selection on the tablet. "Ooh! The Violent Femmes! I love them! We have a giant whale jaw in the club at home, similar to the xylophone. I always request this song. It gets the place pumping."

The opening strains to the song Add It Up started, and I sang along, slowly twisting my hips toward Branko, mesmerizing him. Roan sat back in his chair, watching us with heated eyes. After a slow start, the song rocketed. I bounced up and down on my toes, my arms in the air, head swinging loosely. I didn't think through my choice of songs. Not. At. All.

I spun in circles. Dancing with legs was incredible. I sang every word to Roan and Branko, pointing and teasing as the lyrics became dirtier and dirtier; downright filthy. Both men stared at me, starving, glancing at each other competitively for who would capture and hold my attention.

I flitted to one, then the other, a drunk little butterfly, sipping on the magic they uncoiled toward me. My dancing clearly aroused both, and I didn't want to choose between them. When I kissed Branko, Roan growled in his throat with displeasure. When I soothed Roan, Branko cleared his throat, covering his jealousy. I giggled at the veiled aggression, wondering how far I could push this. The song ended on a furious riff. I grinned, relaxed for the first time in ages, my brain comfortably numb.

I lowered the volume a little, suddenly aware that Anna and Richard might not appreciate punk folk in the middle of the night. Sweaty and happy, I poured more shots of tequila, emptying the bottle. It had already been close to gone. We clinked, and I slammed my shot glass down, slurring. "Who wannsto play a game?" I grabbed the pack of cards from the coffee table and moved the tray to the floor. I shuffled clumsily, daring the guys.

"What did ye have in mind, lass?" Roan's words were a low rumble.

Without a moment's hesitation, I picked a game I might win. "Strip fish. Go fish, but the loser has to lose clothes."

Branko sat forward keenly at the thought of getting me naked. "I don't know this game."

I waved at him through a hiccup. "So easy. I'll go first. Pour some of that mezcal."

And that is how I wound up passed out on the floor in my blue thong and matching lace bra.

I woke to the sound of voices in the kitchen, groaning as a lancing pain shot through my skull. My back was like ice and my front was on fire. Sandpaper had replaced my tongue. I cracked open my eyes, blinded by the pale light of dawn. Before me was a wild array of dark tattoos, luscious and strange as they weaved from one into another. I blinked, trying to focus.

An icicle pushed against my back and I shivered, pressing closer to the warm body in front of me. The icicle shifted, growing harder. My eyes flew wide, and I eased my face around, finding a peaceful, very naked Branko snoring softly. I slowly turned my head, staring at the glistening eyes of a dragon on Roan's wide back. He grumbled, half asleep. "Quit wiggling, lass, unless ye plan to do it on me lap again."

"Branko is freezing!" I hissed. "And he's got… he's got…"

Roan chuckled. "Let me guess. An icicle digging into yer spine?"

"Yes!" I paused, acutely aware of all the skin touching skin. "Um, did we, um…"

Roan yawned. "Do anything? Aye, lass. Feel yer lips. Are they swollen?"

I wriggled up a hand and patted my mouth. "A little. Roan…what happened?"

"Lots of kissing, lass. Branko's mouth probably helped with the swelling. Ice and all that."

My jaw went slack. "Both of you?"

"Aye. With enthusiasm."

I swallowed over the hairball in my throat. "And no one spilled blood?"

Roan chuckled. "Lass, we could either get on board with ye or walk away, and neither of us could make our feet move."

My voice came out as a squeak. "Anything else?"

Roan rolled over, pushing a lock of hair from my sweaty forehead. "We stopped ye from going any further. Threatened to tie ye to a chair, but that only made ye more eager. But there was loads of rubbing and stroking and kissing and–"

I pinched his shoulder. "Shh! Stop. I get the picture. Oh, Gods, my head feels like hot concrete."

Roan snorted, running his hand through his hair, the braid untied early in the game, when he claimed his rubber band was an article of clothing. That much I remembered. He was still in his jeans and stretched, making his ink ripple. I cleared my throat. "So, I guess you won, huh?" I bit my lip, scouring my brain for memories of the card game, but they were absent.

He ran a rough thumb over my bottom lip, tugging it from my teeth. "I'd say we all won."

He rolled away from me and stood, not at all affected by

last night's shenanigans. I scooted forward, only to be trapped by a thick, cold arm that snatched me and dragged me backward, hips pushing more insistently at my backside. Roan grinned at my startled expression before helping.

He lifted Branko's arm carefully, and I wiggled away, Roan placing a pillow where I'd been. Branko snuffled and snuggled into it. I slapped a hand to my mouth to keep from giggling. He was gorgeous, rock hard in all the right places. I threw a blanket over him and pulled on my leggings and shirt just as Anna came through the door.

She smiled at our general dishevelment, and the empty bottles surrounded by gnawed on wedges of lime. Her lips twitched as Branko rolled over, tenting his blanket. She tipped her head toward the dining room, and Roan and I followed, both fighting back laughter at our general dishevelment.

Richard sat at the table, stirring his tea. "Good morning," he said cheerfully, and a touch too loud for my liking. "Violent Femmes? I haven't listened to them in ages."

I sagged into a chair. "One of my favorite bands." I slowly lowered my head to the table, resting on my forearms. I closed my eyes. "Mission mermaids brought back the music, giving it to the local band. Sorry if it was too loud."

Anna said to her husband, "They got into the tequila. Sounded like quite the party."

I coughed. "It was fun, from what I remember. I needed to burn off some steam. Any word from anyone?" The bitter aroma of coffee opened my eyes, and I thanked Veda and all things holy. She smiled, set down my bottle of mixed spices, winked, and headed back to the kitchen, returning with a double espresso for Roan. Mako came through the door after her, carrying a plate of fresh cinnamon rolls, extra spicy. Veda was a goddess in disguise. He took one look at me and started laughing.

He grinned at my bleak expression; me wincing as I sipped

the coffee. He said, "I was going to join you when the music started playing, after I finished my reading, then you shouted 'Strip! Strip! Strip!' Figured I should stay out of that."

I cleared my throat and carefully put my coffee down, slumping back in my seat. Richard cocked an eyebrow and Anna smirked behind her tea. She set down her mug and said, "To answer your question, yes, after two weeks of waiting, I have news."

I sat up so fast the room spun. I braced my hands on the table. "What happened?"

"The third hive is swarming. It's chaos down there. Mako, I'd send you to ask, but…"

He frowned. "But Dad was clear that we shouldn't get involved. Still, we can go look, right?"

I nibbled on a cinnamon roll, forcing my body to take the food. "Do I have time for a shower?"

Mako laughed, ripping off dough and shoving it into his mouth. He swallowed and scrunched up his nose. "You have to. You stink and you'll scare off the bees." He turned to Anna. "I tried doing the ritual you suggested, but no luck. Still no vision of Leif. But I got closer."

That woke me up. "You're doing rituals? Last time, you spasmed and Jelly had to bring you back. She's going to freak when she hears about this!" I snarled at him for his stupidity.

He roared his response, making my brain flinch with his sudden anger. "Well, she's not here, is she?"

Roan growled over his coffee. "Oy, mate, tone it down, will ye? No need to fookin' yell." He spun his scowl on Anna. "And ye knew he was trying to reach the Hellhole? What the fook, Anna?"

Anna stiffly placed fruit on her plate. "We need to understand what's happening to Leif. We want to be ready when Jelly gets back."

Roan shook his head. "Too dangerous, Anna. Far too risky."

Richard hummed in his throat, cocking his head at his wife, a smug smirk on his face. "I told you it was a bad idea."

Anna snapped at her husband. "Oh, damn it, Richard, you stop! I made my decision and I stick by it! I'm here, you're here. We have Roan to do a mental intervention if necessary. We don't need Jelly for this." She jabbed a finger in his face, a creep of color staining her cheeks. "Stop it, Richard. I mean it." He sat back with a contemptuous snort, spinning his teaspoon in the air in frustration.

Well, Jelly was right about them. They did fight, and with vigor.

I stood on unsteady feet and waved my hand at the table. "I can't think straight. I want to punch you for being an idiot, Mako, but my vision is fuzzy, and I'd probably miss the swing and fall over. I'm going to shower. Wait for me." My stomach flipped, the acid of the coffee returning with a burn. I winced and swallowed some water.

Roan said softly, "It'll pain ye to listen, lass. Yer brain is wee tender right now. I'll go with ye and help buffer. I don't want ye hurt."

My heart cracked open. "Thanks, Roan. I appreciate that." I snagged a frosted cinnamon roll and thoroughly dusted it with my spice blend, lurching from the room, pushing through the door to the library with my eyes down. I ran smack into a wall of ice. I staggered backward, and Branko caught me in his arms, squishing me and the pastry against his bare chest, dragging me into the library, away from the swinging door.

He grinned down at me. "How is your stomach this morning?"

"Terrible. Awful. I'd love to get sick, but I'm terrified the return of tequila will make me hurl harder." I glanced over at the two empty bottles and shuddered. He slid a chilly hand into my hair and kissed me deeply. The cool of his lips was refreshing, his magic invigorating, whooshing through my blurry mind like wintergreen.

He took a small step back. I couldn't look away from the intensity in his steel eyes, or the sight of his bare torso. I choked on my breath, staring at his smooth skin smeared with sugar and spices. Branko swept the icing off his chest with two fingers and slowly, slowly slipped them between his lips, keeping eye contact with me the whole time.

My body exploded with sweat. I croaked like a frog. "Gods, Branko." I was so damned hot it was painful. I tripped away from him, hearing him chuckle with my departure. As soon as I was free of his line of sight, I sagged against the wall, panting for breath. My stomach groaned and squirmed as I ran up the stairs as fast as my dizzy body would allow, and once under the cold water of my shower, I noticed something different in my energy. It was fluid.

The fresh air helped clear my head, as did the second coffee laced with my spices, courtesy of Roan. Branko had flown away, saying he needed to run a quick errand. Anna walked with the two of us, Mako and Richard following behind, speaking in tight voices. We slowed as we approached the bees. Loud buzzing filled the air around the hive, and droves of bees staggering on the ground as if drunk. I commiserated.

Anna said, "Let me go first. Stay back, but open your mind to them."

Roan reached for my hand. I froze for a second, thinking he was trying to be affectionate. He grinned. "It helps the connection, lass." Ah. Okay. His warm fingers curled around mine, settling my jumpiness. "Release the block. Just a little at a time, though. Too much and ye'll pass out. Focus on just the bees, keeping the block on the birds. They're right chatty this morning, watching this chaos."

Slowly, I unfurled the edges of my mind, and the voices of tens of thousands of bees assaulted me. My knees sagged, and Roan's voice entered my head. *Breathe, lass. I'm here.* He squeezed my hand gently, grounding me. His magic crept into my mind, cocooning it softly, cradling it in a warm glow, turning down the volume of the noise. Soon, I could make out individual voices, disoriented but determined as they clustered in a gigantic ball, clinging to each other.

I'm so full of honey I could pop, unlike our poor queen, dieting and exercising the past week so she can fly. She must be starving!

Queen Jaima is in the middle of us, right? She's protected?

A rich, warm voice answered. *Yes. You girls have me packed in the middle. It's roasting in here, but thank you for asking, Daphne.*

Several bees chattered about a new place to live, breaking away from the swarm.

Oh, look! It's Anna. Does she have a box?

I glanced at Roan, my eyebrow cocked up, not sure if we should get involved. He shrugged and called Anna over. "Do ye have a box?"

She nodded her head once. "That's handy, being able to speak to them directly. A beekeeper is coming, and she will help them relocate." She tapped her fingers to her mouth. "Ask if they have a preference. I have an option to the north, closer to the water. Or east, near the forest."

"All right, then." He tugged my hand. "Careful not to tread on anyone." We gingerly stepped toward the ball of bees, him speaking in my mind. *Good morning, ladies. My name is Roan, and this is Mori. Anna can put ye near the pond, or the trees. Which would ye like?*

The buzz fell silent for a split second and then roared to life.

One bee broke away from the ball, hovering before Roan's nose. She replied in a high-pitched voice. *I'll confer with my sisters. Please wait.* She flew back to the group, leaving me staring at Roan with an open mouth.

My brain staggered. "How can you talk to them? You're not Fae."

"Shh, lass. I'll tell ye later. Listen to the bees."

As a collective, they discussed the pros and cons of each location, and I stood silently, impressed with their civil democracy. I would have expected Queen Jaima to decide, but she remained quiet. Several bees flew in close to the ball, wiggling in the air as they spoke, reporting what they'd found. They considered the merits of both locations, as well as an adequate tree past the pond. Everyone who wished to speak took a turn.

A decision made, the single bee flew back to Roan. *We will take the north location, please. We will wait for the beekeeper.* He relayed the information to Anna. I grinned at Roan, pleased that we'd helped.

Three bees flew up right to my face, and I stopped myself from swatting at them. In my mind, one of them screamed. *MORI??? It's me! It's Jelly!*

TWENTY-NINE

JELLY

I buzzed around her face joyfully. Roan grinned and held out his hand. Penny, Tabitha, and I settled on his palm, resting our wings. I pulled on my antennae like pigtails, so happy to see them. No one had been out to visit, not that I'd seen, and I'd missed them all terribly. I looked over Mori's shoulder to see Mako with Richard, arguing about something. They both looked angry.

I spoke to Mori and Roan in my mind. *How long have I been gone?*

Mori answered, her eyes gigantic from my angle. They glittered like gold. So pretty. *Sixteen days. Do you have your drop of royal jelly?*

I shook my small head. *Not yet. I was supposed to visit Queen Jaima's hive today, but then this happened.*

Mori frowned. Her freckles looked huge. *So you need another queen? Can you drop in on a different hive?*

I turned to Tabitha, who watched me talk to Mori. "Can you hear her?"

Tabitha nodded. "Yes. Our connection allows us to do it. Unfortunately, only three queens agreed to meet with you, and you won't convince the others, so don't bother trying. They are wary of your magic. And Queen Jaima is obviously engaged at present. She won't receive visitors for some time."

Dread pooled in my stomach, and my abdomen heaved as I struggled for a breath. Roan called Anna over, telling her what was happening. She frowned at me, and I noticed fine wrinkles around her mouth. She leaned close to Roan's hand. "What about bumblebees? They have queens. A colony lives in the woodpile behind the house. You'll see a stack of rotting logs near the shed. Perhaps she will meet you." I could hear Anna's voice as a human, but it sounded disjointed to my antennae.

I turned to Tabitha and Penny. "Will you take me to the bumblebees?" They stepped away from me, conferring in low voices. Meanwhile, I couldn't look away from Roan's eyes. With my bee vision, they were electric green, swirling with magic that lit like small sparks, twinkling as we stared at each other.

Roan whispered in my mind. *I'm surprised yer black and yellow. We have blue bees, too, like the blue mason bee, blue carpenter bee, and blue orchard bee. But they're solitary bees. No hive.*

I tipped my small head. *Roan, how can you talk to animals and insects? I thought only Fae could do that.* I put my feet on my hips. *You always pretend you're confused by Icy. Have you been playing us?*

He winked, the sweep of his eyelashes mesmerizing. *I'm a head Wizard, remember? I can't give away all of my secrets. Some day I'll explain who I am. But not now. Yer friends are coming back.* As he spoke, the skull on his throat moved with butterfly wings, and I wanted to watch it all day. I giggled as I noticed Mori staring as well.

Tabitha and Penny returned, looking grim. Tabitha said, "I'm sorry, Jelly, but we cannot take you. It's too far from our hive and our responsibilities to protect it." She switched the hold of her sword, placing her front foot on my shoulder. "Be safe.

Bumblebees can sting repeatedly, and they may not receive a solitary honeybee approaching their nest."

I swallowed my fear. "I understand. Thank you for escorting me to see Queen Charlotte's flight. And Tabitha, for standing with me during the transfer of power. I'll never forget it."

We bowed to each other, and they lifted away, heading back to their hive. I walked forward on Roan's palm, staggering over the mound of his thumb to sit on his wrist. *I have to go to the bumblebees. It's my only option. Can you carry me? Those birds look awfully hungry. Nice of them not to take advantage of the situation. But I don't want to risk it. Oh, look! The bees are doing a rave dance or something.*

The swarming bees were pulsating rhythmically. The ones on the outside were pushing their bellies up and shaking their wings, sending a rippling pattern across the bulging swarm. Roan said, "That's shimmering. It's a defense strategy. A predator gets confused, seeing the swarm as one creature, and a big one at that. That's why the birds stay back."

The beekeeper arrived, carrying a box and a saw. Roan stepped away to give her room, and I clung to his skin with my feet. She placed the box under the tree branch that held the swarm, the bees clamoring excitedly. She cut the branch, and with a firm shake, dropped the bees on top of the box. They immediately stuck their butts in the air and fanned their wings, calling their sisters to their new home with their pheromones.

A bee from the swarm saw me by myself and landed with a lurch on Roan's palm. "Hey, you're new! Are you coming to live with us? No wait. I'd know you if you were with us." She hiccuped. "Sorry, I'm a little drunk on honey." She waved at the beekeeper. "These humans take good care of us. So, are you coming or what?"

I grinned. "I'm not. I'm just a visitor. I'd planned to meet your queen today, but that's not possible now."

"Sure isn't." She burped. "Okay, then. Bye!" She staggered away and launched toward the box.

I turned back to Roan and Mori. *Carry me to the woodpile please? I'll never make it on my own.*

He brought me up to eye level, dazzling me again with his magical eyes. *I'll cup ye in my palms. Keep yer stinger in yer ass. Ye'll die if ye use it.*

I chatted as he shielded me from the wind. *A bee warned me about that. Their stingers have barbs and they get stuck, disemboweling the bee. And the stinger has a cluster of nerves that keep the muscles moving. The barbs go back and forth, burrowing deeper and spreading the venom. It's like a final 'fuck you' from the bee.* He stopped, and the motion caused me to stumble forward. I barked. *A little warning, please!*

He opened his hand, and I stared into the eyes that I loved most in the world, cobalt blue, like the deep ocean, with sparkles of turquoise shooting around, the folds of colors making me gasp. I wanted to swim in these eyes, drown in the love that stared back at me.

Mako's voice was a soothing balm. *Hello, my savage queen. I've missed you. I've walked to the hives every day, hoping you might see me.*

My heart soared. I clasped my front feet together and gasped. *You have? You came? I haven't seen you! Mind you, we've been so busy. I have so much to tell you. But first, I love you. I love you so much. I'm sorry if I was selfish. I'm sorry I didn't understand what you needed from me.*

He smiled, and his chipped front tooth looked like a skyscraper missing part of its structure. I giggled, wanting to stroke it with my feet. His voice was warm. *I love you too. I understand this swarm has thrown a wrench in the works. Mori says you're going to the bumblebees?*

I nodded, but realized the motion was probably too small

for him to see. I answered. *That's right.* He held out his palm with an inviting smile, and I burst off of Roan's hand onto his, immediately surrounded in lush waves of pheromones. I groaned as my antennae trembled with joy. *Gods, you smell so good. Like heaven. Like home.* He cupped me in his hands, asking Mori and Roan to hold back.

I listened to his warm voice as he walked back to the house. He told me of Mori's mischief, flirting with both Roan and Branko. They'd hit the liquor last night, and that's why her eyes were bloodshot. He chatted about random events until he slowed his pace, his voice dropping lower.

He'd researched volumes of Fae reference books, trying to discover more on the Hellhole, and uncovered some interesting information. He paused and took a deep breath, telling me he'd tried to reach Leif through visions, and that Anna and Richard were fighting about it, taking opposite stances. I stayed quiet, so quiet that he stopped altogether.

He opened his hands and peered at me. *Jelly? Are you okay? You're not yelling like you normally would. I thought you'd be upset about me trying to contact Leif. I expected you to flay me for being reckless.*

His words stunned me. How many times had I interrupted him? How often had I dismissed his thoughts and feelings, barreling over him with mine? I replied softly. *I'm fine. Keep talking.*

It was his turn to freeze. He lifted me up, staring at my tiny face. His eyes were full of suspicious mirth. *Who are you and what have you done with my argumentative mate?*

I'm a terrible mate. I'm too self-involved.

He chuckled. *Comes with saving the world. I'm as stubborn as you, don't forget. Okay, maybe not quite as stubborn.* He cupped his hands again and resumed walking and talking. *I got as close as I could, finding an entrance to the Hellhole from Earth. It's guarded by bats. They told me I shouldn't go any further, so I stopped.*

Is that what you and Richard were fighting about?

He sighed. *Yes. He thinks it was incredibly dangerous without you there.* When he next opened his hands, we were at the wood-pile. Thank goodness he'd carried me. I never would have made it. He looked around, puzzled. *Where should I put you? On the ground?*

Nerves clenched my stomach. I was arriving unannounced to beg an audience with the bumblebee queen. *I can fly. Can you wait? Watch over me while I approach them?*

Of course. Good luck, my queen. I'll be right here if you need me.

I lowered my face to his skin, kissing it as best I could with a mandible. Lifting my wings, I steered myself in a circle over the rotten log, calling out at the gate. "Hello? Hello? Is someone there? I'm a visitor honeybee, but not really, and I'll explain if I may have permission to land. Hello?"

An enormous, furry bumblebee trundled to the entrance, squinted at me, and waved me down. I careened to a stop in front of her. I bowed, as was the custom I had learned. The bumblebee snorted. She said, "We don't adhere to the same protocols as the honeybees. No need to grovel at my feet. What can I do for you?" I explained my quest for my soul piece, and my need to meet three queens, keeping it relatively brief. The bee scratched her ample belly. "Wait here." I groomed myself, wanting to look as tidy as possible for the queen. I didn't even know her name.

"Come on in!" The bumblebee sentry yelled from inside. Security was lax in this joint. I crawled over the scattered, decaying leaves at the entrance, following the sound of the sentry's voice down a narrow dirt ramp. I stepped inside and gasped as my eyes adjusted to the darkness.

It was the polar opposite of a honeybee hive.

Bits of animal fur and feather fluff stuck to the walls for

insulation, plastered with leaves, and the nest was haphazard, just a few disorganized wax cells and honey pots for feeding. The cells and pollen lumps were messy, clustered in groups, not at all like the strict structure I'd come to associate with bees, but the overall vibe was cozy, and incredibly friendly, as groups of bumblebees looked at me with curious kindness.

I waved a foot in the air. "Um, hi. I'm Jelly, and I'm here through magic. Normally, I'm a mermaid. I'd like to meet your queen, if I may, please." The bees buzzed with excitement.

A different bumblebee stepped forward, her large body awkward. "Hi Jelly, I'm Sally. Don't mind the mess. We don't live like the honeybees. We have smaller colonies without the hierarchical division of labor. We all just pitch in where necessary. I'll take you to the queen." She waved me forward, leading me further down a slope.

"May I ask her name?"

Sally replied casually. "Quinn. Queen Quinn."

"Thank you, Sally. I really appreciate this." We entered a warm, dark area where an enormous bumblebee crawled over wax cups, grumbling to herself. She looked up, readjusted the simple crown that was slipping forward on her head, and grinned.

Sally tipped her head casually. "Queen Quinn, meet Jelly the mermaid." I bowed. I had to. She was a queen.

The Queen straightened her crown, so it sat further down on her head. "Hey there! A mermaid, you say? You're a long way from home. Come in, come in. I'm just making some babies here. Oh, careful. Don't trip over those!" She hopped down from her work and edged me away from a squishy blob of fur. "Those are new kids, just hatched. They come out all floppy. It takes a day for their bodies to harden up. Are you thirsty? Hungry?"

I looked around. There was barely any food or honey stored.

Although my stomach growled, I declined politely, not willing to dig into her meager supplies. She looked me up and down. "Magic, huh? I rarely get honeybees coming in for visits, and you're the first mermaid for sure. Well, I'm afraid I don't have a lot of time to chat. What can I help you with?"

I couldn't believe my luck. She was so friendly. I explained my story, and she listened, pulling wax from her belly and shaping cups while I spoke. A couple of worker bees came in and lazily stirred the air with their wings, cooling the eggs. Quinn thanked them before cocking her head. "Fascinating. How can I help you?"

Stumped, I shrugged my shoulders. "Maybe tell me a bumblebee's most pressing concern?"

She sighed, patting a cup to smooth the lip. "That's easy. Humans. We're okay here on the Coven grounds, but the others? The ones who live around ignorant humans?" She ran a foot over her antenna, straightening her crown. "Well, let's start with lawns. Why they insist on miles and miles of grass is beyond me. There's nothing for us to eat. They water it, and cut it, and fuss over it, and then it dies, and they pull it up and lay down new grass... It's senseless."

She returned to her task. "Then there's the dandelion and clover. The humans toss weedkiller on them, or rip them out by the roots. We need those early blooms. Bumblebees especially. When a queen comes out of winter hibernation, she needs nectar to build her strength. Only then can she find a nest and get started making babies. We need that early pollen to feed the first batch of eggs."

She stroked her legs down her thick body. "We're all alone in the beginning. If you see a bumblebee in the Spring, it's a queen. Once we find a place to nest, we sit on our brood cells and shiver our muscles to keep the first worker eggs warm. If it's nasty outside, we keep a little nectar pot for backup, but it's slim pickings in the Spring. We're lucky, though. We can work in lower light, cooler temperature, and even a drizzle. But it's tricky because we need to keep the babies warm, but also go outside and eat, and bring back more pollen and nectar to feed them. It's a tenuous dance of survival."

Her voice hitched. "That's when most bumblebee nests and queens die, where there isn't enough plentiful food. If we can get to the early flowers, we'll make it. But the humans and their chemicals…Tragic. Just tragic, and so unnecessary." She pulled out another wax piece and stuffed it in her mandible to soften before shaping it messily. She growled in her throat. "Killing dandelions and growing grass. They can't even eat grass. It's ridiculous."

She looked up. "Humans like their nature to be pristine and tidy. They rake up all the dead leaves and throw them away. They get rid of the rotting wood and vegetation, sweep up the dirt, and spray insecticides all over their plants. Don't they understand that the poison kills us? Seventy percent of all bees live on the ground and lay our eggs in nests under the dirt." She sniffed, her antennae drooping. "Honeybees get all the attention."

Defeated from her story, Quinn sat down on her big furry butt and cried, great tears dropping from her face into her front feet, her wings shaking as her shoulders heaved. I went to her and hugged her with four legs, standing on my back toes so I could reach around her body as tightly as I could. It seemed right for this queen. My instincts told me she was a hugger. My body was soon damp, and my throat ached as I listened to her sob. It seemed the sorrow of bees met them all, not just the honeybees.

She patted my head kindly and sat back, pushing up her crown and wiping her eyes. "I just get so overwhelmed. I don't understand the humans. I'm also emotional because all my boys just left. I'll never see them again. They're out there on the flowers, drinking nectar, and looking for queens." She cleared her throat. "Like the honeybees, the boys die after mating. Seems so unfair, but they do get to party it up before it happens." She shrugged. "I suppose it's not a bad way to go, all things considered."

She affectionately stroked a cup with a tiny egg inside. "These are my daughters, future queens. I have to feed them three times more pollen to make them really big, fatten them up to survive the winter. Everyone will die in the autumn. But these girls will make it. At least, some of them will. We call them queenlings. Once they hatch, they'll stay here a while before being courted by suitors from afar."

She looked down at the cell sadly. "Once mated, my girls leave. My queenlings will forage for as long as they can to build up their energy stores, but as the nights get colder, the flowers die. They'll find somewhere to burrow and wait out the cold. We have natural antifreeze chemicals in our blood to keep ice crystals from shredding our bodies. Even so, winter is brutal."

I blinked at her. "That's incredible."

Quinn grinned. "Mmm. Our metabolism slows to an absolute crawl. The rest of us will die. The queenlings sleep under the surface like royal seeds. They wait for spring, and then start homes of their own."

My brow crinkled. "Wait…everyone dies except the future queens? Everyone? Even you? Honeybee queens live for years."

She smiled wistfully. "Everyone except them. That's why I get so upset. The humans don't understand how fragile we are." I had nothing to say. She wiped her front feet together and adjusted her crown to sit further back on her brow. "I'm afraid that's all I have time for, Jelly. I have to feed my girls. You're welcome to stay and talk to the workers in the hive. Not all of them forage."

I bowed to her, so touched by her sad tale. She was kind

and generous, doting on her people, feeling deeply for those who didn't share her good fortune of having a safe place. Suddenly dizzy, the world spun as I *saw* the bees and their sacrifices. I felt it to my core. If I had bones in this body, they would quake with the enormity of my epiphany. I kept my face on the floor, murmuring beneath tears of realization and gratitude. "Thank you, Queen Quinn. I appreciate you spending time with me." I straightened, determination in my voice. "I need to return to Queen Isabella now."

She nodded. "Do you know where you're going?"

I smiled, my heart overflowing. "I have help. My mate is waiting outside."

"Your mate? Lucky girl. Take care of that love. It's special."

"Yes, ma'am. It is." I passed through the nest, smiling at the bumblebees who fanned at the walls, swept the floors, and pottered around. They waved at me, turning back to their chores and their chatting. I flew out into the sunshine. Mako was waiting, as promised, his eyes closed as he rested against an oak tree. I didn't want to risk buzzing straight at his face in case he swatted me in his sleep. *Mako? Mako, wake up. I need to speak to Queen Isabella.*

I hovered nearby, waiting breathlessly as his eyes fluttered open. He smiled as I zipped over to a flower, dipping my face into the center and drinking deeply. I was famished. Keeping this body going was hard work. He stretched out his palm, and I settled, tucking in my wings. He said, "I'm not sure which one she's in." His voice dropped, aching with regret. "I'm sorry I didn't join you when you changed. I was sulking."

He cupped me in his hands as he walked. I replied softly in his mind. *We'd just argued, and I wouldn't give you what you wanted. We will constantly challenge each other, and that's a good thing. Learning to work together despite our individual needs will be our greatest strength. But we'll have to fight for that communication. Bending a knee doesn't come easy for either of us.*

You sound so wise, my queen. He opened his hands to stare at me with love and admiration.

I grinned at his expression, even though he couldn't see it. *Can you call Mori and Roan? You can probably reach them faster than me. I'm not sure how far my telepathy stretches as a bee. They saw which one hive I first entered.*

Once he got closer, he called out with his mind, asking them where to go, and Mori answered breathlessly. *We're here now. Go to the pond and you'll see us.*

Mako chuckled. *Why are you out of breath, Mori?*

Roan answered with a teasing in his voice. *Yes, lass, why are ye breathless?*

Her laughter rang through my head, but she didn't answer. I grinned, closing my eyes and inhaling Mako's woody scent while he carried me back to the knoll near the hive. Mako laughed softly and opened his hands. I peered around, finding Mori sandwiched between Roan and Branko, Roan kissing her neck while Branko's hands roamed her hips. I shrieked. *Oh, my goddess! All three of you? When did this happen?*

Both Mori and Roan snapped their heads toward me, Branko oblivious, as he combed into Mori's red curls with his fingers. Mori muttered something, and Branko turned to look at Mako, me perched in his hand with my front feet on my hips. A smile stretched across his broad face, shocking me with its beauty. Roan kissed Mori on the nose and Branko took her hand. Mori sauntered between them, lifting a green square bottle to her lips and taking a long slug.

I waved a leg at her. *What is that?*

Mori grinned. *I got drunk last night. Fun in the moment. Terrible the next day. Branko brought me Becherovka, this stuff, twenty secret spices, and it's amazing. Amazing! My headache is gone and my stomach is steady again. I shouldn't have eaten the worm.* She took another swig. The bottle was already half-gone.

The worm? I tipped my small head. Roan grinned mischievously.

She waved the bottle at me. *Long story. I'll tell you later. If you're back, I assume you're ready to go do your thing.*

Roan pointed to the white box in the distance. *That's where ye first changed, lass.*

I nodded. *Here goes nothing.* I buzzed my wings and lifted from Mako's palm. I flew to the entrance and bowed, relieved to see the same guards as before, scowling with their swords crossed, barring the entrance. They were surly, but familiar.

"Hi! Can you please call Manda for me? She's probably on wax duty with Rachel. Or she might be doing repair work." I bounced on my small toes. The guard glared at me while stroking her antenna. It was then that I realized I never asked their names. "I've passed by you a hundred times, but I didn't catch your names."

The one on the left replied frostily. "We didn't give them."

"Uh. Okay." I think I preferred the bumblebees. I peered over their shoulders, looking for Manda. She showed soon after, giving me a hug and dragging me through the hive.

Her voice squeaked with excitement. "I'm ready to take my first flight! I can circle the hive for orientation."

"That's wonderful!" I was happy to share her joy, but part of me ached for her. Once she was a forager, her life would soon end.

She grabbed my foot with hers. "Isn't it? I won't go far. Just enough to identify the landmarks." She pulled me faster. "Queen Isabella is waiting for you." She tapped the wall in a pattern, pushing the door open for me. I waited for her to come with me. She shrugged and backed away with a smile. "I'm not a queen's assistant anymore. I don't think I'm allowed."

Queen Isabella's kind voice echoed in the throne room.

"Come in, Manda. You may join Jelly. You've been instrumental in her growth." Manda's eyes widened and her antennae flapped. She ran them quickly through the grooves in her elbows and nodded to me to go first. I expanded my abdomen with a deep breath, praying with every small hair on my body that my speech would sway the queen.

THIRTY

JELLY

Manda and I walked up the long walkway toward the Queen, imposing in her black and gold robes, the heavy crown perfectly aligned on her head. She flexed her silver wings as she leaned forward on her pulpit. Her voice was soft. "Are you here for your drop of royal jelly?"

I dropped to the floor, my face touching the hazy gold beneath me. "If it pleases Your Majesty, yes, I am."

"Rise, Jelly." I stood, my face hopeful. She leaned forward. "Tell me what you've learned, and I will decide if you've earned it."

I told her about my experiences in her hive, and how impressed I was with the division of labor, its tidiness, and its organization. I gushed her ability to lead sixty-thousand bees, who loved her and only expressed their dedication to the colony, a seamless orchestration of devotion to a higher cause. She nodded, pleased.

My voice broke as I told her about the second hive. "Queen Candice…" I cleared my throat. "I witnessed a supersedure. Queen Charlotte replaced Queen Candice."

Isabella stroked an antenna with keen interest. "Tell me."

I couldn't help the tear that slipped down my face, swiping it away quickly. "It was heartbreaking. I am still shattered by what I saw. She was only seconds old… To begin life like that… The princesses battled, and Charlotte killed them all, some of them still in their cells." My voice tightened when telling her of the mortuary bees dragging away the princesses, the streaks of liquid on the floor. I rallied in my emotions, suppressing my tears so I could speak. "And then Queen Charlotte had to kill her mother. But Queen Candice didn't fight. She accepted her fate proudly and died in Charlotte's arms. Then Charlotte put on the crown and assumed her role."

I hesitated, unsure if I should share Charlotte's private tears. I phrased it diplomatically. "Queen Charlotte was upset, naturally, but she faced her new role with courage." I wiped my face, determined to speak the next words bravely. "She allowed me to watch her mating flight."

Isabella's antennae straightened above her head. "Did she? That is highly unusual."

I bowed my head, my antennae drooping. "She wanted me to see. She mated with many drones. Seventeen in total, and, and they…and they all…"

Isabella sighed knowingly. "It's awful."

"I watched them all die," I said in a haunted voice. I sucked in a breath and bowed low. "Your Highness, I cannot fathom the magnitude of pain required to be a queen bee." I straightened, my face somber. "And yet, you do not falter. You dedicate your life to the survival of the planet and all her creatures. It is so humbling."

Isabella graciously accepted my words with a dip of her chin. "And the third hive?"

Nerves clutched my stomach. I hadn't seen a third honeybee hive. "Queen Jaima was in a swarm. I understand it's another way that bees reproduce. Her hive had become too large, and half of the ladies joined her outside. Anna had a fresh box for them, and they moved near the pond, to the north."

"Yes, Anna told me. So, you didn't meet Queen Jaima?"

"No, ma'am. But I met another queen, Queen Quinn."

"The bumblebee by the woodpile?" Her smile was broad as she leaned forward with interest, resting her elbow on the pulpit, her chin in her foot.

My heart bloomed with hope. "Yes. She invited me inside her home, and I spoke with her as she was tending to her new daughters, her new queenlings."

"Hmm. And what did you think?"

I paused, wondering if she wanted me to disparage the messy den Quinn called home. But I was protective of the chunky bumblebee. She had been kind, taking time from her busy life to meet with me. I squared my shoulders. "Her home differs from the honeybee structure. Less formal. Far less tidy. But a home all the same. And she has her own sorrows. She told me about the dangers of being a bumblebee queen, waking so early, all alone, struggling to find food. And that humans coat the ground in chemicals, ruining it for all ground-dwelling animals." My throat tightened. "She'll die this winter. She won't live through it like honeybees."

Isabella nodded sagely. "Yes, it is different for them. Much harder, living under the earth." She sat back and crossed her front legs over her chest.

My antennae swayed as I dipped my head in a bob. "Your Majesty, I have a plan. My best friend can move dirt with her magic. I'll ask her to make balls of rich soil mixed with wildflower seeds. And I'll ask my friend Branko, a gargoyle, to fly high and scatter them, scatter them everywhere, over desolate spaces, on lawns, just…everywhere. I haven't seen them myself, but I understand there are spans of bare earth edging things called highways. There could be flowers instead. I want to help grow food for the bees, your majesty."

"What of the chemicals? Won't the humans simply use more? Some of them see the wildflowers as weeds."

Her question stumped me for a moment, but I rallied. "My mate's mother is an internet whiz. I can ask her to create a campaign, highlighting how vital you are to their survival. Humans could appeal to their governments to re-wild vacant spaces. And reclaim their lawns and gardens, growing native flowers without pesticides." I got excited at the possibilities. "Teach them to leave a back section with leaves and logs for ground bees and beetles. Or build tiny houses as shelter. There have to be bee houses, right?" She beamed at my enthusiasm, a waft of her pheromones drifting over me.

I bowed to her again. "Your Highness, I must believe some humans are innocent, doing what's always been done, but maybe it's from simple ignorance. Perhaps they can change. I will speak to Sophia the second I'm back at the house."

Isabella tapped her foot on her chin. "Hmm. The internet. Humanity's hive connection. And you believe Sophia will help you?" I almost jumped up and down with enthusiasm. She let out a small chuckle and said, "Yes, that's certainly a start. I like it." She leaned forward. "Tell me, what do you make of your experiences with the bees, Jelly? Why should I reward you?"

This was the moment. Everything hinged on my next words.

I closed my eyes, breathing out a soft sigh, collecting my thoughts. I met her stare and spoke from my heart. "I believe I understand the sorrow of bees. Despite the murder of queens and the deaths of the drones, not to mention the terror of predators and pesticides, you dance. You split all the chores to make your home run, and your efforts provide medicine, food, candles, and so much more. You work with love in your hearts, caring for each other, for all of us. Without you, the planet would die. Yet even with such enormous responsibility, knowing your life is painfully and unfairly brief, you celebrate, diving face first into flowers. Being a bee… It's the most selfless, gorgeous, devastatingly bittersweet thing I've ever experienced, and I am so grateful to have taken part, if only for a short time. It has changed me forever. I may only be one person, but when we act as a collective, we are mighty. I want to take this understanding back to my hive, back to the people I love."

She smiled, her eyes filling. Finally, after an agonizing moment of silence, she spoke. "Come to me, Jelly, and kneel." I fluttered my wings, closing the space between us as she slid from her throne, standing over me as I bent forward. "You are a deep, sweet soul, Jelly the mermaid, and you deserve to be whole. You work ceaselessly for a better world, just as we do. Your mate calls you his queen, and he is correct. You are a queen, just as I am. It is my pleasure to give you a drop of my Royal Jelly, and for you to reclaim your full soul."

I lifted my eyes in wonder as she somberly rubbed her crown with two feet. An aura of light surrounded her, as well as the thick scent of honey, the golden hue coalescing into a bubble. She gathered the glistening drop in her front feet and held it delicately, lowering it down to my face. "Drink, Jelly. Drink and take the sorrow and the joy of bees into your heart."

I dipped my tongue into the shimmering liquid. The flavor burst in my mouth, fathomless sweetness mixed with the salt of sacrifice. It was so heady the room spun. Her essence settled into me, and the devotion she had for her colony washed through me, so selflessly committed to their success despite the heartache she personally suffered. She understood the bigger picture and her role within it, accepting it without complaint. I wanted to laugh and cry simultaneously, my emotions colliding as they swirled in my heart before dropping into my belly.

My vision turned yellow, a resplendent mixture of lemon,

and amber, and gold. The color of daffodils and dandelions, of buttercups and sunflowers who raised their faces to the light. I inhaled a great breath as my body shuddered, energy zipping past my head, glowing and bursting above it. Lightning flashed through me as my missing piece snapped into place. I blinked all five of my eyes, dazzled by the sensations in my body and soul.

I laughed, overcome with sheer joy as I slid into position in the Universe, a tiny but critical piece. I understood my purpose, throwing myself at her feet. "Thank you, my queen! Thank you so much!"

She patted my head, chuckling kindly. "You are welcome, Warrior Jelly. Take what you've learned and share."

I crawled backward, bumping into Manda, who stood awestruck. "Jelly, you're glowing! You're glowing golden sunshine! You're so beautiful!" She burst into tears and hugged me, both of us shuffling away from the benevolent queen, me bowing so much I stumbled a few times. Bees paused in their tasks, smiling as I passed, patting me on my wings or stroking my body in congratulations. More than one stopped me to touch their antennae to mine, sparks flying around us each time they did.

We went back to the entrance. I trembled with excitement about going home, kissing Mako, and getting Leif. To my utter surprise, both guards bowed. The one on the right sounded gruff. "Fair well, mermaid."

The guard on the left shifted her sword to her non-dominant foot, patting my cheek. "My name is Robin. You've done an extraordinary job, Jelly. I'm so proud of you." My throat clogged with tears as I thanked her and shuffled to the side where Manda waited. I swallowed a few times, overcome.

Manda stroked her antennae against mine, her voice hesitant. "I know you're done here, but will you fly with me? It would be nice to have a friend at my side for my orientation."

I sniffed, my belly expanding, so many tears held in my throat. "It's my honor to join you, Manda. And thank you. I couldn't have done this without you. You're a good friend." We turned to face the wildflowers, the colored patterns and magnified scents too beautiful. I would miss them.

Manda trembled with excitement, tensing her legs. She jumped from the platform, flinging her wings wide. She was a natural, swooping in a circle, and she whooped and screamed with glee as we dove and lifted, the sheer joy of the flight almost maddening. I shouted for her attention. "Manda! Manda! Come and meet Mako!"

I reached out to him, seeing him standing a respectful distance from the hive. *Mako, I'm bringing Manda, my best bee friend.* He broke into a smile and held out his palm. I landed gracefully, if I say so myself, and Manda bumped and rolled before jumping to her feet, giggling.

She swept her antennae through the air. "He smells so yummy!"

"Doesn't he?" I tipped my small bee head, gazing into Mako's blue eyes as he brought us up level.

He spoke softly in our heads. *Hello, Manda. Thank you for taking such good care of Jelly.*

She squealed. *I can hear you!*

Mako's voice rolled over my mind like warm honey. *I was born half-Fae, but being marked by Mother Kokuro allows me to communicate freely with all animals.*

Well, Jelly's right. You're gorgeous! And clearly, you love her so much. I can see it in your eyes. She turned to me, rubbing a foot under her eye. *I can't stay out, Jelly. My first flight is only for orientation. But maybe…come back and find me to say hello when you're done with your mission?* She swallowed thickly. *I pray you'll be successful, Jelly. I pray you survive your trials.*

I reached for her, pulling her close with four legs. *I'll come back. I promise.* Tears caught in my throat. There was a good chance she'd be dead by the time I returned.

She released me with a frown on her fuzzy face, probably coming to the same conclusion. She stroked her foot down my face. *I'll see you when I see you. Be well, Jelly.* She lifted, spinning around Mako's head before darting back to the hive. She screamed joyfully the whole way. I watched her go, my heart simultaneously heavy and light. I sighed a deep sigh, my abdomen stretching wide.

My body began vibrating, trembling to my very core. I shrieked, *Mako! Put me down!* He cupped his hands and released me gently onto the grass. I stared up at a flower, memorizing the vibrant color streaked with runway lines. A ladybug watched from underneath, her mouth full of aphids. I yelled at her to fly away, as I was changing. She lifted her outer wings, her red shell, and a second set carried her away to safety.

I floundered amidst the flowers as my bee body changed with a sharp jolt, leaving me panting, curled up in my human form. My first action was to clutch my throat for the pearl. It was there, back to its normal size, but still silent and cold on my skin. Air rushed into my lungs. I expanded my belly with a bee's instinct and burst into laughter at my mistake. Mako dropped to the grass beside me and scooped me in his arms, rocking me to his chest. I lifted my face to his, grinning from ear to ear. "I did it, Mako. I'm whole."

He dropped his mouth to mine in a blistering kiss. He pulled back with a yelp. "What is that?" His eyes sparkled with shots of turquoise while his hair stood on end. "I'm electrified!"

"That is my full soul. I haven't been whole since the ritual, before we became fated." I fell on him, giddy, and we melted into each other. I didn't care that I was naked, my butt in the air. I was here with my mate, my love, something I'd taken for granted. Never again.

A soft cough interrupted our impassioned reunion, and a light blanket fell on my back. I turned my head to find Mori grinning, pointing her finger in a loop. "I figured you'd be naked." She kneeled in the grass beside us, tracing down my arm. "You're glowing. There's a shimmer on your skin like the best suntan in the world." Her hazel eyes met mine. "Is that the royal jelly?" I nodded, tucking in the blanket before crushing her to me while still straddling Mako. She drew back, her hands on my shoulders, scanning my eyes. "Are you whole? How do you feel?"

I bit my lip, tears in my eyes, my voice catching. "So happy." I wriggled from her stare and dropped my mouth onto Mako's. I'd missed him so much. He moaned from the magic I flooded through him. I put my lips to his ear. "Don't mention Leif yet, okay?" I sat up, chuckling. "Where is everyone?"

He grinned, holding my hips while he caught his breath. "Inside. They tried coaxing Mori to go with them, but she refused."

Mori helped me to my feet. I swayed like a giant. I gazed back at the hive and blew it a kiss, taking Mako's hand and walking forward, my heart freer that ever before. I desperately wanted to regale them with stories of the bees, but I kept quiet.

Mako glanced around my front at Mori. "So, are you going to tell her of your adventures?"

She tipped up her bottle for another gulp. "No, no, I'm sure Jelly wants to tell us her story."

I grinned. "I want yours!"

"Really? I… After all you've been through? I just…I just assumed…"

She assumed I was the same self-absorbed woman who'd entered the beehive. I wasn't. I snuggled her side. "Let's talk about you. I thought Roan wasn't willing to share! What's going on with you three?"

Mori smiled like the cat who'd got the cream, taking

another hefty swig. She was chugging the stuff. "Roan and I had a talk about Goldilocks soon after you left. I told him Branko intrigued me since the first time I saw him. Remember?"

I chuckled. "When he landed during a rainstorm and stripped by the fire? Yeah, I remember. You were practically tripping on your tongue. It was dragging on the ground."

She laughed. "That it was."

I raised my eyebrows. "Well? What did Roan say?"

She dropped her voice to a deep growl, imitating him perfectly. "I canna say I like it, but I can live with it." She slapped her hand to her face. "I almost burst into flames! We've been teasing each other like crazy, dropping innuendos all over the place. There's been kissing…" She grinned even wider.

Mako groaned with an exaggerated eye roll. "So much kissing. Incessant flirting. Her sucking in a breath whenever Branko touches her–"

Mori cut him off. "His hands are like ice cubes!" She laughed. "But I frickin' love his hands. Head to toe goosebumps every damned time." She drained the bottle with a small burp.

Mako continued dramatically, waving his hand through the air. "And growling when Roan growls. It's like living in a wolf den."

Mori bit her lip, and her voice took on an edge of despair. "It's been incredible, so fun. But something changed last night. Until now, I've only flirted with them one on one."

"And?" I pressed her closer to my side.

She stopped, breaking away, and threw her free hand in the air, the other waving the empty bottle. "And I don't remember! I woke up squished between them on the floor in my underwear! Roan said there was kissing and touching, but it's a total blank in my head. I'm never drinking tequila again."

Mako chuckled beside me. "Maybe just not so much. But bright side, Mori, you clearly had fun, judging by the make-out session by the tree. No one's feelings looked hurt, and they were definitely into it."

I giggled, bumping her with my shoulder. "Gods, Mori, I turn my back for one minute and you're shacked up with a Wizardry chair and a lead gargoyle." We approached the mansion. I buzzed with anticipation. We were closer to Leif, closer to his freedom. I wanted to yank Mako and run inside, make a plan, and get moving. His fingers curl tighter. He must be thinking the same thing. But Mori was still speaking, so I tempered myself.

She grinned like a lovesick fool. "Branko made a special trip this morning to bring me this for my stomach. Incredible stuff. He got an extra special kiss as a thank you." She held up the empty bottle. I frowned. He'd flown? And she could kiss him without getting burned from his cold skin? Something *had* changed.

I wanted to question her, dissect and examine it, but she looked so giddy, I didn't want to ruin her joy. Instead, I said, "I'm proud of you. You said you didn't want a relationship, nor did you want a one-night stand. You stated your needs, and the men stepped up, letting you lead the way. It speaks volumes about their character."

She halted, stopping us with the motion. We were mere feet from the front steps. The gold in her hazel eyes caught the sun. "I'm proud of me, too. There's this expectation of one man and one woman, mates, couples…and it seems so confined. You two are fated and blessed, blah blah, and that's what society expects of me. Settle on a merman, get pregnant, do the duty. But it never jived for me. I wanted freedom to explore. And finally, my desires aren't wrong. I'm free to be whatever I want, and I really love who I've become."

She swayed on her feet, stumbling backward. I reached to steady her, but she waved off my help. Her eyes flew wide, and the green bottle slipped from her fingers as she yelled. "Whoa.

Whoa! Oh, shit! Shit!" She shook out her arms as if they were burning. The bracelets around her wrists exploded into blinding white light, arcing over her and shooting to the sky like a comet, the tail popping with fireworks in multiple colors, heavy on green. We all watched, our mouths hanging open.

Veda burst through the front door, clapping with delight. Richard, Roan, Branko, and Anna ran out behind her, startled by the noise and the lights. They paused at the top of the steps to watch the fireworks. Veda cried out in elation. "It worked! It worked!" She dashed down the stairs, clutching her sari to avoid tripping, and pulled Mori into her arms, spinning her around, tottering under her weight. "I am so happy for you! You are unapologetically you!"

Veda suddenly gasped and staggered back, hands outstretched before her, waving them at Mori's belly, then at the empty bottle on the ground. Her bindi spun so fast that sparks flew from her forehead. Her eyes wildly scanned the sky. She shrieked. "Back away from Mori! Get back! Get back!"

Mori stared at her, openmouthed, still shaking from the daze of her bracelets exploding. "Why? What's wrong?" She followed Veda's stare, shading her eyes with her hand. The comet had turned, aiming straight for her. Anna immediately flung up a shield. Branko shifted and roared behind it, slamming it with his stone fists.

Roan's voice raged in my head. *Anna, drop this fookin' thing now! We have to help her!*

Mako slammed me to the ground, covering us with his shield. Terror shredded me. "Mori!" I struggled under Mako, who pressed his full weight on me to keep me from leaping to my friend's aid. "Mori! Gods damn it, Mako! Let me up!" I twisted my head to look at her.

Mori screeched, bolting away from everyone. The wind roared and wailed with the noise of the speeding missile. Veda screamed to her. "Mori, do not fight it! It is your destiny!" Mori turned, her face lifted, arms wide, heart open. A streak of white fur crossed the lawn, leaping for her as the light consumed her body, flashing so brightly it blinded me. The sound was unworldly, a high-pitched whistle tearing into my brain, ending with a crashing boom. And then it went silent. I blinked and screamed her name.

Mako's teeth clenched as we wrestled. I thrust up with my hips, destabilizing him, and squirmed out of the shield, running for Mori. But she was gone, the grass scorched in the outline of her body. I flung myself over the burn patch, tearing it with my fingers while I sobbed. "No, Mori, no! No!"

Anna dropped her shield, and Branko and Roan rushed to my side, Roan running, Branko flying with a loud snap of his wings. Both dropped to their knees, tentatively touching the grass themselves, tracing the shape left behind. I looked at Roan through tear-streaked eyes, my soul smashed with glass that cut and bit and sliced me to ribbons. This couldn't be happening. His emerald green eyes shimmered, and silent tears fell to the burnt grass beneath him. Branko wailed mournfully in a foreign language. "Maly ptacek! Maly ptacek!"

Mako came behind me and locked me in his arms. "Jelly, oh my gods, I'm so sorry. I'm so sorry." His voice cracked. Anna threw herself at Richard. Only Veda looked untouched. Her bindi was still spinning and spitting with sparks. Her head bobbed, and she wore a small smile. I wanted to smack it from her face with my fist.

I roared at her. "What did you do? What did you do to her?!?"

Her face startled at the fury in my voice. She spun in a swish of orange fabric and sprinted to the house without answering.

THIRTY-ONE

MORI

I cy sat back on her haunches, panting. "I knew the bracelets were ready, but I didn't expect it so soon! I figured it would happen later today. They would have been furious with me if I'd missed it." She licked herself frantically. "How did you speed it up?"

I blinked at her, my eyes roaming the sand-colored walls around me, the same as the floor beneath me. I'd been here before. Not in my real world, but in my dreams. It was peaceful, warm, and comforting, three walls rising to a tall peak with no windows to give me a glimpse outside. The smell was earthy, spicy, like myrrh, but I couldn't see the source of the heavy fragrance.

Everything had sucked into a dark hole when the light hit me. I'd woken up here with an anxious cat. I gazed at Icy. "What did I speed up? And why can I still understand you? The bracelets are gone."

Icy blinked back, hissing impatiently. "You sped up your change! This!" She took to grooming again until her pink tongue froze, outstretched from her mouth. She slurped it back in. "Each night, we've traveled here in your dreams. I wanted you calm, and you are, which is good, but you don't understand what is happening right now, do you?"

I casually shrugged. "No clue, Icy. One minute my bracelets explode into a shooting star which then blasts toward me, and Veda's telling me to embrace my destiny, and bam! Here we are."

Icy sat back, stunned. "But you've been preparing…" Her small head shook back and forth. She stared at my befuddled expression. "You're truly confused?"

"Icy, I promise you, I'm clueless. I'm also a little drunk, I think, so my brain isn't working as fast as usual. I gulped down that bottle of liquor Branko brought me."

The ruffled cat marched to where I sat cross-legged and climbed in my lap. "That would do it. I will show you the events that led to this moment, and to answer your previous question, the connection to everything is permanent. Stroke my fur to get it started."

It was like watching a movie screen in my mind. Images flashed and whizzing by until they slowed and steadied. We were back in Bermuda after rescuing Simmi, and I was lying with my head in Roan's lap, not moving. Black lines crawled across my skin. I wasn't breathing.

He was whispering over me, but the words were as clear to my ears as if he stood next to me. "Come back to me, lass. Ye canna go now. Not now. Not when I've just found ye." He rolled agonized eyes to the sky. "Please, take some from me as payment to help her hang on." A gold light shimmered around him and he trembled, squeezing his eyes shut. He dropped his head. "Spirits, I thank ye."

He cleared the tears from his voice just as Jelly and Anna flashed into the room. Roan said, "Thank fook. I'm holding her soul here, but only just. Be quick, lass!" Jelly bit Roan's shoulder, placing her ravaged hand on it to do a blood ritual. She closed her eyes, her forehead creased in concentration. Roan stared at my face, stroking my cheeks with his thumbs.

I gasped as the image changed, and I was curled inside an

oak tree. I was seeing myself in the Sliver, talking to my mom. My heart bloomed at the sight of her face. She said, "Mori, you can come with me, or you can go back. Someone's just bought you some time to decide. You're so special, my girl. You carry a drop of ancient blood in you, and it will make itself known at some point if you go back. You won't remember me telling you this, no matter how hard you try. It will come as a surprise as it's meant to."

I picked at the skin around my fingernail in the vision. "What does the blood do? Where does it come from?"

She shook her head. "I can't tell you, but it's important. Be quick, darling. You need to decide. I love you no matter what you choose." With a kiss to my cheek, she disappeared when Jelly arrived.

Jelly pleaded with me to live. The movie in my head split into side-by-side screens, showing both me and Jelly in the Sliver on the left, and Jelly and Roan hovering over my body on the right. Roan's voice rang through the Sliver. He was using telepathy while I deliberated. His face strained from the effort, but his eyes were sparkling as he spoke to my still body. "From the moment I met ye, I knew ye was special. But when ye split me lip open…oof. Such sass. Very sexy. Come back, Mori. Yer not done here, lass."

I'd called out to him, and he promised to teach me telepathy. I'd chosen to come back. Was it for him? As Jelly and I raced to leave the Sliver, the screen turned singular again. Only seconds from leaving the land of the half-dead, limp in his arms, I'd teased Roan, telling him I should put more enthusiasm into him carrying me to bed. I heard his internal thoughts. *If ye don't survive this, I'll go with ye, lass. I won't leave ye to face death alone. Ye have me.* The screen froze on his tortured face.

Icy hummed in her throat as I sucked in a breath. Her voice

sounded faraway. "Roan sacrificed part of his magic to keep your soul in the Sliver. Normally, you must decide which side you want much quicker. He bought time for Jelly to come in."

"I didn't ask him to."

"Nonetheless, he did."

The images spun forward to countless moments of Roan and me flirting outrageously. With each passing glance or comment, an orange circle in my lower belly grew, becoming a wildfire, stoked hotter every time he looked at me. My body responded to him, but my mouth threw out calculated seductions, teasing and denying him, which he countered with gestures and deep growls.

Icy showed me his softer side.

He was kind in a thousand small ways, passing a towel before I asked, pulling out my chair, offering me food, holding a door, or an outstretched hand to help me stand. Somehow, I'd missed the look in his eyes. He adored me. I always turned it on him, like his kindness was a weakness, tormenting the poor man, yet he came back, time and again.

The screen flashed forward to the basement of the Coven Headquarters with Jelly practicing her magic. He was staring at me from inside the shield, his shirt in his hand. *She has no fookin' clue what she does to me. This lass will be the death of me. I know it.*

We forwarded to my grinding on his lap after Mew disappeared. The ball of orange in my middle was chaotic. My face and body were so stiff as I fought against what my body so clearly needed. Again, Roan's thoughts rang through my head. *Why won't she let go? Am I not doing it right? She's right there. She's so close. Take it, lass! I want ye to take my magic! Ye need this! Yes, oh, gods yes, there she goes. Fookin' hell, she's so beautiful.* I saw him gritting his teeth, holding himself back from joining me, giving me everything, taking none for himself.

The screen froze with me arched back in ecstasy, Roan watching breathlessly in awe. I slapped my hand to my mouth. I'd resisted that orgasm, so frightened it would bind me to him, not understanding I was already tied.

Icy chuckled, reading the message behind my slap. "He's been aching to help you be stronger. Then you nested with the spices, and–"

"Nested? Spices? What are you talking about?"

"Spices lay the groundwork, built primarily from cinnamon and cloves, giving power to create something new from the ashes of the old. You've dusted your coffees with cinnamon since you discovered the drink, but lately, it's turned into a heady blend of five powerful spices. You've been pouring your mix on every-thing, incessantly baking with it. I assumed you were preparing."

I scratched my head. "I've been going overboard, and I thought it was strange, especially when I put it on my eggs, but it wasn't with any thought on my part. What have I been nesting for?"

"For this. Your rebirth. The bracelets Veda gave you con-nected you to everything, Mori. All of it. Green tourmaline is a gateway stone to the devic realm, to the Earth's heart. Once you allowed *your* heart to shine, everything slid into place."

Icy kicked at the side of her neck with a back foot. "Last night, you danced and sang to Roan and Branko. You took their magic with an open soul, and once you ate the transformation grub—" I cut her off with a heavy hand clutching into her fur. She squeaked, and I released my grip.

I fought for breath. "Took their magic… Icy, I don't re-member much of last night." She flashed to the scene and let me watch it unfold in technicolor slow motion action. I was dealing the cards, giggling, telling Roan and Branko I was a master at the game.

She said, "Pay attention to your energy centers. They shift."

My entire body heated from the visuals before me. It started with Roan pulling out his braid, a wicked smile on his face as he watched me stare, my eyes greedy. When Branko stripped off his shirt, the orange ball in my belly turned to lava, pouring out of me. My eyes were living flame as I watched him.

Oh, I'd taken their magic all right. The next song came on, a different band, and I'd given Branko a spectacular lap dance. He'd hadn't been able to keep his hands to himself, spinning me to dizzy heights. Round one of receiving his magic.

The two men had abandoned their competition for my attention, silently agreeing to share me, as that was my shameless intent. The game progressed, me shedding clothing while Roan redressed me in kisses and caresses, flooding me with his magic until I shot to the stars. My body lit up like a beacon.

Branko lifted me from Roan's arms, the card game abandoned. I watched my body shudder under his expert touch. Back and forth, over and over, I soaked in their magic. The night was all about my pleasure. I'd tried to return the favor, but they wouldn't allow it. Eventually, the lava flow at my belly pulled in.

The green of my heart center pulsed with a steady beat, and the red at my base swirled and spun, realigning itself. My energy flowed smoothly through all seven centers, turning me into a languorous ooze of satisfied woman. Both Roan and Branko grinned, pleased with their work. We emptied the bottle of mezcal and the worm fell into my glass with a plop.

I shouted to the ceiling. "To new beginnings!" I chewed on the grub, thoughtful. "May we all be free!" I'd passed out as soon as I'd swallowed, and the men curled around me protectively.

Branko spoke to Roan in a deep rasp. "Do you think she'll remember this? Will she let it happen again?"

Roan sighed, kissing my forehead. "I fookin' hope so. I can't fathom not doing this again. She's changed. The bracelets did their magic. She opened up to us, Branko. She let us in." He gave Branko a good-natured scowl over my head. "Not exactly how I saw it unfolding, but I can live with it. Can ye share? It's what she wants."

Branko coughed out a laugh. "If it makes her happy, then yes."

My jaw was wide open as I stammered at Icy. "Did… Did they know what was happening to me?"

Icy shrugged as I watched the two of them caress my hair, trace my cheeks, and place sweet kisses on me while I snored. Loudly. She purred softly, touched by the tender scene. "They could sense a change in you. You were becoming clear about what you wanted from them. The alcohol slowed your mind enough to break your hesitation. Mori, for weeks they've dissected every gesture, swallowed every sigh, craved every smile you give them. They are desperately in love with you, and before you twist yourself into knots, they give it freely, without expectations."

I had no response.

Suddenly, the images were gone, and I was staring at a smug-looking cat. She wiped a paw over her ear. "When you died in Bermuda, Roan sacrificed a piece of his soul to buy you time. You came back from the dead. He took that as an affirmation that he should pursue you. Branko realized he loved you right before you faced the Fae Prince on the beach. He was in his gargoyle form. You must have made a comment that made him pay attention."

"I was ogling him. I vaguely remember telling him he was a dark horse as I gawped at him. Probably had to wipe some drool from my chin."

"You were not frightened."

"Absolutely not. I found him fascinating, gorgeous. He's brutally beautiful. I couldn't take my eyes off of him. Jelly was standing there in her Fae form for the first time, and I barely noticed. Branko, I definitely noticed."

Icy narrowed her eyes. "Trust me, Mori. Most people would see Branko in his shifted form and run screaming. Your open curiosity must have intrigued him, softened his stone heart. So, you nested, then last night, you shared a ritual, sang—"

"Shared a ritual? We were doing tequila shots! And I sang the Violent Femmes, Icy! Hardly a love song!"

She tipped her head at me. "Certainly not a romantic one, but let me quote the lyrics, shall I?" She cleared her small throat. "Here are a select few. 'I look at your pants and I need a kiss. Nothing I can say when I'm in your thighs. I would love to love you, lover. Why can't I get just one fu—'" I cut her off with a sharp wave of my hand.

She licked her paw. "Pretty straightforward words, Mori. You laughed, and you played and you teased, and they responded, empowering you with their magic, fortifying you, helping you for today. When Branko brought you the spicy liquor, you could kiss him after flying. Didn't you question that?"

I hid my face in my hands. "I was hungover. I didn't even think about being able to kiss him." I groaned to the sand-colored walls. "It was a drunken game of Go Fish, Icy. It wasn't…I didn't plan any of it."

Icy laughed. "You are part of the prophecy that will heal the schism in magic. The world has been waiting for you."

I scanned my sore brain, my heart beating wildly. "No, that prophecy was for Jelly."

Icy stepped from my lap and turned to face me, tail swishing across the sandstone floor. "It specifically mentions you."

"Sure, as a sidekick."

Icy scoffed and stared at me, annoyed. "You are the star of your own life, Mori. You are nobody's sidekick. You are a fantastical creature all on your own. The bracelets connected you to every creature, from the tiniest flea to the grandest whale in the ocean. You became the heartbeat of life." I shook my head, dumbstruck. She continued. "Once you declared you were free of societal restrictions, you gave my Lord permission. Ever since you came back from the dead in Bermuda, the spirits aligned to assist you. Given your heritage, it was only a matter of time until it happened. I am blessed to be the one to witness your transformation."

"Your lord? My heritage? What in the sweet hell are you talking about, Icy?"

She suddenly squeaked a sharp noise and flattened herself to the floor, hissing at me to kneel over. The pale stone walls flooded in sunlight so bright I had to duck my head and squint to see what had startled her. A golden barge adorned with a bird's head floated into the space and settled, causing the light to cast about on the walls like waves.

A buff male body with a falcon's head stepped out, a cobra wrapped around his shoulders, wearing only a shendyt, a leather kilt. Three women followed him. One had a cat's head, another a lion, the third wearing a headdress of cow horns. I fell forward and pressed my forehead to the sand.

I knew who they were. It was the Sun God Ra and his three daughters. Holy shit.

Goddess Bastet spoke first. "Lift your eyes." I assumed she was speaking to me and looked up at her feline face. She was smiling, or baring her fangs benignly, her whiskers trembling from excitement. "Well done, Icy. She's hardly shocked at all!"

Oh, call me shocked. The goddess with the lion's head regarded me coolly. She was Sekhmet, the goddess of a slaughtering rampage, only subdued when Ra ordered seven thousand jugs of beer to be dyed red. She'd mistaken it for blood and passed out cold, stopping the killing. Shit, shit, shit. Had I summoned her last night with my debauchery?

Goddess Hathor, wearing the headdress, laughed at my awed expression. She was the goddess of joy, dance, music, and love. I focused on her face as she smiled warmly. "She's perfect, Dad." Ra tipped his falcon's head to the side and crossed his arms. She leaned closer, and a ripple of her power washed over me. "Do you know what you are, Mori?"

I opened my mouth. Nothing came out. I tried again, tripping over my tongue. "Greetings, great Goddess Hathor. It is an honor to meet you. And yes, I am a mermaid."

The four of them burst into gales of laughter. I'd never seen a falcon laugh before. Nor a lion, come to think of it. As for cats, Icy often laughed at me, so that didn't come as too much of a shock. Ra chuckled. "It was her first time eating a grub. She's bound to be overwhelmed with all this. Girls, give her a minute. She'll figure it out." I looked at them blankly.

I peeked at Icy. She rolled her eyes at me and said, "My Lord, Mistresses, Mori did not realize she was nesting. Apparently, her mother never told her of her lineage."

Ra and his daughters bent their heads together. I couldn't understand everything they said, only picking up the odd word or two. Ancient Egyptian language hadn't been part of my studies, but I'd read the stories and legends.

Hathor looked at me fondly. She counted off on her fingers. "Your great, great, great, great grandfather shared your sentiments about mating. He had many dalliances, enjoying many lovers. Unbeknown to him, one passionate night led to today. To you. His lover for the night found him so delightful, she gave him a drop of her blood as a gift to his descendants. Hardly anything, but enough to call forward your destiny."

I blinked at her. "And what would that be?"

She smiled, tipping her cow horns to the side. She laughed joyfully and looked at Icy with delight in her eyes. "She's truly naïve, isn't she?"

Icy replied with a roll of her eyes in my direction. "Yes, Mistress."

Hathor spoke softly, as if cushioning a blow. "Mori, you carry the blood of a phoenix. Right now, you are dead. The good news is a phoenix doesn't stay dead for long." Every muscle in my body froze as horror raced through me. I was dead?

THIRTY-TWO

MEW

The Boss and I watched the drama at the Coven unfold. Her enormous office wall split into sections so we could monitor the world, and all around us, the lives of the creatures on the planet unfolded. We currently focused on the key players in the now active prophecy on Earth. She watched with a pleased grin. "Coming along nicely, aren't they, Bartholomew?"

I tipped my head. "Yes, ma'am. Although Mori's current situation may send Jelly into a tailspin. She won't understand what's happening. None of them will. Look at Branko and Roan. They're distraught." I wondered how I might mitigate the situation.

The Boss twisted her head sharply, her white hair swishing, dark eyes narrowing. "And you will not tell them what's happening, will you, Bartholomew? The line you've been walking has become terribly thin."

"No, ma'am." Unease crept up my spine.

"I saw you build the fire for Mori, helping her solve the riddle of the royal jelly. Very clever of you, that workaround.

She's incredibly intelligent. She will be a great boon so long as she doesn't become distracted by her men. But I don't think she will. I get the sense that she's come to realize that love, true love, does not mean chains." Her eyes moved to a section of the wall. "You'd better get back down there. Mako will need your help to keep Jelly from exploding. Any advancement on the pearl?"

"No, ma'am. As far as I know, Leoht is still hiding in Kokuro's shell."

The Boss tapped her delicate foot on the floor. "They need her for the Hellhole. For the twins."

"Yes, ma'am."

"Shit." She stood and paced. I watched, keeping my mouth firmly shut. I could force Leoht's return, but it would be a direct interference; one that was forbidden, even to us. She exhaled audibly, a giant heave of a sound. "I will allow you to continue to drop hints, Bartholomew, but I don't want you back here full time. I have enough people fawning all over me. I need you on the ground. Do not cross that line."

"Yes, ma'am." I bowed and disappeared.

Arriving in the kitchen of the coven headquarters, I found Veda bouncing on her toes. She clapped her hands together as I shimmered into being. "Oh, Great One, I suspected you'd come back soon. Did you see?" I smiled at the excited woman in the orange sari, obviously a nod to Mori's energy.

"Quite spectacular, Veda. Your bracelets worked very well."

She bobbled her head with my praise, her smile lighting her face. "How long do we have to wait? Until her return?"

I rubbed the back of my neck. "Until she's ready. Veda, we need to support Jelly and Mako. The others as well. These will be a difficult few moments. It depends on how fast Mori comes back. Come outside with me, please."

Her bright smile dropped immediately, replaced with a furrowed brow and down-turned lips. She shook her head resolutely. "Oh, Faithful One, Mew, I am not sure Jelly wants to see me right now. She looked quite violent when I delighted in Mori's transformation."

I patted her shoulder. "Come, Veda. I will protect you from Jelly's wrath. No harm will befall you." We walked to the front of the house, me having to coerce her with a steady hand as she paused several times. I went first at her insistence. I groaned at the picture before me. Anna and Richard sat on the porch swing, crying as they held each other. The others gathered around a scorch mark on the grass. Jelly was inconsolable and furious. Her eyes swung up.

She slashed her finger through the air, stabbing it in Veda's direction, who partially hid behind my body. "You did this! Where is she?" She wrestled in Mako's arms as he struggled to contain her. "If we can't get her back, I'm going to rip out your fucking throat, witch!"

Veda murmured beside me. "Do you see what I mean?"

I nodded, taking a step forward. "Stay here." I cleared the stairs and strode toward Jelly, figuring out my plan as I walked. As I approached them, Roan stood, barely controlling himself as he intercepted me halfway. He shoved his hand at my chest, causing me to weight my back foot. I held my hands out passively. It did nothing to soothe the man before me.

"Where the fook did she go?"

"I can't tell you," I said, attempting to placate him with my soothing tone. It had the opposite effect, and he moved so swiftly I didn't see it coming until his fist connected with my nose with an outstanding crunch. I staggered back, and he lunged forward, grappling me to the ground, where he straddled me and began pummeling my poor face. I could have easily vanished, but he needed this. His soul was screaming inside. I allowed the assault.

Five, four, three, two, one... everything around us stilled, including the chirping birds and the wind in the leaves.

Roan saw my true form and scrambled off of me as if I'd thrust a hot poker in his eye. Mako hitched in a breath and loosened his arms around a frozen Jelly, who'd been spitting and hissing as she clawed at him to get to Veda. Roan's lungs heaved as he tried to reconcile what he saw.

I sat up, my face normal, with no evidence of his brutality. I grinned. "Only you and Mako can see me. I've paused time. Everyone else sees an irate man kneeling over my pulverized face with his fist cocked. You've got a good punch, Roan. "

His green eyes were wide and wild. He crouched, but stayed on his toes, ready to spring. "Da fook? What the fook are ye?" Suspicion crept over his face. "Yer letting me see ye. Ye let me pin ye. Why?"

"Because I need you to calm down. More specifically, I need Jelly to calm down." We glanced over at the blue-haired woman who had burst into her Fae form, canines bared. Thankfully, Mako had also shifted to Fae and was strong enough to restrain her. But only just. With time on pause, Mako shook out his arms. I called over to him. "Mako, you'll need a good grip on her when we return to normal." He nodded and swept his hair from his face.

I turned back to Roan. "Remember when Mori went to the Sliver, and you offered a piece of her soul to give her more time?"

He growled his reply. "Aye, and I'd do it again in a heartbeat. Does she need more from me? Take it all. I don't care so long as she lives."

"Roan, who do you think retrieved your offering?"

He blinked a few times, staring at the multiple wings that sat folded on my back. "Ye took it?"

I nodded with a smile. "It was incredibly selfless of you, Roan. And here you are again, offering it all for her."

He slumped to the ground, wrapping his thick arms around his knees. His eyes scanned the burnt grass. He made his decision quickly, nodding once resolutely. "Aye. If it means she lives, take me instead."

My smile must have been blinding because he sucked in a sharp breath. I reassured him. "There's no need for that, Roan, but it's a generous offer, and one that won't be forgotten. Mori will be fine. I need Jelly to calm down. She and Mako need to coax Leoht out of hiding. Leoht needs to come back, and Jelly won't be able to travel to her if she's this upset."

Roan snarled. "Where is Mori?"

I chose my words carefully. "Do not be afraid for Mori. We need Jelly to retrieve Leoht."

He squinted his eyes at me. "I don't give a fookin' flyin' fook about the fookin' pearl, Mew! Where is Mori?"

I slid a hand over my bald head, wondering how much I could say. "I have to hedge around my answer, Roan. Read between the lines."

He puffed out a breath. "Mori's the brains of this lot. And she bloody evaporated."

"You're more than the fists you employ so readily, Wizard. Just let your mind wander. The answer will come." Roan leaned closer, watching my face for tells. Mori had taught him well by example. "Mori is undergoing a fundamental change. You and Branko are instrumental in what's happening to her." I tipped my chin at Branko, his stone face streaked with rolling icicles, currently frozen stuck. "Do you know what he was just saying?"

Roan looked over at Branko. "Maly ptacek? I think it means little bird, although I can't be completely sure." He roughed his hand over his chin. "Mori would know."

"Do you remember what you said to her at the pond?"

He shook his head slowly, eyes down as he strained for the words of the memory. "I said a lot of things." He stumped around the potentials. "She liked it. It gave her peace. And the swans touched her heart. She laughed at the ducks. Thought they were funny, especially when I told her about their willies." He looked up with hopeful eyes. "We haven't slept with her. Is that what she needs?"

He was getting off track. I pushed my luck, asking a more direct question. "What did you say later? Right before she ran off?" A searing pain shot through my skull as the boss zapped me. Too much of a hint.

Roan muttered, rubbing his face. "She was lit by the sun, the setting sun." His eyes swung to mine as it snapped into place. "I called her a woman on fire. Caught up in flames."

I sat as still as a stone. My jaw tightened as I strained not to react. It was right there. Mori would have blurted it immediately. He floundered, churning the words over and over, watching me. I'd said all I could say. He'd have to figure it out from here. He scowled at my blank expression. "Can ye give me a hint?"

I swiped at the blood leaking from my nose. "Come on, Roan. Think! Put it together! What happened in Bermuda?" Another lightning bolt slashed through my head, making me groan. A spurt of blood stained my shirt.

He leaped to his feet, his hands fisting. Pacing, he slapped a hand on the back of his neck, urging his brain to work faster. "Little bird. Woman on fire. Little bird. She died. I bought her time. She came back…" I put every ounce of energy I had into my eyes, hoping he could read my enthusiasm. He tripped over the words, watching as my eyes grew bigger and bigger. "She died. She came back. Little bird. Flames…"

He stopped in his tracks, his green eyes enormous. He swung toward me and bellowed. "The lass is a fookin' phoenix???"

I chuckled. "I knew you'd get there. You mustn't tell anyone what I am. Only Mako knows, and if you let my secret slip, my boss will yank me away so fast your head will spin. Get back into position, Roan. You had your right fist drawn back, my shirt bunched in the other. As soon as I release my magic, pretend you're done fighting. Then help Mako restrain Jelly." I looked over to see Mako brace himself around Jelly's frozen body.

Roan hovered over me, his knuckles split, my face ruined. I dropped my hold on time. Richard and Anna rushed toward us, yelling for Roan to stop beating me. He hauled me to my feet and gripped my shirt, shaking me. "How do we get her back?"

I stepped away, wiping blood from my face. "That's up to her. Stop Jelly from gutting Veda."

THIRTY-THREE

MORI

I laughed with an edge of hysteria, certain Hathor was mistaken. "Me? A phoenix? The mythical bird? And what do you mean, my destiny?"

Bastet leaned close, her whiskers twitching as they grazed against a horn on Hathor's headdress. "I marked your friend's back and gathered her story when I licked her blood from my claw. Tell my family exactly what the Fae-Mers Seer told you."

My memory snapped sharply into place. "She was pretty vague. She said, 'We see you having a powerful influence on the world of magic. Do not forget that. Even when all seems lost.' But I thought she was referring to the Sliver, not some secret phoenix blood."

Sekhmet scowled at her father, who regarded us with sharp eyes. She hissed at Icy. "You said she was smart. She doesn't seem all that smart to me."

I bristled. I prided myself on my intelligence. I said, "Forgive me, honored Sekhmet. I am overwhelmed. I'm trying to understand what you want from me." Sekhmet rolled her lioness's eyes. I waved my hand in the air. "I mean, look at me. I can move sand and dirt. That's my only power. But I *am* smart. I've worked hard to understand the different magical races. But as for powers? I have a good scream, but it doesn't explode things like Jelly's."

At this, the four of them buckled into laughter. Again. I inhaled to hold on to my temper. Bastet recovered first. "You think dirt is your strength? Mori, you're an Azkiya'an Maestra Mage." She put her hands on her hips. "Actually, Thoth should be the one explaining this. Where is he?"

Ra huffed a breath. "Really, Bastet? Sun and moon. We can't be together."

I stammered. "Tuh, Thoth? The God of the Moon? Scribe of the Gods? Wisdom, knowledge, science, magic…that Thoth?" I blinked back my shock. "How am I a Mage? An Azkiya'an Maestra? I'm not familiar with that kind." Bastet and Sekhmet both growled in annoyance.

Hathor, the nice goddess, replied patiently. "Your paternal great grandfather was half Mage. He had a recessive Azkiya'an gene. An Azkiya'an Maestra has superior intelligence, the ability to draw connections quickly, and only blooms with the females. It passed to your granny, then your mother, Oxycirrhites, and then to you. Your mother was exceptionally bright. Didn't you notice?" Her headdress wobbled slightly as she shook her head, finishing her thoughts. "Of course not. You were a mere child when she died. I am sorry."

I looked from face to face in shock. "Why didn't anyone tell me?"

Ra lost his patience and thundered. "Stand up." I scrambled to comply. "Your father didn't explain your heritage?" He glared at me with disbelief.

I dipped my head, frightened by his outburst. "I thought we were all Mers. That's all I've ever known."

Hathor lay her hand on his arm. "Dad, her father probably thought he was protecting her. After all, their society shuns non-pure Mers. He didn't want her to experience inferior status."

I stared at her. "So I'm a Mers with Mage and Phoenix blood?" I stuck my thumbnail in my teeth, pacing in a circle. "And what? All this latent magic was just waiting for me? Waiting for me to accept myself? That's insane."

Ra threw up his hands in exasperation. Sekhmet studied her nails nonchalantly, bored with my confusion. "Dad, it doesn't matter that she was ignorant of all this. We're here now." She dropped her hand and leveled her slitted eyes on me. "This won't be easy, Mori. People will want to stop you, kill you, but you have the power to keep rising from the ashes. And believe me, you'll need it."

I paled. "I'm going to die again?"

Bastet yawned loudly and grinned through her whiskers. "Fairly often, if I'd have to guess. Good news! You're a phoenix!"

Ra nodded. "Even better news is that you have powerful protectors. That is their role. Your blood drew them forward, called them like a… siren's song." He chuckled at his joke. "You took their magic. Branko shifts, which allows you to return to the living quite quickly. And Roan's magic has sped up your brain. Oh, girls, remind me to reward Veda's guides. Ingenious, connecting you to all creatures through those bracelets."

I gasped out loud as the pieces slotted together. "If I can come back from the dead…am I stronger than the Fae?"

He turned to his daughters and grinned. "I'm so glad she caught up. I was worried we'd be here all day." He turned back to me, cocking his falcon head. "You do not share the privileges of a Fae, meaning you cannot enter their kingdoms, but power? Oh yes, firebird, you possess great power."

I held up my hands, about to protest. Sekhmet reached the end of her rope with my hesitation. She darted so close I yipped in surprise. She pressed a claw to my heart. "This tender piece of meat glows with the fire of regeneration. It will break and squeeze dry from the pain and suffering you will witness. Yet you must rise again and again with hope despite the odds, and fight for a world of harmony. Do you deny your path?"

"Of course not. I want to heal magic. I want to help."

Hathor stepped forward, her face kind, gently pushing Sekhmet away from me. "Good. Now, get used to dying." She said it so casually I couldn't help but gape. "Each time you do, you'll return here. We will discuss why and how you failed. Then you'll try again." She tipped her head. "You're struggling with this. Your heart is already worried about those around you. I'll offer this advice. Jump in the way. Take the sword. Take the hit. You will come back. They will not."

I thought about Branko and Roan. They were manly men, warriors. There's no way they'd let me die for them. My forehead crinkled anxiously. Ra was antsy, done with this conversation. He lay his hand on my head, pressing until I kneeled at his feet. "Mori Pterois, I claim you as a daughter of the sun, the source of all life." A rush of flames skated over my skin before settling in. "New powers will manifest, Mori. We've never encountered such a strange blend of blood. Between you and your friend Jelly, well, we can't predict what will happen. But your role is important. Good luck, phoenix. See you next time you die."

I choked at that, unable to reply.

They stepped back in the barge, Ra holding his arm out for Hathor, while Sekhmet gracefully leaped in the boat. Bastet had a quiet word with Icy, who nodded and bowed, scraping her small chin on the floor. The walls reflected the light in a pattern of waves, and they simply disappeared. Our three-sided space began shrinking around us.

Icy hopped up beside me, shaking herself from head to toe. "That went better than expected. Ready?" I opened my mouth and fell through a tunnel lined in orange and yellow flames.

We arrived to find chaos. Icy's whiskers twitched. "Stay back here, behind the tree. I want to see what happens. I saw several scenarios." Mako and Roan both restrained Jelly. Her sharp ears rose from her hair, her fingers ending in claws. Roan bled from scratch marks, Mako's shirt hung in tatters, and Anna and Richard blocked Veda behind them. Mew looked like he'd run face first into a bus while Branko slouched on the grass, broken, resignation on his stone face. Everyone's attention was on Jelly, who screamed at Veda like a banshee.

Mew stepped forward, facing Jelly. He raised a hand. "I authorized it, Jelly. If you want to blame anyone for Mori's death, blame me." He gave Mako a surreptitious nod. Mako released his hold, taking Roan with him. Jelly hauled in a breath and screamed, her hand lifted toward Mew in her rage. Orange fire blasted at him, snuffing as soon as it contacted his body. Snarling, she raised the other hand, purple ropes encasing Mew, holding him a foot off the ground. She shot bolts of crimson red at his face, and he grinned, further enraging her. And then, it was a beautiful collision of magic and color.

Squeezing with the purple ropes, orange and turquoise fire lit up his skin. Electric blue zapped alongside pulses of red. She aimed cobalt blue for his throat, as if trying to drown him, while maroon threads raced around his body at speed, searching for an entrance. She yelled at him through a haze of green mist. "Your thoughts are wrong, Mew! I do want to murder Veda!"

All of her magic flowed seamlessly, coordinated in her attack as she stepped closer, weaving the threads, looking for a weakness in the colossal man before her. Mew took all of it into his body. How he could withstand it was beyond me. His smile grew larger, and he winked at her, putting his hands on his hips.

Suddenly, she dropped it all, her hands falling at her sides as she stared at him dumbly, jaw cracked open in disbelief. She screamed in rage and wonder. "Are you fricking kidding me?" She released her Fae form and spun, sprinting in our direction, leaving everyone confused by her abrupt change.

I went to step out and assuage her, but Icy stopped me. "Let her have her moment first. As soon as the men see you, they'll swamp you in testosterone."

Jelly skidded around the trunk of the massive tree, coming to a halt in front of me, eyes blazing from the magic she'd used. She threw her arms around me, sobbing. "I thought you were dead!" She wailed in my ear. "Don't ever fucking do that again!"

I squeezed her hard. "I didn't plan it, if it makes it any better." I wrangled out of her firm grip, as powerful as a giant squid. Holding her by the shoulders, I gave her a small shake to bring her out of her tears. "Did you see what you just did? You wielded the magic, Jelly! All of it!"

She hiccuped, staring at me blankly. "I did, didn't I?"

Icy interrupted us. "Incoming!"

Roan reached me first and spun Jelly away from me. He crushed me into his arms, lifting me off my feet. He murmured in my hair with relief. "A fookin' phoenix, lass?"

I grinned, clutching at him. "Aye. Seems so. Got a touch of Mage too."

A massive gargoyle tore me from his embrace, spinning us, his cold marble arms like heaven on my hot skin as he swept his wings around us for privacy. "Mori…" He stroked my hair tenderly, such a strange dichotomy to the hardness of his body. He gently set me on my feet. I stared up at his fearsome face, thick fangs jutting up from his lower lip. He grunted, pulling his face back to human.

I gasped. "You can partially shift?"

His deep voice shot shivers through my body as he lowered his lips to mine. "I can do many things, little bird." Any response I had died in my throat as he kissed me. I drank his magic like sweet water, willingly drowning, not wanting to surface for a breath. He chuckled. "Roan is breaking his fists on my wings. I should share." He wrapped his arms tighter around me. "But I don't want to." He flinched, his steel eyes sparkling with laughter as he released his wings, shuddering them back into his body.

Roan spun me, Branko's arms still around my waist, and clasped his hands on my face. He growled at Branko. "Don't fookin' touch me, ye bloody ice cube. My turn." His magic poured into me with his kiss, lighting me from within. I felt him nudge at the shroud in my mind. I lifted it to let him in as he sucked on my bottom lip. *Ye scared the fookin' shite out of me, lass.*

I smiled against his lips. *I didn't mean to. I'm sorry.* I glanced over his shoulder and giggled. *Jelly is losing it. She can't break through my mind. Look. She's going purple from trying.*

He chuckled against my mouth, groaning as he pressed against me, but yelped and jumped back. "Fook, man! I told ye not to touch me!"

Branko cocked his head with a snort. "Unless I am mistaken, it was you who touched me by invading our woman's personal space."

My heart stopped. Our woman.

Roan frowned and rubbed his stomach, lifting his shirt to inspect for frostbite, making me hum in my throat at the sight of his tattoos, wanting to trace his scar with my fingers. I patted Branko's arm. He let go. I turned to Jelly, who was standing impatiently with her arms crossed, tapping her foot on the grass. When she had our attention, she snapped. "Roan, you need to teach me the mind thing. You both have me blocked, and Mori isn't contorting her fingers."

Roan quickly explained how to do it, and Jelly stomped her foot. "That's it? That's the almighty block?" She stared at me. "Can I come in?" When I grinned and nodded, she shouted. *All that fumbling with fingers in London! Goddess! I could strangle him! So, what happened to you? Where did you go? Back to the Sliver? And piss off, Roan, you menace. Quit trying to shove in. This is a private conversation.*

I laughed out loud at the storm clouds on Roan's face as she easily blocked him, intuitively closing her mind to him. I replied to her. *We were in a pyramid. Icy took me. It was golden stone, three-sided, so yes, a pyramid, but I didn't see outside.*

Jelly's eyes narrowed. *Mori, what are you?*

I laughed. *A whole lot more than I was told as a child. Come. I'll explain, but first, talk to Veda. She's innocent of any wrongdoing. She helped free me.*

We turned for the house, both my hands taken in larger ones, one warm, one freezing cold. Icy raced across the lawn, and Mew bent down as she jumped into arms, filling him in on our trip. Jelly walked on Roan's other side. I peered around him, speaking only to her. *Did Leoht come back?*

Jelly shook her head no. *I begged her, Mori. She's totally ignoring me.*

That wasn't good. Jelly broke off from us to go to Mako. He didn't seem too shocked to see me, and winked in my direction as Jelly spoke in a low growl, probably angry at him for restraining her. Good thing he did, though. It would have been catastrophic if Jelly had killed Veda. She was a powerful ally, connected to guides with great reach.

Mew held Icy, stroking her fur, making her purr at high volume. He smiled at me. "Hello, Mori. Welcome back." He set Icy on the ground and opened his arms. Removing my hands from my men was like pulling taffy mid-winter. They didn't want to let go, but they did, both of them rumbling their discontent. I hugged Mew, who met me with a chuckle. "Bet you didn't see that coming."

I stepped out of his arms, wagging a finger at him. "One of these days, I'm going to pin you and find out all your secrets. Did you know?" He shrugged his shoulders, making me snort. I gestured with my eyes at Veda, who twisted her fingers together nervously. "She has some explaining to do."

Mew followed my gaze and grinned. Veda disappeared into the house. "We all do. Let's go back inside." I wandered away and stared at the burnt patch of grass, shuddering involuntarily. Branko slid his arms around my middle, stopping me.

His voice was rough. "I thought you were dead forever." His brow pressed down, making him appear angry. "I am no stranger to death, Mori. I have lost many people in my lifetime. But your death…your death took me to my knees." His bitterly cold arms tightened, assuring himself I was still there. He sighed and kissed my curls. "Let's go in."

We were the last to enter. He nodded to the worn velvet chair, my favorite, which was empty, reserved for me. He leaned against the bookcase and crossed his arms, keeping his distance from everyone as he'd just shifted. I took the seat. We were quiet, not sure where to start. Typically, Jelly would speak first, but she stayed curiously mum.

Veda came through the door with Mew, him carrying a tray laden with teapots and cups, her with a plate of cinnamon rolls. Her feet froze on the fine embroidered red carpet, unwilling to cross into the silence, unsure of how we would react. I called out to her. "Veda, I'd love one of those, please." Her relief was clear as her eyes shone with tears. She came to me first.

Hovering over in almost a bow, holding out her sweet of-fering, her bindi spun slowly. "I wanted to tell you. I'm sorry if it frightened you." She glanced at Icy, grooming by the fire, commanding the bench all to herself. "My guides told me the cat had it handled. You are unharmed?"

"I am well, Veda. Probably the best I've ever been. And it did scare me, the light coming for me, but then you shouted for me to claim my destiny. I was ready to stop running from my-self." I cleared my throat, raising my voice, looking pointedly at Jelly, who threw murderous glares at Veda. "I am fine, everyone.

Look. Hale and hearty. As much as Veda started all this with the bracelets, I needed healing. I needed help, and she helped me."

Veda left the treats on the table and sat on the bench, scooting Icy over to one side, and surprisingly, the cat allowed it without complaint. The small sound of teaspoons tinkling against china cups suggested I should speak, as no one else had taken control of the room. I set down my tea. "I have a drop of phoenix blood, given to my grandfather some four generations ago. And it turns out there's Mage blood through my mother's side."

Roan's voice was soft. "Did ye learn what branch?"

"An Azkiya'an Maestra."

He smiled at me. "Aye, that makes sense." Seeing the looks of bewilderment around him, he explained. "A very rare kind. Superior intelligence, and it only manifests in daughters." He swiped his hand over his chin. "So much has just clicked into place."

Jelly's eyebrows raised. "You're part Mage? All this time?"

I grinned at her before turning to Anna. "Let's get down to business. Jelly needs to get Leoht. Everyone else, too. We need to plan our attack and assemble our team for the Hellhole."

Jelly leaned forward. "What do you mean, team? Only Mako and I are going in."

"No, I'm going too. Don't argue."

Roan and Branko shared a look. Roan said, "Then we're going with ye, lass."

Damn it. I suspected as much. I hid the tremor in my voice. "Fine. It's settled. Get Leoht back. Now."

THIRTY-FOUR

MAKO

I sat on the floor between Jelly's knees, my back against the lip of the cushion. She leaned over me, her blue hair draping my shoulders. She slid her hands inside my shirt and placed them on my tattoo. She murmured in my ear. "Ready?" I nodded. Jelly said, "All right. Think of soft silk, of Leoht." We chanted 'OM' in our minds.

Her fingers tightened, and we shot through a tunnel. I sighed a breath of relief at the sound of water pulling through a shell. My vision cleared to find Leoht sitting cross-legged, her back leaning against the dark, luminescent wall. I leaned forward, ready to talk, but Jelly stilled me with a hand on my leg and said quietly, "She goes first." I clenched my jaw in frustration.

Leoht wordlessly held out a strip of green algae taken from the inside of the oyster shell. Jelly accepted it with a nod and tore it in half, sharing it with me. The Fae blinked her purple eyes, the fluorescent pink pupils glowing. Jelly had described Leoht, but seeing her in the flesh was astounding. She radiated magnificent power. I chewed the crunchy substance, the taste of watermelon bursting over my tongue. Energy flooded me instantly.

Her lips curled up in a smile as she watched me study her.

"You are so like your father. Your heart is pure, so good." She turned her strange eyes on Jelly, apologetic. "I'm sorry I didn't go with you to the Seeker or bees. You begged me and I ignored you. After the Hellhole, I just needed safety, and I trusted you would survive. But I'm sorry I wasn't there for you."

Jelly remained silent. I wanted to scratch my head in puzzlement. When had my mate become patient?

Leoht continued in a quiet, melodic hum. "Going into the Hellhole, into that specific room." She shook her head sadly. "I was so overwhelmed. I panicked, Jelly. I felt too exposed, too raw. So many terrible things happened in that place. I had to come home." She stroked the soft flesh beneath her. "I needed to see my mother. You understand, don't you?"

Jelly's turquoise eyes filled with empathy. She shifted to kneel before Leoht. "I do." She opened her arms in invitation, and Leoht's face crumpled as she allowed herself to be touched, melting into Jelly's embrace. Silver tears ran down her black cheeks, reminding me of mercury as they splashed into Jelly's long hair. Leoht reached for me with one hand.

"Mako, come here. You like your group hugs." I smiled and crossed to them, reaching my arms around. Leoht's skin caused a strange sensation to course through my body, and I gasped as thousands of tiny wings fluttered against me. She chuckled. "That's my magic. It seeks energy, and yours is good. It's flirting with you." She sat back against the wall. We resettled ourselves across from her.

Worry edged me. Leoht still hadn't indicated she was ready to rejoin us. She studiously ignored our quiet stares, picking at the greenery on the wall with her claws. I was about to speak when Jelly stilled me with her fingers grazing my wrist.

My mate voiced her doubts. "Leoht, can you do this? You'll need to step out of your pain." Jelly shook her head, her blue hair floating around her as her voice dropped. "I learned that it's easy to get caught up in our own stories, to forget that we're part of a larger collective. But I won't pressure you, Leoht. I want you to make this decision of your own volition."

I stiffened, about to argue. Jelly wrapped her fingers tighter, making me hold my tongue. Leoht slowly scraped at the shell, leaving gouges in the moss. Mother Kokuro broke the tense silence. *I have explained it to her, Jelly. This year, the world has seen multiple hurricanes, extremely destructive, with five of them cataclysmic. Everything is impacted. Someone must rescue the twin girls, and Leoht is the one we have. The Earth will not survive herself without them.*

Jelly leaned toward Leoht, her voice calm. "I don't fully understand the twins' role, or even ours, in the bigger picture, but we need you. Can you separate from what happened to you? Can you overcome your personal horror to work for the whole? If not, we can get Sebastian to take us, but it sounds like he shouldn't go in there."

Leoht went rigid and bared her teeth, making me stiffen, ready to defend Jelly. She hissed at Jelly. "Sebastio will not risk himself for my fear. I want to see Terrun and Vingor punished. I want them to pay with blood. Blood that I personally spill. Does my fury assuage your doubts?"

Jelly grinned savagely. "It does."

A faint whistling sound reverberated through the shell, but as it grew louder, I realized it was a scream. Leoht's face swung up as she cackled with mischief. Jelly and I leaped back as a mermaid with a sky blue tail landed on the silk, causing it to rebound like a water bed and toss us. The mermaid hyperventilated, her tail slapping wildly as she stared at us through shocked eyes. It was my sister.

I yelled at her. "Simmi? What are you doing here? I thought you were at home!"

She rolled over, her tail still floundering. "MAKO? Where

are we? I was swimming in the ocean! I fell through a wormhole or something!"

Mother Kokuro's voice sounded around us, laughter in the tone. *I brought you, child. Hello Simmi. Welcome. I am Mother Kokuro. I wanted you sooner, but Leoht needed privacy. The blood of my daughter runs in your body. Not by choice, but it is there.* Leoht leaned forward from her place on the shell wall to scrutinize Simmi, who turned green under her keen gaze, but stared right back at the dark woman. Mother Kokuro continued. *Simmi, what is different since your captivity?*

I sat up straighter, my eyes narrowed on my sister. She'd waved us off when we'd asked if it had changed her, so we let it drop without further prodding. Simmi glanced at me apologetically. "The magnification of people's feelings, laid bare, even if they're keeping a straight face."

Leoht's face was unblinking, her expression a blank mask. She pointed to Leoht. "You. You're so bitter with injustice I'm amazed you're still breathing." She looked at Jelly's neutral face. "And Jelly is screaming with laughter inside from my expression. I have to admit, that was quite the trip to get here." She looked up at the ceiling of the shell. "I'm also stronger, more coordinated. It's like I have a muscle memory primed for battle, knowing moves as though I've been training all my life. I haven't. Mako's the fighter in the family, not me."

Leoht grinned savagely. "That is from me. My blood is in your veins. I would apologize, but proficiency in combat is an excellent skill to have. As for the rest, my magic has highlighted the empathic strain of your father."

I growled at Simmi. "You said nothing changed. But you're what? A ninja telepath now? When were you going to tell us?"

She rolled her eyes at my tone. "I was planning on never."

Kokuro's voice shimmered through the water. *Simmi, I apologize in advance.*

Simmi's pale blue eyes crinkled up. "For what?"

Oh shit. I grabbed Jelly's hand and dragged her over to Leoht just as Simmi's back arched and she screamed. Encased in white light, we couldn't see her, and every muscle in my body stiffened as I battled the impulse to make Kokuro stop torturing my sister, despite it being a wondrous event. Jelly stroked my hand soothingly, telling me it would soon pass. The scream of her pain turned to a faint whimper as the white light faded away.

Simmi wore her hair long, and she gathered the dark tresses into her fists and looked down at Kokuro's mark. We gasped simultaneously. It looked like a chain draped across her chest, winding over her upper arms and the top of her back. At first, it seemed like a series of multi-colored figure-eights. Jelly scooted forward to see better. I joined her.

In shades of gray, brown, orange, red, and black, spotted yellow, bright purple, dark pink, and one green with horizontal stripes, at least fifty seahorses danced on her skin. Couples faced each other, their tails entwined, resting back to back against other pairs. Right over her sternum lay the same dark circle I had, with three brilliant white stars, guarded by the sliver of a new moon. It hung like a pendant from the tails of the central seahorses.

Simmi gasped, her eyes wide with shock. "Mother Kokuro, what does this mean?"

Seahorses dance for hours each day. So joyful. They are delightful creatures, like you and your lover. So very sweet, your love. But Simmi, he is not who he seems.

Simmi pinked and then paled. "Simon?"

That is not his true name. Ask him to explain how he became the Drifter.

She blinked a few times, flabbergasted. She stammered. "Uh, okay. Okay. I will. I have asked, but he told me it was a sad story, and he didn't want to upset me. What about the pendant below the seahorses? It's the same symbol as Mako's. What does it mean?"

I will reveal that later, my child. You are now a Fae-Mers, one of mine. Learn to shield from emotion to avoid overwhelm. Your father can teach you.

Simmi looked over as I slung an arm around Jelly, squeezing her against me, tears in my throat from Mother Kokuro blessing my sister, bringing her into the fold. My heart was so full. I let go of Jelly to reach for Simmi, hugging her tightly. Simmi laughed at me. "Gods, Mako, settle down. Your heart is about to explode from happiness. Mother Kokuro, can you explain more? What it means to be yours?"

You have the heightened power of a Fae. More speed, more strength, deeper magic. Use it well, daughter. Train hard. Develop the talents you've received.

Leoht nodded in approval, her purple eyes glowing at Simmi. "Your father can teach you to shield your mind, and Jelly and your brother can teach you to fight." She glanced at me and grinned. "He is a strong warrior."

Mother Kokuro issued a warning, chilling my blood. *Terrun and Vingor are aware Jelly is whole. They are gathering strength, bolstering the guard on the Hellhole. You must act with speed.* Mother Kokuro's voice softened, filled with great kindness. *Leoht, my love, you can do this. Face your fears. Destroy the demons.*

Leoht bowed. "I will."

Without warning, she dove for me and Jelly, tackling us on the silk. We whooshed back to our bodies in the library, Jelly swaying in the chair as Leoht resumed her place in the pearl. Jelly grabbed at her throat and spoke to the roomful of anxious faces. "She's back." She dropped her lips to my ear. "Did that just happen? Where's Simmi?"

I searched the room for my sister. She wasn't here. Leoht's

voice pitched into my head, startling me, the tones high and low simultaneously. *You must get her. And Sebastio. Tell Anna to get your father.*

I spoke out loud. "Leoht wants my dad. Everyone else too." Anna nodded once, not needing further instruction, and disappeared in a flash of light. Minutes later, she reappeared with my parents, leaving them reeling. Dad crossed to where Jelly and I were, and I stood to hug him. "Dad, you've missed a lot since you've been gone. We need to talk."

He dropped his voice. "Anna said Mori's a phoenix, Jelly got her soul back, and you've been messing around with vision work. Son…" His voice carried a warning. He tipped his chin toward the French doors. We walked away from everyone for more privacy. I shoved my hands in my pockets defensively.

I sighed. "Dad, I needed to do something. I can't sit around. I wanted to have a backup plan in case Jelly wasn't successful."

"What did you find?"

I opened the door and stepped outside. He followed, and I closed it shut. I spoke quietly. "As we can't access it through the well in the cave, I looked for an alternative. There's an entrance to the Hellhole from Earth. That's as close as I got. It's guarded by bats. I didn't explain Leif, obviously, in case they're loyal to your brothers." I winced at the words. "My uncles. But I didn't get the sense they were."

Dad shook his head. "They aren't. Bats protect all of Fae and don't take sides. Come, we need to share this. Let me explain it to everyone." He opened the French doors. I yelped as Simmi and Simon appeared before us, Anna blinking away again immediately.

Simmi hugged me tightly, her voice low in my ear. "I can't believe that just happened. Do I tell Dad?" I stepped back and cocked my head at her, giving her my best "don't be an idiot, of course you tell Dad" glare. She rolled her eyes and blurted.

"Dad, Kokuro just marked me." She yanked down the collar on her top and showed him.

He leaned closer to inspect the dancing seahorses. "When? While you were home?"

"Yup. Just now. She grabbed me from the ocean. I was floating on my back in the waves with Simon, and then I'm with Mako and Jelly in a giant talking oyster in my Mers form. She claimed me, boosting my Fae power like Mako. An hour later, I was back in the water, although it felt like five minutes in the shell. Simon was going nuts, thinking Terrun kidnapped me again." She smiled at Simon sweetly.

Dad blinked. "What else did she say?"

"A lot of things. Mostly that I'm an empath, like you. Leoht's blood enhanced my magic. I can *feel* people, Dad. It's unnerving. She said I needed to learn how to shield. Will you help me?"

He kissed the top of her head. "Of course." He turned to Simon, his voice distinctly sterner. "Hello, Simon. I thought you were going to Oregon."

Simon's wide smile was genuine as he shook my father's hand and looked over at Simmi, so obviously enamored with her. He opened his mouth to speak, but Simmi interrupted with a laugh. "I wouldn't let him leave. I'm glad I didn't. My impromptu trip to Mother Kokuro rattled the hell out of me."

Simon shrugged his shoulders happily. "She sidetracked me."

I looked pointedly at Simmi, wondering if she'd had time to ask Simon about his real name. Mind you, we'd only been back a hot second, so probably not. She easily read my face. Probably my emotions as well. I was decidedly against my sister being with someone who held secrets, especially as Kokuro had mentioned them. I would never ignore the Mother again. "Later," she whispered. She led Dad to the sofa, and Simon, the

Drifter, excused himself from my inquisitive stare. As much as I wanted his truth, Simmi deserved it first.

Anna flashed in with Gray, who strode straight to me, clapping me on the back. "I shouldn't have left. Mum gave me the highlights, but I need it all."

"Just about to do it." I went back to Jelly and perched on the arm of her chair. I lifted a hand for silence. "We're all here, Leoht included. I'll do a quick recap for those who were gone. Jelly's experience as a bee was a resounding success. Her soul is intact, and she has control over all of her magic." Mom clapped her hands together excitedly and Dad's face burst into a wide smile.

I beamed at my mate, tucking a strand of her hair behind her ear before nodding to our resident redhead. "Mori discovered she has Mage and Phoenix blood and insists she join on the mission for Leif. By default, that means Roan and Branko are also coming." Gray's eyebrows rose inquisitively as he grinned at Mori.

I considered revealing Simmi's marking, but it wasn't my place. That was her story to share. "Mother Kokuro told us to hurry, that Vingor and Terrun are increasing security on the Hellhole. We have to go soon. I found an entrance that lies dormant, rarely used. My Dad would like to explain it."

Anna looked at her husband smugly. "I told you, Mako doing vision work was a good idea." He lifted her hand and kissed it, gracefully acknowledging he was mistaken.

Dad cleared his throat. "Mako spoke to the guards. Bats. The Fae use bat caves as entrances. Long ago, the Fae needed guardians on the Earth plane to protect the entrances to the dimensions, to avoid discovery from the humans. They chose bats, demonizing them, terrifying humans with stories of vampires and eternal damnation. It worked. Most people avoid a cave full of bats. Only a few will dare to trespass. Bats are actually gorgeous little creatures." He nodded his head at Jelly. "They are incredible pollinators, coming out at night to feed on the fruit trees. Over five hundred plant species rely on bats."

"Aye." Roan chuckled, gently squeezing Mori's shoulder. "They pollinate the agave plant for both tequila and mescal." He winked at her.

She shuddered and stuck out her tongue with a gagging noise. She said, "I read a study once that bats eat enough bugs to save the corn industry a billion dollars a year in crop damage and pesticide use. I don't understand why they won't use natural predators over chemicals. Just build a bat condo in the middle of the cornfield, right? Let them take care of the pests."

Dad said dryly, "But then the pesticide companies would go broke." He turned to me. "The abandoned entrance is perfect, Mako. You need to contact Leif through a ritual. Right now. Tell him where to go."

Roan rubbed his chin. "Aye." Anna rose silently, tipping her head at Mori, who followed to gather the supplies we'd need. The room broke into chatter about phoenixes and latent powers. Gray listened with a small scowl on his face. I kissed Jelly's head and crossed to where he leaned against the fireplace.

I copied his stance, casual, stuffing my hands in my pockets. I spoke from the side of my mouth. "Why do you look like you're thinking too hard?"

His eyebrows drew together in concern. "Mori's going to be reckless. She knows she can't die, not truly, and you need to be prepared for her to jump in front of danger. Branko and Roan will try to shield her, and if it goes wrong, they'll end up dead. Forever dead." He raced his hand through his sandy curls. "We need to explain that they'll have to fight their natural tendency to protect her." He looked over at the two men. "They've bonded to her. They watch her every move."

I blew out a breath. "Okay. I'll have a word with them about it. One step at a time. For now, we have to let Leif knows we're coming." With a tip of my chin, he followed my gaze to Anna and Mori, their hands full of candles and stones and bowls. Icy leaped from the bench, trotting toward them.

My heart pounded in my chest as I swept my fingers over my orca's tail. I didn't know if Leif would ever forgive me, or what our lives would look like once reunited. He might shun me for stealing so many years from his life. I clenched my jaw. No turning back now.

THIRTY-FIVE

Vingor had spread the guards along the tunnels to patrol, increasing their numbers. I'd barely escaped this time, but had two more Fae in my growing collection of refugees. Trix and Xeno were incredible, seamlessly taking in every new person I rescued. They had spoken to the salamanders, who willingly gave their lives for us to survive. I didn't even need to trap them anymore. They just marched into the cave and threw themselves at the girls' feet.

Today, I'd found one more Fae hiding in the back of the storage cave. I avoided traversing through the bleeding room after my slim escape, accessing the secondary cave through a hole at the top of the wall. A rarely used side tunnel with sharp, jutting protrusions allowed me to scale the rock. I'd wriggled inside to steal more sacks to use as blankets, and found her. She was barely conscious, nothing more than bones. I didn't know where she came from, but the x on her wrist marked her as mine. She woke long enough to climb, mostly slip, through the hole. I struggled to swim with her despite her frail state. The strange water pulled at me, gnawing at my strength with a forceful vigor I hadn't previously encountered.

Francesco, a burly Fae with blue skin and navy hair, took her from my flagging arms. A former guard, he'd defected, deciding what Vingor was doing was wrong. He'd hidden in a tiny cave, far too cramped for his size, and I'd found him a while ago, high above the mining center when collecting more rocks. It was blistering hot in his cave, almost unbearable, and probably why no one had discovered him. He'd yanked me inside, asking if I was the Ghostfish. I nodded and brought him here.

I shook out my arms and legs, wiping them with a cloth to push the sapping magic from my skin. Francesco shouted with alarm as a form took shape behind me, swinging the Fae on his shoulder and stepping forward. I spun, ready to gut the intruder with my knife. My tensed body relaxed. It was Mako.

"Gods, Mako. Give me some warning." I waved a hand at Francesco. "It's okay. He's my brother." He left, taking the emaciated Fae with him. Mako went to hug me, but I stepped back. I was angry at him, cheated, and I couldn't shake it. Not yet. Mako's face fell. "When are you coming? I have twenty-four people to get out."

A familiar feminine voice rang through the open space, bouncing off the water. "Twenty-four? Leif! That's amazing!" I sagged with relief. My brother's mate made it back. I'd returned to the bleeding room as soon as I'd dared to search for her, finding nothing. It had wracked me with guilt, leaving her there. I repeated my question to Mako, worried about my people.

Mako stilled me, speaking quickly. "Do you remember telepathy? We did it as kids." I nodded, lifting my fingers to my temple, noticing that Mako didn't need to do it. One more thing I'd missed out on, learning magic. I swallowed my bitterness with difficulty.

Instantly, a Fae voice, melodic, hypnotic, burst into my head. *Leif, I am Leoht. I am Fae. You must meet us at the Chiropterra entrance. Do you know it?*

I answered out loud. "The Chiropterra? I have too many people to travel that far. Can't you come here? Portal us directly? We're safe here." As I spoke to her, I stared at my brother, a fully grown man. What did I look like? I'd been a Fae for so long I'd forgotten. I wasn't a child but hadn't seen a mirror in ages.

Leoht's reply made my heart drop. *The magical wards will destroy you. You need to come through the Chiropterra. It's an illusion. I can break it, allowing you to pass.*

Roan spoke next, his voice soft and guarded, echoing around the cave. "We'll try for all of them, Leif, but the twin girls must escape. Ye must get them out." Mako's eyes fell as he scuffed the ball of his foot on the ground. Good. He was as uncomfortable with Roan's directive as I was.

I shook my head defensively. "What, Roan, and leave everyone else? I can't abandon them. No one else can touch the water. I brought them to this cave. I have to get all of them out." My skin crawled at the thought of deserting them. I was the reason they were still alive.

Mako's steady hand gripped my arm. His voice was soft steel. "I'll help you."

Jelly echoed him, determined. "So will I." She had courage. Excellent. She'd need it in this place.

I called to Leoht. "Leoht, do you have maps for the Hellhole?"

Her reply chilled me. *I've been in the bleeding room, and the Chiropterra is just beyond it. Where are you hiding?*

Damn. She'd been here? Tortured? It must have been before my time. "If you pass the bleeding room, you come to a network of tunnels. Two lefts, right, then the center path. There's a pool with a central pillar. Jump on the ledge halfway down the wall. Swim through the tunnel. Can you swim? Are you Mers?"

I am not Mers. I will not touch the water, not even with Mako or Jelly to protect me. The magic is too evil for my type of power, and I would absorb too much, causing a death of horrific proportions.

Mako's jaw ticked as her words crawled over us. He cleared his throat, glancing at me apprehensively. "How bad is it?"

I shook my head. "The magic in the water is different from before. It recently got stronger. I won't lie. It hurts, and it saps your power. But if you help me swim them, we shouldn't be in it too long. Hopefully." I winced, thinking of multiple trips.

Roan's deep voice rang through the cave. "Mako. Ye can't stay much longer. Ye have to go."

Mako looked over my shoulder, staring into the shadows. His eyes were urgent. He spoke in my mind. *The twins are the most important, Leif. We have to free them. They go first. We'll leave soon, so be quick. Get to the bat cave with the twins and we'll work the rest of it out.*

He pulled me into a fast hug, his eyes full of guilt. His body dissolved, leaving me with my arms outstretched, just about to hug him back. His last words faded from my mind. *Don't get caught.*

I dropped my hands to my side, spinning to go back to the cave, finding Francesco staring at me curiously. He tapped his pointed ear. He'd been hiding in the tunnel's shadow, eavesdropping. I gestured for him to join me back near the water. I kept my voice low. "They want to meet at the Chiropterra gate."

Francesco grimaced. "Leif, that's impossible. There's no way you can swim everyone out. You barely made it through just now. The woman you rescued is light as a feather."

I ran my claws through my tangled hair, my eyes downcast, giving him my back as I thought out loud. "They can only enter through the bat cave. They'll be escorted by a full Fae, Leoht, and she—"

Francesco spun me around to face him, horror in his eyes. "Leoht? Leoht is coming here?"

"You've met her?"

He slowly shook his head from side to side, his ratty navy hair falling forward. He looked haunted. "Met her? I served with her." He looked at me forlornly, his cornflower blue eyes glowing. "I'm the one who brought her here." All the life seemed to fade from him, his shoulders drooping forward as he grasped his head in his hands. "I betrayed her."

I clasped my hand on his shoulder. "You changed, Francesco. You are a different man now."

His lips turned down. "You don't understand what they did to her. She wasn't just bled through needles. Her torture was far worse. Vingor let the guards feed from her directly, making them more foul, more powerful, just demented. They bit her daily. Over and over." His blue face paled, edging with green.

My blood ran cold, as did my voice. "Did you?"

He shook his head wildly. "I couldn't do it. I pretended. I whispered to her to scream, and clamped my lips on her neck, half hidden in her hair. Finally, after weeks of her torment, I couldn't take it anymore. I knocked out the other guard, drowsy after drinking her blood, and ran for the cave above the mine. That was the day I defected. I wanted to take her with me, but I didn't have the courage. I sent a bat with a message for Prince Sebastio, warning him, but I left her there." His eyes filled with tears of shame and guilt.

I frowned. "Francesco, how long have you been here?"

He cleared his throat, standing up tall. "Too long. But I need to redeem myself. This is my chance. How will we get everyone out? Even if you could swim everyone, moving two dozen exhausted people through the tunnels is an unsurmountable task." He paced, scratching his chin. "We have magic, although given the state of us, I'm not sure we're enough to outwit the guards."

I grabbed my hair in my hand, bunching it. "We have to

try. This is our only shot. Let's see what powers we have collectively." We jogged through the tunnel to the cave. Everyone gathered together, their faces alternately terrified and hopeful. I stalled at the assembled crowd.

Francesco said sheepishly, "I might have mentioned we are escaping."

I called Trix and Xeno to the side, keeping my voice low and soft. "We are being rescued. It means we have to swim through the water again." Both of them nodded, their brown eyes solemn. I tugged a hand across my face. "You are the priority for some reason, probably because of your Amphibi blood, and no one has explained why, but you go first. We leave soon."

Xeno grasped my hand. "If we survive this, we will tell you everything."

She and Trix moved among the crowd, urging everyone to eat what supplies we had left. I turned to the group of Fae. "None of you deserve to be here. You all have an x on your wrists, stolen for your blood, which means you have potent powers. Is there anyone who can cloak?"

Two Fae raised their hands. One of them, gaunt and barely functional, with green skin and enormous gold eyes, spoke in a rattling voice. His name was Ceru. "I can." The other, an exhausted female named Gedina, also confirmed the gift.

I kept my face blank. "I just rescued you both. You're drained."

Gedina snarled. "I will fight. If it means getting us out of here, I will fight."

Unease grew in my stomach. She could barely stand. "What else do we have?"

The old Fae lady, who called herself Flower, grinned. "Glamor. I can create a fake wall. The guards will run right past us if we creep from cave to cave."

A young Fae lifted his hand. "I teleport." Now that was worthy of excitement.

My eyes lit up eagerly. "Can you take people with you?"

Doocan was one of my earlier rescues. His blink reminded me of lizards' eyes, with thin slits down the centers. "I've only done it with my sister." He glanced over at Trix and Xeno. "She's about your size."

More Fae clamored about their powers, although many complained that after their bleeding and surviving on salamanders, they were weaker, but they would try. Hope prodded my heart. I had everyone press back as far as they could, and etched a map in the dark stone using the tip of my knife, outlining the Hellhole tunnels. We formed a rough plan for our escape. I would have liked to be more prepared, but we didn't have time.

Doocan studied my map carefully. He met my eyes, confident. "I'm going to take them together. I may need to stop twice before the Chiropterra." He pointed to two locations, both smaller caves.

I crouched over the map. "That will be fine. The guards rarely go in those." I looked over at a short, squat Fae named Malgo. He blinked orange eyes at me as I singled him out. "Malgo will project his voice, confusing the guards, leading them on a chase far away from us." I turned to another Fae, her skin a dusky rose. "And Wilamena will cast a silencing bubble on the ledge near the water to muffle any noise we make. Wilamena, can you also cloak?"

She nodded enthusiastically. "But only a few at a time, and only for a short while. I'm too weak to do more. But if a guard runs past, I can hide us. If they stop and look closely…" she shrugged her shoulders, her open palms to the air.

I scanned the faces around me. "So we're clear on the plan? Doocan teleports Trix and Xeno straight to the bat cave, returning with my brother and his mate, who will help me swim you out. Mako looks like me, and Jelly has long blue hair and tur-quoise eyes. I'm not sure what Leoht looks like. She's full Fae, the one dropping the ward so we can get out."

Francesco replied softly. "Tall, pitch black skin, purple eyes, white hair. Ferocious personality." His eyes dropped to the floor, as did Flower's jaw, but she said nothing.

"Thanks, Francesco. I swim Malgo and Flower out first. They hide here." I pointed to a cave across from the pool. "Malgo throws his voice to reverberate over here." I pointed to a location far from our route. "I'll take Gedina, Wilamena, and Ceru next, to support Flower with cloaking and glamor. Hope-fully, Mako and Jelly will arrive by then. If Doocan has the strength for it, he can teleport the smallest of you to the entrance. Otherwise, we'll have to sneak."

Francesco said what everyone was thinking, myself in-cluded. "Are you strong enough, Leif? To be exposed to the wa-ter this much?"

I gave the only answer I could. "I'll have to be."

I stood and clasped forearms with Doocan, who looked barely older than twelve. Still, he was tall for his age and wiry with lean muscle. "Be swift, Doocan." He nodded and shivered his body, his skin quickly changing to a shiny black that matched the color of the walls. I stepped back to give him space.

He grinned, blinking his lizard eyes. He tipped his head at the twins. "I'm Amphibi as well. Chameleon." He turned to Trix and Xeno, frowning. "Anything in your magic I should be care-ful of?"

Xeno giggled. "Don't kiss us. Our saliva will paralyze you. Other than that, don't eat us. That would definitely kill you."

If he wasn't all black, Doocan would have blushed. He swal-lowed and bobbed his head. "No kissing. Got it." He took a deep breath and wrapped his arms around the two girls. With a nod to me, they vanished.

I turned to Malgo and Flower. "Let's go. Everyone waits by the water. Malgo, get on back, Flower on my front."

She cackled, fanning her face with mischief. "You're a young stud, my Leif. Draping this old body against yours makes my day." I snorted a laugh. I steadied my thighs and crouched. Thankfully, Malgo was a slight Fae, undernourished. Flower clung to my neck, her legs around my hips.

"Hold your breath." I jumped into the water, my tail snapping into place, and swam hard through the tunnel. We came up and waited. No sounds. Malgo leaped up from my shoulders, landing on the ledge, and hauled up Flower.

She patted my cheek. "Be safe, Prince Leif. We'll see you soon." I opened my mouth to correct her regarding the title. I didn't want to be associated with the royal family, but she'd already scooted away to climb the wall, darting across the walkway to the cave. I closed my lips shut and dove back into the icy hot water, pumping my tail.

Gedina and Ceru shuffled on their feet, both sliding into the water with a hiss as they kept contact with my skin. Wilamena wrapped her arms around my waist, hanging off to the side. My entire body was thrumming. I ignored it, taking all three through the tunnel. We surfaced, and Ceru helped Gedina as they scrambled away. I pulled myself up on the ledge for a reprieve from the water. It was sucking the life out of me. Wilamena panted next to me. Her voice was faint. "Why is the water so painful?"

"I don't know. It's some kind of magic." A shout spun our heads, and her eyes widened in alarm. She gripped my hand, and I held my breath as two guards flew past us, chasing Malgo's voice. I suppressed a shudder. "So far, so good. Stay brave."

I slipped into the strange water, my whole body aching, returning with two more Fae. Ceru darted out of the cave to pull them up. Wilamena's body was rigid with anticipatory anxiety, just waiting for us to get caught. I changed to legs and hauled myself up, creeping down the tunnel, praying for a glimpse of Mako and Jelly. I'd hoped Doocan would have brought them by now.

With no sign of them, I slumped next to Wilamena, willing my body to stay strong. My arms and legs felt useless, like noodles. But I couldn't quit. I leaned forward to push myself back in the water, but Wilamena stopped me, her dusky skin dark against mine. I was painfully pale after fifteen years without the sun. "They will be here soon, Leif. Rest a moment. You can't see your family again if you're dead."

An abrupt laugh stuck in my throat. "Wilamena, I've been dead to them for a long time. I'm more worried about living."

THIRTY-SIX

JELLY

Now that she had a chance at revenge, Leoht wouldn't stop prattling inside my head. *The guards will be incredibly strong. Like the Eaters, don't let them break your skin. Definitely fighter skills. It's good you trained with Mew. You have your blood as a healing potion. Be ready to use it if anyone gets hurt. If you need magic, weave it together, use it all at once. One strain at a time won't be strong enough. Can you do that? You did it when we fought Terrun.*

Her breath hitched with his name. The pearl pulsed a few times. Crying? I reached out to her gently. *Leoht? Are you okay? He won't be there, will he?*

Her reply came quickly. *Can you ask Sebastian where he sent him? Now?*

I looked over at my father-in-law, his face tight with tension. He was speaking in hushed tones to Mori, Roan, and Branko. The men looked thunderous. I joined them, catching the tail end of their conversation, basically telling them to let Mori die if it came to it. They turned as I approached. "Leoht's worried about Terrun. Please tell me you didn't send him to the Hellhole."

Sebastian's reply edged with anger. "I banished him to the farthest reaches of Fae. It's a barren place, all ice, inhabited by monstrous creatures. I hoped that in his weakened state, he could not defend himself. If all went to plan, he is nothing more than a pile of bear shit."

"Bears?"

"Polterbears, like polar bears, but three times the size, with six legs. Earth polar bears can run at twenty-five miles an hour. Polterbears easily move at seventy. Let's hope I sent him straight to a den of hungry ones."

The pearl rattled at my throat, laughing. I grinned. "That made Leoht happy." I watched as Mori picked at the skin around her nails. I took her hand gently. "So, do we need to let you be our shield in the bat cave? Is that what I just interrupted?" Roan scowled, and an icy chill rolled off of Branko's skin. I tipped my head, studying them. "You two have to trust her. She won't throw herself away lightly." I lifted my eyebrows at my best friend. "Right Mori?"

She squared her shoulders, all Warrior. "I will not. But if one of you dies trying to protect me, I will find you in the afterlife and throttle you. Understand?" Both men rumbled in reluctant acknowledgment. She narrowed her eyes at me next, and I nodded.

Simmi and Simon joined our group. She cleared her throat. "I'm going too. I can swim." Sebastian opened his mouth to protest, but Simmi cut him off, holding up her hand. "Leif is my brother, and Mako's Hai Matau connects us, so I won't get lost. I'm not a child, and this is not up for debate. I'm going." Sebastian wrapped her in his arms, holding her head to his chest as he swallowed.

Simon spoke sharply, almost with a bark. "I'm going with her. When I'm shifted, I can see in the dark. And a bat cave will be pitch black."

Sebastian shot him a look of gratitude, squeezing Simmi and letting go, gently pushing her to Simon's side. I nodded to Simon. "We'll take all the help we can get. But Simon, I'm calling you Drift from hereon. Simmi plus Simon? It's too confusing. Unless there's something else you'd like us to call you?" Simmi stared at me with incredulous eyes, annoyed.

Simon answered with an accompanying growl. "Drift is fine." He kissed Simmi's head. She glowered at me.

Anna came close, her face solemn. She held out vials of an orange liquid. "These are for night vision. It won't be as crisp as a Shifter's vision, but it will help in the dark." We tossed them back, the flavor like cherries and carrots with a residual linger of something bitter. She handed out squares of strange fabric. "Drape it over your shoulders. It will act as armor, shifting to accommodate your tails."

I shook it out and pulled it around me. It morphed and contained me like a leotard from head to toe. Only my face was unprotected. I flexed an arm, barely able to sense it. Branko and Drift refused the armor and the night vision potion, needing neither, as they would shift once we landed. Anna said, "I have the coordinates to the mouth of the cave. Gates block it off, but I can enter inside, beyond the barrier."

Mako slid up beside me, snaking his arm around my waist. He dropped his lips to my ear. "Do not die, savage queen. I will not survive it." I squeezed his forearm, twisting my neck to kiss him.

I studied the people staying behind. Sebastian and Sophia clung to each other, frightened for their children, but terribly proud. Richard and Veda stood together with serious faces, her twisting her sari in her fingers. My eyes wandered to Gray. He lounged at the side, his hands in his pockets, looking frustrated. He caught my gaze and shot forward, brown eyes blazing with gold. "Bugger this. I'm going as well."

Anna balked. "But Gray, your magic is persuasion. We talked about this."

He took her gently by the shoulders. "I appreciate you want to protect me. Fae magic can manipulate me, yes, but Mum, I can create fire. Might be helpful in a dark cave. I'll stand guard with you at the back of the cave, far away from the entrance, away from any rogue Fae."

Her lips pinched together for a second before she sighed, glancing apprehensively at Richard, who approached and smiled at his son, holding out the magical cloth and a long dagger. "I suspected you wouldn't stay behind, and I'm grateful. I'm proud of you, son. Take care of your mother. We'll be ready to receive everyone here." Gray slung the square on his shoulder, downing the potion as the armored fabric slipped around him.

Anna flung a powder over our group. I sneezed. She explained as she waved in front of her face. "Disinfectant. We don't want to harm the bats by bringing parasites or bacteria into the cave. Drop the shielding on your minds so we can communicate silently. Sound off." One by one, we confirmed our connection. She blew out a steadying breath and held eyes with Richard, probably saying goodbye. Her voice clipped tight. "Very well. Hold hands."

We disappeared from the warm library to a freezing cold blackness. We arrived without a sound or a trace of light. Anna had muted her magic, using more than she normally would for transporting. The space echoed with thousands of high-pitched chirps, far too similar to the battle cry of the young bee queens. I shivered as my eyes slowly adjusted to the dark cave. Branko and Drift both shifted into their alternate forms, and multiple gasps of admiration flew through the excited bats when Branko's wings snapped out.

With my mind open, the squeaking noises came into clarity. Alarmed and intrigued by the sudden visitors, the bats shouted at each other. One dropped from the ceiling and hovered in front of my face. His voice was velvet and thunder, not at all what I expected. "Human, you are not welcome." I toned the rest of the bats down to background chatter. "You bring disease to the caves. The white-nose syndrome."

"I am no human, Guardian." I bowed my head respectfully. "And we are disinfected through magic. We post no threat to you. We are going into the Hellhole."

The bat made a clicking noise of irritation. "You cannot enter. You are not pure Fae. You'll never get past the wards." The pearl shuddered at my throat, stealing my breath and my voice, and Leoht appeared at my side, wild, fangs bared.

Her strange voice warbled in the cave. "But I can." Everyone in our group gawked at her except for Mako, Simmi, and me, familiar with her form. She wore head to toe black leather and razors on the edges of her claws. She looked over at Branko and winked, tossing back her long white hair. "Hello, handsome monster," she said in a singsong voice. He blinked at her, his stone jaw slack. Mori giggled.

The bat tipped its small brown head, staring at Leoht. "Lady Leoht. I am surprised to see you here. After your rescue, I thought you'd abandoned Fae forever. Vingor visits often. I haven't seen Terrun in some time. You know we are impartial, but I feel I must warn you."

Leoht's voice was a symphony of sound, even as she whispered. "We are here to rescue innocents. Evacuate your cauldron of bats. I don't want you caught in the crossfire. Everyone, stand still."

The bat sent out a series of high chirps, and en masse, thousands flew for the hole in the ceiling. Not a single one touched me as they swooped past in a frenzy. After they left, the sound of silence dragged down, haunting me in the eerie stillness.

Leoht tugged at my hand. "Let's go." I held in a yip as an enormous white wolf took point at Leoht's side, ears twitching.

Leoht prowled forward until she held up a fist. We all stopped, huddling closely. Leoht spoke softly in our minds. *This is the first round of wards. They hide the entrance. Stand back while I break them. There will be no alarm. That only comes with the next one, and I cannot stop it. If Mother's information is correct, it does not give them our location, only that there is a breach. Where is Mew?*

Summoned, Mew shimmered into form, nodding at her to continue. She looked relieved to see him and said, *Mew takes the twins. Mako, Jelly, Simmi, and I help Leif. Branko, Roan, Mori and Drift, take the rescued Fae to Anna and Gray as fast as you can. If anyone attacks you, kill them. Do not let them slice your skin. Is everyone ready?*

With Leoht's question, Mako, Simmi, and I turned full Fae, broader, taller, meaner. Leoht rolled her shoulders back and began to hum. Goosebumps broke out on my skin as the first magical shield warped and shimmered, releasing a noxious odor and a blistering blast of heat. The cave wall was an illusion. We stood at the gate to the Hellhole; the archway made from a glistening black stone with veins of red running through it. The air was steamy, making my skin slick under my magical armor.

She crooned to the shimmering stone, her hands making a pattern in the thick, humid air. Pressure built against my body, pushing me away. I gritted my teeth and leaned into it. Leoht hissed and spat a word, and a pulse of magic slammed through me. Leoht whispered. *That releases the holding spell. Even those marked with an x may pass through.*

Leoht crept inside, beckoning us to follow. Every nerve in my body resisted with fear, but I squashed it with a snap of teeth on my cheek. We'd gone three paces when a tall boy stepped out of the shadow and eyed our group warily, two small girls behind him. I couldn't differentiate the boy from the cave walls when he closed his eyes. Leoht said, "Who are you? Where's Leif?"

The boy spoke quickly, eyes darting at our faces. "I'm Doocan. Leif's getting the others, and I was supposed to teleport you to him, but I…I can't. I don't have the strength. Getting Trix and Xeno here took everything I had. But I'm returning with you. I owe Leif my life."

Mako said, "You did well, Doocan." The twins remained pressed against the wall, hesitant. Mako stepped forward, drawing a small blue ball of light in his hand to show his face to the twins. "Remember me? I'm Leif's brother. You saw me in the ceiling. There's a giant bald man just outside the archway. His name is Mew. He's going to take you somewhere safe." Their eyes trailed over his shoulder to settle unnervingly on me, just behind him. They stared into my soul.

Xeno said on an exhale, "You. We've been waiting for you. We need to talk. It's urgent."

I wavered under their scrutiny, as though every shred of my being became bare. I gave myself a shake to come out of the trance. Leoht growled at their backs, hustling them forward. I hadn't seen her slip behind them. She whispered, "I dropped the spell. You won't get hurt. Go. You can talk to her later. Go!" Leoht gave them a small push.

The girls held their breath, simultaneously glancing back to look at me before facing forward and stepping through the entrance, hand in hand. Mew immediately swept them up and disappeared into thin air. The tension in my shoulders eased. Leoht steadied her breath and whispered to us. *If I tell you to run, you come straight back here. Don't worry about me. Does everyone remember the turns?*

I wanted to argue, to tell her I'd never leave her, but I swallowed the words with the glare she gave me, nodding obediently. We crept forward, Doocan bravely leading the way. Leoht's skin was even darker than his, and I would have lost track of them if Leoht's hair was black. I glimpsed inside a cave, spotting three empty chairs, and the urge to scream and retreat to the entrance almost overpowered me. Leoht resolutely did not look inside, but her fingers gripped mine. I squeezed back.

From nowhere, a knife slashed at my shoulder. It bounced off the armored cloth covering my skin, and I gripped the thick wrist in my left hand and twisted hard. The knife clattered to the ground, and the broad Fae in black armor inhaled to call the alarm to his colleagues. Before I could grab my knuck from my hip and silence him, Leoht sliced through his neck with her razor-edged claws. Black blood gushed from the wound, and I spun to my head to avoid the spray. I grimaced and dropped him. Leoht watched with pleasure as the guard gulped his last breath.

We dragged him away from the entrance, smearing the floor with his blood. I stepped around the dark puddle, about to give Leoht the all clear, when voices shouted and feet thundered. Leoht pressed us against the wall of the bleeding room, splaying out her arms to touch Simmi, me, and Mako. Doocan blended into the wall seamlessly, holding his breath and closing his eyes. Everything went blacker than black. Leoht was shadowing us somehow.

Fortune was on our side. The guards turned down the tunnel ahead of us, going the opposite direction. If they'd come any closer, they would've seen the opening to the bat cave. Leoht sagged with relief, motioning for us to move, and picked up the pace. The deeper we went, the hotter it became. The stench of sulfur was overpowering, burning my windpipe, and I took shallow breaths to spare my lungs. Finally, we sped on light feet down the center tunnel, stopping when we reached the water. I hissed in my mind. *Where is he?* More footsteps bounced through the cave walls, disorienting me. It seemed like the guards were everywhere.

"Psst!" The noise came from my right. I whirled to find an

old lady Fae beckoning me. She hunched over, peering around the wall, her eyes lit with rebellion. She hustled us into the cave, lifting a finger to her lips as guards raced by. She dropped her hand and sagged. "Are all of you Mers? He needs help in the water. He won't say it, but he's exhausted."

Leoht stared at the woman incredulously, her purple eyes swirling with silver. Were those tears? "Flower? What are you doing here?"

Flower flung herself at Leoht. "I thought you were dead!" They embraced tightly, Flower's arms shaking from how hard she hugged Leoht. She cleared her throat, becoming strict. "Leoht, avoid the water. Those three can go, but not you. It will burn off your skin, child. Stay here and help me."

Flower turned to me. "Swim fast. Don't dally. Leif said for us to wait here for everyone." Flower did quick math and her mouth turned down. "There are eighteen left in the cave. With four of you shuttling…" She took a deep breath. "Well, swim fast. You'll have to make several trips."

Two more Fae staggered into the cave. One of them smiled weakly at me and strained to speak. "Blue hair. You made it. Leif has gone back for more." Mako, Simmi, and I crept from the cave. We discovered a slim Fae perched on a shelf halfway down the wall. She held a finger to her lips, motioning us closer, pointing to the black water. We jumped the short distance, landing silently beside her thanks to her magic. More footsteps and shouting echoed around us. The Fae woman frantically waved her hands for us to go. Alarmed, the three of us slid into the water, shimmering our transformations quickly, slipping under the surface.

The water was terrible, a living entity, dragging at my skin. The armor Anna had given me did nothing to repel the sensation of icy fingers reaching for my bones, while a strange heat lit up my nerves. I swam harder, popping up inside a cave to find Leif hovering at the edge with two Fae clinging to his body, about to jump in. He staggered back and dropped them as Simmi came up for air.

She scrambled from the water, changing to legs as she climbed, and launched at him. He caught her and clutched at her, his face twisted as he kept from crying. His voice choked. "Hey, Sim Sim. You have boobs."

Simmi laughed through her tears. "I have boobs." She stroked a hand on his cheek. "You look the same. Older, but the same, save for the fangs and the pointy ears, and the total lack of personal style. Your hair is a mess." She glanced around her and shuddered. "But let's catch up once we're free of this shithole."

"Hellhole," whispered one of the Fae.

"Same difference." Simmi hiccuped and wiped her eyes. She cleared her throat. "Who do we take next?"

Leif scanned the group of Fae huddled together. "Whoever you can carry." His eyes settled on a huge Fae with blue skin. "Actually, Mako, take Francesco while you're fresh. We need him to fight if the guards find us. Simmi, take the two smaller ones. Jelly, whoever you can lift." Without another word, he grabbed his two Fae and jumped into the water.

We loaded up, Mako taking the massive male on his back, a smaller female on his front. Simmi grabbed three children, shushing Mako when he tried to protest. She followed right after him. I motioned to two middle-sized Fae, both female. They clambered onto my body, and I shifted when I hit the water. The water was fiercely magnetic, leeching my power the longer I touched it. I swam faster.

Mako was waiting for me and helped push the Fae up to the ledge. We both heaved for breath. I didn't see Leif or Simmi. The thin Fae with dusty pink skin hissed at us, shooing us away from the ledge. "Get in there! She's going to kill him!" We scrambled up the wall to find bedlam in the hidden cave.

THIRTY-SEVEN

JELLY

I staggered in, immediately running across the cave, alarm boosting my muscles. Leoht had Francesco by the throat, pinning him to the wall. The large Fae did nothing to defend himself, hanging limply in her grasp, his tiptoes barely touching the ground. Beside her, Leif held a blade to her neck menacingly.

Flower and two other Fae waved their hands at the cave entrance, glancing nervously at each other as they tried to muffle the noise of her shouting. Everyone else stood well clear. I hissed through my teeth. "Leoht! What are you doing?"

"He betrayed me." Her purple eyes swirled with fury.

Leif pushed right in her face, shifting the edge of his knife. "Drop him. He's a friend. He didn't bite you. He defected. Drop him!"

Leoht didn't drop him. She shook him instead, making Francesco's eyes bulge as she squeezed. She growled the words through her fangs. "Did he tell you how he watched them attack me over and over? Did he tell you he did nothing to help me? That he left me there? He's a traitor to decency and I should snap his neck now."

Leif pressed, and a thin trickle of silver leaked across her dark skin. Her purple eyes slid to his face. She snarled, a rattling noise like a snake with a warning.

I threw my hands in the air and whispered sharply. "Oh, for fuck's sake! Both of you, drop it! You can fight it out later when we're not in the bowels of hell! We're not done! Both of you! Stop it!"

Without taking her gaze from Leif, Leoht opened her hand. Francesco dropped to the floor, wheezing. Leif drew back the knife but not his body, edged with threat. She sneered at him as she smeared silver blood from her throat. I ventured to touch him, pulling him away.

He raised one side of his lip in warning, staring at my hand, and Mako stepped closer, ready to defend me if his brother attacked. I spoke in low tones. "Leif, pull it together. You're not alone anymore. If you want us to free all these people, temper yourself." He snatched his wrist from my grasp, throwing an ugly look at Mako, who hovered near me protectively. Leif stormed from the cave, throwing a clawed hand in the air.

Mako muttered, "Fuck. Exactly as I feared."

I blew out a breath. "Give him time, Mako." I pointed at Leoht. "Do not kill anyone!" We paused at the entrance, and hearing silence, slunk back to the ledge for another trip. The magic in the water sapped my energy far faster than the short return swim warranted. Without shifting to legs, I pushed my two Fae onto the ledge and went back.

When I resurfaced in the cave, only six Fae remained. Almost there. Mako and Leif organized two each, Simmi taking the smallest of the group. I motioned for a woman to climb on, willing my body to keep going. I shrieked underwater as a fluorescent orange eel brushed against me, giving me a shock that set my teeth on edge. Its power hit the Fae as well, and her body clung awkwardly to mine as I struggled to keep swimming. Black spots danced in my vision by the time I reached the ledge. Mako and Leif surfaced. Mako nodded to me. "That's it. That's the last of them."

"Where's Simmi?" I scanned the dark water.

Mako spun his head, his hands under the thighs of a Fae, pushing him to safety. "She was right behind me."

I dove in a panic and saw flicks of orange surrounding a blue tail. Over there. I swam to her and my heart gripped. She was unconscious. The eels were feasting on the skeletal body of the Fae she'd been carrying. I grabbed Simmi around the waist, pushing a breath into her as I hauled her as fast as I could. The water was electric from the swarm of eels, and my mouth tasted metallic, my whole body drained.

We reached the ledge, and I didn't have the strength to climb out. My tail flailed, and my head slipped under the water. Leif pulled out Simmi, and Mako yanked me under my arms, dragging me into the cave, still in my Mers form. *Jelly! Jelly!*

His voice was so far away. Then his lips were on mine, pouring in what scant magic he had left. I stopped him, taking just enough to shift to legs. I crawled to Simmi, unconscious on the floor, and bit my cheek hard, snapping at her lip to tear her skin. Leoht came up behind me, laying her hand right over my mark. Fae power rushed into me, and I transferred it to Simmi. She coughed and vomited brackish liquid, all of us grimacing.

Leif went to a hole in the cave wall and retrieved a pair of worn trousers and numerous sacks for everyone. I wished I had the armored cloth to give them.

Simmi wiped her mouth and groaned. "Gods, get me out of here." She shifted to legs and sat up, spitting on the floor. Looking around, her face fell, tears wobbling in her voice as she spoke. "She didn't make it, did she? That last Fae? The one I was carrying?"

I answered with a sigh. "No. But it was fast. She probably died as soon as she lost contact with your skin." Simmi's eyes filled. I hushed her. "Don't fall apart. Not yet." Mako helped her up and held her around the waist when she swayed. Leoht lifted me onto unsteady feet. I said, "We can't use telepathy with everyone, so no speaking."

Our ragtag crew huddled at the mouth of the cave, Leif taking the lead. "Malgo, do you have anything left?" A short Fae with yellow corkscrew curls and orange eyes nodded from where he leaned against the wall. "Send them to the mines." Malgo's mouth stretched open in a silent scream. Leif turned to the rest of us. "Flower, Gedina, Ceru, keep us cloaked. Everyone, go as fast as you can."

Those of us with remaining strength hauled up the weaker Fae, carrying them piggyback as we shuffled down the dark tunnel. I carried Wilamena, the rose-colored woman who'd silenced our swimming. Leif paused, listening. The sounds of shouts came closer. His voice rose in alarm. "The guards figured out it's a trick. They're turning back! Hurry!" We took a second right.

We were halfway down the last tunnel, so close to freedom. We dashed past the bleeding room, several of the Fae tripping over themselves when they realized it. I gripped one by the arm and yanked her forward. Mako carried a Fae while dragging Simmi around the waist. She could barely place her feet in front of her. Leoht sprinted ahead and tossed her Fae from her back before spinning on her heels, her purple eyes flashing with menace as she ran past us in the opposite direction. I stumbled on my feet, wanting to help her with whatever she'd seen, but she snapped at me coldly. "Get out of here!"

I ran with legs like lead and threw Wilamena through the entrance. Roan caught her and rushed away. Mako and I turned without speaking, racing back toward Leoht, adrenaline attempting to boost our depleted muscles. Hot on our heels were Francesco and Leif. Stony arms yanked Simmi to safety, accompanied by an outpouring of cursing from her. She was about to follow us, but Branko decided otherwise when he saw the state of her. A bark from a wolf cemented it.

Leoht stood about ten feet from the bleeding room, bracing her body for battle, her white hair lifting with electric energy. She was vibrating. I fumbled to speak, to ask her why she turned back, when she lifted her hands and snarled. A tall Fae stepped into the tunnel, lighting up the ceiling with a menacing red glow, highlighting the rage on Leoht's face.

He was gorgeous, an older version of Terrun's beautiful glamor with the same silky dark hair, his lithe body dressed in snake-like black leather, and he wore rings of stones on every finger. His bone structure…It was obvious that he shared the same blood as my mate. Three silvery scars marred his left cheek, reflecting faintly under the eerie light. He spoke in a deep, sing-song voice, reminiscent of Terrun, making nails skate down my spine. "Well, well, if it isn't the whole family."

Leoht's voice burst in my head. *It's Vingor. I'm using your glamor. He thinks I'm Simmi.* Mako stepped forward to stand beside Leoht.

Vingor laughed, a strange discordant sound, and gestured inside the room. "You killed my guard. Pity. He was a good one." He tipped his head curiously. "Are you two trying to stop me? Where is your father? Too cowardly to face me himself? He probably knows I would skin him alive. Those were my last words to him." His eyes swung to me as I stepped next to Mako. He smiled at me, a charming expression but for the darkness in his eyes. "Look. It's the little mermaid who attacked my brother. This is a wonderful coincidence. I came by to check on my latest donors, and low and behold, I find you instead."

"Hardly donors." Leif growled, his body pulsing with rage as he pushed to stand next to me, Francesco at his side. We stood in a tight line, five against one.

Vingor spoke with false sincerity, eyeing up Leif. "The

elusive Ghostfish. How lovely to meet you, *nephew*." He spat out the word with distaste. "You've been the consummate pain in my side. The magic recognized you, no matter how I tried to alter it." He sneered. "You with your Mers blood. That's how you hid for so long. You could swim through the tunnels." He waved his bejeweled hand through the air dismissively. "You can't stop me, children. I'm too powerful, especially with all the magical blood so generously given to me."

Francesco vibrated with anger. "Stolen, you mean. You're a monster, Vingor."

Vingor sneered at Francesco. "And you. Traitor. I think I'll kill you first. Let them watch what I do to those who betray me."

Leoht spoke quickly. *Pull on your magic. When I shout GO, hit him with everything you have and run for the entrance.*

I spoke with desperation. *Leoht, I don't have much magic left after swimming.* Mako echoed me.

She replied with cold venom. *Whatever you have, use it. We're taking him down. Ready…*

Vingor chuckled at us, flicking his fingers at the ceiling, making the light brighter so he could see us better. He stepped closer, his grace casual, as if we were old friends. His eyes were black with red pupils and made the breath in my lungs freeze in terror. Mentally, I called to Kelbazi, Bastet and the Mother for help, forcing up every drop of the Surfecti magic inside me. Raw power writhed, coiled like an agitated cobra as I inhaled, preparing to scream. After the water, I probably had one good shot left.

Set…

Vingor looked over our heads at the entrance. I didn't turn around, but I'd bet Roan, Branko, and Mori were standing on the other side. Vingor frowned and narrowed his black eyes, puzzled. Leoht chose that second of distraction to strike.

"GO!" Leoht swept her razor-sharp claws at Vingor's face, making him step back as he clutched at his cheek. I whipped at him with my magic, binding him with a purple rope, lighting him up with orange and turquoise flame. I hit for his center with blasts of red, plunging cobalt magic down his throat.

Mako added his magic to mine and stilled it, blocking Vingor's airway. I kept my hand steady, letting the power of my violence pound at the wicked Fae Prince. He tore at my ropes, freeing himself, and bellowed over the thick water we tried to drown him with. Leif jabbed for his heart with a knife, working in tandem with Leoht perfectly as she swiped again, but Vingor swerved, knocking the knife from Leif's grasp, ducking under Leoht's claws.

Francesco, far faster than I would have expected, dashed behind Vingor and slashed at his legs, dragging vertically from thigh to calf with a blade. It must be a vulnerable spot for all Fae. I dropped all the rest and let Drift's maroon magic dive into his flesh, ripping and tearing at will like a frenzied wolf. Vingor fell forward with a roar, sending out a pulse of dark magic that made mine stutter and fail, seizing it as if sucked into a vacuum.

Leoht's roar mangled my brain. *RUN! He has too much power! We can't take him. Run before he recovers! Go!*

We thundered down the tunnel. Roan, Mori, and Branko were on the other side, beckoning us with waving arms, screaming for us to move faster. I glanced over my shoulder. Vingor was standing up, bracing himself against the wall, and he was furious.

Suddenly, Flower stepped from the cave wall, dropping her glamor. She had a steely look in her eyes as she stared at Vingor, her ancient mouth twisted up in malice. I cried out her name and Leif faltered, trying to turn and haul her with him, but she sidestepped him.

Her voice was thunderous steel. "Leave me! Now!" Mako and I both grabbed him and pulled. Flower's voice echoed against the cave walls as she spoke to the wounded Fae before her. "You are filth, Vingor. You and your brother, Terrun. If I'd known what you were going to become, I'd have drowned you as babes in your baths."

There was a beat of silence, and Vingor spoke with something like regret. "You shouldn't be here, Flower. I never called for you. You came and couldn't leave. It's your fault what happens next."

I glanced over my shoulder to see Vingor strike out at our fleeing bodies, a twisting spear of black and red shooting from his palm. I tried to lift a shield to defend Flower, but my magic failed. A spark of turquoise was all I could muster. Flower took the full brunt of Vingor's magic, her frail body shaking and jerking with the impact. She crumbled to the floor in a heap.

Leoht wailed a tortured cry and gathered her magic for a returning blast, but she had nothing left to retaliate with, having used so much to break the wards. Vingor effectively crippled us with the pulse he'd sent out. Leif tore himself from our grasp, turning around. When he saw Flower's still body, he dropped to his knees. Mako grabbed him and dragged him by the waist.

Leoht sprinted for the entrance to the cave with me right behind her. She spun, weaving her hands, trying to create a shield for us, but she was too slow, too drained. Vingor shot another bolt, incinerating Flower's body as it aimed straight at us. Time slowed down. Leoht reached for my hand in what was surely our death. But in a flash of red curls, a warrior cry in her throat, Mori shoved us to the side, knocking both of us down. Her eyes glowed gold, her hair rising around her as she spread her arms to take the hit.

But Vingor's magic didn't land on Mori. Instead, it collided with an inexplicable wall of white and gold, ricocheting to the ceiling.

Mew.

His expression was one of painful surprise before he

collapsed, rolling onto his back, eyes staring wide at the ceiling. Mori screamed, the furious sound causing blood to leak from my ears and nose. Her entire body lit with spitting fire. She flung her hands at the cave entrance, aiming to get through to Vingor. We watched with loose jaws as she did. Orange and red flames burst into the opening, burning the walls, racing toward him, but before it could touch him and turn him to ash, he leaped into the bleeding room, clutching his ruined leg.

Frustrated, Mori roared again and fisted her hands, raising them, ripping rock from the floor and filling in the entrance, stunning us with the fury of her actions. The flames around her body snuffed out, and she dropped beside Mew, her hands scattering over his face and body. She yelled at him. "Mew, you stupid idiot! Why did you do that? I was right there! I was ready!" He didn't reply. He lay as still as the dead. I stared, waiting for him to sit up and laugh. He didn't.

Mori kept talking to him, her hand smoothing over his shiny bald head. "You've been such an incredible friend. I can't believe you sacrificed yourself for me. No one's ever done that before." She half-heartedly punched his unmoving chest. "You dumbass! You knew I'd come back! Why did you jump in front of me?" She choked on a sob, squeezing her eyes shut.

Mako ran over and collapsed to his knees, his breath coming in heaves. He shook his head. "He can't be gone." His face crushed as he met Mori's pained stare. He groaned through a tight throat, "It's impossible. He's invincible." He lay his fingers on Mew's neck, his head dropping forward as he pulled back his hand.

Mori's eyes overflowed. She stroked her hand over Mew's bald head and gently closed his blank eyes. As she did, her tears ran freely, dripping onto his face in splashes. She reached for Mako's fingers, holding them over Mew's lifeless body, her other hand still stroking his cheek. Mako leaned over, broken, steadying himself with a hand on Mew's shoulder. Together, they wept. I crawled over and wrapped an arm around Mako, resting my hand on Mew's chest, right over his heart, my cheeks wet with rolling tears.

Branko and Roan paid their respects. They kneeled, and each lay a hand on Mori's shoulder and another on Mew's body, saying goodbye. Simmi sat at his head, stroking his forehead with trembling fingers. Drift whined and settled next to Mako, his wolfish chin on Mew's thigh. Leoht fell at his feet, her hands firm on his ankles as she whispered a Fae prayer for the dead. Francesco crouched beside her, laying a heavy hand on Mew's shin, joining Leoht in the prayer.

Leif stood dumbstruck, not knowing who Mew was, but came to us and touched his fingers to Mew's, thanking him for his sacrifice. We stayed in silence, save for the sound of our choked crying as we struggled to breathe through our loss.

Mew was gone.

I closed my eyes, my heart shattered. He saved us. He died protecting us, and I could never repay the debt.

First a grunt, then a chuckle, then a full-on bray of laughter. Mew sat up, right as rain, causing us all to fall backward. He said, "Aw, look how much you care! Mori, that speech was so touching!"

Mori punched him in the face, which made us burst into laughter, edged with hysteria. Mako helped me to my feet, shaking his head at Mew, giggling as he wiped his face. Mori remained kneeling, still in shock.

Mew groaned, rolled over to kneel, and stretched. Six perfect wings flung out of his back, filling the cave with gold light. He flexed them, testing them. We stared and stared, all of us with our mouths hanging open. I noticed that Roan didn't look surprised. Suspicious.

My voice was shaky. "You…you…how?"

He giggled. "You pinned me for over five seconds."

Mori screeched. "While you were dead!"

Branko tipped his head to the side, studying Mew's magnificent wings with barely disguised envy. "What are you, Mew?"

He spoke jovially, as if chatting over tea. "Seraphim." He beamed at Mori. "Thanks for bringing me back so fast. It would have taken a few days otherwise. That bastard's magic really stung."

Mori's eyebrows drew down, the freckles on her face piling on top of each other. She massaged the knuckles on her punching hand. "What are you talking about? I didn't do anything."

He smiled. "Ah, Mori. This is going to be so fun. First you shoot fire from your hands, breaking through to the Fae dimension, which, technically, you shouldn't be able to do. Then you lift rocks from the floor to seal off the entrance…rocks, Mori, not dirt. You drove up a sheet of solid stone. And then you bring me back from the dead." He grinned at her cheerfully.

She shook her head, still confused. His smile was glorious. He said softly, "Phoenix tears, Mori. You bawled like a baby over my corpse and your tears fell on my skin."

She sat heavily back on her knees. "Phoenix tears. Immense healing powers." She looked at him in a daze. "Enough to bring back an angel?"

He patted her knee. "Seraphim, but angel will do. I would have come back anyway, but you saved me time and a great deal of pain. Thank you, Fire Maiden."

Her eyebrows shot up before her eyes rolled back and she slumped over. Roan cradled her in his arms, checking her pulse. "She's alive. I think she just fainted." Roan stood, Branko fussing over her, and Mako and I pulled Mew to his feet. He swayed and wrapped heavy arms over our shoulders.

Leoht and Francesco bowed at the waist. Mew said, "Oh, thanks, but stop. I'm not into all of that. Leoht? I'm pleased to meet you in person. You are as glorious and fabulous as I expected." He grinned at her, softly shaking his head in wonder. "Spirit of the Fae." He turned to the broad blue man beside her. "And Francesco, glad to have you on our side." He stared at the two Fae. "You need to make up. Now."

Francesco and Leoht locked eyes. Francesco spoke first. "Leoht, I am so sorry. I didn't understand what was happening until it was too late. And then I just went with it. I wanted to learn more, maybe stop it. But Vingor…"

Leoht softened. "He is too strong. You did what you had to do for survival." They clasped forearms. "Earlier, when I had you by the throat, that was reactionary. I'm sorry, too."

Francesco tipped his chin down. "I would have done the same thing."

Her voice cracked at the edges. "Come with me to the entrance? To say a prayer for Flower?"

His face twisted with grief. "She was your friend."

"She was my childhood guardian. She must have followed me and could not leave."

Leif crept forward. "May I come? I liked her. She always tried to make me laugh in the middle of the horror."

Together, they kneeled at the shimmering wall of black stone Mori made. Leoht extended her hand, removing the razor, and carved a flower into the rock with her claw. She sang a melancholic lament, her voice echoing around the cave. After a moment of silence, she wiped her face, stood, and walked toward us. Francesco followed. Leif strode to us, his lips in a furious, firm line, upset we hadn't all made it to freedom.

We staggered to the far end of the cave, Mako and I helping to drag a limp Mew to where Anna and Gray were waiting alone. Gray paced while Anna rested against the wall. Leif reached them first. They stared at each other before moving as one, meeting in a violent embrace, gripping each other. Anna started crying, and Gray thumped Leif's back. Gray's voice was rough. "Can you change back? Or are you permanently Fae?"

Leif stepped away and concentrated, the effort a strain on his face. He opened his eyes and shook his head. "Not yet. Maybe…maybe once I see my parents. Maybe then."

Anna dotted her eyes with a handkerchief she produced from somewhere. "It doesn't matter. Come. It's time to go home." She reached out her hands.

Leoht lifted her fingers, stilling us. Her jaw clenched and released as she struggled to find the right words. "We saved many from a terrible fate." She turned to Leif. "It's not enough. We need to finish him, but we will need far more power."

She turned back to the group. "Thank you all for your courage. It was an honor to fight beside you." With a small nod of her head, she shimmered, her body fading into a deep black streak of smoke, bolting for my throat. I staggered backward as she resettled into the pearl. Her voice strummed through my head. *You did well today, Jelly. Your magic was perfect. Cohesive. Sadly, not enough to kill Vingor, but we'll work on it.*

I called up to the solitary bat on duty. "We're going now. This entrance is out of commission." I paused. "Thank you. For pollinating. And for insect control. We appreciate all that you do for us."

The small brown bat gave me a bow before stretching out his wings. "Thank you, Warrior Scyphozoa, daughter of Kokuro, child of Bastet, and honorary bee. And thank you for your future missions. All the Earth appreciates it." I paused at his words, wanting more, but Mako and Gray grabbed my hands. Anna's magic flared around us, and we disappeared, leaving the Hellhole behind.

THIRTY-EIGHT

JELLY

I expected frightened, shivering, displaced people, clinging to each other. What I found was far different. Anna transported us into the foyer, almost sagging to her knees with exhaustion. Richard was there, ready to catch her. He traced her hair from her face and kissed her. He broke away in a gruff voice. "Thirty-something trips in a single day…You are remarkable, darling." He kissed her again, his magic returning color to her pale cheeks.

The Coven had set up triage, with multiple witches attending the rescued Fae. They were hooked to IVs of multiple colors, dragging their rejuvenation potions on poles as they stopped at the cots of those who needed to lie down. Mostly, they looked enlivened, joyous, and chatted excitedly to each other. A few were out cold, witches murmuring healing spells over their bodies. It was the first time I'd seen so many witches in the house. Wait. Fae-Witches. Three of them had pointed ears.

An unfamiliar witch beckoned Branko and Roan, who still held an unconscious Mori. They followed her into the study, not looking back. The witch paused at the door, whispering, and Roan and Branko nodded, closing the door behind them. The

Fae clustered around Leif, hugging him, petting his head, tears of joy and gratitude on their faces. As one, silently, they parted, creating a line on either side of the door to the library.

There, in the doorway, Sebastian and Sophia stood together, staring at Leif, all of them blinking, barely breathing. They ran forward as Leif sprinted toward them. They bound themselves to each other, bodies trembling, pressed tightly as they cried. Sophia kissed his face over and over while Sebastian stroked his head, murmuring through tears.

Happiness flooded through me, almost taking me to my knees. It definitely stole my breath. Mako wrapped his arms around me, his chest on my back, the strength of him keeping me upright. His muscles shook, his body vibrating as the reality of our success soaked in. His voice was rough in my ear. "We did it, savage queen."

I turned in his arms, wiping the silent tears from his cheeks. I had no words to capture my elation. But he saw it, his cobalt blue eyes flaring with recognition. "I haven't seen you like this for ages. You look happy."

I spoke through my tears. "So happy."

Sebastian called us over. He crushed me in his arms, his chest heaving. His deep voice cracked as he tried to find the right words. "Jelly. Thank you. Thank you so much." Love poured out of him and into me.

"You're welcome." I squeezed back harder, thinking of my father, Tro, and now Sebastian. How lucky I was. Life gave me more than one father. I put all of my strength into my hug, making him shudder as he gulped down his tears. His arms loosened, and he turned me to face Sophia, whose beautiful face was even more striking because of the raw emotions she wore.

"You're a miracle," she said in my hair, her embrace encompassing. "I can never express how grateful I am that you came to us. You've healed us, Jelly." She stood back, cupping my face in her hands, stroking my wet cheeks. I hiccuped through tears of happiness as I tried to reply but couldn't. I was too overwhelmed. She leaned in and pressed her lips to my forehead. She released me with a small sob, her breath catching in her own joy.

Simmi hit my body next, flinging herself at me. She popped my spine as she lifted me off my feet. "That was crazy! You were amazing! Anna was just about to teleport my group when you blasting out your magic. I was too far away to see. Did you kill him? Is it over?"

"It's not. But we all got away." The pearl pulsed twice at my throat. My voice dropped. "Well, almost all of us. I'd like to hold a ceremony for Flower."

Simmi's voice wavered. "And for the one I failed."

Somber, I said, "We were all running out of strength, Simmi. No guilt. There was something evil in the water. We all did our best, and we got all of them, save two. We should be proud." The pearl pulsed once. "Leoht agrees with me." I held her face in my hands. "No tears. We did well. You were so brave, Simmi."

She swallowed and nodded, but I knew that look. She would carry that Fae on her back forever. Leif loomed behind her, his blue eyes sharp on my face. He was still in Fae form, but his dangerous edge had softened now he and his people were safe. Simmi stepped away, drawn back by Sophia. Mako stood with his father, all of them watching us.

Leif cleared his throat and gave me a half-grin. "We haven't officially met."

The corner of my mouth tweaked up. "We were a little busy."

He stood awkwardly, not sure how to greet me. I could sense that he was uncomfortable with anyone but his immediate family touching him, and we weren't familiar enough to hug, but a handshake seemed insufficient.

I smiled. "How do you greet a Fae?"

He puzzled for a moment. "We clasp forearms."

I nodded once. "Let's start there." His face broke open in a smile of relief. He held out his arm. I copied him, my grip firm. He reached out his other arm hesitantly, as if nervous to be too forward. I held that one too.

His voice was raw. "What you did…you and Leoht…Thank you. You were phenomenal in there. And I appreciate you intervening with me and Leoht. I'm glad I did nothing rash." His fingers tightened, and he tugged on my arms, bringing my ear to his lips. Humor rolled through his words. "Do you, by chance, have a sister?"

I threw my head back and laughed. "I do, in a way, but she's spoken for." I looked around the room. "And she's still missing."

"The Phoenix? The woman who became fire and passed out?"

"That's right. Her name is Mori. Excuse me, Leif, I need to go check on her." I met his eyes and squeezed one last time. "I look forward to getting to know you better." I nipped across the foyer, Mako joining me, and pushed open the heavy wooden door of the study, immediately yanking it shut, blinking at Mako like I wanted to scour my eyeballs.

"What? Is she okay?"

I coughed. "She's more than okay." There was a squeal of laughter followed by a deep moan from Mori. "They're restoring her. Vigorously." I scrubbed at my eyes. "I will never unsee that."

Roan's voice floated through my mind, laughter in the tone. *Should've knocked, lass.*

I pounded on the door, shouting. "Get dressed!"

Several fooks and a deep laugh came from inside. The door flew open and a radiantly glowing Mori beamed at me. "Keep your hair on, Jelly. We're coming." She paused, looking back at Roan and Branko with a coy smile. "Well," she added with a drawl, "one of us did." Roan's eyes flashed with heat and Branko chuckled. She looped her arm in mine, a spring in her step as we crossed the floor, dodging cots with sleeping Fae.

From the foot of the stairs, the twin girls watched us with sharp curiosity, Mew leaning casually on the curling volute at the bottom of the railing. Mako's voice was low in my ear. "They've been speaking with Mew for ages. Your name kept coming up."

Xeno stepped forward, casting her voice powerfully in the foyer. "All Fae and witches besides Anna, please remain here. The rest of you follow me." She swept toward the library before turning back, pointing at Francesco. "Francesco, you come, too." We glanced at each other, shrugged, and followed.

We entered the library, and I guided us to a sofa, Mako sitting beside me, Mori on my other side. Trix waited patiently. Soon enough, Roan and Branko entered. They stood behind us, and I twisted to see them as identical statues, arms crossed, faces stoic.

Trix nodded, and Mew entered last, closing the doors behind him, throwing up a silencing block from prying ears. Trix spoke with the confidence of someone far older. "We conferred with Mew, and Xeno and I may offer a partial explanation for who we are and what we need from you. You must determine your course of action without our direct influence, but we would like to give you some background to help you understand the depth of the situation."

Xeno reached for her hand, weaving their fingers together, and continued. "There is a prophecy. Centuries ago, magical races remained exclusive to each other, commanded not to mingle. But love overcame law, and secretly, the races began mixing. Only a few Fae stepped outside of their race, creating Fae-Mers, incredibly powerful beings. You met them in Bermuda. And Sebastian and Sophia created an equally powerful family in the Pacific."

Trix said, "The prophecy states a mermaid would take on the impossible task of fully absorbing Fae magic, transforming to become an entirely different being. She would bear the Spirit of the Fae, and the Mother would mark her. We assumed it would be one of the Bermudian Fae-Mers, as they have existed far longer, but it seems we were mistaken."

Trix beamed at me. I swallowed uncomfortably, crossing my feet at the ankles. "There is always a catalyst that starts a revolution, one rallying voice. Leoht woke you up, Jelly, demanded you act. You were already a warrior, and she pushed you further, bonding you together. Mother Kokuro saw your gumption and claimed you." She nodded to Mako. "She also claimed Mako." Her eyes swung across the room. "And now Simmi."

Everyone stared at Simmi, who cleared her throat and said, "It's true. We haven't had time to discuss it. Mother Kokuro marked me just before we went to the Hellhole." She squirmed in her seat. "I haven't been totally honest with you all. Since my kidnapping, when Terrun force fed me Leoht's blood, I have more power. Like, a lot more. I haven't said anything because…" She crinkled her nose. "Well, Jelly's always got some crisis. I didn't want to add fuel to the chaos." Her voice dropped away as she glanced at me apologetically.

I had to laugh. "I swear I'm not trying to be the center of the universe. Trust me, I'm the eternal reluctant heroine. But if my chaos means we've activated something that can help the Earth, I'm all in. Xeno, please, keep explaining."

Xeno pushed back her long hair. "Mother Kokuro granted full Fae magic to Jelly, Mako, and Simmi. Leif, your transformation to full Fae happened when you fell into the Hellhole. Something in your genetic pattering knew you'd need it to survive." All eyes turned to him. He shuffled under the attention, awkward. "Leif, your uncles yanked you into the Hellhole. They sensed your bloodline and stole you, hoping to provoke your father to attack. You touched an entrance, wired for Sebastian's blood, and it dragged you in."

Trix's voice was soft. "It was never about your longing for Mako's necklace." Leif frowned, his long fangs snagging on his lip. "Leif, you could swim the waters because your blood gave you royal protection. Same for Mako, Simmi, and Jelly. If anyone else had jumped in, they would have melted. You never questioned it?"

He looked bewildered and gave a ragged answer. "I was just trying to survive. So long as I was touching someone, they were okay in the water." He ran a clawed hand over his face. "But that makes sense now. Flower," he choked on her name, "Flower suspected as much. She told me I looked familiar, but she never hinted at my family."

Sebastian sighed sadly. "Flower was like a granny to us. She worked as a childminder in the castle, running what was essentially a daycare for Fae of a certain caste, including us and Leoht, who was a Queen's guard." He added softly. "My mother's guard. And, true to her soul, Flower sacrificed herself to save you."

Trix swallowed, nodding. "And her one life changed the course of history." She turned her brown eyes on me. Trix wiped the side of her hand under her cheek, catching an errant tear. "All of you have trusted your inner guidance, doing what was right, just like Flower did. That is where true power lies."

Xeno smiled at me, blinking her enormous eyes, so large in her small face. "You've spent your life defending the oceans. Mako as well." She turned to Sophia and Sebastian. "You met at a logging protest, falling in love at the top of a tree. Sebastian, you left the Fae, and Sophia, you left the Mers. Disgusted with the politics, you took a stand and unknowingly created three powerful children."

Xeno pointed to Drift. "You roam the land, helping wolves survive deforestation and loss of habitat." She added quietly, "At a great personal cost." He nodded solemnly, his face uncharacteristically sober as he dipped his chin down.

Trix smiled at Mori. "Mori has dedicated her mind to understanding the commonality of all magics. Her unique blend has awoken, ready to tackle the worst of the world." She sighed. "Your burden is substantial, Mori. It will be painful at times. Remember to keep your heart light." Mori swallowed thickly as Branko slid a hand to her shoulder.

Trix continued. "Simmi created something to wake the humans, and her inventions will change the world." She winked at her. "You have only just begun." She pointed to Roan. "Nuclear bombing demonstration as a child, where you lost your mother. You transformed your grief and became one of the strongest Mages ever to live. Your mind's power is phenomenal. I know you've only shown them a small piece."

Xeno smiled at Gray. "You battle in court using human law, using your brilliance and natural charm as your weapons, fighting against destructive corporations. I imagine you sneak a little persuasive magic in there sometimes." He laughed. With a nod to Branko, she said, "Lead gargoyle. Your kind remains intentionally cloaked in mystery. Perhaps at some point you will share your story. Thank you, protector." Branko slightly bowed his head at her praise.

She looked at Anna. "You led many rituals to make all of this happen, provided safe transport and shelter. You continue the work of the witches before you, guiding those who seek a higher purpose." Then to Richard, "You are the wind, unseen, working behind the scenes. Thank you for your efforts with Gaia." Richard gave her a small bow, not disclosing what she was referring to.

My curiosity piqued, I leaned in, scanning everyone in the room.

I had *so many* questions.

She turned to Leif, who stood uncomfortably under her gaze, twitching and fiddling with his fingers. Both Trix and Xeno bowed deeply. Trix said, "Leif, you rescued countless innocents, sheltered them, and fed them. For those who could slip past the wards, you helped them escape. You believed you deserved to be in the Hellhole, that it was a punishment for your emotions. That assumption is incorrect. You are innocent. Once you can understand that truth deep in your soul and forgive yourself, as well as the others you hold accountable, you will find you can change back to human form."

Leif swallowed, his eyes flicking to Mako. Xeno sighed, her gigantic eyes sad. "It is seductive to fall into victim energy, asking yourself, why me? Yet, your experiences shaped you, honed you like a blade, allowing you to be someone entirely different, able to rise to impossible challenges, digging into your true soul to find your integrity. Sometimes, awful situations turn out to be blessings. I think each of you can appreciate that."

Xeno tipped her chin to the Fae standing beside Leif. Francesco straightened, his cornflower blue eyes glowing. She said, "And you turned your back on evil. You could have been the Head Guard for Vingor. You could have had unfathomable power, but you said no. Your heart is pure." She nodded to Sebastian. "Francesco sent the bat, warning you of Leoht's captivity." Sebastian gasped and bowed to Francesco, thanking him.

The twins scanned over each of us. Xeno said, "Thirteen new keepers. The prophecy predicted a team of mixed magic. They would come together, putting their differences aside for a larger endeavor; saving the Earth. And now, here you are. It has begun. All of you are Gaia's warriors, and you've lived your lives as such, with brave hearts and great courage. Today, we make it official. Do you swear to defend the Earth? To give her your life in fealty?"

All of us nodded in agreement, not a single one of us

hesitating. Trix grinned, staring at the cream drapes. "Actually, Xeno, there are fourteen. Doocan, you can come out now."

Halfway up the curtains, a shimmer of pink marred the pale background, and a blushing Doocan stepped forward, his skin turning brown, cheeks still on fire. "Sorry," he said. "I was curious. If you want me to leave…"

Trix patted his shoulder. "You should be here, Doocan. You risked your life for us. Do you swear to protect Gaia?"

Doocan straightened his shoulders. "Always."

Trix and Xeno joined hands, weaving their fingers together and pressing foreheads. Their skin glowed butter yellow, light rising off them like sunbeams, engulfing the room in the sweet scent of rich dirt. My skin prickled from the power they exuded. Suddenly, together they shouted a word, a command.

My left thumb burned, and I drew it up sharply, watching as a symbol appeared. It resembled a pine tree, with dark green slashes wrapping around a black central line. Mori hissed simultaneously as a similar mark formed on her skin. I whipped my head right and left. Everyone shook out their hands. Everyone except Mew, who smiled from ear to ear.

Roan scowled from behind me. "What the bloody fook does this mean?"

Xeno and Trix broke apart. Xeno stared at us with her earth-colored eyes.

Trix followed her. "We must calm Gaia. She reacted badly to our leaving, and we will need additional support to soothe her. She needs to feel respected. We need to defend her from Vingor's attacks."

I frowned, confused. "What is Vingor's ultimate plan?"

Francesco raised up a hand. "I was close to Vingor, one of his main confidants. He bled Fae for their magic, changing decent humans into puppets, monsters with no heart. They've done it for years. These Eators infiltrate the system, becoming leaders in human governments and influential corporations. They are greedy, abusive, and destructive, influencing others, making all the humans ignore the cries of the planet in their never-ending pursuit of more. But it's worse. They created an army of manipulated animals. They started with the rainforests."

Xeno's voice was ominous. "We've seen them. They stole us and gave us to Vingor." She shivered.

Francesco stepped forward. "Razors. The creatures are called Razors. Vingor forced Fae power into the wildlife. It's a huge operation. Destroy the rainforests and you wipe out Gaia's natural climate regulation."

Richard added in a quiet voice. "Twenty-five percent of modern medicine comes from rainforests, and seventy percent of plants with anti-cancer properties come from the Amazon. Eliminate the rainforests and humanity will die from the unnatural diet they consume. As far as wicked plans go, it's bloody brilliant."

Mori paled. "Francesco, what are these Razors?"

Francesco leaned forward. "Green anaconda, the world's largest snake. Typically, they are thirty feet long and weigh over five hundred pounds. Gorillas, normally six feet tall, and over four hundred pounds. Black caiman, the largest species of alligator, can grow to twenty feet and weight over six hundred and fifty pounds. Harpy eagles, the largest and most dominant raptor in the Amazon, can fly fifty miles per hour. Now add Fae magic. A lot of powerful, powerful Fae magic. Are you getting the picture?"

Xeno's thin body vibrated with rage as Francesco kept speaking. "It's central to the plan. The Hellhole was where they bled the strongest Fae. They did it there, so the Fae rulers, Queen Raya and King Handsraj, wouldn't discover them. According to Vingor, there are limits on how much power he can siphon, so he took it underground. Then, he goes to the rainforest. The Amazon is where Vingor's operation is located. That's where we'll find him."

Mori's freckles bunched together as she filtered the information. "I don't understand. If Vingor and Terrun turn humanity towards destruction, and they continue to pillage the Earth, and Gaia responds through natural disasters, how does this serve them? Won't she destroy everything, leaving them with an uninhabitable planet?"

Francesco slowly shook his head. "Gaia always rebounds, but she will be exhausted. If Terrun and Vingor can enslave her, they rule everything."

I recoiled. "They want Gaia herself? What, her soul?"

Trix nodded, a tear slipping down her cheek. "She is the oldest energy, an ancient goddess of creation. With her under their control, they will be the most powerful beings alive. It's all about control. They hunger for absolute power."

"But why?" Mori leaned forward in her seat, her eyebrows tight together. "Why do they need it?"

Sebastian gave her a sad smile. "Why do humans need five yachts? That's the point. They don't. It's a craving for power."

I voiced my thoughts with an edge of apprehension. "Look, I've been down this road. At one point, I wanted Terrun to destroy humanity. I believed the Earth would heal if they were gone. If they wanted ultimate control, why not just kill humanity now?" I chewed on my cheek, embarrassed to have admitted my past beliefs.

Mew rubbed his head, stepping forward. "Humans are one of Gaia's creatures, and she loves them deeply. She is proud of their creativity. Music, arts, literature, dance. She loves to see their expressions when they climb mountains, or scuba dive, appreciating her beauty. Humans have the capacity to be awed by her, and it gives her great satisfaction. The animals exist on instinct, but humans sing her praises. Like any goddess, she likes the admiration. By turning them against her, she feels forsaken, driving her to madness. Vingor is simply being cruel, breaking down her spirit."

Trix cleared her throat. "Listen closely. If the rainforests die, all of us die. If the oceans die, all of us die. If the bees die, all of us die. We must stop the dissolution of human empathy for the Earth. We need them to care again. It's the only way Gaia will survive."

I sat forward. "So what do we do?"

Trix answered with a sinister grin on her face. "We disrupt their corruption and return Gaia to peace."

I chewed on my lip. "But how? Where? As you say, the ice caps are melting, the forests are burning, the ocean is suffocating. It's everywhere, and humans are inhaling resources at an accelerated rate. Where do we even start?"

Xeno frowned. "We cannot help you with this part. You must decide your own course of action."

Mori's eyes swirled with gold. I could see the wheels turning in her head. "You're from the rainforests, and you say that unnatural creatures are living there, so I will assume that you're dropping a hint, a big one."

Francesco pulled on the tip of his ear. "It's the central location for Vingor's operations, but it's vast, easy to hide in. Few people go into the Amazon rainforest besides the indigenous tribes. Vingor has centers all across the planet. We could attempt to overthrow the main one first, but it's massive, from what I understand, and we may not be enough. It might make more sense to destabilize the smaller centers first."

The room broke into debate, discussing the pros and cons of the various centers, the approach, and the skills we had for each terrain. I ran my fingers through my hair. I whispered to Mako that I needed some air. He gave me a quick kiss and turned back to the room, listening to Drift talk about the Arctic.

I reached out to Mori's mind. *Walk with me? I have a promise to keep.*

She nodded, and we slipped out the side door, away from the rising voices, now moving to the merits of a full attack or a stealth approach. Mori reached for my hand. "Where are we going?"

"There's someone I want you to meet." We walked toward the hives, me pointing out the flavors of different flowers, as well as the strange coloring only available to a bee's eyes.

She dropped my hand, pushing her nose into a fragrant rose. Her lips quirked. "You've changed, Jelly. In a good way. I like this improved version. You're not demanding to be in charge of everything."

I laughed. "Thanks. Here. Let's sit here for a moment." I pulled her down, about ten feet from Queen Isabella's hive. It didn't take long for the bee on my mind to find us.

Jelly? Jelly, can you hear me?

I held out my palm, and a bee laden with yellow pollen smoothly circled and landed with elegance. I lifted my hand up to my eyes. Her ragged wings showed battering on the edges. I swallowed my grief. *Hey, Manda. I wanted you to meet Mori. She's been my best friend since we were merbabes. Mori, this is Manda. She helped me stay sane in the hive when I was completely overwhelmed. I wouldn't have succeeded without her friendship.*

Manda giggled. *You give me too much credit, Jelly. You are a queen. It's your destiny.*

Mori grinned at the small bee. *You have no idea. She might be one day. A true queen. She's mated to Fae royalty.*

I squinted my eyes and frowned. *Okay, let's not go there quite yet.*

Manda stared at Mori. *May I see your eyes up close?* Mori held out her palm, and Manda flew over, perched on a finger. *You're touched by Ra. We are sisters, then.* She pulled her antennae with her front feet, bouncing excitedly. *That means we will meet again. I'll see both of you in my next incarnation.*

Incarnation? I asked.

Mand nodded vigorously. *Indeed. Remember, I told you honeybees are the go-between for the Spirit world? Well, if I've made friendships with creatures beyond my own, I will get to return to find them. I don't know how or when, but we will cross paths again. Our work together is not done.*

I leaned toward her. *How will I know it's you? Will you come back as a bee?*

Manda waddled to Mori's thumb, stroking the green slash marks. *Doubtful. I may be a different animal, or a human, or a magical being. Gaia will decide when I die. At least, that's what we believe.* She flew back to me, landing on my wrist. *Lisa is gone. She fell among the flowers as she wished. The ants carried her away in a wonderful ceremony.*

A pang of sadness shot through me. I nodded, understanding it was the way of bees. Manda smiled, the sides of her mandibles twisting into her familiar grin. *Well, this pollen won't unpack itself. I need to get back to work. I'll see you when I see you. Nice to meet you, Mori. Take care of this one. She's a firecracker.*

I laughed. *Actually, Mori's the firecracker, but I appreciate the sentiment. Bye, Manda. I hope we find each other soon.*

She buzzed around our heads in a circle three times, blessing us. She gave us a Mers farewell. *Until my sisters. Until.*

I bit into my cheek, swallowing down the tears that had sprung to my eyes. Mori wrapped her arm around my shoulders.

"Isn't it incredible?"

"What?"

Mori smiled, a laugh burbling up from her throat. She waved a hand in the air. "All of it."

I leaned my head against hers, my heart full of sorrow and love. "It certainly is."

AUTHOR'S NOTES

Sigh. I loved writing this book. I have multiple bee tattoos, my favorite being a fuzzy bumblebee with flowers on her wings. You know what to do. Keep part of your lawn wild, and if you don't have a lawn, put a native flowering plant on your balcony.

Tell your local representatives about barren spaces and how wildflowers can improve them. Talk to your neighbors about the importance of dandelions and clover, and see if you can start a riot in your own backyard. If your HOA demands lawns, put up some planters with native plants.

I've signed up for the Pollinator Partnership, www.pollinator.org, to earn my Pollinator Steward Certification, giving me a deeper understanding and appreciation for these magical creatures. I will start with my own backyard and see where it takes me. Sign up for my newsletter for updates and photos on www.andieholman.com.

If you'd like to connect socially, you can find me on BlueSky, under the handle @authorandie.

Thank you so much for your support. Reviews help small authors be discovered, so please take a moment to pop online and write a few words. I certainly appreciate it.

Bee kind, bee good, and bee happy.

Love,
Andie

ACKNOWLEDGEMENTS

As always, my husband is top of the list. His constant support and love keeps me going.

My friends lift me up, encourage me to keep going, and squeal with excitement at all the right places. Love you.

My thanks to Kenneth Zink, my fearless editor, who reduced me to tears when his notes said I'd nailed it with this one. Thanks to Richard Ljoenes for his gorgeous cover, and to Lorna Reid for her impeccable formatting.

Thank you most of all to my readers. Your kind notes and reviews make my days brighter.

BOOKS IN THE LAUGHTER OF THE SUN SERIES

BOOK ONE: THE MERMAID'S WRATH

The ocean is dying. A mermaid vows to save it.

The Mers are barely surviving in a magical marine bubble, isolated from the rest of the world. Jelly, warrior mermaid and champion of the sea life, battles against the choking, accelerating pollution, living beneath the Great Pacific Garbage Patch.

When Jelly's mind opens to terrifying premonitions, she must leave the ocean, collaborating with estranged magical beings on land. She's seen one of theirs in a vision, a woman abducted for the power in her veins, and Jelly's black pearl is the key to this woman's freedom.

The pearl, passed down through generations, holds a secret, and when it wakes, it sends Jelly on a tumultuous journey on the surface, changing her life forever.

BOOK TWO: THE SORROW OF BEES